# The Hoffman Affairs

# The Hoffman Affairs

A NOVEL

## BETH SCHORR JAFFE

R.BECKER
PRESS

Printed in the Unites States by R.BECKER PRESS







Cover painting by Julius Schorr

Book Design by Duane Stapp

ISBN 979-8-98650-48-1-0

Subjects: Family Saga, WWII, 1960s New York City, Paris, immigrants, drug abuse, Jewish family

Library of Congress Control Number: 2022913752

Dedicated to my grandparents:

HYMAN AND BECKY BECKER

*Russian Immigrants*

and

DAVID AND HENRIETTE SCHORR

*Romanian and French Immigrants*

# Contents

"For in the end, it is all about memory, it sources and its magnitude, and of course, its consequences."

ELIE WIESEL
*Night*

# Part One

# 1

# How We Met



*Paris, 1942*

*<u>Henri</u>*

The first January of liberation, our rooms brimmed with only the cold. The black market had disappeared from Paris along with the Germans the previous August. This had not turned out to be a good thing. The black market surplus once available for us to fill up on was gone, and prices were so inflated we could afford nothing above the ration. There was no coal to heat us, nor could we afford the luxury of burning even sawdust. We cooked carrots and turnips for our daily soup between noon and one thirty. We had not enough gas to heat the coffee of burned barley. Hoarding the weekly ration of less than half a pound of meat and half a pound of butter, we saved for our Sunday meal.

Monika taught me to say grace and cross my chest, warning me to always do this. She was adamant about praising the Lord. She told me I would doom us to hell if we did not continually ask for God's blessing. The custom was unfamiliar to me, and the power she gave Him was frightening. I forfeited the rituals of my parents, of my lost family—what little I remembered. Without religious guidance or knowledge of real calendar time, of the holidays, the fasts, the blessing of a new week—to hand my burden to the cross was comforting in its magical relief.

I was eleven in Paris, 1942, when the Nazis took my father away. But I believed that if Papa were dead, they would have buried him here, at the cemetery of Montmartre, with other great men of France. I'd spent days looking for his grave, and when I didn't find it, I was sure he had to still be alive. Crying, shivering, a stone bench became my perch. By the end of October, as it was, the foliage had not yet fallen—yellow and red and orange. The wind blew dried brown leaves across the mounds of freshly dug graves and headstones. A hard, pointed leaf, looking petrified, briskly swept up into the air, blowing so fast through the cemetery, it was impossible to follow with my eyes. I began to weep for Papa. I wore only a shirt and short pants, with Papa's old red wool scarf wound around my neck. He'd not needed his coat the day they took him, so I had it in my rooms, but I had not worn it that day. If only I could lift myself from the ground and go back to sleep in the coat.

It had been three weeks since Papa was being pushed down the road. I was his only son; my mother and older sister, Jacqueline, gone already for six or seven months. They had left early one morning, as was their ritual, for the baths before I left for school, and were abducted along with the other women. When my father was taken, I was with him, but he had pushed my head down hard when he saw the SS coming, almost knocking me to the ground, the dirt of the road smashing my nose. It smelled of horse manure. Before I could lift my head, he had disappeared. I was small enough to crawl under and between the crowds. Hiding finally behind the butcher's icebox, watching the screaming women inside the grocery as they were marched away.

Aunt Monika, I came to call her for a while, was a German girl wandering through Paris when she glimpsed me crying. On the day we met, I was sitting on a stone bench and she sat next to me, lifting her skirt above her knee. She asked, "You are alone?" As I nodded, she ran her pointer finger down my cold cheek. Monika told me she was fifteen and had been in Paris for several months. She didn't know exactly how many. She had had some job, she said, but no longer. "I will do things for you if you show me a clean place to stay." Even at my young age I could tell she was one of those girls—a seductress, Papa would say—but I ignored her intentions.

Monika was alone, her blond hair twisted in braids and pinned to the top of her head, her watery hazel eyes fixed on me. Her skin was like a smooth, bleached stone. A striped dress clung to her emaciated body. White torn-off sleeves from another garment swaddled her arms. She wore white pointed shoes that had no heels, but I saw by their rounded bottoms that they once had been high-heeled. Easter shoes, my mother would have called them. When Monika opened her mouth, she spoke first in German and continued in perfect French. They had given her a fine education as a girl in Germany, I later learned, and she also spoke English.

I had lived the past weeks by myself in Papa and Mama's rooms on Rue de Rochechouart. It was a clean and modest apartment. From the kitchen window, over the roofs, we saw the white bell tower of the Sacre-Coeur. Sunday mornings, Mama would have finished her day's work by the time the first calling for Mass rang out. She seemed always to be awake. My mother's sister, Jeanine, and her husband used to live a few blocks away on Rue Riquet, above the baker's, with the awning that had always been unrolled to block the sun from his window pastries, and blocked the view of the street from my cousins' window above. Their apartment smelled of hot bread. All the family I knew from my father had already fled the city. I did not know where they had gone.

A companion would be wonderful—even though she was German she didn't seem threatening—so I allowed my weak, loose grip to weave her tiny fingers. When Monika and I reached my rooms, I asked her to make soup from the carrots and cheese I had. If she could do that for me, I thought, she could stay. She could, and it was good, and she cleaned my mess, and we set up house together.

With my curly reddish hair and blue eyes like my father, I could safely pass as a non-Jew. Monika never spoke of the Jewish situation. She was Christian, she declared, and this little information was all of her history she would share. From me, she only needed the comfort of my rooms. Otherwise, she seemed to move within and about the city with an air of entitlement. My cousin, Bernard, a soldier in the French Army, was thirty-three when the Germans killed him. I would encounter the women who knew my parents on the street sometimes, but they would not speak to me. "Go, Hen, go," they whispered to me, hurrying past. I was not their Jewish friend anymore. I suppose they tried to protect me in this way, pretending I was a stranger who was living with a German relative. Only two months after they killed Bernard, they too vanished.

♦

## 1943

In winter, when the electricity was turned on at the lunch hour and our grayish apartment filled with light from our kitchen bulb, the yellow dots in her hazel eyes came alive. She would not admit to being cold. My skinny body gave me no protection, and Monika knew this. She let me hold her around her shoulders and stand barely an inch from her as she cooked. There was no milk to buy, but as children we were allocated four eggs a week, which I gave to Monika who drank them raw. She tapped the shell so swiftly and straight that she removed the top half, then poured the egg down her throat. I would have gotten ill watching anyone else do such a thing, but I indulged, fascinated as she extended her neck backward and swallowed the yolk in one gulp. She told me her mother taught her to do this as a little girl. This was all she ever said to me about her mother. When I asked where her parents were, how she parted from them, she slapped my cheek and told me it was no concern of mine. With her slap came a draining of all the blood from her face. She looked as if a knife were pressed to her throat. What frightened her so? I hurt for her but, selfishly, more for myself as she hid her secrets from me. I could easily speak of my mother and sister, Jacqueline. What was she hiding?

Monika walked with me through the in-between days of attacks, taking careful steps in and around the city, and spent nights by my side through the peeling quiet of the approaching raids.

## 1945

By spring, fighting throughout France had ceased to concern Paris, and we could begin to find meager employment. Monika found jobs in the theaters as a ticket saleswoman, or cleaning the floors and kitchens of the cafes. When she sold tickets, she dressed well: the theater owners loaned her clothes for the evening. The theaters were the only places in Paris that were crowded; customers escaping into the silvery life of Mrs. Miniver. On the nights Monika worked there, I waited up for her by our front bedroom window. Sometimes I waited until after dawn for her return. She never fooled me with her excuses. I knew the Americans were with her. All the American journalists thought they had a right to claim our women. After all, the Americans had won the war for us. They had freed us and brought light back to our streets, so now they invaded in droves—all the intellectuals, writers, artists—to take our women. That is how I understood them. I could not blame her for wanting the things they brought for her. The clothes, the clean, beautiful, soft underwear, soft as old table linen—someday I would provide them.

It was May when my cousin Manny came to Paris. When Monika

opened the door and I saw a man standing before us, with the glare of the sun shining in around him, he looked so much like my father in his height and posture that I thought, *Papa, oh Papa, you've come home.* Monika looked stunned. I had shown her a picture of Papa. But when I went to examine him up close, he was so young. And his beard was days old. Even in the worst times, Papa would not have a day-old beard. This man smiling at us wore his army clothes, United States Army clothes, pulling his belt tighter and standing so straight, waiting for us to speak. His dark eyes stunned me. Papa had blue eyes.

The soldier's "bonjour" was hard to the ear, as if he had tripped over a rock. He asked me if I were Henri, and explained in English and some irritating French that he was my American cousin. He was not my father, and chagrin fluttered around my stomach. Grimmer still, in looking at his dark and familiar face, opening as it was to us—as if a gift, permanent—I felt then my father would never come back.

Monika's face blushed, and she flitted into the room, jubilant to have him in our home. She was a beautiful eighteen-year-old girl, and Manny was a handsome soldier—a savior, really. He hurried to explain how he knew our address. "Nadine. My girl. She wrote to me with your name and some old addresses. She got it from my sister, Hildie, and sent me a letter listing my relatives on your father's side." His eyes moved from Monika to me. "This is my third furlough to Paris, and you're the only one I've found. There's no one else on the list to look for." He looked down at his shoes, and Monika closed her eyes, whispered a prayer, and crossed her heart. Now, on top of everything else, he made her sad.

He looked back at her and finally asked, "Is there anyone else from your family here or have they been taken?"

"I am German and not one of Henri's family. I am not a Jew. But yes, they are all gone." She moved close to Manny, closing the door behind him, edging around him to the open window so he would have to turn away from me to let her pass, and she whispered briefly to him. He responded with a shallow nod. I could not imagine what kind of secret she would have for him that I did not already know. I walked into the room, taking a seat on the sofa, and pretended not to have seen this. My humiliation would stay buried, but I admitted to myself his immediate winning of her trust.

Monika went to the kitchen to prepare a meal for Manny, who sat next to me on the sofa. He was polite and didn't rustle my hair or tickle me as he might a small boy. He said something to me in English, but without Monika to translate, I just smiled and nodded. Monika used up all the food she was storing for the next week, and set the table with our only clean bedsheet, which was once a window drape, and took out my father's clean handkerchiefs—embroidered with an H for Hoffman—as napkins. While my cousin tried to speak with me through his broken French about his home, I only half listened and half spied on Monika. She helped to translate and kept dropping things because she could not stop looking at Manny. He smiled a lot, and as the room began to fill with smells of pungent pig scraps and sweet cheese, he finally reached in his shirt pocket and gave her a chocolate bar. She took the brown-wrapped candy and placed it near her plate on the dining table. I must have dropped my mouth open in envy, because he looked at me with dulled eyes. He reached for the gold chain around his neck, pulled it gently up and over his head. When he handed it to me, he said, "This will keep you safe all your life."

I looked at his gold charm, this protection, attached to the chain with twisted metal, its original clasp gone. How could this rectangular piece of gold, with its little cutout in the back revealing rolled up paper with foreign writing, ever keep me safe? I had never seen one this small before. We once had larger ones on our doorposts, all of them buried when the war started. I remembered my father digging quickly behind the build-ing. Then I saw on Manny's charm the worn tracing of a Magen David. It looked beaten down into the metal. I went to return it to his neck—slip it back over his head. He cupped my hands with his and shook his head. "Please, Henri. This is from my girl at home. It's kept me safe, you see? I can't think of anything else I'd rather give you than this." Monika translated and added a nod to me to accept his gift. He was teary eyed and said, "You seem to be our family's survivor."

Did he already know none of them would come home again? I was still hoping. He squeezed it into my palm and kissed my cheek. Monika's smile had grown thin as she translated back and forth for us. I knew it had disappointed her when she heard more of his sweetheart in America. My shoulders relaxed, overcome with relief.

She brushed the sheet-drape on the table very flat with her hands and stood at attention, to signal us to come. Stained across Monika's face was the embarrassment of the mock table covering.

Early in our life together, she had removed my mother's linen drapes to use as bed coverings. When we wanted cover over the window, she hung my Papa's woolen overcoat from hooks on either side of the frame. She said it gave better protection from the cold, which it probably did. I loved to peek from the corner of the fabric out to the street and smell my father's skin on the cuff. But now, in this late spring heat, it hung lopsided. From its high hook, it looked like someone was hanging from his neck. I thought of my father and what they had done to him. I had heard stories on the streets. With a knot in my stomach, I turned back to Manny to see my father's face alive on his.

Manny showed no sign of recognition of the urges he had in so few minutes sparked in Monika. I saw. She sat on the chair closest to the stove, allowing Manny to sit at the head of the table. I eyed him sideways, with my head facing my plate as I tried to eat. He was tall and thin with thick, wavy hair that had a trace, here and there, of pearl gray. His black eyes were surrounded by heavy, dark lashes. He did truly look like an American movie star.

We had no fruit, but there were creamy Camembert and day-old breads, some ham Monika had gotten somehow from the end of town, where the roads from the farms enter the city. Last week, she had gotten some fowl. And she had the chocolate that Manny had just given her. My cousin pulled an apple from his coat pocket, cut it in half, and gave Monika and me the pieces. I saw her blush. Did she take this to be a romantic gesture? She ate the apple right then, before she tasted her own food. What little juice it held she let drip from her mouth and turned to him.

I didn't know much about women, but I was almost fifteen, and my heart sped and my hands sweat, witnessing the powers of her simplest conjuring. If Manny felt nothing when she wiped the apple from her lip, then he was surely a man deeply in love with that girl of his.

Monika had watched me grow taller over the years. Every year, she grew more beautiful, and I loved her. I wanted her more. She wanted Manny, and he wanted someone ten thousand hours away. It had escaped me that I was so much younger than Monika. She was tiny and thin, and I believed that she needed me. I served as a decoy for her when she went to steal food, and I sang my old songs to her when she couldn't sleep. And sometimes, lately, when we walk so freely down the street, I pretend to be her lover—her husband—carrying her packages and watching behind her as she crosses the avenues. Now this soldier had come in and given me something for protection, when it was clear to all of us, I was the only protection we needed. Hitler had not gotten us, after all. Paris had been liberated, and we were fine.

"Let me put that on you," Manny told me, as he picked up the chain from the table and reached to put it over my head.

"Won't your girl at home be angry when you return without her gift?" I asked. "When you tell her you have given it away to some stranger—who is alive and perfectly well?" Monika translated what I said, and I was glad to have reminded them both of Nadine.

"What a wise young man you are." He rustled my hair. "But she won't get mad at me when she hears that I've found you. My coming home to her is all the luck we will ever need again."

Light diminished through the rooms with the sunset, and we settled into the parlor. I did want to hear his stories of war and heroism and liberation, and Monika seemed only to want to watch his face. His black eyes became half covered with his lids as his voice created words for us to hear. Until he found us, fellow soldiers who fought beside him knew his stories as their own. Now Manny could absorb the impact of telling his tales, let them run through his blood and chill him. His memory, hard as bone, declared itself as a newly grown appendage—which, like my memory grasping for home, had grown tentacles through the years. His reach for connection irritated my spine, and I shivered.

"It was the closing weeks of last May," he began. "They stationed us in Bath, England, in what turned out to be a 'marshaling area' for the US First Army. Something big would take place, but everything was top secret."

I can still feel the pounding in my chest when he said, "top secret." He scooted his chair closer to me and grasped my hand. Monika sat curled on the sofa with her bare toes exposed beneath the edge of her hem. She may as well have been nude.

He continued in a hushed tone, his eyes nearly closing. "No one knew when or where, but it was general knowledge that there would be an invasion of *major* proportions. In the first week of June, a train to Southampton transported us to our embarkation point. Jeez. That's when this little mezuzah came in handy." Manny shifted his gaze toward my neck and held the gold charm in his palm.

"What do you mean, cousin?" Monika asked.

"I was supposed to be on the first ship out. They had called my name, and I was already lined up to embark my ship. Then this MP—Military Policeman—came running to the line, yelling, 'Manny Hoffman, get your fuckin' ass off the line and report to mess!' The *mess* is where we eat.

Excuse my cursing, but that's what he said." Monika told him it was all right and to please continue. She looked delicate enough, but she could hold her own on the streets with her mouth. "So I cut off the line and ran the hell back. Would you believe that they needed a damn trumpet player for the USO show that had just come? I was a stinking bugler, and they called me back to blow that horn in a show because their guy had pneumonia. I stayed back five days for that." I couldn't tell if the dropping of his facial muscles was a sign of his relief or guilt.

Manny listened to the end of his sentence and looked sideways, as if he were waiting for someone else to continue his story. "That brass saved my life. That was June sixth. My entire battalion was wiped out." He nodded. "On June eleventh, I embarked the *Leopoldville*, and they told us that as soon as the weather and the Channel calmed down, we were gonna join invasion forces in Normandy."

"So were you a hero?" I dared him.

"I can't say that, no, but there were close calls." Manny adjusted his back and pulled his hand through his hair. He looked taller and more handsome by the minute. "My last close call was when FDR died, on April 12. It was the same day a GI I knew drowned trying to cross the Rhine in Bonn. The bridge had long since blown away," Manny waved his hand to show how long ago it had been, "but this young guy from Atlanta, Georgia, tried to cross by foot on the pilings, twisted cables, concrete. He slipped off, fell into the river, and drowned." Monika hardly reacted, just nodded her head. I could feel the soldier suffocating under the water and my chest tightened, though I tried to mimic Monika's stoic face. I wondered if she was just being brave to show Manny she knew about war, or if the boy's death really had no effect on her.

"I was walking through the occupied city with another soldier, Paulie, when we heard the news of both deaths.

"We drove from camp toward the PX to buy cigarettes, the place we go to eat and buy stuff. They had stationed us in Germany a few weeks, since crossing the Rhine in March. And now, we find out that the man we knew as President our entire lives would not greet us welcome when we returned home. So I say to Paulie, that makes two."

"Two what?" Monika asks.

Manny says, "Two dead people, Roosevelt and the drowned guy from Atlanta. We'll hear about another one before today is out. You know, death comes in threes."

"Yes, I believe that!" Monika said.

"So," Manny caught the intensity of our stares and continued, "we were musicians. We knew of a shelled-out apartment house near the church of St. Remigius with musical instruments. Creeping in through a broken basement window, climbing over the debris in the dark stairwell, we kicked and tripped our way through to the first landing." Monika gasped. I doubted it was so difficult as he made it sound.

"I grabbed a dented trumpet, while Paulie came away with another trumpet and a piccolo. Shipped home." He waved his hand bye-bye. "The piccolo would be for my niece, Claudette. She could dance around playing songs she'd make up. She's a little actress."

Shrugging my shoulders, "That doesn't sound very scary."

"Oh no, it wasn't until stepping off the curb, a soldier checked up and down the street for traffic and started toward us, when I saw a stick or tube of something blue flying between us, and then a loud noise popped. I jumped back. When I opened my eyes, I saw this little kid close to me was bent over and lying still. Another boy turned in circles in the middle of the street, shrieking!" Manny mimicked the sound of the boy, AHHHH! I ran to the downed boy, scooped him up, and saw him bleeding from his belly. The red was pumping out fast, and seeing it oozing through his shirt, I turned to see Paulie with the other kid, who seemed to be okay."

Monika and I sat staring at Manny—she biting her nails, me thinking more about Manny's thoughts and desires than the bleeding boy.

"I screamed, 'He's bleeding!' I'm thinking shrapnel, or he'd been shot! I looked up the street to where I'd last stood with Paulie and the soldier was pointing.

"Fucking kids playing with a concussion grenade. This kid fell on it and the goddamn thing exploded. Shrapnel hit the MP behind the PX gate. Blew off his arm. Before help could rescue him, he bled out."

Monika whispered, "Three."

By now, Monika had moved closer to me at the end of the sofa. We did not touch, but I smelled the chocolate left on her breath, caught in the air between us, pulling like a tightrope. Her yearning for Manny made me furious. He must have thought the rage in my eyes arose from fear of his story. Monika pulled her uneven blond curls off her neck and brought them down over one shoulder.

It was only seven o'clock, still so early in the evening. I figured he had a year's worth of stories to get through and he would never leave.

"So tell me, cousin, how did they let you come to find us?" I asked, hoping it would remind him he would soon have to leave.

"They gave me this pass, my last before I go home, and my company motor pool got me from Bod Kissinger, Germany, to Luxembourg. There, by train to Paris and the army's GI bus to a hotel in Montmartre." He then pointed to the chain around my neck. "As soon as I stepped off the bus in front of the hotel, a man comes up to me, Toulis he said his name was."

"Ah, the baker," Monika chimed.

"He was trying to get some cigarettes or stockings or other things he could sell. I have nothing." Manny shrugged. "I told him that my uncle, your father, David, lived on Rue de Rochechouart, and he said it was just a few blocks from his own house. He brought me right here." He smiled a little. "He warned me. I would not find what I was looking for."

Manny had used the word "house," but our home was a four-room apartment above a store. It was over a bazaar—a five-and-ten-cent store.

"Important house, this place is," Manny informed us. "This is where my parents and your parents were married. The same place where my sisters Hildie and Fanny were born."

I waited for translations and nodded politely. As Manny spoke, the room darkened and a dry breeze blew in over us. The window was open and we could hear mothers, bending from their railed terraces, shouting for their children to come in for the day. Manny seemed to become chilled. He wrapped his arms around himself and asked for some water. Then he asked for a blanket. Monika reached over to him and touched his cheek with the back of her fingers. "You are burning," she said. I feared he had gotten this three-day pass and brought pneumonia with him.

Monika helped him lie on the couch, and I removed the sheet-drape-tablecloth from the dining room table to put under him. She told me to sit at his side and not move. Before I could even remember to be angry, Monika disappeared downstairs to demand a neighbor run the three blocks to get a doctor. She returned, a wet cotton handkerchief for his head already in her hand.

The doctor brought with him some syrupy liquid and some pills, Monika set up a chair next to the couch to keep watch, and they sent me, sullen, out of the apartment to sleep at a neighbor's. Monika would be alone with him now. Her compassion for him tore me, but he looked so gravely ill, empathy snuck like a kitchen mouse into my heart.

—◇—

## *Monika*

He reminded me of Henri during our second winter, when he had that frightening fever. As I had done for Henri, I did for Manny. I became, by some twisted default, the woman of the home, the mother, caregiver. With Henri gone downstairs, I washed my hands in the basin of cold water and wrung the cloth through it for Manny's head. Waiting for his fever to rise, afraid of how ill he might become, worrying that after all he had lived through, he had come to us to die. Before he awoke in the middle of the night, I had already composed the letter to his Nadine, describing his valor and his tragic death in my caring arms. As though I had known him all my life, my eyes filled with tears, and I prayed to know him for the rest of it.

Then, thanks to God, his fever broke on its own, for when he awakened at about three in the morning, his head was cooler and he was lucid. It was only a one-day sickness after all, one that had arrived and risen to its crisis by the time he came to us.

When he opened his eyes in the middle of the night, he smiled at me. Taking my hand in his, he said, "Tell me your story." I was overcome with pity at his neediness. He asked me of what I had whispered to him when he first arrived, what I had kept from Henri.

"You said you escaped Germany alone."

This was the first time I spoke about it. Manny had to understand. "You are aware of the Nuremberg Laws?"

"Not really. I've heard the words thrown around." His voice was no more than a whisper.

"My mother is the Catholic, my father a Jew. In 1933, it was passed that there could be no interracial marriages. I was seven years old. My mother taught school and my father owned a furniture business. Some new, some antiques. A good business in Cologne." I took every occasion to remember the small things. Most of all, I could smell his pipe, because the smoke from it lay on all the cushions that traveled to customers' homes when they bought a chaise or sofa. I knew if I could find something from his shop, still I would be able to smell my father. "By 1938, my mother had lost her job, because of her marriage, and my father's shop had gone out of business. We didn't live in a Jewish part of the city, and no one would buy from him. No one was *permitted* to buy from him."

Manny put his hand to his forehead and was still for a second before he spoke. "And so you all came to Paris?"

"Oh, no. No. We had saved money, but not half enough for the tax to emigrate. But my mother, she had the coloring like me, she was able to get vacation visas. We had always prayed in church, and I didn't know any part of me was Jewish. I didn't know about Jewish, good or bad. We got as far as the border when the Germans stopped us. But you have seen enough of this war."

Manny turned onto his side. He took my hand. "Your hands are cool. What happened to you?"

I was so relieved he wanted to know more about me. "They, the Germans, said my father had defiled the race. They said he would have to go back to Berlin to face the charges." I cried now for my father for the first time since I came to this apartment, as I recalled that morning.

*"Papa please, I beg you, Momma, I will go back to Berlin with you. We must stay together." I feel I will up heave my dinner as my father insists, "You and Momma will go to Paris. You will blend in and be safer there. You will obey me and go!" We pack a small bag of clothes and some memories, photographs, and perfume, and head for the train, Momma and me. We stand in silence as the train makes its way into our station in Cologne, and I hold my mother's coat and I cry into her pocket. As she takes me to the steps of the train car, I feel the ripping tug from my father's arms down in my belly, and I squeeze Momma tighter. "Please, please!" Then she pushes me onto the car, jumps on behind me, and as soon as the train picks up enough speed to hold me on, she jumps off, leaving me.*

Manny stared at me, eyes popping, mouth wide open, as if I had just been stabbed to death in front of him. I put my head on his chest. As I listened to his heart pound, he rubbed my back—a touch gentle but reaching that place in me where lovers could convince you to murder— until his hand moved to his face to wipe his tears.

"And you ended up here by yourself, a little girl. How old were you?"

"Not a little girl. By the time I got to Paris a few days later, I was a woman. A fourteen-year-old woman." I cocked my head, posing for a snapshot he could keep, and took a breath.

"Did you ever see them again?" Manny stroked my cheek, and in the time it took his fingers to slide from my cheek to my chin, I fell in love with him.

"No, I have not, will never see my poor Mama and Papa again. I believe they are dead. People come and go through Paris. I have met the other Germans who have tried to escape. Not only Jews, you know. Half Jews, related to Jews, bought furniture from a Jew. They were all criminals in Hitler's Germany." My hair was sticking to my forehead and my cheeks. I had to push it back to find my breath. "I was told by a man I serviced from the resistance about a year later that both my parents went to Berlin. My mother had taken ill with a chest infection or such. They didn't keep you alive if you were sick. She was sure to be dead. They are both killed. They are both in graves with the other criminals."

The Germans loved an adolescent Aryan, and I had to survive. They loved it more—I learned from other girls—when you told them you were half-Jewish. I told Manny of meeting them at the strip clubs where I danced behind the blackened windows of the old cafes in Pigalle, every night standing center floor in front of tables full of my countrymen, my German fathers and sons, removing my simple clothing to the music of an adagio piano that played in my head, beneath the light of a single bulb, exposing myself, offering myself in exchange for any trash they could throw to me. Then taking a Nazi, or two, to a backroom where he would have me—quickly—for the payment of some cigarettes that I could sell, or for a piece of cheese he had put in his pocket for me. I told Manny how I got so sick from the men—they burned me with cigarettes and bit me—and then came to find Henri at the cemetery, and how he came to save me. Of course there were other nightmares I could never expose. After many minutes, I turned to look at Manny's face. He was studying me. Watched me as men did, his eyes traveling over my face and shoulders, his lips slightly parted. I had to rest, and he let me sit closer to him, following streaks of headlights that flew past outside the window like angels fleeing hell.

"And you, is it Manuel?" I broke the spell. I had seen Manny's jaw tighten as I told him of the prostitution. I was not ashamed of this, as I was of my other sins—things no man, no person, can be told.

"Call me Manny."

"So, you are a musician, you say you play the trumpet. Do you miss playing in a big American band?"

He laughed, then swallowed the sound as if it embarrassed him. "The only thing I want to do now is go back home to my girl and marry her. If I could have that, I wouldn't care about or want anything else."

"You will have that." I took his hand to my cheek. I would not be writing to Nadine of how he had died in my arms.

Manny shivered and curled again into the blanket I'd tucked around him. "Tell me of your family back home," I said, hoping this would lull him into a peaceful sleep.

Manny tried to bury his flushed cheek into the pillow, closing his eyes. But he shuddered and shook his head quickly, as if freeing a bee from his hair. Then he sat up straight and leaned tight into the sofa. "My mother died after giving birth to me; twelve years later, really.  But it was because of my birth. She was forty-two when she had me. I was her fifth. I have two older sisters, and two brothers died of diphtheria before I came." He coughed to clear his throat, and I gave him water to sip. "My father, it seems, had no real regard for her health. The doctor had told him that another pregnancy might kill her. She had sugar. Diabetic." He looked at me to see that I understood the term. I did, and nodded for him to go on. He swallowed and looked away from me when he said, "After she died, my father disappeared with another woman."

"Tell me when the war took you?

"July 1943."

"You left your Nadine crying by the side of a ship?" That's the image we had seen in movies.

Manny smiled. "No, I was in my sister Hildie's house, where I had been living. The heat had wiped out everyone in the house. My older sister, Fanny, had just undone my niece Claudette's braid," he smiled again, "and smelled her shoulder. Fanny is a smeller." He laughed. "She smells everything to make sure it's clean." His eyes rolled up and he counted on his fingers. "Yeah, Claudette was eight years old, and I shook, even in that heat, holding that green army blanket. 'Stop shivering, Uncle Manny,' she whined.

"She begged her mother, Hildie to let her bring me *her* blanket. She was quite possessive."

"And Hildie and Fanny's men?"

"Hildie was abandoned by her husband when he was discharged from the army last year, and Fanny never got hitched. Hildie is tiny, both of them with blue eyes, red curly hair, and freckles. Irish Jews." He giggled, but I didn't understand. "I managed to get my mother's dark hair and eyes." Manny looked out the window as if he were finished with his telling, but no. "My parents moved to Brooklyn—before I was born—from here, where my father, Joseph, had been a women's clothes designer and my mother was pregnant all the time. And sick. Dead almost ten years now."

"And Nadine?"

He began crying. "Nadine is the love of my life. She's shy. Lovely. She fits next to me as if the next numbered person in the world's plan." He raised his hand in the air. "Above me."

I was so taken with his story, and I kept falling.

# 2

# The Liberation

## *Henri*

After Manny left the apartment to go back to his base, my life with Monika resumed. It took a few days for her to stop looking out the window, praying for him to come back.

The streets were growing busy again. Monika was small but walked with power. Her narrow feet charged the pavement with each step, and her squared shoulders swayed side to side. Even in a braid, her blond hair reached her waistline. The men. They followed her. Courted her.

Mssr. Toulis, the old baker who had directed Manny to us, became my friend. Oddly round and tall for a Frenchman, he taught me to drive his car, a small Simca, so I was able to find work as a taxi driver. The metro was still not fully operational and the need for taxis was great, though until the middle of 1946, I was not allowed by law to take on anyone who was not ill, pregnant, or held an official position in the government. Monika found a job as a sales girl in the Galleries Lafayette. They hired her above all the other girls because of her face and figure. She'd also told them her father had owned a dress shop and she was experienced with customers. At the shop, she soon became involved with a man. He was an American journalist, infatuated with her. This man, this writer who had not fought, but who had come here after he finished his education and thought he would see our heavenly city, drink our wine, have our women—this thief—brought his pipe and books to Monika. He wrote about politics and talked about music, art, and sex. I would listen, and the things he wrote as truth were fairytale. He would never know about life in Paris during the war.

When he first went into her bedroom, I was left to sleep out on the couch with a blanket and pillow. I cringed from the sounds, but concentrated to hear them. His French was deplorable, so Monika spoke in English. "No" is the same either way, and though her cries were weak and muffled, I understood that he was taking something she was not willing to give. The curtain that served as a doorway to her bedroom did not connect wall to wall. I had to be sure he was not hurting her. I had to be sure her "no" was definite before I would run in to rescue her.

Their shadows revealed that she didn't look encumbered or in danger. He stood above her in the bed and held her hair behind her head. The blond curls were like black spiders down her back in the dark. I know she saw me because she briefly turned her head toward me and smiled. I didn't know if this was a thing women do. Do they like you to watch? I could smell his tobacco breath when he panted, and I could see her long neck glistening with sweat when the street lamp found it. With his sudden loud grunt and her breathless fall against her pillow, I ran to the couch and pretended to sleep. And when he left, maybe an hour later in the middle of the night, my heart was still pounding and I had no choice but to go to her, and I screamed and threw her things across the room. Monika kept her arm across her eyes and cried, sobbed, and spit. I thought she had spit at me for peeping at her. "You smiled at me. I saw you! You wanted me to watch!" I challenged her.

But then she told me, "I am spitting him out. I am spitting his filth from me."

I was so relieved, so humbled. I thought, of course this can only be her devotion to me. I was meek, but had to ask why she allowed me to watch her. I thought she would tell me she wanted me to learn how to be with a woman. But she said it was to prove to me that it meant nothing. That it was as though I were watching her prepare a meal. Only many years later could I comprehend how that explanation was a peek into her psyche, an opening that allowed some buried rot to ooze out and warn me. But I was too young, too stupid, to understand. When she invited me that night, I slipped beside her in her bed.

With my back to her as I dozed, she began. First, she started waking me by pulling on strands of my hair. When I reached behind my head to swat the crawling thing, she grabbed my fingers and put one in her mouth. I awoke fully and knew what she wanted. I was terrified and too excited to speak. She stroked my back as she had when I was small and frightened, and left me alone. I lay there and could only breathe hard, but didn't move. Something was stopping me from turning to her. When my eyes were closed against the dark, I saw my mother's face.

It was two more nights like this until she insisted I turn to see her. She whispered that she saw me bathe from boyhood, and that now she saw me as a man. That was when I turned to her. Facing her, not able to respond with words, I followed her direction, and—risking with her the chance of pregnancy—I found the place she wanted me to go. And when my eyes were forced to close by my release, a weight I had thought was natural, a weight I could not have dreamed I could cleave, lifted.

# 3

# Life in Paris

*July 1948*

## *Henri*

Monika was twenty-two. I was soon to be eighteen. Our daughter Jacqueline, named for my murdered sister, was now three months. With a full head of black hair, she resembled neither of us, but she had a sweet face—small and delicate features, except for her enormous, smoky brown eyes that followed me everywhere. Monika and I had married during her third month of pregnancy. The baby was colicky, and Monika nursed her every hour to keep her still. I drove a taxi by day through all of Paris and a city autobus half the night to bring home enough money for rent and food. Jacqueline was at the doctor, it seemed, every other day for this or that, and that cost every extra franc we had. Monika was sure there was a serious problem because of her crying, though the doctor reassured her it was the normal case, sometimes, for babies to voice their opinions forcefully and *constantly.* "Someday she will have something important to say, so be happy she has a strong voice and healthy lungs," the doctor admonished her.

I'd arrive home from work at three in the morning and I only had three, occasionally four, hours to sleep before I had to drive the morning rush hour. Monika—exhausted, dehydrated from the constant nursing—would lay Jacqueline in the bed next to me and go to sleep on the couch. I knew my wife needed her sleep, but I missed her next to me in bed. We had not made love since before the birth. The baby seemed at peace nestled beside me; it was the only time during the twenty-four-hour day she would rest quietly. Monika told me she physically ached for my arrival home from work and swore she could not get through the next day if it weren't for my soothing effect on our daughter. I deeply sensed how fearful Monika was for her child's well-being, bringing her to her doctor visits, the yielding of her breasts. Yet the blank look in her eyes when she turned her child over to me in the night, the way her arms would caress herself with their emptiness, saddened me.

—✦—

## 1950

France was politically unstable once again, the streets bereft with talks of involvement in America's Korean War. The nights had been filled with Monika's nightmares about her parents and lovers from the war. Just five years after the liberation, Monika filled our home with canned food, and all basic staples, and began filling her nights with clandestine meetings. I chose not to believe she had lovers. I coddled Jacqueline, and she clung to me, and I spent more time home from work; she was so afraid I'd never return, and I could not trust Monika to stay with her. Monika was, it seemed to me, a lazy mother. She would give in to Jacqueline's tantrums, of which there were many, just to quiet her. She would leave her alone during her naps and wander outside the home.

As the Korean War raged on, the French volunteer force was finally called upon to aid the United States. I wanted badly to show Monika I was also a hero. "If you leave me alone with this child, one of us will end up dead!" she declared, staring at me and stamping her hand on the dining table. That was that.

Monika's ongoing correspondence with Manny brought little mention of his Nadine, except for her miscarriages, nor any good news at all—until one day in 1953, after the Korean War had ended, when word came from Manny saying he had work for me, that his hardware business was thriving and he could use my help. He believed immigration would be easier for relatives and that we could live comfortably on the salary he offered. Monika said she was happy to leave Paris behind. It elated me just to think about taking Jacqueline and her mother away.

Monika longed to see Manny again, but now that she would, she couldn't get her things in order. First she had to find the right traveling clothes for herself and Jacqueline. Then she couldn't decide on the right case to carry to hold Jacqueline's daily requirements. She gathered blankets, little sweaters, and knitted hats. She cried every time she looked at herself in the mirror. She'd yell, "I'm not beautiful anymore." And I'd yell back that she was.

It took her three months longer than me to get her travel visa approved because she was a German citizen. She complained she had no clothes for America. I bought her new clothes. She feared the new jet aeroplanes, so this meant first getting to England to take a ship to New York. Finally—five months after Manny had written—the three of us were on an old cruise ship turned warship, turned back to cruise ship, leaving our days of play and nights of fear; the rooms that froze us, comforted us, and allowed us to be lovers.

"You will remember that your cousin Manny is a devoted husband to Nadine, and you'll not fuss about him," I warned Monica. I felt secure in my manhood, my fatherhood, but Monika was so beautiful.

"You just get me over to America! You will see what a woman can do for herself. I don't need Manny, or anyone!" Monika was too brave.

I wanted to work hard for my cousin. I had bound into America determined to devote my life to whatever it took to care for Monika and to raise Jacqueline safely.

# Part
# Two

# 1

# The New York Assembly

## *Monika*

My younger husband, Henri Hoffman, and our toddler daughter, Jacqueline, met Beatrice Giordano as soon as we arrived in New York City. Our arrival was on the cusp of spring. As winter faded, spring was showing off and everything was cooing. Beatrice, her husband, Tommy—a steady customer at Manny's hardware store—and their eight-year-old son, James, lived in the two-family brownstone they owned on East Seventy-First Street and Second Avenue and offered their empty street-level apartment to us as Manny's cousins.

The Manhattan neighborhood around the home was clean and comprised a mixture of narrow brownstone houses with seven-step stoops, broken up by brick six-story, pre-war apartment buildings. Neat and evenly spaced trees sprouted in front of each property, garbage pails were kept out of sight behind black wrought-iron gates, little girls drew chalk games on the sidewalk, and boys pounded Spalding balls against the stoop to compete for nickels. I had thought the city location would be exciting, and convenient. I was pleased to have a few stores interspersed along my street: an Italian delicatessen, a dry cleaner, and on the corner, farthest from our stoop, there was a dealer of antique furniture in a shop much like my father had in Cologne. It was a reassuring portent, but it was also a reminder of what I had lost as a girl, and now again as a woman.

I wanted to get a job after the summer as soon as Jackie began school. Even though she had already turned six, Jacqueline would begin in kindergarten, and I would try to teach her as much English as possible over the summer. Jacqueline was told we would do the three S's: shop, sightsee, and study all summer. Hopefully we would not have to experience the predicted heat wave of 1953. Aware I was anticipating discomfort of some kind but wasn't sure what about America would bother me most, I was ready to start with the hot summers. At least I would see Manny.

Our first trip to shop at a big American department store had me in shivers. Macy's on Thirty-Fourth. Paris was sophisticated and beautiful, but nothing had prepared me for the likes of Macy's. I dressed Jacqueline in a sweet purple pant set, with a matching little vest and short-sleeved white shirt. "Momma, first we go to the shop for me."

That had not been my plan, but I agreed.

But soon after we arrived at the children's department, Jacqueline was nowhere in sight. I screamed her name and ran from rack to rack looking for her. The cashier was at her station behind the register. "My, my little girl is gone. They took her. She is gone, call the police!" I started pulling clothes off the rack near the register. "Jacqueline, Jacqueline!" No response. A lone store guard appeared in minutes and began a wide search of the floor, finding Jacqueline under the racks of the boy's suits, 7-14. When I grabbed her, screaming in her face, Jackie peed her pants.

Once home, I started moving furniture around our small apartment, rearranging drawers, and scrubbing the old appliances. The thought of entire days alone in the city with my daughter made my skin crawl. I would have to work outside the house before school started. Hopeful but wary, I had an instant friend and confidant in Beatrice, with whom I looked forward to sharing Jacqueline's dramas and Henri's considerable faults. She helped get Jacqueline enrolled in summer camp at the local Y. Beatrice had already been working for a few years, and she wangled me a job interview in Bellevue Hospital. We could ride downtown together on the Second Avenue bus. "I am what you call here, a 'people person,'" I told personnel. They gave me a job dealing with visitors on the psychiatric floor. Anything to get away from that stuffy apartment. I tried to imitate Beatrice's simple and sensible style of dress, to get comfortable in a plain skirt and blouse, but I would look in the mirror and add a scarf, costume beads, dark stockings instead of the drab beige that Beatrice wore. By the time I finally got out the door, my look was satisfyingly as far from Beatrice's as I had the means to make it. Self-conscious of all the comfortable strangers on the bus, I thought they somehow knew and disapproved that I had come here to find refuge, and they reminded me of my alien status daily.

Henri wouldn't drive. He had been afraid ever since his first month in New York when he crashed the taxi he had been driving for extra cash. He was drunk with excitement, and nothing else, at having this cab to drive and freedom to pick up whomever hailed him—so different from what he contended with in Paris. A small girl ran out into the street, and he hit her, his fender smacking her hip and leg. She didn't die, but it paralyzed her, and he's never been able to shake himself of the guilt. From then on, inconvenienced, I had to drive him around occasionally, but at least I had the car to myself when he rode the subway to Manny's store in Brooklyn.

With two working parents, living in the middle of New York City, Jacqueline grew spoiled and unruly—wild with romantic plans of becoming a singer. She learned lyrics quickly. Sharp and gifted, she could read French and English by the time she was seven. Sometimes she embarrassed me, singing on the buses and the trains, in the streets and late at night out the windows. Her voice was powerful, as the doctor had warned it would be, and Jacqueline wanted everyone to hear her. I shouted at her to stop; I couldn't stand her voice. It was like sirens in my ears and reverberated in my sleep, waking me and invading dreams with scenes of girls dancing on tables in the backs of barrooms.

She was nearly twelve when I finally stopped shouting at her, right after Jacqueline woke and screamed in the middle of the night.

"Henri, wake up! Jackie is crying." We ran from our bed to her cries, where we found her bleeding from a gash in the back of her head.

Henri grabbed her and told me to bring the car to the front of the house. "What happened, my baby?" he asked.

"Someone came in the window and hit me with a baseball bat, papa." Dazed and bleeding, Jacqueline seemed to be dreaming.

Henri, trembling, screamed toward my shocked face as he carried Jacqueline to the car. "The girl says that someone came in the window and hit her in the head with a baseball bat. Who? What?" As if I knew the answer. "I noticed the window was open about a foot." Henri held her with her head in his lap in the back seat as I drove.

The examination from the emergency room brought suspicion from the doctors. The bruise did not look like someone hit her head with a bat; the injury was too narrow, too sharp. Henri questioned his daughter about what had happened, questioned me about what the emergency room nurse had asked him. She hinted Jacqueline was lying, and the girl concocted the story in the aftermath of what had actually happened. This insinuation would eat away at what was left of the family.

Before leaving the hospital, while I filled out forms and spoke with doctors, Henri caught Jackie's elbow in a lock and stared into her eyes. "Tell me something you would not tell the nurse. Tell me anything." Jacqueline pulled her father to a seat in the corner of the waiting room. She told him that one night months ago, he and her mother were doing sex in their room. Jackie came to the door of the bedroom. It was dark, and he didn't see her. But she said that I was facing her and did see her, and that I didn't tell Jackie to go away.

As I approached, the two separated their close cuddle but held hands.

"What are you two conspiring now?" I asked.

"We're just so tired, and Jacqueline is in pain. She wants to go home. Go to bed." Henri said.

After the night Jacqueline first spied on us making love, I threatened her, telling her I knew what she had done. I told her that to wipe the image away she had to repeat the voyeurism until it didn't make her so sick inside—till it was nothing. Then the devil would get fed up with her, and God would forgive her.

Now, as we walked back into our apartment, I offered to put my daughter to bed, but Jacqueline went wild. First she tore all the sheets from her bed, then threw the bedside lamp to the floor and started screaming. As Henri contained her in a lock hold, she blurted what I had done. Henri now understood—immediately, feeling as sick as when I tried to convince him to  watch me and that man in Paris, to prove the act meant nothing. His knees gave, and he knew he was culpable—most immediately, for Jacqueline's suicide attempt by crushing her own head.

"Our love-making means nothing?" Henry whispered to me, "You have to leave."

He does not know better? Still a boy. Jacqueline is the child. It is my duty to teach her about such frivolities, not to still be teaching Henri.

I told everyone a baseball bat caused the injury. I said I had found Jacqueline in bed. "No one knows what happened," I lied to Beatrice. She let us put metal gates on our window after that. But she heard the constant yelling. Within a month, I told her, "I've agreed to be the person at fault for my family's unhappiness. I will be the one to leave."

My struggle to maintain a normal American family had finally ruptured into such unintended chaos that on a mild autumn day in 1959, a month after the night of Jacqueline's attempt, I left home committed to support myself, and determined to teach my daughter, *my* daughter, whom to trust.

# 2
# Attempted Treatment

## *Claudette*

As I performed my one-act plays, Manny and Nadine, my mom and aunt filled the seats of my makeshift auditorium in the garage. They tried to make the absence of my father, Ben—who had never returned after the war—at my shows somewhat less featured. But when I sat in bed at night and reviewed my performance, his absence was that much more painful. There were other men to come see me—Manny always encouraged neighbors—but I couldn't help witnessing my mother Hildie's down-trodden face—alternately leaning her head from left to right through the show, until she seemed awakened by the applause. She sat proudly enough, but I embraced her loneliness just as she did. I'd overheard my mother late at night with my Aunt Fanny in the kitchen, trying to guess where my father had gone. Worried that he might even be dead. She had heard from several men who knew him that the last they knew he was in California, working as a maintenance man or a carpenter for a Hollywood studio; didn't know which one. But he'd had no contact with anyone at all since 1946. I was sure that if he died, the army would have contacted us. Surely my mother knew that as well.

At seventeen, I started entering and winning local beauty and talent contests and did some vocals for radio commercials: Greenpoint Brooklyn Savings Bank, A&P Supermarket, and other local concerns. For extra money, I would babysit little Jackie once her father came to work for Manny. There was a twelve-year gap between me and Jackie, and I easily pretended that she was my little girl. After Monika so suspiciously and permanently left her and Henri, with Jackie on the brink of adolescence, Henri had called the Hoffman women—urgency and panic in his voice—to report that Jackie had just started menstruating, practically crying his words into the phone, *What do I do?* I took twelve-year-old Jackie into her bedroom and sat her in front of the make-up mirror the girl's mother left behind, and as I applied a little bit of shadow and rouge to her face, explained her new monthly routine. When we were done with the woman-to-woman chat, we snuck cigarettes from Henri's pocket and smoked out the bathroom window. Jackie was petite, even for a twelve-year-old, as if she were the runt of a family of several children who ended up with the tiny genes—because, though slight in build, both Henri and Monika were taller than average. But her brown eyes were big and playful, and her skin was pale and unmarked, like Monika's. Such a delicate and cute girl. She looked quite comical smoking.

Jackie spent most nights crying for her mother's return. She would stand in the vestibule, between the interior door and the front door, and weep through the white sheer curtain on the door's window, banging her head against the wood molding and pulling at her hair. At bedtime, Jackie would sneak into her closet, grab a sweater, try to creak open the vestibule door silently—which was impossible—and curl into a ball in the corner of the small, tiled floor space. I would try to talk her into coming inside, but Jackie would cry and threaten to bang her head against the glass window and cut her face. I sat just inside the door and watched her until her eyes closed, her lashes glistening with tears as she fell into a loud, snoring slumber.

Night after night, Henri would call and ask me to stay with them until "the baby," as Henri still called her, fell asleep. By the time Jackie reached sixteen, she was spending some nights out. Henri called me to sit with him until his daughter came home. The waiting necessitated finding things to do—poker and smoking Marlboros, usually—and things to talk about—my stagnant acting career—as the hours drudged through a night of looking out the window ten times an hour. We sometimes had to wait until the next morning.

Henri and I were drawn together by the limits of our lives. He was on perpetual guard duty over his daughter and never spent an evening out. He'd come straight home from work, prepare dinner of spaghetti with butter or eat take-out Chinese food, and make himself comfortable in front of the television, kept company by the wine he bought on sale that day. I spent all day looking for acting work, calling my agent first thing in the morning, hopping the subway from one audition to the next, when I could get them. With less than a handful of acting offers a year—commercials, bit parts on soap operas where the girlfriend loses at love, an occasional walk-on when a television show shot in New York—earning my share of room and board at my mother's with part-time work as a checker at A&P, left no time or money for entertainment beyond the conversation of family.

I was getting very comfortable spending evenings with Henri, watching TV when Jackie stayed in, otherwise playing cards and keeping window watch. One night, when Jacqueline didn't come home at all, exhausted from worry and hungry, we shut our eyes instead of standing watch by the window, finally giving in to sleep.

Awake in Jackie's bed while Henri tossed in his, a room away, I could hear his half-smothered moans of frustration and went to him. From my limited experience with other men, I knew that what I felt now had nothing to do with familial compassion. The fitful feelings encouraging me to rise from my bed and go to Henri—how I needed to make sure he was all right, wanted more than to be relieved of the dreadful heat that was folding on me in Jackie's narrow bed—a heat that did not lift by merely throwing the blanket to the floor—and remained warm even when I remembered we were related.

His room was unlit, with shades pulled, but I saw the shadows of life illuminated by the light at the front of the house. So innately sharp was my sense of light to dark, I could make out the deep-plum-colored lump of his clothes on the floor, abandoned there in a fit of exhaustion. I heard his breathing strain to remain even; he knew I was there. I wore only an old T-shirt found in Jackie's room. Trying not to shake the bed, as if he were asleep, I slid beneath the duvet and lay rigid. I was not with my cousin Henri. I was with a man to whom I'd become close over years of friendship, a survivor of the Big One, a hero, a mild, sweet—albeit passive—and good man, and I wanted only to become close enough to him to vanquish his suffering, and mine.

We stirred, and Henri turned toward me, whispering as I lay beside him—how he'd been picturing Jackie lost in a subway, or even dead, down in the hollow of night. His guarded, hushed fears broke open. As I tried to soothe him, pushing his hair away from his eyes, he reached for me and held my arm briefly. Once again flat on our backs, we eventually fell asleep.

The windows on both ends of the apartment had been open, and the cross-ventilation pulled a closet door shut with a bang. "Is that Jackie?" Henri asked. It was quiet. I sat and listened, turned, and my hand accidentally slapped him in the head. He started and shouted, "What?" not remembering I was there. We both laughed. My laughter turned to giggling, and I found no reason not to kiss him softly. The suppleness of his lips made me smile, and he seemed to relax. His head slid off the pillow onto the bed, loose, as if I had slashed his throat. By morning we had become lovers.

Even though I loved Jackie as if I were her mother, Henri didn't trust me to know why Monika had left so abruptly and wordlessly, or why Henri got custody of their daughter. Jackie insisted that she didn't know why her mother left. But whenever I asked, and I had asked often, Jackie would cough, a sound that was deep and hollow, as if she were trying to spew up an inflated balloon. My eager curiosity over the circumstances of Monika's departure was never more deeply buried than the surface of my hairline.

When I was with Henri upon his daughter's return from week-ends with her mother, Monika would appear at his door—yawning and sighing, dressed in her loose-fitting house clothes, but fully made-up face—and little Jackie would scoot out of the car with her head down, her shoulders shrugging in what seemed a nervous tic, responding, "I don't know" to a question that wasn't asked. At about fifteen, Jackie came home from her mother's especially bitchy and wired. Chewing the inside of her cheek, she'd brushed past her father without saying hello. I gave her a look of reproach, and Jackie snarled—her face swollen, blotches on her pink skin, and black rings seemingly imbedded around her eyes. Both Henri and I confronted Monika about her condition, to which Monika, as always, reacted with tears and indignation. "I can't handle her. I try, but she goes and does what she wants."

By the time Jackie turned sixteen, she randomly refused to see her mother. A month would pass without a visit, then Jackie would call her mother crying about this or that, screaming about how no one under-stands, and Monika would meet her in a local playground and take her back home with her. The dire need to see each other would soon lose its fire, and they would separate again. Their sudden cravings to connect ignited periodic cycles when Jackie would get into trouble at school, then with police, over minor assaults and drug possession, and Monika would bail her out.

Cute no more, Jackie's face seemed drawn and sullen. Her dark, playful eyes were bloodshot. At seventeen, she randomly smirked at empty spaces. She often talked of the lines darting around ordinary objects. The mice in their apartment, which could have been true. I was with her one night, just over a year ago, when she walked out of the bathroom complaining of people yelling in what was a quiet room. And once I watched as she put out a fire on a perfectly content chair, whipping at it with a kitchen towel. Juxtaposed against the hallucinations were her eerie silent hours, when she crashed into inaccessible preoccupations with her own thoughts; sitting mute in Henri's living room, her thin arms wrapped around herself, her brown eyes watching the corners of the room. When I asked if she was all right, Jackie said nothing. The doctors considered the strong likelihood that her odd behavior was drug induced. What drug? There were differences of opinion.

I knew nothing of street drugs but was afraid she was shooting heroin, or using the mysterious LSD—but Monika appealed to various psychiatrists at her hospital to investigate the possibility that Jacqueline was schizophrenic. Monika had studied the books in the medical library and was convinced that Jacqueline did not listen to her mother's reasoning because she was, basically, insane and a pathological liar. "How do you expect her to cooperate with me and the doctors if she can't put two true thoughts together?" Monika had asked me.

"I don't know what to think. Maybe it's a little of both the drugs and illness," I said, taken aback by Monika's sense of Jackie's condition, and her conviction in her daughter's mental illness.

For the past year, they had been investigating, took blood, gave her trials of anti-psychotic drugs—at least when they could hold her down long enough for the doctor to stab her with his needle. And although Monika oversaw these pharmaceutical interventions, it was I who had to accompany Henri when the psychiatrist attempted electro-convulsive therapy on his daughter. Jackie was scheduled for a minimum of six treatments, but when I saw her emerge dazed and limp on a gurney from the first procedure, I pleaded with Henri to discontinue the series. It was stopped. Within weeks of the ECT, Jackie became more disrespectful to everyone, cursed her teachers, ignored her father; she seemed absorbed, like sugar in tea, into the life of a drug addict—illegal drugs and legal—first leaving home overnight, then out of contact for days at a time.

It all became too much for me to watch. With Henri's time and concern spent almost solely on his daughter's needs, and Monika's demands, I packed my bags and left for California. Either I was an actress, or I wasn't.

# 3

# Failed Treatment

## *Monika*

For what we prayed would be her final happy years of high school, Jacqueline had fallen headfirst into her illness and addictions. Henri and I weren't sure when the heroin started, but it had already led to several attempts at intervention: a psychiatrist, medication, threats. This morning, I needed to speak with Beatrice and dialed her extension at work.

"Why don't you meet me after work, and we'll try to find her downtown?" Beatrice offered. "And get an appointment with her shrink. She's overdue." Mid-senior year, Jacqueline had officially moved out, to an apartment in the East Village.

I ignored Beatrice's suggestion, already looking over my shoulder at nurse Stephanie and preoccupied with thoughts of this miserable job. After thirteen years, I had yet to feel respected. I told Beatrice on the phone, "On top of this garbage with Jackie, that nurse Stephanie gets onto my back about her files, until I had the last straw and talked to my supervisor. When I go back to my desk, Stephanie is talking to a patient's grown son. They whispered about the care of his suicidal mother. As if they will make a difference! The woman needs a kind word to hear. So, I decide to bring his mother tea during my break and visit with her. I had first to make sure Stephanie didn't see me, because she tells me, 'it is *beyond* the *scope* of your abilities to *assist* with the infirmed.'" I felt goosebumps from the air conditioning, and rubbed my arms.

Borrowing medical books from the doctor's library and copying passages onto lined paper in my notebook, I outlined Jacqueline's symptoms—audio hallucinations, inappropriate mood response, ambivalence—and showed the doctor how they manifested in her behavior. The doctor would then show me the needle marks on Jacqueline's arms, between her toes. When I nodded at them, as if they were right about her, the doctor suggested Jacqueline be put in a hospital, behind locked doors. Henri agreed—he told Claudette he felt it was his daughter's only alternative, but I refused. I would take charge of my daughter. I would watch her and be there for her and keep her at home. Henri had legal custody of Jacqueline, yet he would not dare enforce his desires against mine. Predictably, Jacqueline made promises and worked out deals—I'll go back to school and get a part-time job and go for counseling—and I consistently swept her off the floor and gave her another chance, writing in my notepad and redlining  paragraphs in textbooks, beginning a tally of the indications that she had a serious psychological problem.

She was seventeen when she came staggering home to her father at four in the morning, with alcohol on her breath, claiming that she was modeling for a painter in a West Side studio and he had paid her a hundred bucks. She had the cash on her, but little else. When Henri walked into her room that night to check on her, she was asleep, uncovered and sprawled across her bed. Her night-light was on and he couldn't help but notice that though she was still wearing her dress, she had no panties. He confided to me that he had thrown a blanket over her quickly, but had been too embarrassed to question his daughter about underwear, so he let her sleep. Henri said he was deeply troubled, that he saw her declining every day, that he was losing his grasp of fatherhood, more and more letting her slip from his protection. It seemed to me that the evidence of the missing panties had shown him the inadequate relationship he had with his daughter. How could he keep her under control if they never confided in each other? I felt a flurry of entitlement scurry up through my chest, as I tallied yet another advantage of my maternal status. I had no problem at all asking Jacqueline about missing underwear.

Months later, I was jolted awake late at night when Jacqueline phoned to announce her plan to go to Germany, asking questions about her bank account and airplane schedules to Cologne, as if she were going to move there and live happily ever after off some secret fortune she had inherited. I feared she would actually get the money for the airfare and I would lose my deluded and high-strung daughter to the vastness of Europe. I had declared to Henri the heart-sickening observation that our daughter was having psychotic episodes, but harder to accept—though I had to admit this to myself—a more indisputable fact: my daughter was crazy with heroin.

By the time Jacqueline turned eighteen—and as far as I knew, had never known any shore but the Manhattan side of the East River—she believed once again that she was bound for Germany in a few days' time. But there was no such bank account for airfare or a place to live, and there was no one there she knew.

"We're going to attend Jacqueline's funeral one day. I'm sure of that," Beatrice frequently told me. "Jacqueline is going to bring us such pain. A kind of pain you never knew—even in your war-torn Paris!" I never felt Paris was *mine* in the first place, and for my friend's information, I *already* felt more pain than I had ever known in Paris.

Today, just a day after Jacqueline had resumed the insane talk about Germany and complaining about the rain in April in New York, I picked up the phone at work to hear my daughter's raspy voice, amid snorts of mucus and tears, telling me she'd been beat up and hit hard in the head by somebody—another derelict-druggie, I assumed—and she needed money for *medicine*. And I said yes—my daughter was my daughter; I responded to her as if every new story were a new beginning, as if my daughter had never told a lie or disappointed me. I didn't give a damn if Beatrice or my vague-minded ex-husband Henri disapproved. This was still my living, breathing child.

Jackie, as she now insisted was the only name she'd respond to, had no car or money for transportation, so I put on my sweater and lipstick and prepared to leave work and pick her up in the East Village, at an apartment that pained and frightened me because it was so filthy, where Jackie slept on a bare mattress that she picked out of some vacant apartment building and had sex on with some despicable and useless man/boy she lived with, whom I had seen hitchhiking on the FDR Drive with a cigarette in his mouth and Jackie at his side. I almost crashed into the highway divider that night when it registered that the shabby girl was my own daughter, and now I was to drive into that squalor to get her and then take her to some facility she had told me about.

Afraid of the horrid conditions, I decided Henri should do this with me. So, shielding the telephone receiver from the snoopy nurses who hovered over me, I called Henri at the hardware store and asked him to take the rest of the day off and go to his apartment, where I would retrieve him. Henri agreed, as long as Manny okayed it. He was still the hero I had met so many years ago. Still the handsome G.I., and I believed a lonely man.

I pulled up to Beatrice and Tommy's brownstone and waited for Henri to make his jaunty walk down the steps. I loved that he at least retained that walk, a residue from when he tried to look tough during the war. Some children had chalked the numbers 1 through 6 up the stairs. Tommy had tried to teach Jacqueline stoop ball when we first arrived, but she was too impatient to learn to hit the step in the right place to get it to bounce back. The top landing was swept clean, always clean, and Beatrice had painted it in stripes of red, white, and blue. I didn't like it. I thought it looked silly, but she must have had her reasons. A nice flag would have been my choice if you want to be patriotic. Manny had a flag in front of his house. He was so proud of his country. I was so proud of him. I felt dejected, as I did every time I studied the building I had loved when we first moved here. It looked virtually the same in 1965 as it had in 1953. Except for the damn stripes!

Even before he opened the door to the car, Henri was speaking. "Jeez. I saw her last night. She looked like hell." Henri told me that her eyes had been glassy and her skin looked dry and dull. Her hair was bobby-pinned around her head haphazardly.

Affronted, I asked, "What do you mean? When did you see Jacqueline?" My voice picked up volume, and I could hear my foreignness coming through my English words.

"I just told you. Last night!" Henri said. "She came by with some guy in a suit." I examined the incredulousness on his face, his drowsy eyes rolling. He went on. "Can you believe what she tells me? She said they were going *dancing*." Then he looked at me with the corners of his lips turned down, as if dismissing the likelihood of his daughter telling the truth. "Do you *believe* her?"

"So, why did she come? For money? Did you give her money?"

"I gave her ten bucks because she looked like *death*. What can ten dollars buy?" Henri asked. "I didn't know what to do for her."

"Well I'll tell you! Put that together with the money she makes by prostituting herself"—I had come to believe she was doing that—"and she'll have enough for a bag of something. That's probably when she got attacked, when she tried to buy drugs!"

Henri's face rearranged itself into contrition. "I am sorry, sorry to God for giving her the money." The tears streaming down his face made me hope he had learned a simple lesson: he could not care for her properly. The heart and soul of Beatrice spiked through me: hard, straight. A boss.

"Do you see, Henri?" My cheeks felt pressurized, ready to breathe fire. "You take the easy way. All the time you do this. You treat her in a way you *think* is kind so she won't yell at you! Do you see why I must manage her?" Henri looked away, out the window. He did not seem to have an answer. "I judge better when it's time to give her money and when she's better to go without." His eyes and mouth cringed toward the center of his face, crushed, but I made no move to fix his shaken soul. He had abandoned me, and he deserved nothing unless he was willing to give something back to me.

On our way to Jackie's, we had a long conversation, so the ride was pleasant. I caught him glancing as I fussed with the tight ring of curl falling against my cheek, trying to tuck the ends behind my ear. I had tiny ears, like baby's ears, each fitted with a large, costume pearl earring. My hair had just been cut into a chin-length, bouncier style, letting soft curls fall about my face, with bangs cut just short of my eyelids; they were always powdered with blue-gray shadow, making them seem heavy over my hazel eyes. I once overheard Tommy tell Beatrice, "Monika has bedroom eyes." I wasn't sure what he'd meant, but I liked the idea of it.

As we inched down Park Avenue, Henri said I reminded him of better times, that I still looked young; that my face remained smooth, no lines. Henri talked about work. He was doing more of everything so that Manny could leave him to take over completely if necessary, if ever Manny needed to be away to care for Nadine at the hospital. Henri had been taught to take inventory and order stock, to tally the daily register receipts, and write checks to pay vendors. He was even given the authority to fire and hire employees, in an emergency—which he confessed impressed him more than any other responsibility Manny had ever entrusted to him. I scoffed, "Very nice, Henri. Maybe you can get your daughter a job with you. Watch her all day."

"You think?"

"Yeah, Henri, that would make Manny sooo happy!"

Stopped at a light on Twenty-Third Street, a bus driver ran his engine in my ear, so I had to shout. "How is Nadine feeling, by the way?" I asked.

"The last few weeks have been rough," Henri told me. "She's back in the hospital."

"And Manny?" My head turned forward so that I stared down Park Avenue.

"It's his trial. This is where he's been made to pay his due." Henri shook his head sympathetically. "Everyone has to."

As he spoke, I kept pulling on my narrow skirt, making sure it covered the tops of my knees. I still had trim, muscular legs, with hair so fine and blond I didn't bother to shave it, but was in the habit of keeping them covered below the knee. "I would think Manny has already paid his due." I sighed, sing-song, and pulled once more at the hem of my skirt. What do you think he did in the fucking war? You idiot, I thought.

When we got to Jackie's building, the gray brick tenement that stood in the shadows of Thompson Square Park, we parked the car and groped our way, sometimes hand in hand, through the dark hallway of the ground floor. The doors to some apartments were open, and peering in we could see the general condition of life in that place: mattresses on the floor, torn plastic window shades half off the windows. Cats.

"The smell is unbearable," I growled to Henri. He remained stoic, even when we got to the apartment that our daughter was supposed to live in. When no one answered the door, we tried it, found it unlocked, and peeked in. Taking a few steps farther into the apartment, we called for her. There was no answer. Breathing too deeply, overcome with the stench and stupidity of Jackie's existence, I started shaking and crying, but Henri was there to hold me. I whispered a quick blessing under my breath, and kissed Henri's cheek. All my repulsion for him vanished, like a mother kissing her missing, dirty child.

Driving uptown with him, I had wanted to go back to his house and enter it; to sit with him, feel his warm arm and smooth skin; skin that is always as smooth as my own. But he needed to return to his work. "I've thrown away enough of my and Manny's time," he told me, and jumped out of the car at Fourteenth to catch the subway back to the store in Brooklyn. He told me we could go out and look for her again that night. A poke of promise, and as if we'd shared a long goodnight embrace, heat rose in my chest. Although I could still feel the disappointment of his dismissal floating in my gut as I rode home, when I passed through the door into my apartment, I let loose my bridled hopefulness and laughed. How funny it was that my turmoil could also bring such joy because I had ended up spending time with Henri. Maybe it was just meant to be that Jackie would give us so much trouble, we would always be together. Even five years after our divorce, I felt real acceptance, real comfort, only when I was close to Henri. *Always, you will need me to be the strongest one.* The thought brought me peace for the remainder of the afternoon.

Walking into the hospital for work the next day, Beatrice and I were confronted by the usual wave of nurses that brushed by us as though we didn't exist. Beatrice worked in the billing office and had no personal contact with patients; she praised the Lord for this daily. Although my job title was "receptionist," I knew my responsibility was certainly more than a welcoming face. The parents of sick children, the children of sick parents—they all stopped to tell me their tales. I was naturally friendly, charming toward everyone. But as I made it clear to Beatrice, my various bosses, and anyone else who would listen, those nasty nurses and social workers tried to make it impossible for me to form bonds with the families. In spite of their efforts to alienate them from me, some of the parents of kids who were repeat admissions really did think of me as family. The nurses never knew that I had slipped them my home phone number, that they sometimes even invited me into their homes. There in the hospital ward, I had to keep my place. I knew I could be fired for my extracurricular involvement in patients' lives. The day before, I had complained once again to Henri about the different colored lab coats—how all of the staff was so possessive of sickness: "The white-coat physician—heal thyself; the blue-coat pharmacists—drug thyself." Henri had laughed.

Stephanie, or as I loved to call her, Nurse Wipe-My-Ass, possessed a tone of voice that was just rude toward me. "Mrs. Hoffman, put the chart closer to the edge of the counter so I won't have to bend in over the typewriter. You know I knocked over a cup of coffee onto a file last week because you keep the charts so far in. Okay?" I could actually feel her smugness on my skin. "Ugly with meanness," I would tell Beatrice. I knew the nurse was envious of my looks, because every time I spoke with the hunky pharmacist and he gave me doe-eyed attention, Nurse Wipe-My-Ass came over to remind me to get back to work.

Just as I got comfortable at my desk that morning, the phone rang. Jacqueline spoke before I had a chance to say hello. "Mom. Me. I ripped the stitches out in my head. The doctor made them too tight, and now it's fucking bleeding. I'm in pain. Call that freak at the clinic who stitched me and tell him he has to give me more Demerol or something. Will you do at least that for me?"

"Jackie, where are you?" I whispered into the phone, afraid for her, but still I felt like killing her.

"What the fuck kind of answer is that? *Where* am I?" She yelled into the phone. "Are you gonna call him or not? Just tell me or I can hang up and fucking cop 'em off the goddamned street! For Christ *fuck*ing sake!" Then she hung up.

I sipped tea to calm myself. I could not get used to that—that kind of mania when she missed her prescription medications, and I knew she was using heroin.

While Beatrice and I took the hospital elevator down to go home, I cursed Henri. He had not returned my calls, and I'd grown frantic during the day. We got off work at four in the afternoon, so the traffic home had not yet fully built up. From the time we left the hospital, I pleaded with Beatrice to get off the bus with me; I felt desperate not to be alone in my apartment in the event Jacqueline phoned again. Before the bus came to my stop, Beatrice agreed to stay with me, but not without comment. "Shame on you, Monika," she said, poking her finger into my thigh. "Cursing Henri. Save your lot of frustration for that…that *confused* daughter of yours." Beatrice tsked, looked up, and whispered, "Poor little Jackie."

My apartment, the same one I'd been in since I left Henri and Jackie nearly six years before, was a one-bedroom on the ground floor of a pre-war building off Second Avenue and Forty-Ninth. Since that autumn day in 1959, Henri wouldn't even let me inside his home. He got to stay in the apartment because he agreed to my divorce demand to say he "abandoned" me.

The apartment was situated just about halfway between my job and my family, and Tommy knew the landlord and was able to finesse a kindlier rent. I had made it as comfortable as I could on my income, but it never became home. The kitchen was big enough for an ice-cream table and two stool-sized chairs. But it was meant to accommodate only me, and Jacqueline, when she came to visit, or Beatrice. The few things Henri had let me keep from Paris—the cotton embroidered tablecloth with flowers, a cherished German-made vase that held one stem—made the main room look homier. I ultimately used the tablecloth to cover the couch because of the picked-at fabric. During one of Jacqueline's fitful times, she sat all night and picked at the threads on the seat cover until there were holes. The sight of that destruction made me cry for three days.

The kitchen faced the small owner's yard, and from springtime on, sunshine still filtered into the room at five in the afternoon. Beatrice sat at the table, and I put up the water for tea. I stood over the pot, watching for it to boil.

"Why don't you come sit until it boils. It'll whistle," Beatrice told me.

Although I needed to stand to allow my disappointment with Henri height enough to reverberate through my body, space enough for my voice to carry, I released a loud "Ahhch!" and reluctantly sat out of politeness. "This attack on Jackie didn't have to happen. She was here with me a few nights ago. I sat right there on my couch and told her, 'Sit on my lap.' She's so skinny, she's like a twelve-year-old. As I rocked her, I said, 'Let's sing, little Jackie.' And she let me sing to her, and she cried, *Mommy, Mommy, I'll be good. I promise.* She soaked in a warm tub and allowed me to rub her back with violet-scented oil. She even rolled the yellow ringlets of my hair around her fingers. I felt she would come back to me. She would be Jacqueline again, and she would finish high school and maybe even go to college! In the morning, what good had it done? When the first light came, she tricked me into bringing her back downtown."

Beatrice just watched me as I stared, and I *let* Beatrice watch as she grew excited, wanting her to feel as I felt, to appreciate what other women have to endure. Without warning, my lover rose to mind, as he had late that Monday night after Jacqueline had disappeared again. I could not share the sweetness he brought to my days. I willed those thoughts to disappear and concentrated on that morning. *The sun had just come up, and I thought, "Oh, praise God, what a beautiful day." Jackie and I could walk through the park down at Kips Bay, and maybe she'll remember how she loved the ducks when she was little. When she was our sweet girl. We would collect different wild flowers—how I love those colors, and we would make an arrangement, set it on the table in the kitchen.*

"I went to Jackie, still sleepy on the living room couch, curled in the blue cotton sheet," I told Beatrice. "She's always so warm at night. She began mumbling something about getting to her apartment for something important she left there. I believed her. Why shouldn't I believe her? We had just spent the night together. She had just cried in my lap!"

"You're a fool, Monika," Beatrice muttered.

I was disappointed that Beatrice had chosen to insult me at this time of distress. I continued nonetheless, telling how when we reached Jackie's street, she got out of the car, raised her hand into the air, and waved a twenty-dollar bill, which she had stolen from my purse. As I watched—choking, temporarily paralyzed—in no time there were hordes of scum around my daughter, calling out to her, offering her drugs for her stolen cash.

*Hey, girlie.*

*Hey, mama.*

*Jack-o-leen.*

"Rat-bastard whoring little bitch," I swore at the windshield while I gunned the gas pedal and just left her there, heading uptown to Henri's apartment.

I parked at a meter on Second Avenue; my steady heartbeat had already resumed, as I strolled down the street anticipating my visit with him. Maybe we will sit and have a glass of wine, or he might play for me the new records he's bought at the Sam Goody next to his store. I strode the walk I worked so hard in my teens to achieve, with my back straight and my strides even, elongated and careful as my foot hit the pavement —a person could pick me out in a crowded street from a block away. I passed the neat brownstones, counting flowers in window boxes, imagining the owners: dull lives if they were white flowers, passionate if they were purple. As I got closer to Henri's place, my stomach started to turn. I had to force myself to burp.

He had been waiting for me, sitting on the steps with a face hanging so low and so pale; angry at me already because he'd be late for work. I remembered what I was doing there, and I walked slower.

"So, Henri, you still will not let me inside?" I stood on the next-to-last step.

He ignored my remark. I noticed his cigarette-holding fingers shaking as well, and I dropped my smile.

"Can't we please go inside and talk about this? I insist you allow me into your home." I felt the sweat accumulating in my armpits. I wished I could at last get used to the *idea* of shaving them.

Henri just shook his head. It astonished me that his determination to keep me out ran so deep that even in time of such crisis he would not capitulate. "I've been painting," he said. "The living room and kitchen are a mess. We can only sit on my bed. I don't think we should go in."

"Oh for heaven's sake, Henri. I think we can sit on a bed together." I put my arm under his and pulled on him, laughing, to stand up and let me in. He stood reluctantly and walked in, allowing me to follow behind.

Entering my first American home after an exile of six years, I expected to be greeted by the scent of my own perfume, incense from Jackie's room, or maybe the awful odor of a gym bag containing my daughter's dirty soccer uniform. All smells dead for more than half a decade, but as alive to my senses as though I had left yesterday. I put one foot beyond the foyer into the living room and smelled paint, overcome with the sheer fumes of oil, of molten rubber and singed electrical wire. The kitchen table and chairs were draped with sheets I had bought on sale at Macy's, and the countertops were covered with newspaper. There was not so much as the smell of popcorn, which Jackie had Jiffy-popped every day after school, giving the house the permanent aroma of a movie theatre lobby. Not so permanent, after all. I swayed, lightheaded from the dour evidence of a life discarded. Mine.

Walking carefully among ladders and pails, we found our way to his bedroom. I sat on the bed and bounced a little, smiling. Henri stood.

"So, what should we do about Jacqueline?" I asked. Henri closed his eyes and wiped his forehead with a handkerchief.

"Henri! You knew it would come to this! It was inevitable. So, now we don't have to wonder when could it come?" I sat higher. "She is what they call the junkie."

He sat beside me, and I was titillated by his weight in the bed with me. Henri put his arm around me. I leaned in toward him and started praying at once that he would take me, throw me down on the bed and just make love to me. I had another man, a man I loved, who did not need to be treated like waste, the way Henri did as a child—but I relished having sex with him.

Henri removed his arm and kissed my forehead. He sat staring at the floor and chewing on his lower lip. "Shall we go and try to find her now?" He stood and motioned to show me the door. He said, "If something really bad happens to her it will kill me, you know."

Yes, I nodded. I knew.

# 4

# How Well the Children Played



*Monika*

Just an hour later, Henri and I were back at Jackie's apartment and re-trieved her from her bed—her blouse torn off at the shoulder, her dun-garees hanging just below her navel. Her face wore shadows of screams, and her eyes were dark as the bottom of an ashtray.

"You see what happens when you ask me to stay at her place?" I heard Jacqueline tell her father.

"Shush now. You get quiet before you get in your mother's car. And shush! shush!" He pursed his lips and breathed hard. Henri led her by her elbow out the door and onto the street while I ran ahead and brought the car around.

I screeched to a stop as a spot opened in front of her place. Jackie climbed into the back seat, and Henri grunted while he bent to slide in next to me. "So where were you last night, Monika? Jackie said she sat awake all night trying to call you, waiting until you got back home—at *three* in the morning. Is this true?" Henri asked.

I pulled my head back, his gall—Henri thought anything that had to do with the two of us was his business. He was fuming. I knew he'd do little more than chide me for my absence. I said, "She's crazy. I was home until she was well asleep. And am I not allowed to have a date? Just like you to look to fault me instead of comforting your baby girl from the drugs or her god-knows-from-what torn shirt!"

"Just checking." Henri had frowned at my temper, then turned to the back seat and told Jackie to stay put and keep calm. She gave him the finger, the act sugar-coated with her smile. "Nice," Henri said. "I want you to know that I am thanking God you are safe, even if you are nasty with me."

"If you must know, I've spent the night out on dates before. Are you happy now?" That, I knew, had been more than he wanted to know. I wanted him to know everything. I wanted to scream it into his face after he rejected me this morning. Scream at him: See who wants me!

Henri reached into his pocket for a cigarette. He held one out to the back seat and Jackie grabbed it. "Anyone I know?" he asked me sarcastically.

"Not now, please." I'd keep my secret, at least from Jackie, a while longer. I turned off Houston Street, heading uptown on Sixth. Greenwich Village was crowded with kids cutting school. They looked happy. They looked happier than Jacqueline. Girls crossed the street holding hands, some twirling in circles as they went. Boys laughed and pulled their mop-top hair off their faces, just getting used to the management of it kept so long. I looked at the teenagers laughing, dressed in pants that were too tight and tops too transparent. Some were obviously high on dope, but most were just kids pretending they were on their own and free in the big bad city. Fools, I thought…recalling the city of my adolescence, which had raped my childhood. From the back seat came the disapproving, exaggerated gags from my child.

"They think they're so cool, with their make-believe drugs. They all still live at home with their mommies and daddies, eating every goddamn meal with a silver fork," Jackie growled. She closed her eyes.

Henri blew smoke out the window and threw the butt into the gutter. When we got to his apartment, he leaned over the seat. "So tell me, what do we do with you now? Where will you stay tonight?" Jackie gave him her cheek to kiss, and looked at me. I hoped she would tell him she wanted to go home with her mother. "So what are you going to do? Who will you stay with?" he asked her once again.

"Mom, I can stay with you, or, you know, I could go back to my place." Jackie, wide-eyed, looked as if she knew there was candy waiting at my apartment.

"Yes, of course," I said. "Why don't you go back to your place, so you could buy heroin and shoot up." Through my tears, I looked in the rear-view mirror to see Jacqueline roll her eyes. "But you'll stay with me again tonight. I'll be there with you tonight. We'll have to come to an arrangement about tomorrow."

"Yeah, yeah. We'll make *an arrangement.* I gotta get some sleep anyway. Yeah, so I'll sleep. Okay?" Jackie stretched her legs across the back seat and crossed both arms over her eyes.

"Well that's settled then." Henri scooted out of the car. "You stay with your mother and sleep. If I find out you stole money again from her, I'll put you back on the street." His easy, say-anything way out. I wondered precisely which of us he thought he was fooling.

"Yeah, like I care." Jackie rocked back and forth in her seat, starting to sweat. She pulled at her shirt, ripping it further.

"It's the withdrawal talking, Henri. She's going to need the fix real soon."

"*A* fix," Jackie snarled. Then I heard her mutter, "Jeez."

"Well, that's just not going to happen," Henri declared, as if he had any idea anymore about what kept her alive. He might as well have claimed to control the sunset. "Are you able to handle this, Monika?" Henri didn't even know what it was like for his daughter to withdraw, except for my recounting the day after, over a telephone at work, each of us distracted by and protecting ourselves from people who needed us on the job. He turned to face his daughter. "Please behave yourself, Jackie. I love you." He blew a kiss. "You can go without this stuff. Be strong for me."

"Come sit here, up front with me." I watched her in the rearview mirror to see if she would move. When she climbed over the seat and got into the front beside me, Henri hurried around to my side and held his fist to his ear, telling me to phone him later. "I'll take care of her," I mouthed. I drove away and left Henri to his mess of a home.

During the ride home, we hit one red light after another. The wind had kicked up, and a paper cup flew up and hit the windshield. We both jerked at the quick tap on the glass and the shadow of it passing. Jacqueline was shaking with chills. "We'll be home soon, sweetheart. You just hold yourself together." I squeezed her hand and nodded.

"You'll let me, Mom? You'll let me take my stuff? Promise me, please please please," Jackie chanted through her shivering as her hand lay tense under mine.

In the apartment, Jackie sat at the small kitchen table. I offered to call a doctor from work, a psychiatrist who had seen Jackie before. "Dr. Melone is your best choice here. He could get you back on medication and clean you right up. What do you think about that?" I knew what my daughter thought about that. She wanted only to get drugs into her veins and feel relief.

"You promised me. You said you had some and would give it to me." Her eyes were bloodshot, and her hair was matted and darkened with desperation.

I went into the bedroom to get the stash from a cardboard cigar box under my lingerie.

The parents of patients were not the only friends I had made at the hospital. I had befriended the patients themselves, many of whom were addicts, many of whom had visitors who were addicts, eager to share information on purchasing drugs in return for the promise of favors, such as sneaking them in for carnal visits with their incarcerated loved ones. The drug had been so easy to attain. Having the dealer come right to the hospital, ostensibly meeting me for lunch in the cafeteria, handing me a paper lunch bag—I knew it wasn't any harder for Jacqueline to buy drugs than it would be for her to buy bubble gum, just more expensive.

Along with the box under my lingerie lay clean needles stolen from the hospital, alcohol, cotton balls, tourniquet, antiseptic ointment to rub on the wound, a spoon, and a box of matches.

Handing my child the things needed to calm her, I stepped out of the room.

"You watch me, Mom. You *have* to watch me," Jackie told me before she touched the needle to her skin. "You'll see. It's nothing." I turned and watched Jackie put the needle into the skin above and between her breasts. I didn't think this was normal, even for a junkie. What do I know? I didn't speak. Jacqueline's hand shook as she pushed the syringe, and she watched closely, looking mesmerized, gratified that she'd hit a vein, until the needle was pulled out. Closing her eyes and dropping her head, she waited for the flush of heaven that would immediately envelope her. Her hand reached over her chest and the blood trickled, running around the curve, stopping under her nipple, encircling it like a kiss.

Within a second, her face was at peace and her hand was warm to my touch. "You're okay now, baby?"

"Yeah, Mom. Thanks." After a while, Jacqueline stood. "It was like watching *nothin'*, right?" She swooned and gently hugged me. "I love you, Mommy."

# 5

# No Holding Back



*Henri*

I sat in my bedroom as the onset of evening melted into my head like ice on blistering skin. This night no different than the previous hundreds of nights I'd spent alone, long before Jackie had drifted from me. Disappearing, evaporating. Come home from work, shower and eat, change channels on the television, settle on nothing, pick through the fridge looking for spoiled food to throw away, then rummage through the clothes on my bedroom floor for pieces to take to the laundromat. All this and only an hour would have passed. And so I'd sit with a drink and wait for sleep to come.

Tonight, in my darkness, I reached for the phone. I felt my heart send a hot ripple to my throat. It was the same pain I'd felt when, at ten years old, on my knees with my sister, digging holes in our small garden behind our apartment in which they'd bury the small *treasures* of Judaica—a Kiddush cup, mezuzah, and a few gold stars on chains—in a rush of dirt and dandelions, I had looked into my mother's eyes and saw in them not strength and hope but the splintered bones of her broken spirit. Now at dusk, the shards of defeat stabbed into my groin with longing. I called Claudette.

"It's me, hon. Can you come…?" Was I panting?

"I've been waiting for three days to hear that. Should take an hour if I take the subway. Henri, I've missed you so much."

Had it been so long as nine months since I breathed in her excitement to be with me? I smiled into the phone, my head relaxed and dropping. "We'll go to a movie and have something to eat. Make it a homecoming celebration. How's that?" I knew there was no way that would happen. We were second cousins, after all. We could not be seen in public, me pretending not to be in love with her.

An hour later when the doorbell rang, I woke and jumped to my feet. The house was completely dark, and I couldn't find my way to the door of my room. The banging at the front door shook me to turn on the light switch, and I felt the teasing poke of excitement in my belly.

She stood at the doorway in her dungarees and white cotton blouse. Through the etching of the glass that looked like stars sitting on little sleds, was the silhouette of her hair, twisted into two braids, hanging behind her ears. The door was heavy oak, and the deadbolt was tight and hard to twist open. I had to push it against the jam to release the lock and pull it open. The air that surrounded her had, in one minute, caught her fragrance, and the smell of lilac jumped the threshold before she moved, powdering my skin, preparing me.

I kissed her cheeks as she walked in, pushing hard with my mouth. At thirty years old, she appeared to be no more than seventeen. California had trimmed her face, but she returned more golden. From the quick sweep of her eyes and the twitch of her nose, I knew she could see and smell the mess of paint and drop cloths, but she sauntered in without comment, to the only livable room, my bedroom.

Barely awake, I excused myself to get a drink from the kitchen. From the hallway, I turned to look at her and watched as she straightened the bedding and turned on all the lamps. I followed her gaze out the window into the light of a room across the alley, where she watched a child practicing a violin; she was hitting herself in the head with the bow every time she scraped out a bad note. The light of the girl's room shone only over her head and onto her music stand with sheet music; I imagined my cousin saw the girl in the spotlight of Carnegie Hall. I smiled. The girl, maybe twelve, had finally been doing well, with no mistakes when I returned, a bottle of wine in one hand, two glasses held by the stems— clicking—in the other. Claudette was tall and narrow but with round buttocks, and her dungarees fit tight around them.

"You look lovely, Claudette." I put my handfuls on the dresser and went to her.

Just weeks after Jackie's shock treatment, Claudette was offered a bit part as a nurse on the television show *Dr. Kildare*, and she left us all and moved to California. This job was a tremendous break from the rejection she had steadily received in New York. She accepted the part without hesitation. If she became successful, I would move with Jackie to California and no longer have to live out our romance in secret. Our life in New York had been spread thin—as if gold leaf had been poured upon barn straw, and it was cracking. Jackie was ruining the lives of everyone around her. In California, our roots and history would be unknown, and we could start over in a warm place. We'd get Jackie into treatment, out of the reaches of her mother. In the meantime, Claudette and I would write and call. The studio had promised her a vacation; she could come home during the hiatus of the show.

Claudette was gone for nine months. The job ended, and there didn't seem to be any more work, so she was on her way back to her mother's house in Brooklyn. She was evasive when I asked her what really happened. Claudette shared with no one the disappointment she felt when she realized the shameful and painful place she had run to. Directors ridiculed her, producers ignored her, and other actors offered her drugs. She was encountering an existence that looked more like *Jackie's* life than was naturally tolerable. She'd throw her mother and aunt off her back with answers like: "It was too lonely for me there. The parts are too demeaning. I want to work on Broadway." She didn't reveal how much she missed me—and Manny.

She had tried to look for her father while she worked in LA—to the best of her knowledge, he was transported from the South Pacific to California and stayed there—but found nothing. An extra she met on the studio lot dabbled in private investigation and made some calls for her to the Army and Social Security Office. Claudette entertained no grand expectations even if she had found him, seen him. Her father didn't know her anyway, she thought, so the meeting would have been, at least for him, shocking.

Tonight was our reunion. Claudette had doubts as to why she was agreeable to be with me like this. She loved me, but it was not a clean love. There was always a nuance of shame between us. I put my hands around Claudette's waist and kissed her neck, my cheek brushing her face. I could sense her blush was not all from pleasure. Guilt-ridden, turning from me, as if looking over her shoulder after a theft, "I missed you. It's been three days since you called, since I've been home." Claudette gently kissed my neck in return.

"The last two days we had trouble again. I'm sorry." I smelled her perfumed neck and slid my hands beneath her shirt.

"What's happened to her now?" Claudette asked, knowing it had to be about Jackie, breathing hard but keeping a poker face.

I dropped my hands and sank onto the bed. "Same shit. Her mother takes her downtown to that shit-hole apartment, and she buys drugs right in front of her. Right in front of her. It keeps going, getting worse. What will be with that child, I don't try to imagine anymore. Her mother tries, I guess, to help, but—poof!—she escapes." I opened my hands into the air, letting go of my magical parental doves, then pulled Claudette to the bed. She fell on top of me.

She would take longer than me to warm up to intimacy. Nine months in California had been a long time to think, a long enough absence to test life without me, a generous stretch of time to allow the pitfalls of this unamerican relationship to allow seeds of doubt to grow. Yet even at first glance of me tonight, I felt her caution turning to ash beneath her damp skin. Upon my touch, I felt her curiosity erupt. "Tell me why you and Monika really divorced." She straddled my hips, and she teased me. "You'll tell me, Henri. How horrible a thing could it be?" She put a hand on each of my shoulders and pushed them down into the mattress. "Come on, Henri. For god's sake, I'm the one in bed with you! You've trusted me with your daughter's welfare, but you won't trust me with your *past*?" She released her grip.

I reached up and rubbed the heel of my palm around and over her left shoulder. Her back arched as her thighs tightened against my hips. I knew a tinge of electricity rushed through her. I crunched up and kissed her navel, then said, "Not horrible. *Inhumane.*" I rolled to the side so that she toppled off and we lay face to face. I felt the abrupt detachment.

Before I could speak, I put my hand to my throat. Claudette's forehead perspired. "You can tell me anything, of course you know that, but you can also have this secret if you want." She seemed lost to specify what she wanted.

"I'll try to tell you, but you have to remain still. No questions."

"No questions, I promise." Sitting, she crossed her legs and propped her fists under her chin, keeping her head from shaking. When she had to listen to bad news, her head quivered.

My throat was in pain. "Okay," I coughed and looked away from Claudette. "When it happened, I had to change my world. Up, down, I didn't know what was crazy anymore." Claudette's fists tightened and her stare locked. "One night, when Jackie was about eleven and a half, Monika and I were making love. Jackie came to the door of the bedroom. It was dark, and I didn't see her." Claudette's heart rate must have jumped as she grimaced, tightened the hold on her head, and tried to picture the scene. To put Henri with Monika made her jealous and was hard enough, but the rest, the rest was impossible to imagine. She closed her eyes, just whispering, *Oh, God.* I sat up, leaned over Claudette, and held her face. I was finally talking and didn't want her to move her eyes from my face. She kept her promise and asked nothing.

"Monika told her that she would tell *me* if Jackie didn't do whatever Monika told her to do."

"So what did Monika tell her to do?" Claudette whispered in spite of herself.

"According to Jackie—and this is where there is room for disbelief, or at least speculation because the night she told me about it, she was on painkillers and had a slight concussion."

"Concussion? Painkillers?"

I had to explain about the trip to the hospital and take a gulp of air.

"What are you telling me, Henri?"

"I'm telling you that Monika would sneak Jackie to the doorway when she knew we were going to make love, and she would have her watch."

I tilted my head back to draw breath, then clenched my jaw. Rubbing at my day-old beard, pulling my face, I looked to Claudette. "Could you believe such evil in a mother? She warned Jackie not to close her eyes because the devil and God would see her, and she would never be absolved from her sin. How did Monika come up with this half-ass bullshit?"

"Henri, no! Did Monika really believe that? Is she crazy? Tell me you found out and smacked her and stopped her."

"I think it happened two or three times before I knew. Monika is supposed to be a religious woman—I mean, she's so big on crucifixes all over and thanking the Lord for everything—but how can she believe such…such a disgusting experience for a child, her child, wouldn't be harmful?" I let go of her hand—I'd grabbed it somewhere in my confession—and gave her distance. "I will never believe that what she had Jackie do was meant for Jackie's *benefit*. There is something terribly wrong with that woman." I hit my forehead with three jabs of my fist, like teaching the idiot kid in me a lesson.

Claudette took my hands. Her hands were shaking. "How did you find out?"

"The night that Jackie tried to bust her own head open against the metal window frame. You remember those stitches she got in her head?" I shook my head, staring into the moonlit room. "Can you believe she watched us? Watched me, her father, in such an intimate way? And Monika knowing she was there. Putting her there, with all our bareness. It must have seemed violent and filthy and, *uch, uch*, I cannot sometimes even look into Jackie's eyes." I walked to the window, talking into the glass pane. "Even I felt violated by Monika. Not that it matters. It's only Jacqueline that matters here. Can you blame me for not letting Monika into this house? Can you blame me for not wanting Jackie to live with her?" I checked Claudette's face.

"I can't understand this. This is too much to take." Claudette came to me, buried her face into my shoulder, and shook until she wept.

I felt paralyzed. "This is how the drugs started, I'm sure, with those first painkillers." I made the sign of the cross over my chest, saying, "I thank God Jackie finally was able to tell me, and I was able to put a stop to it."

I told Claudette how I had brought Jackie to the emergency room the night they found her with her head split and bleeding. Jackie, under the influence of painkillers, was able to first tell the nurse what had happened. In shock and disbelief, the nurse had asked me if it could be true.

"No, no, I told her—the girl was hallucinating from the pain drugs they'd given her. But once she was bandaged up and back at home, Jackie told me she remembered what she had said to the nurse. Crying hysterically behind the locked bathroom door, Jackie told me that it was true; she had seen us. And that her mother forced her with the fear of God to watch. All I did was hug her and hold her until she stopped crying. I grabbed Monika and asked her to admit it or to tell me her daughter was lying. She said that Jackie was exaggerating. She said it only happened that once by mistake and that Monika told her it was a sin, that Jackie had gotten into her own head to watch again and again."

I now looked at Claudette and waved a finger into the air, as if an old rabbi making a fine point. "But there was such a sparkle of excitement in her eyes, such energy to explain and *discuss*, that I knew it was Monika who was lying. I slapped her cheeks. Both of them." I had wanted to spit. "When we woke in the morning—I stayed with Jackie and slept on the floor next to her bed—Monika was in the kitchen making veal stew, as if it were just another normal day."

"You're telling me you let her stay here?" Claudette leaned her shoulder against the window, looking dizzy and trying to keep steady.

"It was a mistake. But you see, we'd been together almost all our lives. I wanted to make sense of it, to half believe each of them, to forgive both."

"And so," Claudette asked tightly, "what did it take?"

It had taken more than disgust, I explained. I could no longer touch her, even casually, for fear that Jackie would see us. The smell of her flowery perfume made me sick; the sound of her breathing made me cringe. Jackie was sullen, buried in some dream of who knew what; staying in bed all day; refusing food. Monika would cry every day, and I would start to calm her—an act borne of some long ago need to spare her feelings— but always I ended our talks by threatening her. "I told her I'd kill her for what she'd done. I wouldn't have, never could hurt her, but I knew our marriage was over. I took everything she had in her drawers and closet and threw it into the vestibule. She slept in that vestibule that night. I locked the inside door so she couldn't get back into the apartment."

"She stayed there all night?"

"Yes. Jackie and I went in the morning to see Manny and Nadine in Brooklyn. I carried Jackie out of the house and stepped right over Monika on the floor to get out. We stayed with Manny overnight. Manny didn't ask why."

Claudette now knew why Jackie would stand in the vestibule and cry. "How can you look at her?" Claudette asked me, her face twisted, trying to look as ugly as possible. "This is more than I ever—how does *Jackie* look at her? My god!" She covered her eyes with her hands. "She should have been arrested."

"Remember how she cried for her to come back?" I said.

"Remember? I held her almost every night."

"I'm telling you, Monika has a great power over that child. So I work with that power. I work with it to help her."

"And I'm sorry to say Monika has power over you as well." Claudette buried her face in her hands. "But Jackie was always worse when she came back from Monika. She should *never* have been allowed to see Jackie again. My god, Henri. Why have you *allowed* this to go on with her?"

I could only stand stiff with regret. "I kept them apart for a year. You don't remember. Jackie was having such nightmares. She begged me on her *knees* to see her mother. She even took back *everything* she'd said. Told me she made it up. I knew she hadn't made it up. What child would make up such things and then try to break her own head on a window sill?" I was caught and helpless. I had no answers and no truths. "You must remember the childhood we had. How she had been abused. Watched. I felt pity for Monika." I genuinely did not feel the need to apologize to Claudette. "One night it was enough, I couldn't take Jackie's crying anymore. I let them see each other at the playground the next morning." I gulped my full glass of wine.

"And you were able to let go of Jackie's hand? You were able to look at Monika and *let* your child go to her?"

"*Let* her go?" I chuckled. "She ran so fast to her mother that by the time I looked at my empty hand, Monika had her arms around her. After that—well, you know what after that."

She knew. I leaned so far forward, my head was between my knees. I went to sit on the recliner and Claudette followed, sitting on my lap. She leaned into me. Darkness had fully lowered, leaving the purple gray of sky to fall solemnly over the streets like a tallis on a coffin. The little violinist was no longer playing; no light shone over an innocent shoulder.

6

# With Open Arms

## *Manny*

I kept my left hand under Nadine's armpit and held her hand with my right as I walked her from the hospital room's bathroom back to bed. This was our goodnight ritual. Over the past two months, Nadine's condition had grown dire; the cancer that had been cut from her breast three years ago was now residing maliciously in her lungs. Every morning I visited her before work, then, at three in the afternoon, leave Henri to handle business at the store and drive down Rockaway Parkway, past the comfort of the kosher hot dog and knish cart near the subway station, the small convenience groceries and fruit stands, and neighborhood shops like John's Bargain Store. The white brick and black canopied façade of Brookside Hospital stood out like a modern structure of hope, but mine was dwindling. I'd park in the lot across the street, stop at the vendor's in the hospital lobby for coffee with cream, three sugars, and a Danish, gulp my hyperglycemic breakfast, and proceed to the elevators. Stiff with sweetened courage, I'd get off on the third floor for another surreal visit with my wife.

After I helped her back from the bathroom, I lifted her legs onto the bed and covered them with the light cotton blanket, then sat beside her and held her hand, watching as she closed her eyes. Fingering the thinness of the blanket, I thought about our bed at home, the comforter Hildie had bought us for our wedding. This bed seemed inadequate. All of this was inadequate—the painkillers, the bed, pillows, room, lighting, the shades. Even the slow progress of her disease was inadequate. It was as if Nadine's cancer were a roller-coaster car at Coney Island that was dangling in the balance, half off the rails. I wanted something about her condition to change dramatically—change enough either to give her comfort, or kill her. This cancer became our neighbor, enrolling its children in schools in her lungs, walking the streets of her body. After swallowing my tears, I asked her, "You uncomfortable, hon? Are you sure this blanket is enough?" Her moaning was constant, but soft, conscious enough to be polite about it.

"Comfortable and warm enough." She opened her eyes and tilted her head toward my face.

I rubbed my forehead with my index finger and thumb. I was already exhausted. The fear of awakening to answer a call from the hospital kept me from falling asleep last night, most nights. It was almost nine o'clock, and I was torn between wanting to stay and wanting to escape. Our empty house on bustling Kings Highway terrified me. Being alone at night felt like sitting in a foxhole, listening for the one sound in the darkness that would signal all hell had broken loose, the first enemy shell to blast open the black sky, sprouting white hot bullets pointed at me. "Sleep, sweetheart." I slid my hand under the blanket and found hers. "Tomorrow is supposed to be really hot." I looked up at the television, which was on, but mute. A chattering young actress sat with Merv Griffin, flirting with him in the greenish black and white. "Henri's hocking me about getting the store air-conditioned in time for summer. What d'ya think?" I didn't look at her face for an answer.

I wasn't expecting her to speak; I was just trying to fill our visit with normal sounds.

She cleared her throat weakly. "Yes. Henri's right. Air-conditioning would be—" She tried to breathe. "It would be good."

I knew how hard it was for her to maintain this ridiculous conversation. "How about I shut the light and TV now?" I pulled the chain for the light over her head, then pushed in the knob of the TV, ending the ingenue's seduction. Nadine lowered her eyelids against the daylight, and I could see tears leak from the corners of her eyes, sliding onto the sides of her nose. I put my head against her cheek on the pillow. "Don't cry. Please, don't worry. You want me to stay all day?" As soon as I made the offer, I felt a stab of fear that would cause her to worry even more. Worried that I'd thought this was the end. I was relieved when she shook her head no. "I'll be back by three. We'll watch the early news together." When I lifted my face from the pillow to look into her eyes, to offer her a smile, I saw she had fallen asleep.

I focused intently on her face and imagined kissing her eyelids, her nose, and her lips. Without touching her, I moved my mouth from shoulder to shoulder, to belly, to knees and toes. When I had envisioned kissing her entirely, I lifted my bag of garbage—cold coffee and uneaten Danish—and went to work.

## *Monika*

The night had made its full descent, and I was feeling edgy. Jacqueline had skipped out as soon as she woke up this morning, and I have no idea where she's gone or if she's shown up at Henri's. Beatrice was a dear and came home from work with me again. I think something is going on at her house. She isn't usually this helpful to me. "I don't understand why Henri hasn't returned my call," I said to Beatrice, tapping with the paring knife against the Formica counter. "Maybe he's busy at work. Manny is pissed that he misses so much time because of Jacqueline." I wrapped the leftover carrots and Beatrice rinsed the frying pan of burnt fish.

"I don't believe he would be *pissed*," Beatrice said. "Manny always spoke well about Henri. More than any man I know, even Tommy, Manny's patient and fair minded."

I could feel myself blush. I loved hearing other people's love for Manny.

Beatrice wiped her hands. "He's been covering a lot of the slack while Manny runs to the hospital morning, noon, and night. Poor Nadine," she sighed, shaking her head. "I spoke to Hildie when she came by to visit Henri with rugalach, and she said that poor woman is near the end. Very near."

My chest swelled with impatience. "I know all about it. What do you think, I don't find out about my family? I talk to Manny all the time." I sniffled, inserting the carrots in the refrigerator with a punctuating thump.

"I didn't know you speak to him. I thought after the divorce you lost touch. Because, you know, he's so devoted to his cousin Henri."

"I *see* him too, if you must know. And I've visited with Nadine in the hospital. She's the one, after all, who wrote Manny to find us in Paris to begin with." Reminding myself, with a soothing swoon, that Manny had been on a war-long search for us.

I could see Beatrice eyeing me, a tinge of suspicion in her squinting eyes. "I'm glad for you, keeping in touch. What d'ya have to talk about with them?"

I leaned back against the sink, lifting the towel to my face and wiping my forehead of sweat, trying to think of something I might speak about with a neutral tone. "I tell Nadine about Jacqueline. I lie, of course. Nadine'll never get well enough to know the truth, and since she only had Claudette and Jackie as *pretend* children, I can't break her heart. What would be the point?"

"True. You're thoughtful doing that. Pretend children?"

I licked honey from my fingers; I'd drenched the carrots with it and would find drippings around the kitchen for a week. Struggling, I continued, "Nadine thinks she's such a disappointment to Manny. How she never had a child, and now with no breasts." I turned to Beatrice with tears in my eyes. "They butchered her, you know. She showed me the scar. It's a monstrous mess." I blew my nose in the dishtowel. I had been truly horrified at the sight, putting my hand to my breast, remembering. "I couldn't speak a word of encouragement after I saw that, except to tell her that everyone loved her no matter what." Everyone did love her, but now I looked out the kitchen window to hide my face from Beatrice, afraid the other woman would read in my eyes my own question. How could I?

We worked silently, except for a shared sigh over Nadine, straightening the kitchen and mixing lemonade.

"Can you stay a while? Will Tommy mind?" I asked, an affect of self-pity in my voice.

"After twenty-six years of marriage to the same woman, the only thing he minds is me telling him more work needs doing. No, he won't mind. You know, I really want to hear about the man you've been out with lately. At least *you* get to go out. I haven't been to a movie in a decade."

The phone rang and I jumped. "Please don't be Jackie," I said. I picked up, and, in case it was Manny, spoke a throaty "Hello." When I heard who it was, I made my words choppy, hushed. "Oh my Lord… Yes I know." I moved around the small kitchen table, trying to get privacy, tangling the phone wire in my hand, pushing my bangs off my forehead, torn between being discreet, and saying what I wanted—to hell with Beatrice. "Any improvement at all?"

He told me she was comfortable but weak, that she said it was okay to go home for the night. He'd see her in the early morning.

"So you can come over tonight?"

Beatrice walked closer to me and mouthed, "Who is it?" I shook my head and tried to wave Beatrice away, but she stood there. With her focusing on my face, I could not hear a thing Manny said on the phone. But I could see Beatrice's cheeks flush. It was out.

My nosy friend burst with accusation as I hung up. "Monika! Tell me it isn't Manny that you've spent nights with! Tell me you wouldn't *do* that to Nadine!"

I inhaled deeply, sighed, as a tremble crept its way down my arm into my fingers, spilling tea from the cup I tried to hold. "Tell you *I* wouldn't *do* that?" Poked into rage, I pushed up on my shirtsleeves and stepped within inches of Beatrice's face. "It's Manny who's married to her," I seethed. "If anyone's *doing* something to Nadine, it's him, not me!"

"Then it's true? You're *stealing* a husband from a sick woman?" Beatrice gulped. "And you're *in love* with Manny, aren't you?"

My brain spun so wildly, it seemed my vision doubled. I didn't know where the wall ended and the floor began. Titillated, and defensive, "Listen to me, Beatrice. Sit." With my hands gently on Beatrice's shoulders, I led her to the sofa, pushing her down. I softened my tone. "You're not being fair. You have to see this from my side." I patted my chest, trying to set the pace of my heart. "I have been in love with Manny since the first day I met him in Paris. I would never have been with him at all if it weren't for all the, you know, the other things that just happened. Life has a way."

"Life has a way!" Beatrice looked at me hard. She whispered, "You are in Never Never Land. You think his wife will be dead soon, so why not *take a flying leap?*" Beatrice started yelling. "Tell me it's not too late to stop you from doing this!"

"Please, Bea. Even in Paris I would have." I shook my head and started again, thinking so deeply beneath years of loneliness, I had to close my eyes against the darkness. "I am not a vixen. I *do* have a heart, and I am *entitled* to have love in my life." I jammed my index finger into my palm.

"Do not forget what I've sacrificed, who I've lost, and what I've gone without so that Jacqueline and Henri could have a good life here in your *Greater* New York City!"

I lit a cigarette and plainly, as if reciting a recipe, explained to Bea how the forces of God and all His knowledge had brought me and Manny together.

"Three years ago, when Nadine got breast cancer, before I'd even heard of her surgery, I dreamed that she was screaming in pain, that she was cupping her breasts while faceless men in dark uniforms ripped suckling babies from her." I stopped and stared at the floor, to appear as though I were watching the dream, the dream I was in fact making up for Beatrice as I went along.

"That's so gruesome." Beatrice said, and shuddered. Watching my face—her mouth drawn, her eyes watery—I could feel Beatrice's anger shift to fascination.

"It was a horrible nightmare. So I decided to call Nadine. See, maybe we could be friends after all these years. Sure enough, when I called her and Manny to ask how things were with her—to catch up on their lives—he told me the sad news." I nodded. "I'd asked Manny if I could see Nadine, if I could comfort her, and he welcomed the effort."

Beatrice seemed caught up in my fairytale fate, listening intently as she looked me in the eye, seeming to appreciate that life *has a way* of entering through dubious doorways. She asked, "What, exactly was Manny welcoming you to do?"

"I know my way around a hospital and was able to help Nadine through her stay." I went on to explain how I and Manny kept the nurses hopping. We took shifts on the weekends: one would stay while the other took care of business outside the hospital. Each weekend for a month, until Nadine could go home, I was there for her lunch and afternoon walk through the hospital corridor, while Manny paid household bills and ran personal errands. His sister helped in the hardware store with Henri on Saturday and Sunday, and the women stayed with Nadine during the week."

"Strange that Hildie never mentioned this to me," Beatrice said evenly.

"Once Nadine was home and settled into her treatment routine, I stayed away," I said proudly. "They did not need to know that my feelings from years ago came back." I felt myself blush and looked at the floor. "I was afraid he'd reject me as he'd done in Paris. I wanted to be near him."

Only six months after her first surgery, Nadine was back in the hospital with unbearable pain. The cancer had spread. Manny called me, sobbing and threatening to shoot his brains out if anything happened to her. I told Beatrice that I went to him and cried with him. "Believe me when I tell you, Bea, he was a man with fear. *Worse* than in the war!" I shook my head, and whispered, "Worse."

"And while he was grieving you seduced the man?" Beatrice asked flatly.

"No, Beatrice. I did not seduce the man while he was grieving. I seduced the man while he was *cooking*." I giggled, but Beatrice didn't smile. My eyelid started to twitch, and I squeezed it shut to try to control it.

I told her we started sharing meals together on Sunday nights. Sometimes I would go to Brooklyn and sometimes he'd hop on the subway straight from the hospital and bring take-out food. One night he hopped on the subway but forgot to pick up the food, so he cooked.

The kitchen, I reminded Beatrice, is tiny. I explained how I stood beside him, handing him utensils as he pan-fried steaks and sautéed mushrooms and onion. The onion had made my eyes tear, so I left the kitchen to wash in the bathroom. When I was walking back to the kitchen, I stopped in the doorway to look at Manny's back, and at his shoulders, their tight movement as he cooked in the small space. I walked to him and ran my nails down the back of his shirt, from his neck to his waist. "That's all I did. I swear. It's all I did and all it took. He turned right to me and kissed me. You know, really kissed me."

We had kissed and then stopped kissing, trying to make nothing of it, attempting to eat. We had gotten through the salad when we looked at each other and saw we both had tears in our eyes. "I know mine were from joy," I said to Beatrice. He reached for my hand; I stood from the table and went to him, sat on his lap in the tight space. We kissed again, and in what seemed a rabid fluster, he lifted my sweater. I had thought about it so often, had imagined his hands, his body inside mine for so many years. "I would have collapsed if he hadn't taken me then. We made love on the floor."

Beatrice's mouth was open, and her eyes were closed. After she gasped and opened her eyes again, she said, "Monika! Didn't you realize he was just lonely? Don't you know he will always and only love Nadine?" She rose, covering her eyes with her handkerchief.

"*I* was lonely. Don't forget that Henri *discarded* me. Does it count that *I* was lonely? Does it matter who Manny will *always, only love* if he can still show such affection, and *passion*—yes—for me?" I caught my breath. "You see what happens to marriages that are for *always*."

"It all sounds reasonable when you say it like *that,* but there is something wrong, very, very wrong," Beatrice said. Her hands searched the air. "I can't put it into words that would withstand your argument, I feel there is something…" She lowered her arms, sat on the arm of the sofa, and I could sense my friend's sympathy.

I went into the kitchen to get a plate of jelly doughnuts. Returning, I put the plate on the sofa cushion. "Here. Dessert. I thought in case Jacqueline came I would have these for her." Beatrice took a bite, piercing enough so the jelly squirted above her lip.

"Uh-huh. So, what's the situation now? How deep are you two into this *affair?*"

"We see each other once or twice a week, *every* week. And we talk *every* day. He's the most generous, warmhearted man I've ever known."

"And how does he define the relationship between you and himself? Does he call it adultery?"

My upper lip and neck sweat as I stood to face Beatrice more directly. "Look. He found me in Paris because Nadine *sent* him my address. *He* brought me over here. If his wife dies and we end up together, it's like she sent him to me so he'd have me when she was gone. Like she knew he would need me. That is fate, no?"

"First of all," Beatrice said, "and I will be making an important point, so please pay attention. First of all, his wife—your cousin Nadine—is not dead yet! You do see how that fact would throw off your little theory of *life having a way?*"

"Yes, well, nothing is perfect." I brushed crumbs from the top of my blouse, showing her how I regarded her point.

"And, Nadine sent Manny to find *Henri*, not *you*. And Manny wanted to help *Henri* when he brought you all here, not *just you*. Do you see how this is not really about *you?*"

"Me or Henri. Same difference."

"It is a very big difference. And if you loved Manny from the first, why did you marry Henri? What was that about? He didn't even have money, and he was only a boy at the time."

"Henri and I were *put* together. We had a child. There was God's hand in that too." I made the sign of the cross. "The other men," I spit and Beatrice jumped, "that came before Henri and I became lovers. Henri knew—he knew everything I'd done to stay alive, both before we met and after, and he could love me the same. What other man would have? Am I not right?" I lowered my eyelids, and held them closed for a second until I heard Beatrice breathe. "I wanted a good man like Manny. Henri was young, but he was a good, kind man." My mouth was dry, dusted with powdered sugar. "And I was tired of feeling like an illegal alien. Paris was not my home. Could never be my and Henri's home. My home in Germany was destroyed. Emptied. I was an orphan, I am *displaced.*"

"I won't press you about your life back then, that you *refuse* to go into." Beatrice knotted her fingers and rubbed her palms hard enough to start a fire. "But I don't know, Monika. This is a real shock, and I must be straight with you, it's a big disappointment to me." She pushed back her plastic-toothed headband, clamping her hair down tight. "Here you are—living a good, clean life, trying to take care of *the* most difficult child, doing important, important and wonderful work at the hospital–and then you do this scandalous thing. It's *shocking*."

"I'll tell you what else is shocking, Beatrice," I said through clenched teeth. "It's shocking that you never said anything bad about Henri's affair with Claudette! Now tell me you didn't know. And they are *blood* cousins."

"Second cousins, and of course I know. We live in the same building. It's totally different, and you know it. Neither is married. Neither has a spouse who is dying."

"Well, excuse me for thinking incest is disgusting and much worse than the normal love that I have."

We sat for a while, looking at the blank screen on the television. When Beatrice got up to go home, I felt like a child, "Are you still my friend?"

Beatrice kissed my cheek. "Monika, tell me. Why is it you say it brings you joy to be with Henri when Jacqueline gets into trouble? Do you still love him, too?"

I felt swayed by her question. "I remember who made love to him first. Until Claudette, it was *only* me. And I know when I walk into a room, *he* remembers too." I looked up, to see something in the emptiness. "We share a spirit."

It was nearly nine o'clock, and the streetlights left a dull orange path on the sidewalk. The spring air was getting sticky with humidity. Children were out later than usual, windows bled the voices of televisions turned up too loud, and women sat on their stoops and yelled whole conversations about personal matters across the street.

# 7

# The Hot Flood

<u>*Henri*</u>

The hard banging at the front door made me start, tightening my hold around Claudette's waist. At ten o'clock at night, I was usually asleep since I was responsible for opening the hardware store at six a.m. these days. I smoothed my hair, buttoned my shirt—left Claudette on the moonlit rocker, cautioning her to stay in the room quietly, then closed the bedroom door behind me and padded down the hallway. I saw Beatrice peering through the glass as I turned the corner. Now I was wide awake.

"Beatrice," I said with a smile, which faded as I got closer and saw the look on her face. I turned the latch with effort, pulled and pushed, and finally swung the door open wide. "What is it, Bea? Is it Monika?"

"Oh, Henri, for goodness sake. Is everything about Monika?"

"Well, it appears to be. No?" I tried to smile again but my false ease was uprooted by her tone, which teetered on the cusp of hostility.

"Can I sit a little with you and talk?" Beatrice's arms were folded across her chest as though she were cold.

"Please dear, come in." I quickly brushed dried paint chips off the sheet covering the sofa and glanced down the hallway to the closed door.

She scrunched her face and I wasn't sure she'd sit, but she brushed the sofa again herself and sat on the edge. "You know how I feel about all of you, I'm sure, but you know, hon, I can't help but ask myself over and over how such a terrible fate could have befallen Jacqueline." Beatrice tapped her blunt-cut fingernails against the arm of the sofa. "I was just coming home from Monika, and the child stopped me outside and asked me for money." She described how Jacqueline had sniffed hard, as if fighting a runny nose, and scratched the back of her neck. "She smelled awful and was thin as an underfed ten-year-old boy."

"Holy shit. I'm sorry, Bea." I thought of Monika, and the omission I had made in not calling her back—that I had caused this incident by assuming Monika would report an arbitrary crisis, one of many that she thought couldn't wait.

Beatrice rubbed under her nose as if she were still trying to wipe away the smell of Jackie. She explained how Jackie had approached her on the street and begged for money and how Beatrice had to hold back on her sympathy—she didn't have money to feed the girl's habit, and besides, she had stolen ten dollars from Beatrice's wallet just last week. "She showed up at my door, hungry. You weren't home, so I offered her some macaroni and cheese for lunch, and when I left the room for a minute, she grabbed the money from my bag and ran out the door!"

I listened, stunned at this story that had come rushing into my house, and began to feel sick to my stomach. I'd heard enough and wanted Beatrice to leave.

Thinking about Claudette in the next room, I was no longer paying full attention to my landlady's account of tonight's encounter with my daughter, when her sharp voice cut into my daze. Beatrice said she had turned to look into the street, and that's when she felt a pull on her arm. Her handbag fell from her shoulder, caught at the crook of her elbow, and Jacqueline yanked at it hard enough so that the strap burned Beatrice's arm as it was ripped from her. She turned around to see Jacqueline running down the street with her bag. "'Get back here!,' I screamed at her, but she kept running."

I shivered and crossed my legs and arms tightly. Besides having its contents squeezed into the center of the floor, the room was poorly lit, with only one working bulb in a two-bulb lamp. Beatrice tilted the lampshade to free more light. "Is it just that she fell in with the wrong crowd? Is it all just *happenstance* that one thing led to another and before we knew it she was gone?"

I shook my head and rubbed my face with sweaty hands. My beard made a sanding noise. "All things in her life—starting with me and her mother." I thought about the admission I had made about Monika to Claudette just an hour ago. I was back on the witness stand so soon.

"Henri, why would you say such a thing? You and her mother. I saw two devoted parents when you lived here together. Why aren't you and Monika together, Henri? This is the thing that's so puzzling to us all. What happened?"

I hissed out a sigh. "Bea, if I wanted you to know, if Monika wanted you to know, you would have known already. You—of all people—would have known from day one. Let it lay."

"Lie."

"What?"

"Lie, let it lie, not *lay*."

Now I was getting pissed off. I had to take care of things with Monika, to call her at least, and I had to attend to Claudette. I shook my leg restlessly, urging her to discern my impatience so she'd leave.

"But your daughter—"

"Monika has a grip on Jackie now. She's always calling the doctors and the social workers. She'll get it all worked out." Enough said.

"You can't think it's that easy."

"I didn't say it would be easy! I said she would get it done! She has to. There's no one else."

Beatrice sat forward, her hands clasped on her knees. "So what if Jackie dies first?" Beatrice caught her breath amid tears. "She's dying, Henri."

I looked at her face but couldn't focus. She was right, of course. I felt as I did when Private Manny Hoffman first came to my door in Paris and brought with him his belief that my parents were never coming back. A great dread filled me, making me feel like the lost son I was.

I kept my voice soft. "I cannot bear to think of that right now, tonight. Please go, Beatrice. It's late and I get up so early, you know." I looked to the ceiling, opening my mouth wide, and sucked in the warm turpentine air. "I'll reimburse you for what she took. You can add it to my rent bill."

"Yes, Henri, I know I can, but I won't. I do apologize for waking you up now." Beatrice's voice had cooled. She stood. We kissed each other's cheeks. Putting my hand on her back, guiding her to the door, she rubbed the back of my hand as we parted. "I'm so sorry I upset you. There's nothing I can do to help?"

There were black edges to everything, and I had to squint to absorb any light. I put my hands in my pants pockets. "Excuse me being secretive."

"I understand. Tomorrow. I'll see you tomorrow?"

"Sure. In the morning when I leave, I'm sure you'll already be out sweeping the steps, so that by the time the sun rises we will all be presentable."

She shut the door herself. When Beatrice was out of sight, I locked it, pulling down the small linen shade Monika had made years ago to cover the door's window. She had taken the fabric from a skirt she brought with her from Paris. Monika pressed narrow, pointed pleats into it so it would lie flat and look tailored, sophisticated, and not ruffled like the eyelet curtains on Beatrice's windows, she had said.

I looked up to see the reflection of Claudette's silhouette backlit in the windows. She wore only a sheer white T-shirt. Her braids undone, her hair had fallen to her waist. She held her hand out and walked toward me. "I heard everything between you and Bea. I'll never tell a soul what you told me about Monika. You know I'll never tell." Her voice was low and dramatic, but real.

"And how do I stop telling myself? How do I make it so I don't know what I know?" Plodding to the kitchen, I reached for the bottle of Chivas a customer had given me last Christmas, washing down my shame.

Claudette frowned, standing next to me by the kitchen sink. "You think I might have a drink with you? Huh?"

My body slumped toward gravity, as if I were an inanimate object. "Now two women I respect more than any other women in the world have asked me the same thing on the same night about Monika's sudden departure."

Claudette kissed my neck behind my ear. "Come to bed now or you'll never get up in the morning."

"You should date other men. I'm too old for you." At thirty-four, married, divorced, with a daughter who was nearly eighteen, I felt much older than Claudette.

"You're only four years older than me." She said. She brushed a curl off my forehead, and I tried not to flinch at the maternal gesture. "And before me, you'd only known Monika, right?"

"Yes. And before me, Monika had been with the whole of France, Germany, and an occasional American," I said and laughed. "I was so young, I could have forgiven anything a woman like Monika might have done." Might have done then. But now? I wasn't sure.

"It was the war. I'd forgive her anything too, if I didn't know what she would become. But let's just forget about her life for tonight." Claudette arched her neck, as if trying to look elegant, but an itch overcame her and she had to scratch furiously under her nose.

I had to smile. She was still such a girl. "And if you didn't know what I've just told you, you'd forgive her now for being with Manny?"

I put my forefinger on her lower lip to touch her pout, but quickly realized I had not thought before speaking. The sickening thought that was circling in my gut just snuck up and had spurt from my mouth. Monika and Manny had been a secret, especially from Claudette. "I wasn't—"

She pulled away, staring until the words sank in, her chest visibly rising and falling. "That's not true, Henri. Why would you say such a hateful thing about Manny?" She fell back and leaned on the covered kitchen table. "Manny and Monika." Her face turned red.

She ran to the bedroom. Who am I to repeat gossip? It seemed everyone at the store knew, and Monika has been seeing someone. Still, I should not believe the gossip. I could hardly believe it myself.

I followed her, watching as she threw on her dungarees and shirt. "Nadine has been sick for a long time, Claudie. You know she's not getting any better."

"Is that your justification for deceit and betrayal? When somebody's useless in bed, let's fuck somebody else?" I grabbed her arm as she passed back through the bedroom, and she squirmed to get out of my grip, making her way closer to the front door. "You suck. You really do suck. And that sleazy, sick demon of an ex-wife you have. How *dare* she?" She twisted past me and stumbled into the kitchen, then sank to the floor and began to sob into her hands. "What? Did she tell you this? Rub it in your face to make you jealous?"

"It could be just rumors, but so many people have said something. In the store, they laugh at Manny, and I am so embarrassed for him. It could be false." I didn't believe it was false.

I sat beside her on the kitchen floor. "Is it Manny? Is it because you think he is a god? He's only a man, Claudette. And Monika is a stunning, driven woman. She's wanted him since the first time she met him."

Claudette's eyes narrowed and stared. "Do you know she's a devil? Do you know she has a vial of poison for a heart? That if it weren't for her, you'd have a healthy and beautiful daughter?" She slapped her hand over her nose. "This fucking apartment stinks. I can't even breathe in here."

"You won't tell him. Claudette—you must not tell him about Monika and Jacqueline back then. Say it." I held one of her wrists, and she slapped my face with her free hand. I let her go. "Promise me you won't tell him about them."

"Why? Manny would die if he found out I knew this and didn't tell him." Her eyes darted around the room, as if looking for the phone to call him right now. "I should tell everyone. I should tell the goddamned authorities and have her locked up for this!" Claudette stood, pulling her dungarees out of her crack. "Henri, I'm leaving now. You make me sick, and I can't stand the smell of this place. Just let me go."

Her words stung hotter than the slap to my face. "Promise me, Claudette. This is bigger than how ugly a person can be. Jacqueline still needs her. She's trying to make things up to her. Too little and too goddamned late, but I tell you I couldn't take care of Jackie myself."

"What about me?" Claud screamed back. "I would have taken care of her!"

"She wanted her mother." I looked down at my fists, knowing this hurt her. "Monika knows everything about her disease. She's an expert on schizophrenia. She knows more than the doctors she drags her in to see. She reads everything and documents everything, and you must not get her into trouble. Please, Claudie."

Claudette's face twisted. "I don't know what I'll do. This is just, just too big to keep to myself." Her voice softened, edged toward crying. "But the next time we speak, I'd like you to tell me why *you* still need her. Because if you can't come up with an answer, I'm done with you." She blew her nose into the bottom of her cotton shirt.

Pushing and pulling on the heavy door, she turned back to wince at me. "And this color you painted everything looks like *shit*! How *apropos*."

From behind the slammed door, her words stabbed like needles through the paint dust. "Schizophrenia my ass. She's a junkie."

All the rooms had been given their final coat days ago. Claud was right—the apartment stank, and the avocado color was putrid. Claudette would keep their secret. We had, after all, kept our own secret from Manny. If she told Manny about Monika, I might as well take Monika and Jackie and leave on the next plane to France. Our lives in this family would be over. The thought wafted through me, as a fleeting relief.

It took two hours to remove the paint-dripped sheets, push the furniture back against the walls, and vacuum. By one a.m., I was able to stretch across the couch and pull the telephone onto my chest. I'd lost Claudette. Panic subdued only when smothered beneath discomfort, as the pounding in my temples became a migraine. I sipped whiskey with one hand and with the other, dialed Monika.

"Hey."

"Hey? What are you doing up? You'll never get out to work in the morning," Monika scolded me.

"Fuck work. Fuck Manny and his business. Fuck you and your secrets. Fuck me."

"Henri, you're drunk. You're talking as a madman. Did Jackie come by? She saw Beatrice tonight. Well, I guess you know that. Is that it? Because, Beatrice called me. That yenta. Listing her ridiculous suggestions for caring for my own child. I told her I'd pay her for the purse *and* its crap, and *I* would take care of Jackie, *danke*."

"Stop talking." I shook my heavy head, disgusted, as if Monika could see. "You better move your Bavarian ass and get our daughter into a hospital or something. Beatrice and Claudette *know* you're screwing up, and in the middle of all this our daughter is killing herself." I took a short sip of my drink. "People are asking about *you,* Monika. I don't know how much longer I can lie about this." I didn't know how much longer Claud would lie about it.

"Lie about what?"

She was as delusional as our daughter. "Lie about what? You know what you're lying about, and so will other people. You better get Jackie onto the straight road, because people are starting to think long and hard about you. I do believe, my beautiful ex-wife, you are going to hell." I coughed so hard I spilled whiskey and sat in a wet mix of truth and lies. Thinking about her with Manny, I dropped the phone and disconnected Monika.

———✧———

# *Manny*

It was six forty-five a.m., but the cancer floor had no need for Eastern Standard Time. The dozen or so patients had their own timetables of pharmaceutically induced sleep and intrusive arousal from it, as doctors and nurses paraded from room to room in their end-of-shift drowsiness, poking patients one last time before the day shift arrived. I saw a nurse heading toward my wife's room and ran to catch her so I could wake Nadine myself.

Wearing a soft blue work shirt that Hildie laundered for me—soft to the touch because she had an electric dryer, and pressed with sharp creases down the middle of the sleeve—I was grateful to look like a man ready to go to work in a hardware store and tend to his customers with dignity. I had awakened this morning to a call from Monika and felt ashamed at the prospect of kissing my wife. Beating the nurse to her door, I quietly slipped in.

The blunt orange glow of sunrise lit the room, limning the pale green walls and blue metal furniture. A countryscape hung on the wall across from her bed, but its muted browns and greens lending no sense of grace or enchantment to the room.

Nadine was already awake and greeted me with a blink for a smile and a tap of her fingers on the cover sheet. Her eyes were glassy, their shine in dispute with her dull, sandy skin. I walked slowly to her side and lowered my face to hers. It was hot.

"Does she have a fever?" I asked the nurse, who had crept up immediately behind me.

"I'm afraid it spiked a few hours ago. We didn't want to bother you during the night. The doctor put her on additional antibiotics." She shifted her eyes sideways, suggesting we go into the hall to speak.

Nadine caught the look. "I'm not blind," she whispered. "Just tell us here." I lowered the side rail of the bed and squeezed in to sit with my wife. Her body heat bled through the sheet and my pants. This is not a fever, I thought…this is death. "When is the doctor coming back? Is there a way I can talk to him now, by phone? You really should have called me when this happened." I was nearly breathless.

The nurse glanced at me and then into the hall, distracted by movement and the sound of wheels squealing like a strangled cat. She stood still, intent on monitoring the passing annoyance. I couldn't remember this one's name or I would have shouted it to get her undivided attention. A moan came from the next bed and reminded me that I needed to be courteous and calm. The other patient was a younger woman who played rock and roll on the radio all day long. Now those Beatles were on. Nadine liked this music, though I didn't get it. Lifting myself from the bed, as if peeling a soggy paper-lace doily from a serving-tray, I said, "Excuse me, sweetheart, just for a minute." I kissed her forehead, walked a few steps toward the nurse, who was still looking into the hallway, and placed a gentle hand on her shoulder.

The nurse jumped. "Oh. I'm sorry, Mr. Hoffman. It's a woman who's sort of senile and she doesn't understand…"

With bowed head and closed eyes, I tried to stay calm. "Never mind out there. Tell me about Nadine." My legs went weak, and I reached to hold onto the wall.

The nurse spoke so softly her voice was barely audible, and Nadine slapped the bed as hard as she could manage, making a weak thump. The nurse smiled, almost with shame, and went to Nadine's side. "You have a lung infection, sweetie pie, a pneumonia. And the doctor might want to drain the fluid later." She looked into Nadine's eyes, then into mine. "We'll give the medicine a few more hours to bring the fever down." Touching Nadine's hand, the nurse let her bright face slip into dismay.

Nadine would die today, and I had no control of the shudder rattling my chest. I climbed back into the bed and aligned my body with hers but couldn't make myself touch her skin. She was just too hot. "Don't worry, Nadie. I'm right here." I covered my eyes with my arm so she wouldn't see me cry.

The nurse withdrew, and we lay like this as the sun rose fully between the drapes that never got pulled closed anymore. Nadine was in the bed closest to the window, and I felt the color spread slowly over our bodies. It felt heavy but soft, like Hildie's thick cookie dough rolling over us.

Nadine fell into heavy sleep, and my breathing tripped over the erratic rhythm of hers. The deeper she slept, the harder and more gurgled her breathing became. I closed my eyes and swam with her. The sun beat on my eyelids, and I embraced the burning and basked in her liquid locution, joining her in the stuporous fuss of dying. A wind, late for the season, started to kick up outside. Air pushing against the window rattled the glass in its metal frame; its random but confident and dependable intrusion reassured me that there was a plan—a plan offered by fate that we were called upon to accept. I was happy to be aware of my part in it; pleased now to know that all these things—the timing of her fever, the rise of the sun, the hum of the wind and the snugness of our communion—had all met at the arranged time, and that in the exact moment of her release, we will have completed our roles in the design of her death. I did not need to be responsive now. I did not need to think of anything or anyone now. We were in the hot flood together.

The wind suddenly halted, and I wondered if I had caused it by not doing my part. Then Nadine spoke in her half sleep, and the nurse pushed the bed curtain open, and by some mistake of mine, fate's perfect orchestration broke. At that moment, I opened my eyes in a state of total disturbance and thought I saw Monika. She was all around me, poking in through the window, whispering to me from under the bed, her head thrown back, laughing her ferocious laugh.

The nameless nurse asked, "Mr. Hoffman? Are you okay?"

I didn't want to answer her, did not want to have to answer anyone. "No, I'm not okay. What do you want from her now? She's sleeping." My whisper was angry, and I spit out my *she's sleeping.*

"Well, I'm really sorry, sir, but I have to check her temperature and pressure again."

I thought she felt less hot, and as my lips met her skin, an awful smell—a mixture of ammonia and urine that sheathed Nadine's body— gagged me. "She's cooler."

"Good. That's real good. Let me check." The nurse walked toward the bed, and I got up and allowed the senseless ritual. It would be a three-minute wait. My eyes drifted to the greeting cards lined up along the windowsill. Flowers. What makes them think a picture of a vase with flowers will cheer her up or help her "get well soon?" The cards' well-wishing and hopes for health that my Nadine would never be able to realize taunted me. With the nurse's back to me, I collected them, folding one into the other, and dumped them in the trash.

"You're right, Mr. Hoffman. She's down to a hundred and one. She was one-oh-four during the night." The nurse removed the thermometer and began to wrap Nadine's arm with the blood pressure cuff.

"So what does this mean? Will the pneumonia clear up? You think she'll be able to come home?"

"Don't know, hon. Maybe, but Dr. Janssen will have to decide. It will be days anyway. This doesn't clear up overnight. The most we can hope right now is that he doesn't have to drain the fluid. That presents all other kinds of risks of infection and discomfort. She doesn't need any more discomfort." She took Nadine's hand and squeezed it, as if emphasizing her own commitment, like a teacher with a slow pupil.

Nadine was awake again, blinking drowsily in the glare. I drew the curtains. The room darkened dramatically, allowing me to dismiss the flaring images of Monika into the sun's shadows. Floating in thought, the linoleum floor began to rise into my face and the music from the next bed began a one-note drumming.

"Manny, tell me a story," Nadine whispered. "And get me a wet cloth so I can wash my neck and face." Trying to boost herself a little higher on the pillow, she began to cough, first a shallow clearing of her upper throat, then inch by inch down into her chest she reached for an opening, trying to do the breaststroke through a swamp. Her futile efforts only made things worse and soon she was unable to catch her breath or stop the spasm that punched its way from rib to rib.

I could do nothing but mutely brace her against the wrenching, until she fell into her pillow and her chest rose soundlessly. "Please Please Me" played in the next bed and I watched as Nadine's face fell back into a more relaxed mask. "You want water, Nadie?"

She didn't respond, except to take in a bare breath. Her eyes glazed over, and I could see fluid starting to seep through the pores of her arms.

"Shit. I'm going to get someone now, Nadie. I'll be right back." I ran to the doorway and yelled to a nurse I had not seen before, "You! Please. I think my wife is choking."

The nurse was heavy, and trying her best to run toward me. I stood back against the door to let her pass, her ballooned arm rubbing against my chest as she rushed past. Swiftly, lifting Nadine up, leaning her over the side of the bed, and slapping her middle back with a thrusting jerk, she got Nadine to cough up the fluid. I watched, dumb at the violence of it. "There, there now, darlin'. You need to get that up from you and get your breath back. Yes, that's it." She lowered Nadine back onto the pillow and turned to me. "You run a cloth through with cool water and bring it here." As I turned away to do as she told, I could hear the nurse mutter to herself, "No help in this hellhole."

Hellhole? Do I have her in a hellhole? I looked around the pale green room and saw a used tissue near the bed of the younger woman. Has it always been this filthy? I went into the bathroom and wet a towel. Running the water, I held my hands under it and saw my face in the mirror. My black hair had gone gray, my lashes darker. Nadine and I were aging into polar opposites. I grew stronger from my laborious job, my fuller face making me appear healthier. I'd been out walking with Monika, and my skin was tanned. My lust for her caused flashes of blinding anticipation. My love for Nadine had defined me since I was a boy; I had measured the degree of my attachment to the world by the touch of her hand. But sex with Monika had become too consuming. The relief she provided left me tortured by the deceit. My longing for her didn't know about Nadine or hospitals or promises and vows. Now her face suddenly came up from the drain, with a dimpled smile and her freckled white skin, and I shook, turning the faucet off and wringing the soaked towel.

As the nurse placed the wet cloth on Nadine's neck, I remembered Monika in her apartment in Paris, administering the same remedy to me, as I lay before her, a formidable American soldier who had brought with me an inexplicable fever. And just as Monika had done two decades before, the nurse said a prayer, crossed her heart, and asked me if I would like to see a priest.

"We're Jewish. You think we need a Rabbi?"

"Oh. With that dark coloring I thought—well, clergy is always comforting. Who should I call for you?"

"No one. I'll sit here with her and tell her a story. Thank you, nurse…" I turned up my palms at not knowing her name.

"Nesbit. My name is Mrs. Nesbit, and you are very welcome, Mr. Hoffman." She straightened her nametag. I hadn't even noticed the nurses wore nametags. "Oh, Hoffman. I guess I should have known you are Jewish. So sorry, I made the sign over her."

"It's all right. Any prayer is a good prayer."

She smiled and again said a blessing and crossed her heart. I didn't know any Jewish rituals to perform. I thought to call my sisters.

Nadine was lying close to the edge of the bed and nurse Nesbit had again raised the railing. Pulling the chair close to her, I whispered, "Now I will tell you a story, Nadie. You want to hear my story?" She nodded, and I saw the commencement of a sweet and grateful smile she was determined to maintain. I reached under the cover and laid my hand across her stomach. "Once upon a time, a man fell in love with a beautiful princess," I began. I knew the story did not have a happy ending, but continued to tell it the way we had lived it.

It was now seven-thirty a.m. and I thought of Henri in the store, which reminded me of Monika again. I rubbed the back of my hand on my wife's sweaty cheek and continued our tale. I told of the wedding of Manny and Nadine, how it was planned and performed in five weeks from the time I came home from Europe and was discharged from the army. I told of the many times we tried to conceive a child and my sorrow at the loss of three pregnancies. She nodded gently at this, and I leaned in to kiss her lips. "You made it up to five months once," I said, "and we began to think of names. And even though it ended badly, those weeks of picking names and looking forward to the joy of it still made those times happy for us. I would rather have that loss with you than a child with someone else." I was speaking of the third and last time she conceived, about six years ago. From then on we had trouble in bed, after so many fears and disappointments. We lay together every night and watched TV, picking on snacks and eating pudding that Nadine had cooked in the morning and let set while the two of us worked in the store. But I could not ask her for sex, afraid it would remind her of her failing, and from what I could determine, she felt no urge to offer it.

"Do you remember what names we picked, Nadie? I bet you can't remember the names." I knew she did, but was too weak to speak them. Her eyes fluttered. Her breaths sounded as if she were trying to suck water from a damp paper towel. It would be such an extraordinary effort for her to say those two names that it might be the last words she'd ever speak. I knew she liked hearing them, and so I said them for her, "Linda for a girl, and Phillip for a boy. You remember." I nodded and smiled at the nonexistent infants' faces. It was as though they had indeed been born, and deeply loved.

"Well then, after that, we decided to work really hard and use our money to travel. So we saved and saved for that trip to California. I was so happy to take Claudette with us. Of course, it was probably that trip that gave her the ridiculous idea to live there and try to be a star. Beautiful she is, yes, but so few become stars. You know, Nadie? You know so few become real movie stars, like Marilyn Monroe. And look what became of her."

I looked at my wife and saw she was motionless. I put my hand to her chest and felt the pounding of her broken heart. My chest felt heavy, and my heart pounded heavier and faster than hers. "Open your eyes, Nadine. Open your eyes and tell me you forgive me. Nadie, Nadie. I love you, please open your eyes." I put my thumb to her eyelid and pushed it open. Her plain brown eyes were clouded over, but they were not yet the eyes of death.

Nadine caught a full breath and turned to see my face close to hers. "Hi baby," she said softly. "A story?" She smiled. "A happy ending?"

"The only happy ending is when you come home with me. Then I will tell you the happy ending." I offered my pinky to make a deal, and rubbed it across the tip of her nose.

"Stop," Nadine whispered. "I won't. I don't want to. Just stay…until the end. Okay?"

"Nadine. You have to come home. You *will* come home." I shook my head at her.

"I dreamed." I watched her falling away; it was like seeing an egg roll out of its nest to the tip of a branch that was too high for me to reach and break the fall. "You asked me to forgive you." Nadine shrugged, her shoulders barely moving. "Should I? For what?" Like a frightened child hearing scary stories in the middle of the night, she spoke the sentence softly, and her face and hands gestured only when something inside her moved of its own will.

"Do you think you're leaving me, Nadine? Do you feel you can't try more or harder? Do you want me to call Claudette and my sisters to come?"

"No one else, Manny. Just me and you." She cleared her throat gently, "I've tried…all I can. I can't do this anymore." Her eyes filled. "You'll let me leave, won't you? You won't keep the ending from me… so I'll wait to hear?" Then she whispered, her voice as neutral as if she were telling me she knew my name was Manuel Simon Hoffman. "I forgive you and Monika."

"You know?" I started to cry and lowered the rail to sit in the bed with her. A lump swelled in my throat as I kissed her forehead. "You'll leave knowing we are connected forever? You'll know that when I die I'll be buried next to you, you who will be my only wife, eternally. Our souls were fused a long time ago, Nadie. No matter what these bodies have or haven't done with one another, it is our *souls*, Nadie, that are together."

She nodded yes. I stopped speaking to cry. I was afraid she could sense the wild lasso whipping around my head, arresting vulgar visions, keeping ugliness from hurting her now. I could feel my head shaking in the struggle.

I sat up straighter. "Nadine?" She was still. I shook her, but she remained still. There was no beat of her broken heart when I reached inside her damp gown. There was no pant of shallow breath. I heard nothing, except the wind outside the window, and the creaking of wheels out in the hall, and the uninterrupted drum of rock and roll from the next bed.

# Part Three

# 1

# Shiva

## *Claudette*

My mother and I left the cemetery swiftly to rush back to the house: set up the food, cover the mirrors, and place pitchers of water on the stoop for mourners to rinse their hands before entering. I stood in my mother's doorway, holding the door open for the steady stream of mourners who had already formed a line outside the house, heads lowered and covered with yarmulkes or lace. Ceremoniously, hands reached up to pass a kiss onto the door's mezuzah before accepting my practiced "Hello." I saw by their puffy eyes and sagging shoulders how they adored Nadine, offering a sad smile, or a comforting nod of recognition, yet the procession seemed oddly pretentious in its even and soft-tempered rhythm. They'd been expecting this; they were prepared.

Nadine's parents had been dead for years, and her house in such disarray from Manny's untidiness and absence, the Hoffmans together decided to sit Shiva at Hildie's house. It smelled of cinnamon cookies. Manny's sisters' ovens—always licked with flour, cinnamon, sugar, eggs, and honey—were turned off during the day today for the first time since Yom Kippur.

Watching the devastation, I greeted visitors with a nod and "Thanks for coming." Then, when I saw the last of the family coming up the sidewalk, I went to sit down, leaving the door unlocked. Manny walked alone, sunglasses on, his hands holding a handkerchief to his nose. No matter the *Plan* Manny had been mumbling about into my ear during the service—something about events unfolding in a cosmic, pre-set order, so that everything that occurred was meant to be at that exact time and place—I couldn't forgive him for his affair with Monika and would not look at him as he walked through the door. While he rinsed his hands on the stoop, I looked past him for Monika and was surprised that she hadn't already attached herself to the torn black ribbon on his lapel. Would Manny be kissing her tonight? Would he run to his whore so soon? I wished Henri had never told me. Most of all, I wished it had been Monika who died. Thank God that dickmonger is staying away today.

I was eight years old the day my uncle left for the service, and I had tried to make him look at me, dancing in the corner with a makeshift lampshade hat on my head. I wanted him to smile. I hadn't been told where he was going or for how long, but my heartache popped in bursts of possessiveness like little bombs in front of me. My father had gone and never returned. I gave Manny a hard, numb hug. I had grown thus far having studied the displays of misery, watching my mother cry too many times. I could see Manny suffering then and I saw it now.

Fanny put out the tray of cookies they baked the day before, and someone had sent two giant platters of thinly sliced layers of smoked fish and bagels. The air was warm, and the open windows let a breeze ride over the serving table, softly crinkling the Saran Wrap over the foods, rustling the paper doilies' fringe around the cookies, ruffling the drape over the mirror in the hallway. The starched cotton snapped hard in the gust, and I jumped. It seemed to me that the people in the house today stood still—poised in place—while objects flirted and talked between themselves.

"Hey, gorgeous movie star," boomed in my ear. It was Jacqueline. Spruced up in a clean white blouse and navy blue skirt, all she needed was knee-high socks and she could have passed for a normal kid. Her legs were bare, covered only with scrapes and scabs. "I made it. Don't I look *spiffy*? My mom dressed me up." She pressed her lips into my cheeks and gave me a smoochy kiss. Her lips were parched, and small jagged pieces of skin abraded my cheek. Her hair was pulled into a severely tight, waxy ponytail, and I could tell that it was dirty.

I also suspected Jacqueline was coming down from a high; her eyes were bloodshot and her hands shook when I held them, but she accepted a comforting hug. The thought of her abuse made me want to pick the little girl up off the floor and carry her to a warm beach, thousands of miles away from Monika and Henri both.

"Are you okay, Jackie? I mean, are you high on something, or down here in hell with the rest of us humanoids?" I looked deep into Jackie's eyes, searching for the movie that was playing in her head, and ran my fingers over Jackie's inner arm.

"I'm down, *dowwwn* here with you." Her eyes met mine for an instant. She cleared her throat. "I am sorry about Nadine. I know she meant the world to you." She kissed me again. "I never could get close to her, you know. 'Cause mom hated her so much."

I shuddered; it was as if Monika's soiled aura loomed over her daughter's head. I jutted my chin and assumed the pose of my mother: shoulders squared, hands clasped across my stomach. "I don't want to be doing *this*, welcoming people to your funeral, Jackie."

"No chance, Claudipoo. I'm goin' out in a *ball of fire*. You'll have to sweep me up and blow me away." She covered her mouth to hide her hiccup laugh.

I pulled her by the sleeve. Jacqueline giggled, a sound that was weak but audible to the others congregating near the doorway. As if we two girls were planning to sneak out from a children's birthday party to smoke, we slid into the kitchen. "Come and sit with me at the table. We haven't talked in a very long time," I said.

Jackie put her head down on the yellow speckled tabletop. My stomach fell as my mind retrieved my little-girl goodbye to Manny before he sailed for England, when he sat, shivering and sick, at this very table. That horrid, stiff, green blanket lay over his heart. I pulled Jackie within an inch of my face. "Don't leave us, Jackie. Don't leave *me*." I swallowed hard, then whispered, "You're like a daughter to me." I tried to recall how long it had been since I'd taken care of the girl. I began to cry and flick at my blouse button with my thumb, frustrated. Looking up, I saw that Jacqueline's face was blank. "Are you listening to me? Jacqueline! Are you listening?"

"It's *Jackie*." Jacqueline raised her head and looked at me, then peered out the kitchen window for a second and turned back to me. "Like a *mother*? You got the wrong creds for that one, cuz." She gagged and hugged herself, as if out in the cold. "Coming down to you, Claudala. I'm coming down." Her voice was soft and sickly, but it held a hint of self-mocking. Then her cheeks became puffy, as if her mouth were filled with water. She tried to get loose from the table and chair and run for the bathroom, but she didn't make it, and I watched as she heaved onto the linoleum floor.

"Oh, Jesus," I bounced to her side. "What is it? Oh, Christ. Come into the toilet." I pulled and pushed her toward the back bathroom. "Fucking asshole mother of yours. I hate her. Do you hear me? I hate your mother and I will hate her forever!" Jacqueline was kneeling over the toilet, then sliding to the floor, crying into the hem of her pleated skirt.

I slammed the door behind us and locked it to keep out curious mourners. "Why aren't you in a hospital? What is your mother thinking, letting you live on the streets?" There was no answer. "Jacqueline!" I pulled on her hair as she gagged over the toilet. "Are you going back to see her? Because if you go back there every time you get like this, and she doesn't get you hospitalized"—I clenched my jaw—"I'm never going to speak to you again! Jacqueline, do you hear me, damn it!" She had stopped vomiting, so I grabbed her shoulders from the back and spun her around. Her breath hit me, and I let go.

Jacqueline's arms were shaking as she crawled to her feet, then started kicking at the bathroom door. "Fucking shit they sold me. Let me out of here! Where the fuck am I? Let me out!" She took the doorknob and started shaking the door back and forth.

I knew how the door's rattle would reverberate through the house and unlatched the hook for her. The door swung open, and Jacqueline fell out into the hallway, where Fanny—who was mopping the floor and listening—gasped, as if she had an unexpected burp. At shoulder height, Hildie crouched beside her, lips pursed. Fanny leaned against the wall, wide eyed. When Jacqueline saw them, she screamed, "Move!" and raced past them. I pursued, through the dining room, into the foyer, and out to the street. Jacqueline got to the corner and made a left by the time I had gotten out the door. I ran after her.

A block away, I watched as Jacqueline tripped over the curb and fell. I sprinted, but before I had time to catch up, she had sprung and ducked, disappearing. I quit and stood there catching my breath, looking up to see the rear windows of the old synagogue, its corner pane cracked and splintered. Jacqueline was gone.

The house overflowed with the friends of Nadine Anne Hoffman. In the living room and dining room, it looked as though people had been hired to stand and mark, like black horizontal pegs, every square foot. Backs were pushed into corners and perpendicular rows of mourners lined the walls, three deep on each side, until some extraneous piece of furniture met them. Manny sat, leaning with his left elbow on the arm of the couch, his chin propped on his fist.

He raised his right hand to greet guests, but otherwise sat still and soundless. All through that first afternoon without Nadie, when he needed to cry, he simply got up and went into the basement bedroom. Before his sister Fanny had moved into this room Manny had built for her, while she was still in the process of selling her own house, he and Nadie spent the first months of their marriage here. Manny was still trying to get a bank loan to buy the store downtown. Nadine worked as a school secretary—a position she hoped to leave when they had a baby, and then return to, so as to be near their child when he started school—but that salary alone could not pay the rent. There was no toilet or sink in their basement bedroom, so after they made love at night, they would sneak up to the shower on the first floor and wash under the water that dripped so slowly it took them half an hour to finish washing together. Sometimes they enjoyed it too much and started making love again. For all their modesty, washing quietly so that Hildie and I wouldn't wake and know what they had done—when he saw my reddened face in the morning, my eyes looking elsewhere as I spoke to him in a flurry of silliness—he knew what I had heard, and he blushed.

—⬦—

# *Manny*

I could easily recall the warmth of our connection and the comfort of being with the girl I had loved since my adolescence, who had grown into a dignified woman. But I couldn't remember the physical part, couldn't recall any excitement or urgency. And now I couldn't help but compare what I didn't remember to what I felt with Monika.

Since yesterday, Monika had stalked my mind. On my first trip to cry in the basement today, she was peeking at me from the storage space under the stairs; later she spooked me from beneath the springs of the hi-riser, giggling and taunting me with her exposed breasts.

I sat on the floor at the entrance to the storage room during that first trip downstairs, about the same time I'd heard the commotion of Jackie vomiting in the kitchen. Monika had been giggling. Closing my eyes, I reached into the dark space, feeling for her legs. I was lost for a few moments. My eyes filled and my chest heaved.

All day, nonstop, the Hoffman family friends joined me on the couch. I refused the customary hard bench the Shiva dictated, because I was not religious in any other part of my life and didn't want Nadine to think she had caused me additional discomfort. "So Manny, what now?" asked Mr. Cooper, who, like everyone else, seemed to want to know this. The question burned my gut. It was as if they were all referring to the fact that Nadie had known about Monika. Did everyone know? I checked their faces to detect disgust. No, they didn't know. I looked around for Claudette and caught her eyes just as she came back into the room, her face flushed. I raised my hand for her to come and sit.

"I was chasing your little cousin. Don't think about it now, Manny. Later. We can talk about Jacqueline later. How're you holding up?" Her lips were tight, trying to suppress her heavy breathing, but the rise and fall of her chest was still clearly visible. She clasped her hands and looked around the room. Hildie reached over the back of the couch, put her hands on her daughter's cheeks, and kissed the top of her forehead. Claudette reached up, turned, and stretched backward to kiss her mother's double chin. I will have to face them when the truth is out. Their disgust will punish me enough for a thousand years. I took a shallow breath and prayed, begging for Nadine not to be shamed.

I looked up toward the sound of the front door opening, "Have you seen Henri since the cemetery? I hope that fool didn't think I wanted the store open today."

"No, no. I think he wanted to buy some fruit or candy to bring here. Do you need him now?"

"I just want to make sure he doesn't bring Monika back here with him. You know, ask her to drive him here or something. I don't want her here."

"Why, Manny?" She whispered under her breath. "Why don't you want her here?" Claudette lifted her head and looked at me squarely, challenging the terseness in my voice.

The first shot had come that fast, and I thought, *Oh shit, God!* I knew Claudette from the day she was born and was able to read her face so well that I could discern from the lines around her mouth the difference between being very angry and very, very angry. Now she was very, very angry. "Come into the basement with me." It took effort for me to be gentle with her. My affair would hurt her more than Nadine's death. She idolized me, if not in a romantic way—I was still the war hero come home—unlike her own cowardly phantom of a father. So close were we through the years that on sad days, when I held her, I'd seen her eyes change color from faded gray to brown. "I want to talk to you, sweetheart, in private," I said. We stood and walked toward the back of the house. She peeked over her shoulder.

The forty-watt bulb at the top of the stairwell shone to the bottom step, filtering through the room, leaving more shadows than light. Getting to the bottom, Claudette bent down to pick up some used tissues I had dropped on my way back up this afternoon. "Who's been down here besides Fanny? She never leaves a mess." Her voice was uncharacteristically loud. Claudette sniffed around and wiped the banister with her index finger. She was acting bawdy, almost obnoxious in her tone.

"It was only me, Claudie. I was down here before. I didn't want to get emotional in front of that whole bunch. You know, they'd all try to *comfort* me." I shuddered at the thought.

"You don't need comforting? Is that why you don't want Monika to come, because she might try to comfort you?" Claudette's voice rose, but then, as if someone whispered in her ear to stop, she mumbled, "I'm sorry. This isn't right. Not today."

I bit the inside of my lower lip. "What's not right today? Tell me what's eating you, why you're looking at me that way. You can tell me anything, Claudette." I sat on the bottom step, crossed my legs Indian style under its lip, my elbows braced against the stair behind me. *Come on, hit me with it already, before I choke to death.*

"Nadine was just buried. I don't feel right."

"She'll still be buried tomorrow and the next day and forever. Just say what you need to." I stood and walked to the wall in front of me, leaning my forehead on it, shouting into the paneling. "Speak, Claudette!" I turned to face her.

"How dare you order me to speak? Who ordered you, ever ordered you to do anything?" Her voice was blunt, and she came two steps closer to me. "You order Henri, and you order, you order…" She took two more steps and was nearly under my chin. "And I know you sleep with Monika. I *know*, Manny, all about everything!" Her eyes bulged, wet.

I burst into sobs. Claudette leaned her shoulders against the wall and crossed her arms on her chest. Speaking softly, she said, "Manny, I should let you explain. Come sit with me and explain." I let out more sobs. "Manny!" It seemed she couldn't help herself; she continued, right into my ear, "Why did you do that, Manny? Why did you have an affair and become an *adulterer*? Do you know what kind of woman Monika is? Do you know what a demon she is? Manny, answer me!" Now she was crying in heavy sobs.

My back fell to the wall, my speech was garbled with saliva. "How do you know?" I wiped my nose with my sleeve.

"Henri told me, okay?" She straightened her spine. "That's right. I believe by accident. Some accident. He said it was rumors, but he'd never believe a rumor. Why? Who else would tell me?"

"She knew."

Claudette's face drained, right there in front of me. She knew I meant Nadine. She leaned toward me and abruptly rammed her head into my chest.

I cried again into the top of her braided bun. "She told me before she died."

Claudette pulled away a bit and looked into my eyes, puzzled.

"I asked her to forgive me for things, and she said she knew nothing that needed forgiveness. I don't know what I said next, but then she said, 'I forgive you and Monika,' and she was gone."

Claudette bowed her head.

"Do you think maybe she was just guessing? Maybe it was the only woman who came to mind?" I put my knuckles against my lips. Was I trying to keep myself from screaming?

Claudette squinted in thought. Her hair was falling from the bun, and frizzy strands, damp with sweat, curled on her neck. "I don't know. I would take Nadine at her word. Henri thinks everyone knows. But what's important is that it's true—you have gotten yourself into a mess now, Manny, with an evil, filthy woman."

"Don't be jealous, Claudie." As I went to take her hand, the room lit up. We had only turned on the switch that lit the stairwell, so when all at once the fluorescents came on, it seemed like God flashing a bolt of lightning—warning us to shut up.

"What's going on down there?" Fanny called from the top of the stairs. Before we could answer, I saw the hem of her brocade dress descending over her twig-like ankles, up to the bottom of her apron. She stopped mid-flight and bent her head down past the overhang to look into the room. Her hand went automatically under her large, soft breasts to support them. "Manny? What are you doing down here? Is everything all right?"

"Yeah. We're okay. Claudette and I just wanted to be alone. We'll be right up." I turned to Claudette, nodded toward the stairs for her to follow me.

"Because we heard some yelling up here. We got concerned. Don't mean to interfere."

"You're not interfering. We're comin'." I reached the steps and Fanny offered her hand to me, turning it this way, then that, to encourage me to grab it. I was still the baby, always. I met her fingertip to fingertip. Claudette was coming up behind, pinning loose strands of hair behind her neck. She was raising an eyebrow, as if in a sarcastic commentary at the sight of the brother and sister, hand in hand. When we reached the landing, I kissed Fanny's perfumed powdered cheek. "Mixed berry?"

"No. Violet and lilac." She raised her chin to get her cheek closer to my nose.

"Nice. You smell very nice."

I saw Henri standing with an older man at the fireplace, trying his best to be polite and listen to the man's opinion about something important enough that he was waving his fist in the air. I noticed this often in the store—how Henri could make intense conversation with anyone. People loved his accent, and they enjoyed when they helped him find the proper English word. I'd found—one year when we decided to do some spring-cleaning—that Henri had been keeping a vocabulary list under the shelf near the cash register. Now, I waved to him to come and make himself comfortable on the couch. I took his shoulder and we embraced, my arms firmly encircling his. "What can I say, Manny? She was the best. At least you know you had the best." Now his French accent made it sound all the more cheapened.

He's riding me, I thought. He knows about Monika and me, and he's riding me.

Yes. I nodded and motioned to Henri to take his seat next to me on the couch. "I had the best and she only got me." I wanted Henri to be aware of my shame, but he looked at his glass and rattled the ice, making no allowance for confession, asking immediately what the end was like. We talked of the final hours and about the competence of Fate and the realization of its Plan for me and Nadine. Henri blinked and nodded, drank schnapps, and allowed me to ramble. "You should have heard the wind, Hen. It was as though it were trumpeting me to attention, saying, 'Watch as she goes from you.' I guess it could have, just the same, trumpeted her miraculous recovery?" I rubbed my face wholly with the palms of my hands, reached into my pocket for a handkerchief, blew my nose, then slapped Henri on the leg. "Well, my boy, looks like you got yourself a week off. Why don't you take Jackie to the Catskills for a vacation? Get her out of the city, away from those scumbags she hangs around with." The knot in my stomach tightened as I worked to keep Henri off the subject of my affair.

Henri grimaced, burped from the sip of plain seltzer he had switched to. "Yeah, *right*. Monika wouldn't let me leave town with her. Are you kidding?"

"I thought you had legal custody. What do you mean she won't *let* you? Has something changed?" Monika was so tough on Henri. It was beyond me to know why.

"Legal shpegel. Don't mean shit when your kid's a junkie and you run out of drugs. Monika at least tries to get her to the doctor and stuff. You know it—Jackie is a sick girl. But Monika thinks she's schizophrenic, whatever that is. She reads a lot and knows about that shit. You know, she's practically a shrink herself in that hospital." I forced a smile, but what he was saying sickened me.

I was well aware of Monika's diagnosis of Jacqueline. She talked about it incessantly, even in bed. Every time Jackie showed up high or hurt or just broke and tired, Monika filled me in on her plan for this doctor, that program. Much as she talked, there never seemed to be any movement toward getting her better.

"She was here today, you know, Jackie was," I said, my voice soft and half-hearted. "She got sick or something. Flew outta here in a blast. Claudette tried to catch up with her when she ran out."

Henri shook his head. "Jesus. I haven't heard from her today." Henri's face fell, and he put his fist to his forehead. "You know, I'll stay if you need me, but I really should go now. Something I have to get to in the house. Okay if I see you tomorrow, cousin?" He rose, bent over and kissed my cheeks, then hugged me as I had hugged him. When he bent down to me, he looked like a boy. "You're only human, Manny. Nadine knew that, and she loved you. You keep this up too long and make yourself so low, you'll end up buried with her." I stood, momentarily speechless, until Henri whispered, "Taking Monika was not the same thing as her taking what was yours and Nadine's. Look, Manny, you needed what you needed. You never cheated Nadine out of your love. She knew that. That's all that matters." He slid his hands into his pockets.

Touched by my cousin's gesture, hoping there was sincerity in Henri's offer, I wondered how many of those words had come from discussions, maybe with Monika, or with Claudette. I certainly didn't feel his justification. I took Henri's elbow and walked him through the room into the foyer. Straightening Henri's tie amid some chattering grievers primed to depart, I leaned in and whispered to him, "Henri, don't hold it against me, about Monika."

Henri whispered back, his words clean and shameless, "Manny, I hold *nothing* against you, but we'll talk later." We shook hands and Henri asked if Claudette had left for the day. He hadn't seen her. I felt my stomach turn when reminded of her and shook my head, wondering myself where she had gone after the basement. She was right behind me when we came up. I simply shrugged, I didn't know, and Henri walked into the early evening breeze.

Soon after Henri left, I watched as Claudette reappeared and hurried to clear off the dining room table, without looking directly at me. "Claud. Where ya been hiding? Henri was looking for you."

"Oh, I just needed to take a nap, so I could give mom a break tonight. Tough day for her, you know." She looked at the floor.

I suggested she stay for the evening so we could talk, but she waved off my attempt as if she were refusing a horrible chore, like cleaning up Jackie's vomit. She rushed out for home as soon as the rooms were clean. She had just recently rented her first two-room, third-floor walk-up apartment in Manhattan, and I guessed she was eager to get back to it. I too became anxious to leave and said my goodnights and stepped out onto the cement porch, its fresh coat of brick red surrounding the emptied milk bottles. I hesitated on the top step, trying to shake Monika from my head before stepping foot into my own house. Claudette will have to come around. I'll make this up to her somehow.

The earlier gusts that hinted at rain had died, and it was a calm, just-the-right, sixty-degree night with a clear sky. I looked up and started searching a thousand stars, as if I might see Nadine swinging from one.

Hildie's prize rose bushes, survivors since before the war, flaunted some red buds, distracting my eye from the yellow glow of the porch bug light. I walked down the five steps to the sidewalk, stopped at a budding rosebush, kneeled and pounded on the dirt with a fist, making sure it wasn't loose, making sure nothing would surface tonight.

# 2

# Lost

*Monika*

Jacqueline lay snoring on the sofa as I looked out my living room window into the murky night sky, feeling confident that God blessed me for my kindness. I felt His glow, and hung my head to thank Him, grateful for my strength. Jacqueline had come a few hours after paying her Shiva call, appearing at the front door at about eight o'clock in the evening. I just smirked at her, noticing the skirt she had borrowed from me was on backwards, the back hem lifted higher than the front. Her white blouse was mis-buttoned and had a dark red, crusty, circular stain near the cuff.

"Just come in and get out of my clothes that you ruined." I waved her in, as if she had shown up drenched from an unexpected April downpour. I saw no point in questioning Jacqueline. Wherever my daughter had been, whatever she had done, I was too exhausted to hear about it. I helped her remove the soiled clothes, pulling the skirt down around her feet. "You want something to eat? You want first to shower?"

"You want to *shower first*. Get the grammar right already, for Christ's sake." She shook her head and tsked at me before dropping to the floor and crouching, arms folded around her waist in chills.

I threw the clothes onto the floor next to the hamper, away from my own, retrieved a new shirt from a shopping bag, tore off the tags, and gave it to Jackie to put on.

"It's stiff and scratchy. What the hell kind of fabric is this?" Jacqueline pulled the collar of the new shirt from the back of her neck and ripped off the labels.

"It's clean. If it itches, give it to me and I'll give you something softer. Something I've worn. Come on. Give it." I stuck my hand out to her at chest level.

"No. It's good. Got any Fiorinal? My head hurts." Jacqueline scratched hard on her forehead.

Out of the room and back in a minute, I returned with four tablets and a glass of orange juice. I handed them to Jackie and took a place on the sofa.

Jacqueline sat next to me, in her clean shirt and panties, drinking her juice and yawning. I took her hand and waited for the drug to dull the tension. When the pills started working, she put her head into my lap and I sang her a German folk song about a farmer in love with a dairy maiden, German words interspersed with English and French, until the child fell asleep. As Jacqueline snored with the lush, wet whistle of a baby, I thought back to my phone conversation with Beatrice earlier, when I had complained about Henri's lack of consideration for me. "Of course I have no legal right to interfere, but does she go to him when she's hurting? No. Does he extend any hand at all to encourage her to reach for him? No."

I had asked Beatrice these questions before. Beatrice had answered them before: "He's not a mother, Monika. You are the mother and as the mother, legal guardian or not, you have to make it your business to take control of that girl." How? Beatrice didn't really know, other than to *get thee to a nunnery*. My heart fell into its ominous ditch of impotence and only wanted Jackie to stop shivering.

This evening—on the eve of Nadine's burial—I had anticipated spending time alone. As Jackie snored on my lap, my mind was wild with possibilities: Nadine had left a room empty, and I could fill it. Or Manny and I would leave the United States and start a life in Germany. Or he would leave me and let me rot on my own. I wanted to call Hildie and offer my condolences. I wanted to grieve and be comforted in the arms of Manny's family. Maybe I would clean a closet, scrub the oven. Hildie would love to hear that I spent the night cleaning. Then I could have that lunatic Fanny come over and smell it!

By eleven o'clock, having eased myself out from under Jacqueline's head, I had changed into my pajamas and stood at the front window. The phone rang, and as I turned to get it, I crossed my chest and kissed a crucifix on the wall with my fingers to seal my prayer that it was Manny. Jackie stirred on the couch, cursed a "sloppy fuck," and I quickly picked up the receiver and said hello, as though I were out of breath from doing chores round the house.

It was Manny; the crucifix had answered my prayer, and I dragged the phone from the living room into the bathroom. "How are you, sweet one?"

"I'm not doing so great." Manny's voice was soft, falling into a whisper.

"Oh, I wish I were there. I wanted so much to be there to help send Nadine to her resting place, to make it easier for you and the family. *My* family, as I think of them." I sighed, dragging the phone cord over so I could sit on the toilet seat, pulling my pajamas tight around my neck, becoming modest.

"This is a nightmare. Nadie is really, really gone." He started to cry, and I heard him blowing his nose away from the mouthpiece. "You have to remember, Monika, that the worst of this is that Nadine is gone."

"I know that, Manny. Of course! Do you think I have no heart at all? I never wanted it to end for her this way." I was crying now. I let loose my collar and unbuttoned the top two buttons, giving myself room to breathe. I heard him breathing heavily, and the sound spawned fingertips along my spine. "Manny, don't stay alone. I'm afraid for you. Come here tonight."

"Don't be absurd." His voice had gone clear and sharp. "You don't get it, do you?" He spoke one word at a time, as though each were a sentence unto itself. "I-love-Nadine-and-only-Nadine-and-I-am—sick-with-grief!" He hung up. He'd never spoken to me like this, and I was frightened.

I dialed his number back. As soon as he picked up, I spoke. "I'm sorry. Forgive me. It's just that I have such a need to hold you. I love you, Manny."

He was quiet. I was ready to tell him how human contact is healing, how the positive support of a loving partner is key to overcoming grief. I heard the tinkling of a bottle against a glass rim.

He finally spoke. "Monika. Jesus. I have to get through this night by myself. I'm exhausted and weary to my bones. There's so much other shit, so many things going on, it would kill me to spend another brain cell thinking about it. I'll call you when I wake up, okay?"

"I'll be thinking of you all night. I love you." I kept my voice shallow and breathless, almost asthmatic. I did not betray my melancholy.

"Okay. Goodnight. And look out for Jacqueline tonight. She's wandering around stoned." He sniffed hard. "Claudette talked to her, but she ran away."

"I have her here already. She's sleeping on the sofa." I explained to him how no matter who else tried to intervene, it would always be me who would ultimately have to do the cleanup. I was my family's mop and pail. He responded with only a sigh.

I hung up softly but felt the prodrome of doom. I went and sat next to Jackie on the sofa and stroked her hair in an effort to rouse her. She started smacking her tongue against the roof of her mouth, then shuddered, her arm twitching, and turned over on her back.

"Hey. What time is it?" she asked. Clearing her throat, she sounded like an eighty-year-old smoker.

"It's twelve."

"In the day?" Jacqueline coughed with a deep wheeze.

I rubbed the inside of her baby-skin arm, a sickening reminder of her infancy, and told her that it was midnight. "Do you feel shaky? Do you think you'll be sick again tonight?"

"Yeah, I forgot, oh shit! Claud said if you don't take me to the hospital, she'll never speak to me again. I'm not going to any fuckin' hospital. She could ignore me till World War Three, I am not goin'. Fuck her. And fuck you if you think you can get me to go." She stood and pulled off her panties, dropping them to the living room floor. "I gotta go pee." Halfway to the bathroom, she stopped moving and turned toward me, opened her mouth to speak, then shrugged, disappearing into the darkness of the bathroom.

I picked up the panties and went into the kitchen to get her a drink, dropping her damp underwear in the trash. Before I opened the fridge, my attention was stolen by the smell of a frying pan left dirty in the sink and by the shelf of chipped and dusty shiny ceramic figurines I had gleaned from my old apartment. I swiped hard at the pan's handle, sending it across the counter and onto the floor, where it spun until its bottom found its center, and rocked back and forth, causing a metallic racket that hurt my head. When it stopped, I collapsed at the table and burst into tears. I pretended not to notice Jackie when she came into the room.

"Got any more juice?" Jacqueline opened the refrigerator and started pushing things around. She cleared her way through the food with the back of her hand.

"What are you doing there in my refrigerator? Are you brushing dirt off the tops of the food before you have any?"

Jackie's knees were bent, and she stood for a few seconds completely still, with her eyes closed and her mouth open. Then, as if awakened, she continued pushing bottles and Tupperware in the fridge. The bottle of milk fell out and crashed on the floor.

I jumped. "Jackie! Watch what you're doing. Go sit in there, and I'll get you what you want. Go ahead. Go!" I held my arm out long and straight, directing her into the living room.

Jacqueline turned to me, her face dissolving into a snarl of disgust. She lifted her hand and slapped my face. "Fuck you! It was an accident. Don't talk to me like you have a right to tell me what to do. Who do you think you are, my *motha, motha* fucker?" She spat on the floor. "Get me a fucking broom and a rag, and I'll clean up this *accident!*" She sniffed a big blob of snot up and threw her chest out. "Cry over spilt milk, do they in Ger-man-eee?"

The sting on my cheek was hot to the touch, my mouth open in shock. I ran into the bathroom. The old bolt made a loud knock as I twisted it into the latch. I leaned over the sink, trying to catch my breath, and gagged. I heard the sound of glass hitting glass as Jacqueline cleaned up the broken bottle. Splashing cold water on my face, examining my cheeks for red fingermarks, I sat on the toilet seat to compose myself. "What do I do now?" I shouted at the mirror. "That girl is mad. Totally schizoid." Claudette wants her in a hospital, and Beatrice. They don't get it. They'd put her through withdrawal is all, and then send her back out. She'd freeze to death.

I'd have to get Jacqueline back to her own apartment, tonight, before she got sick again. I put a firm hand on the bathroom doorknob, sucked in my stomach and went back into the kitchen to help her with the mess.

We packed a bag of cookies and bread, along with a suitcase filled with clothing donations from Beatrice. I tried to say calmly, "If you are going to behave in such a rude, awful, hateful way, then you have to go back to your apartment downtown." Although I had skipped this barbed path dozens of times before, I continued to recite the same lesson. She thanked me for the lift home.

The drive downtown at night was horrendous, but I had no heroin left in the house and couldn't tolerate another night with Jacqueline getting sick on me.

"Are you set for the night? You think you'll be getting sick again tonight?"

Jacqueline was wiggling in the passenger seat and blasting the car radio.

"I'm gonna need a fix in the morning. So you have *got* to give me money. I'll get real sick if you don't give me money."

"I will give you twenty dollars if you promise to call home tomorrow."

"Sure. Yeah, right. Call you tomorrow. And tell daddy I might see him tomorrow too. Tell him I need to get some things from my room. George wants me to move in with him downtown *totally*. So I have to show him, you know, like…good faith, and bring all my stuff." Jacqueline smiled sarcastically directly at my face.

I nodded but wouldn't promise that Henri would allow her to remove any other stuff from the house. Where East Seventh Street met Tompkins Square Park, couples lay on park benches half-asleep. In the shadow of the street lamps, I saw the braless lump of a middle-aged woman's breast beneath a shirt, and the nest of a man's beard as he leaned on her shoulder. I tickled Jacqueline's cheek. "Daddy wants you to move back with him. I suppose that's out of the question."

"Out of the question." Jacqueline chomped on a piece of bubble gum she'd found on the dashboard. "And I need more than twenty bucks."

"You want more for that George, don't you?"

"I told you. He is not on drugs. He's my *mentor*." She smiled to herself. "Like that word? He taught it to me. He said he could get me off the shit if I'm living with him. He needs *complete access*. His words. Neat, huh?" She closed her eyes and seemed to sleep spontaneously.

Neat. I turned down St. Mark's Place, venturing into the darkest part of lower Manhattan. The streetlights seemed to know there was hellish life in these buildings, because they were dimmer than the other streets, as if the dirty little panties of runaway daughters screened the light. One street lamp lay flat on its back, people pausing when they encountered the length of steel on their sidewalk, stepping carefully over the beast so as not to fall en route to shooting up.

"We're here." I shook Jacqueline's shoulder to rouse her. "I don't see any lights on in your building. Where could George be?" I muttered "shit" under my breath.

"It's late. He's probably asleep. Has school in the morning, you know. I told you he's a student."

"Uh-huh. *Law* school, you told me. And *which* one does he go to?"

"I don't know. NYU, I think." She looked at me. "What? You don't believe him? Cause you're a damn saint, right?"

"I believe him, Jacqueline." No time to get her started.

Jacqueline popped the door and got out. She leaned in, remembering, "The money? You got the forty bucks?"

"So now it's forty?" I reached into my wallet, mumbling, "I can barely afford my own groceries! Here's your forty. If you want to go back to Daddy's, remember that he wants you."

Jacqueline said "adios," and walked into the street, then bolted away from the apartment she shared with George, the law student, toward the park benches on the Bath Street triangle. My mind let her vanish as quickly as her shadow had.

"So many things," Manny had said. What else? So many things. Claudette must have been a basket case at the funeral. She must have gotten worked up because Jackie was stoned, and because I wasn't there and she didn't know why.

A sick acid climbed into my throat. The acrid taste of too much tea. My pulse got rapid and the taste rose, causing me to swerve the car at the corner of Houston and Allen, avoiding a window washer standing in the middle of the road, wearing a purple wool cap that stunned me because I was sure it belonged to Jacqueline.

I know what he meant by so many things. Manny. He's told Claudette! That was what this was all about. Claudette knows we have been together. She's sick because she has pictured us making love. "Ha!" Claudette's jealous.

# *Manny*

The clock in the hallway had not yet struck midnight as I clutched the phone receiver after hanging up with Monika, which meant it was still the day that Nadine had been buried. I could be alone with Nadine, could count the minutes—only minutes, but still some time—to be together on the final day I'd seen her bodily form. Standing with my sisters in the chapel while Rabbi Berger said the blessing as they closed her coffin, covering her forever, my eyes traced the outline of her body, wrapped in its plain white sheet, trying to memorize all its features. How wide her shoulders spread, how far it was from her shoulder to her fingertips, how long from her torso to her toes. She was tiny under the covering, like the body of a child. My tears wet her sheet.

Lifting myself from bed, unable to lie still, I roamed in circles from room to room. I lifted our wedding picture from the table at the entrance to the house. The eight-by-ten frame felt heavy pushed tight across my chest. Following the night shadows on the walls and floor, I made my way back to the bedroom. It was a small house, intended for a small family. The dining room was really a space meant as an anteroom to the living room. Everything was dusty, and I apologized out loud to Nadine about the mess. She was so tidy. Having slept on the living room couch these last weeks, at least the bed was still made. The patchwork quilt lay tight over it, its hem tucked in around the foot. I took the corner of the top sheet and carefully pulled it down so only one side, my side, was unmade. Lying with the metal picture frame resting on my belly, eyes closed, I saw her glowing beautiful face waiting to kiss me under the chuppah. We fell asleep together, on this last day.

# Monika

It was after one in the morning by the time I got home from Jackie's. Not a time to call and wake Beatrice. I turned on the transistor radio, more news about the fighting, and I boiled water for tea. I'll call in sick for work—tell them there's been a death, I can't come in. It would not be a lie. Bringing the steaming cup into my bedroom, I sat to catch my breath before undressing, savoring all the events that led up to my conviction that Claudette knew about me and Manny. It elated me, filled me with satisfaction. The curtains that hung over the only southern window blew into the room, accompanied by a humming sound, like a harp string plucked and vibrating. The musical note was delivered with a sweeping draft that lifted the hairs on my arms and slammed the bedroom door shut. As I rose to close the window, I was stricken with the same nauseating dizziness that afflicted me when I smelled Fanny's drugstore perfume. I felt the start of a migraine: a pain in my left temple struck once, only once, then the ache spread to my entire head.

The Fiorinal bottle on the night table was empty. Jacqueline. Twenty minutes later, the pain really would not dissipate. Unable to sleep, heart pounding, I pictured walking into work, spitting on Stephanie, and taking over the nurse's job. More dream than fantasy now, the sixteen-year-old patient, Sophia—the little Italian girl who tried to cut her wrists open—was crawling onto my lap. She was kissing me on my chin, trying to open my blouse to drink from my breasts. I unhooked my bra, but when I looked down to guide her nursing, my breasts were gone and the young girl started pulling at my skin with tiny hands trying to make the nipples come out. I woke myself screaming out, "Momma!" and realized I'd fallen asleep. I ran my hands over my chest to make sure I had breasts. The train's whistle signaled it was leaving Cologne; I felt my mother push me from behind, up onto the train. "Papa." My hands grabbing the metal window frames of the train, I shook them until the glass shattered. I woke fully and remembered Sophia. She was to be discharged from the ward in the morning. I had promised her and the girl's mother to be there. The father had the hots for me, so I'd been keeping a friendly distance. He had come to the hospital only three times in Sophia's six-week stay, but I felt his attraction. At least show up for work until the girl has left. I'll cough all morning, and tell the head nurse I'm not feeling well once the girl is gone.

Thunder startled me from sleep. It was after seven, but darkness filled the sky out the window. Lightening was flashing across the room. My head still foggy from the pain, I wrapped myself wearily in the top sheet and pushed toward the shower. A loud thunderclap sent me darting into the bathroom, and I locked the door. There was no window here, and I felt instantly safe. As I turned on the water, the rushing noise blotted out the thunder; I was able to step into the stream and feel the heat and wet cover me, my face up into the water, hair stuck to my neck, the tail end dripping a fine ticklish line down my back.

*Manny is behind me now. He shampoos my hair with green herbal soap, and I am suddenly in a heavenly garden. Squirming a little, I roll my head under his fingers as they work the tension from my scalp; I giggle at the lightness of his touch, how it tickles me. Ready to play, I take the shower attachment and turn to shoot him.*

The spray jolts me, and I blink open to the blank look of the pink ceramic tile.

Pinning up my hair, I fought to keep my fingers on my head, I was so drained. I made up my face, ready to go to work and help that dear patient Sophia get discharged into the hands of her loving mother and neglectful father. I had watched enough doctors' wives to learn about fashion and style. Accustomed to wearing whatever was inexpensive or handed down to me, I came to this country dressed in blouses and soft colors that were too elegant for fad-obsessed New York City. I could carry any style and look beautiful, but I felt it hard not to stand out as an alien imposter, so uncomfortable in this costume of a new white man-tailored shirt and pale yellow straight-line skirt, tight enough though to cup my backside.

And now I was primed to face the dreary hospital, its self-important staff, and a mother retrieving her damaged daughter. I could see similarities in Sophia's family more than they knew, and today I would send them home along with my own sad story. They would learn about Jacqueline. They would have to sympathize. Then they could become confidants, comrades in heartache. Sophia's father's attentions had already pledged his allegiance, but I needed to recruit the mother. I'll trade my secrets and humility as long as it takes to get *something* from them.

# 3
# Come and Go

## *Monika*

"I had to work all day, a dreadful day. And now you are here? What?" My daughter was perched on the curb in front of my building, sitting in the shade under a blooming maple. When I saw the shadowed marks on Jacqueline's face, my first thought was that a bird shit on her.

"I'm not going to Germany. My funds have been stolen," Jacqueline announced.

"Get up from that filthy curb." I hefted the grocery bags onto my hips. "Come in the house. I have packages. They're heavy. Come on, Jack, get up!"

Jackie stood and shuffled her feet to the front door. "Did you hear me? I'm not going." She followed me into the house, holding the door open for herself with her shoulder. "Seems the guy holding my things sold them and now there's nothing left." She followed me through the apartment and went straight into the bathroom, sitting on the toilet in the dark. "Mom? Come talk to me."

"I can hear you from here." I put the packages on the kitchen table and talked loud enough to reach the bathroom door. "You're not going to Germany. Well, that's really too bad. Are you eating dinner here with me?" I opened the windows to the still air, added water to some flowers in a vase, fixed the arrangement, and bent over to smell them.

"This is important. I need to get my things and my money," Jacqueline yelled from the bathroom.

"There is no money, Jacqueline. Where would there be money from? And who do you know in Germany? You never went to Germany, Jacqueline." I had read that when patients were delusional, you should not try to explain reality to them. I was tired now and didn't feel like feeding her fantasy and playing psychiatrist. "You were born in France! You're French!"

"I never said I came from fucking Germany. You're from there, aren't you? You forgot to bring any shit back with you and now some guy has all your money, *my* money, and sold all my things, and I'm left with nothing."

And the plot thickens. Now she's got *details* of this theft. In the light of the hallway, my stomach turned at the trail of pocks and scratches that coped the front of Jackie's forehead, nose, and chin. "Jacqueline! What happened to you? My god, you've been beat up. Oh, dear Lord. Sit here and let me look."

Jacqueline shimmied her shoulders away from me, as if she hadn't come here to be with me. "Get outta here, will you? I fell off a bike. Jesus, you think everything is so major." She turned back into the bathroom and squinted at her face in the mirror. She looked like someone had drawn on her with crayon—colored in thick and thin lines, in varying shades of dried blood that rolled from pink to brown. "Shit. I got a broken tooth. Fuckin' crappy piece of shit."

My throat closed so tight, the pressure felt as though it were trying to expel my tongue. "Who did this? I demand to know where you've been and who did this, or you're going to have to leave. Did George do this?"

"I said I fell off a bike."

"You don't have a bike. Whose bike?"

"George's. He has a bike he takes to class. You want to come see it?"

"George's bike, huh? Just wash up good. Take my toothbrush and clean your teeth. I'll call my dentist." I got close to Jackie's face and took a better look and couldn't help crying.

"You think he'll give me Demerol?" Jackie asked, as she brushed her broken front tooth.

"If we're lucky, he'll give us both Demerol."

Jacqueline remained washing in the bathroom as I tried to stay calm enough to speak to the dentist. Of course, he was unavailable and would have to call back. Disgusted, I went to her bed. Jackie and Sophia, the teenager who was supposed to be discharged today, blurred in my exhausted head. The girl did not get to go home after all. She had been so afraid to return home that during the previous night, she got hold of a nurse's knitting needle and tried to bleed to death by sticking holes into herself. She hardly produced any blood at all, but it was enough of a demonstration to keep her hospitalized for at least another week. I sat with her parents, Camille and John, for the length of my lunch hour. During that time, between bites of hospital tuna sandwiches, we three discussed the pitfalls of parenthood. Through the lunch hour, our chairs shifted closer and closer to either side of John, until, at the conclusion of the meal, we were all sitting on one side of the table in a huddle.

Sophia's parents learning about my daughter demonstrated clearly—reassured me, if not her doctors—that she was schizophrenic. Her psychiatrist's primary diagnosis, that Jackie was first and foremost a drug addict, got it backwards. "It is her mental disorder that is the *cause* for drug use and prostitution," I said, pounding my index finger against the table. I further clarified her diagnosis by reiterating that *illness* was the reason she took drugs and lived on the floor in an apartment downtown, and not the other way around.

"You don't say," Camille said, shaking her head and taking my hand. "And goodness gracious, you must know—my lord, you see it *all* up there." She sniffled hard and squeezed my hand. "And the doctors, they don't see it the same? They don't agree with you? You know, it takes a while to diagnose. My Sophia wasn't diagnosed as manic-depressive for two years. Not until *two* attempts." Camille held up two diamond-clad fingers and wiggled them.

"Sounds to me like it's all because of the drugs," John said flatly.

"Yes, well, it seems to me people are too fast to blame the drugs." I tried to put him in his place. "I know what she was like *before* the drugs. She had delusions then as well. Oh, I do look for strength in the Lord." I made the sign of the cross over myself.

"What kinds of delusions? Did she see dead people or talk to the wall?"

I began to think the woman was an idiot and was going to believe anything I said with conviction. "Delusions. You know, of persecution. It's a subject I don't feel comfortable talking about here and now. One day, perhaps, I'll tell you. But believe me, she has given her father and me reason to suspect mental illness long before the drugs. Going all the way back to when she was just a little girl. Self-destructive, completely unaware of danger." I shook my head at the trauma. "I'd find bruises on her. She could never remember where they'd come from. Like she walked around in a daze, you know?" I stood and lifted my tray from the table; Camille and John followed suit. Turning back toward them as they trailed in my footsteps, I asked, "Have you heard of a split personality?" They nodded their heads. "Wait till we get upstairs. I'll explain it all to you. It's not what it sounds like. I've got books under my desk."

We returned to the ward that held Sophia. I was joyous about the new friends I was making. John was an attorney, and no doubt I would someday need legal advice for Jacqueline. He had great promise as a friend. He knew lots of people, and I could probably get him to do all sorts of favors.

Camille and John went to their daughter's room, bringing her their lunch leftovers. She was a girl with the plainest features, nothing notable, except for her heavy black eyelashes around pale blue eyes. They didn't make her pretty, but she had that one distinguishable feature.

While they were in with their daughter, I grabbed my textbook from under my desk, a green soft-covered volume simply titled, *Handbook of Psychiatry*. I turned to the section, "Fundamental Symptoms of Schizophrenia." As soon as they finished their visit, I pulled Camille and John into the sunroom and recited the symptoms on the list that corresponded to Jacqueline. She, Jacqueline, spoke illogically—how her thoughts would shift from one subject to another without pause or obvious connection. Her delusions included her current belief that she was going to Germany to get her money. She laughed in the face of tragedy and never cried, she loved and hated the same people simultaneously, and she was impulsive and indifferent.

Camille told me I had made a brilliant and difficult diagnosis and that someone should listen to me. John just sat with a rude air of doubt, his arms folded across his chest, his head still. A set of parents who were emotionally drained, exhausted with doctors and false starts.

Now, reliving a successful day with John and Camille from the softness of my bed, I banged my elbow on the night stand, as if just awakened, when the phone rang. It was the dentist calling to say he could see Jackie the following morning. That meant she had to sleep over. I was hoping Manny would come tonight after sitting the second night of Shiva. Well, Jackie could be put down, as though she were five, and Manny could still come and visit, to talk about our future.

Jacqueline appeared at my bedroom door. "Can I lay with you?"

"Sure, sweetheart. Come here." I sat up a little and fluffed the pillow for Jackie to share. Her bruises were raw, but at least she had cleaned her face and brushed her teeth. "You look beautiful tonight, except for that tooth. The dentist said he'd see you in the morning. You should eat and go right to sleep."

Jackie sat up abruptly. "No, no. I got to get back. I'm meeting some people, and I can't let them down. George is having a goodbye party for me. I think I will go to Germany after all." She was soft-spoken, matter of fact, and scratched feverishly at her head.

"Really? Well, how do you expect to go downtown and get back uptown to go to the dentist in the morning?" I pulled Jackie's hand away from her head. "Stop scratching so hard. You'll make yourself bleed."

"Don't touch me. And I don't know how I'll get back here. You never even asked me if I want to go to your dentist. And I don't want to go." Jacqueline scooted out of the bed. "I'm goin' home. I'll take the train or bus or somethin'. I don't have any money, can I have some, please?" She looked straight into my eyes.

"What is *wrong* with you? You came here looking for help, and now that I offer it, you want to leave. You *just* wanted to sleep in bed with me!" I climbed out of bed and stood to wrap my arms around her. Jackie held her arms out to keep a distance. "If I take you home, you have got to get back here by seven in the morning so I can get you to Dr. Davis!"

Jackie smirked and rolled her eyes. "I didn't come here for help. I came here to see you, that's all."

"Well, you've seen me. And now I want you to come back in the morning."

"Yeah. Absolutely. Seven o'clock. I won't even go to sleep tonight, just watch that clock tickin' and get here on time."

"I'm not kidding. You'll be here? Maybe George can ride you here on that *bike* of his on his way to *school*." I waited for a raised eyebrow, a smirk, wide-eyed reality to reveal itself in Jacqueline's eyes.

"The bike is busted up, from my fall. I'll get here, for fuck sake. Just get me downtown. I have to get back and see my friends."

"What friends? Who exactly are your so-called friends?"

"George's friends."

"Do you love him, Jackie? Is that was this is about? You think you love him?"

She explained to me about George. She didn't love him. She loved no one. Love was some made-up bullshit belief sold by poets and parents, and other thieves who profit from and soothe a guilty conscience. She was going to live her life without loving another human being. George. Where would she get those thoughts on her own?

Frustrated, but kind of relieved that she was leaving, I drove her back, just as I had the night before. On Houston and Second Avenue, I saw a man sitting in a rocking chair—a "For Sale" ticket hanging from its slightly rotted, bent wooden arm—in front of his "antiques" furniture store. The street corner contained a gated lot that held old plumbing fixtures and odd pieces of clipped architecture: ornate iron gates, marble cornices, broken columns and capitals from various eras. This neighborhood. Jackie's broken neighbors. And we watched the woolen-capped window washer standing in the middle of the road with his rag and spray bottle, waiting to shine my windshield. I was panicky and Jackie was laughing. The light didn't turn green. It stayed red and stayed red and Jackie began getting agitated, first rocking back and forth in her seat, then repeating, "Come on, come on." She flicked her head toward me. "I'm gonna have to jump out, mom. I can't wait here like this. They're waiting for me. George is having a party."

"Oh," she said, "and I have to see my man Clifton." As the light remained red, my darling daughter explained that Clifton was sort of her business associate. A tall, muscular, beautifully faced black man. Dark, she said, almost iridescent. "He shined like a black Cadillac." She had seen him that morning.

She reached for the button on the door. I grabbed her arm. "Jacqueline, don't you move from that seat. There is no one waiting for you, so just sit there and tell me what the hell happened to you. Did Clifton hurt you?" I was on fire.

"No. Gotta go." The light remained red.

"Tell me how you got hurt or I'm turning around in the middle of the street here and taking you to the hospital!"

She nearly ripped off her shirt in frustration and stared at me. "I got beat up by a little Spanish guy who gave me ten bucks, okay!" She held my arm and confessed how she sold herself, got men through Clifton, and how this guy pushed her face into a brick wall.

"He's a pimp? Clifton is an actual pimp!"

"What should I do? I have to get money for Germany!" She popped the door open and ran across the three lanes, her body dodging cars, hopping over the curb, vanishing from sight. It was eight o'clock and a yellow full moon stood in complete view in the dark, clear sky. Cars started honking for me to move across the intersection. A pit bull barked from behind the fence, and an old woman tapped the hood of my car to signal she was crossing the street in front of me. I instinctively turned east toward the FDR Drive and headed for the Brooklyn Battery Tunnel.

I didn't know what time Manny would come home from sitting Shiva at his sisters' house, but I was going to wait. I had met with him before in Brooklyn, but only at a restaurant near the hospital, never at his home. I drove along the narrow Belt Parkway, ships in the ocean under the vast Verrazano Bridge. The coming of May hovered over the surf, quieting it. I fixated for a moment, catching the swerve of the car, as the moon's reflection stained a flat, luminous spread of gold leaf across the water.

Manny and Nadine lived on a block on Kings Highway—which wasn't a highway at all, just wider than a typical street—that had been built sometime after World War I. The houses on his block were red brick or gray stucco, and each had a similar façade: two windows on the second floor, centered above the large picture window on the first, with the entry door to the left or the right, on a porch made of the same material as the house, the whole property and its tiny gardens protected by a wrought-iron railing. Having been there so few times, and so many years having passed, I wasn't absolutely sure which house was his. The streetlamps were brighter here than they were in the city, and some boys played stickball in the middle of the street, parting to the sides of the road to let me go by. Two girls leaned against a car, watching the boys, and smiled as I cruised toward them. I stopped in front of them and rolled down my window. "Excuse me. Can you tell me where Nadine and Manny Hoffman live?" I smiled my New York smile.

One of the girls came up to the window and bowed to speak directly into my face. "I have some bad news," she said in an urgent teenaged voice. "Mrs. Hoffman passed away a couple days ago. Their house is that one." She turned and pointed to a small red brick house with a lawn that featured one crabapple tree and a green-and-white awning, lowered halfway across the cement porch.

"I'm so shocked to hear about Nadine. I knew, of course, she was so ill, but I hadn't heard. I'm from out of town." The girl looked at my plates. New York. "Well, out of Brooklyn anyway."

"Mr. Hoffman's not home yet, but if you want to wait, you can park in his driveway. He won't mind. He's such a doll." The other girl had come over to listen, and when this one called Manny a "doll," they both giggled. I nodded at them, stunned at these young girls' attraction to Manny.

I drove the car into his driveway, turned off the ignition, and sat back, waiting. No one else in the family had died since we came here from France nearly two decades ago—but I believed Manny said he would sit for a week. It would be all right for me to visit him, since he had so many more days left to pay his respect. A woman next door sang an Italian lullaby out her kitchen window; I turned to the foreign words and saw the singer's husband kiss her neck in view of the street.

I rolled up the window, then slumped into the seat and tried to think of a way to get Jacqueline and George together at my house. Maybe he really was a law student. Maybe it would turn out cozy. Maybe the boy would graduate and marry Jacqueline and we could all live together. Or Manny and I would marry, he'd take us back to Germany, find my parents' burial place, raise our child. Anything was possible. The young girls on the street whistled and cheered for their winning team member.

An hour passed as I watched the kids throw the ball to each other, shout "hooray," finish their game, and retreat to one of the houses. There were four boys and two girls, and I wondered how they were going to work out the kissing game with that ratio. Lucky girls. When the door closed behind the last straggling boy who had been left to collect the equipment, the headlights from Manny's car came around the corner. My stomach churned. I forgot I had to vacate his driveway so he could pull in. He parked his car on the street. His head tilted down as he walked toward me.

"Monika, what are you doing here?" he mouthed through the glass of the windshield. He did not look happy to see me.

I rolled down the window. "I missed you. You didn't want me to come to Hildie's. What was I supposed to do? Not see you? I'm not supposed to see you now?" My eyesight got blurry with tears.

"You can't come in. It's not right. I'm sorry, but this is out of the question." He stood waiting as I stared at him, blinking. "Come to Hildie's tomorrow. Okay?" He was breathing hard, as if he had run to my car.

"I work tomorrow," I said. What made being together acceptable when Nadine was sick and not acceptable now that she was dead? "What if I park around the corner and then walk to the house? Is it safe?" The sweat on his brow and the weak look around his jaw told me I could work my way in.

He looked around the street to see if anyone was out. "Yeah, it's safe. Park on the side street and come up to the house from that side." He pointed to the end of the block that was closest to his house. "Don't get yourself noticed. Just come up to the door. I'll leave it unlocked." He grabbed his key chain tightly into his palm and turned to go inside.

I rolled up the window, turned off the radio, started the engine, and crept to the side street. Before getting out of the car, I checked my face by the light of the rearview mirror. Struggling to slow my heart rate, I took deep breaths and sat still. It didn't help. Maybe the walking would calm me. I straightened my skirt and focused on the small house with the red brick. He had revealed nearly nothing about the contents of the house, how it was furnished, what the colors were. Knowing Nadine, it was probably beige, with small furniture and small accessories, everything neat and unimaginative. I'd finally gotten Manny's love, and his passions. If only I could give him the baby Nadine stole from him when she couldn't hold it in her womb, share this child in the kind of marriage Henri stole from me when he took my daughter away.

The door opened easily; there was no pushing and pulling the way there was entering Henri's apartment. I slipped within the narrowest opening I could make and closed the door, turning the deadbolt behind me. The hallway led to a small room that didn't really feel like a room but had a small dining table and narrow chairs, just as I had anticipated. Impressed with myself, I noticed a painting on the wall hanging off center—children frolicking in a park. I thought of a happy time when I and little Jackie and Henri were in our tiny room in Paris, and they played roly-poly with a pink rubber ball. Grieving my own loss, I walked toward the light into the kitchen, where Manny stood at the sink filling a teakettle. He turned, nodding for me to take a seat at the kitchen table. It was a warm golden oak. Two of the four chairs were pushed snuggly against the wall with the table flush against them. A smudged set of glass salt and pepper shakers sat in the middle of the table, a stack of white embroidered napkins between them, probably from Fanny. The table, I discovered when I put my hand down, was sticky. "Can I have a sponge?" I asked softly.

"I'm sorry, Monika. Let me get that. I really haven't been taking proper care of the house." He began to sponge the table around my place.

As he bended to clean, I put my hand to his face and tried to kiss his cheek. Manny pulled away, stopped wiping, and stood cold and flat, looking at me.

"I only wanted to give you a little kiss on the cheek." I put my index finger to the corner of my eye and sniffled. "I want to comfort you."

Manny put the sponge on the table, sat in the other chair, and took my hand. "I'm in shock, Monika. I'm in emotional shell shock." He lifted my chin with his hand. "This is going to take some time here. You can't expect me to bury my wife and jump into bed with you the next day." His eyes were steady but empty.

"You jumped into bed with me when she was in the middle of dying. I know you love her. I know you will always love her. But what does that have to do with us, and our lives together? Are you going to stop seeing me?" I stood and walked to the stove, two feet away, and poured the boiling water into the cup with the tea bag. I was crying and wouldn't turn around.

He had to have heard me, unless he was truly in shock, but he didn't ask me to turn around. Didn't come over to me or say my name. I returned to my chair. "You haven't answered me. Are you going to stop seeing me?"

Manny gazed down at his fingers, as if looking for his veins to give him an answer. "I think for now, yes. I am not going to see you for a while. I'm in pieces. Claudette is in tears over this, you and me, and I can't deal with that. Not on top of Nadine. Do you understand?"

That pain on the right side of my head from the night before erupted, rapidly spreading to the left, pulsating in my temples so that it punctuated the pounding in my chest, and I broke into a horrible tremble. "Understand? Oh my god, Manny. I love you. I want to have a baby with you. Claudette is in love with Henri, her own cousin, and you're worried about her crying over you and me? What is it with the men in this family? Lord have mercy on all of you!" I didn't know if his look of shock was from the force of my anger or his response to hearing about Claudette. I didn't think he had known, and for the second that it took me to tell him, I wanted him to know, but now I regretted hurting him.

The thump of the kitchen chair being thrown aside made me jump back and make a dash for the front door. I turned to him, and he grabbed my shoulders and held me as close as he could.

Sweat leaked through his shirt onto my cheek, and for a second I stood petrified, wondering if it were blood. "I'm sorry I said that," I said through tears, my fingers running gently over his cheek. When I turned into his chest and breathed him in, we both started to sob. Our tears seeped into each other's clothes. I was so happy. I rocked him and took his head to my cheek. As his tears fell, I caught them on my lips. "Please, stop crying. I'm here and I'm not going." I don't care if you cry all night, I thought. I'll stay and be here when you stop.

Standing in the little dining room under the brass hanging lamp, lit and dusty, I waited for Manny to decide where we'd go from here. A minute or two passed. He took a deep breath and walked me to the couch. It was covered with a turquoise sheet and two down pillows with no cases. It was obvious he'd been spending his nights here.

Nadine's blue canary hopped restlessly in his cage by the window. He pecked on the small mirror and chirped a song that had no cogent pattern, yet the little bird was able to replicate the notes three times in a row.

We sat with the length of our legs touching. I held his hand on my lap. Thinking he was deciding how to say what he wanted from me, I allowed the silence to continue, focusing on the rate of his pulse. If this went on for too long, I thought I would kiss his hand. After some minutes, I nudged closer and woke him out of his dreamy world and into speech.

His pulse was not slowing when he sighed, then asked, "So, what's this about Henri and Claud?" Manny yawned while he spoke, making his question sound casual. He was never casual when it came to his niece, and I knew if we were ever going to get back to talking about the two of us, I had better answer him about Claudette.

I squeezed his hand, and my voice echoed his casual demeanor. "Beatrice knows, it's not some great secret. I don't know why your niece hasn't confided in you. Maybe she knows it's not normal."

He adjusted his position on the couch. "What exactly is it that Beatrice and you seem to know? You're not being totally clear here," he turned his head and looked at me more directly. "Unless you meant in the kitchen that they're being intimate. Are you saying that?"

His hand tensed in mine. "I am saying that, Manny. She and Henri have been lovers for years now." I went on talking rapidly, explaining that I didn't think Henri could possibly take the relationship seriously, but according to various impressions from Beatrice, who'd seen them together many, many times, Claudette thought she was in love with Henri, and he with her. And that was most likely why she left her career in California to come back. "He'll never marry her, you know. Even if something as dubious as cousins together is acceptable in these changing times, in *these* United States."

"They're *second* cousins," Manny said to the air. He sat still, in thought.

Quiet, hesitant to remind him of my reason for being angry, I was even more hesitant to *have to* remind him that we'd been lovers. But my heart raced, my thoughts occupied with designing a tactic I could use to get him into bed with me tonight. Manny let go of my hand and clasped his own together. With his elbows on his knees, he rested his forehead against his fist, speaking into his own lap. "This is too much. How could he be so crazy to do this?" He sat, biting the inside of his lip and looking into the room, nodding as though counting off ways to kill Henri. "I'll talk to Claud tomorrow. This can't be as serious as you make it."

It was not me who made it serious, but I decided to drop the subject and prayed he could let go of it tonight. The windows were open to the warm night and the street was quiet. Then I heard a dull tapping in the kitchen. It sounded like a tiny rubber ball—the kind Jackie had used to play the game Jacks—dropping against a metal drum. The rhythmic bounce of water from a faucet. I wanted to get up to adjust the handle and make it stop, but instead I took a deep breath as evenly as I could through my nose, preparing to speak. "Manny? We should talk about—"

"About us," Manny said, as if my breath reminded him that I was there.

"Yes, about us."

His voice raised an octave. "Can't you understand my emotional state, my confusion?" And softer, he added, "You've been a bright light in my life since the day we met. I don't ever forget the night you sat with me in Paris. I know you thought it was my deathbed." He smiled sadly.

"But?"

"But I'm incapable of feeling anything but grief right now. And now this, with Henri." He took my hand again. "You know you stir great feelings in me, urges. I admit that freely, but I could not bring myself to touch you now. I couldn't bring myself to."

Flushed with panic, my skin burned, and I could sense my head quivering. "So you think it would help you, help *us*, if we didn't see each other for a while? Say it to me already, straight out, if that is what you want." I prayed, *no, no, don't say it.*

"I, I'm at a loss. I just don't have anything to give."

"Just say it, Manuel! I am not a child. Tell me your desires, what you want me to do, and I will abide by them." I waited for an answer as he sat motionless. Sitting too close to him—looking at his straight, elegant, and dark profile—I was aroused, yet I kept my stiff pose. I tried not to let my quickening breath be heard.

"Please don't do this," Manny's voice sounded as if he were pleading, but he didn't move to push me away.

I kissed the back of his hands, and gently pried his palms apart to kiss his fingers. My heart pounded when I looked up to see his eyes closed. He looked so tired. I didn't want to speak anymore.

Manny made no move to return any tenderness. The canary chirped more and more urgently, as if alerting his entire species. When Manny started to doze, I rose and without a word, walked to the bathroom, where I stripped and stepped into the shower. When I was clean and powdered, I walked nude to his room and got into the disheveled side of the bed—alone with his things, the stillness in the room, dense with horrible thoughts. The imprisoned air holding a sound you strained to hear, needed to hear.

The lamp in the other room had been turned off. Squinting, I searched the purple blackness, trying to put the room into focus. Where was the door, and which side of the room was I lying on? Not being able to picture the depth of space between the bed and the door, I panicked. Clutching the sheet to my chin, I thought I heard Jacqueline crying down the hall. Under the sheet, I listened frantically for sounds of the fading moans of a dying baby. This is when it all began to return to me.

Still—pretending to sleep so he wouldn't hear me, so he wouldn't rush away in shame or guilt—I waited, praying, urging him, through whatever mental telepathy I had, to come lie next to me, tell me to wait for him until he was ready, tell me he loved me and promise our time would come soon. When I stopped listening to my heart long enough to listen to the room, all I heard was the sound of the front door open and close.

# 4

# Gone Astray



*Claudette*

My apartment was part of a three-family brick house wedged in between two other three-family brick houses on Twenty-Ninth Street and Second Avenue in New York City. I lived on the top floor and had to walk the three flights. The entire third floor was supposed to be one two-bedroom apartment, but the landlord had split it into two. I loved this space, my street. In the mild weather of spring, neighbors would sit on the stoops, as if in a stadium, and watch the shadows of the day blur under the full maples that stood like landmarks to each stoop, until the current of men coming home from work tapered off, well after the setting of the sun.

After leaving Manny at my mother's house, I came home to find Henri on my stoop. Exhausted, when I reached the steps, I just plopped down next to him and bowed my head. We talked about where Jackie might have gone the night before. Henri said, "She's probably with her boyfriend downtown. Where else could she go?"

I neither looked into his silvery-blue eyes, nor let his skin touch mine. "Her mother," I answered.

The air was clear, and a strong breeze carried the East River's coolness across our faces. While Henri spoke, I picked at budding plants in the window box, and simply refused to show him a crumb of familiarity. The silence around us was so heavy, it forcibly held us in place. Henri followed me into the entrance, walked me up the stairs to my apartment, and I allowed him to stay the night because I just didn't want to be alone.

I woke first in the alcove that served as a bedroom in my tiny apartment—a cooing pigeon on my windowsill. Little woke Henri besides the irritating buzz of his own alarm clock, and I let him sleep, pulling the blanket over his naked leg, not really wanting to talk to him about Manny or Monika or Jackie. I had not yet forgiven him for keeping it from me for so long. I had not yet forgiven him for telling me.

Dressed in Henri's *Manny's Hardware* t-shirt, I drank instant coffee in a cup from a mixed set of dishware Hildie had given me to stock the kitchen cabinet. I wondered if I'd ever have a full set of anything. There hung one cabinet for dishes and another cabinet under the sink for household products. A beige vinyl shade covered the window, a rug with a picture of a bouquet of flowers Fanny had hooked lay in front of the sink, alongside two chairs with a wood-grain, Formica-topped snack table between them. Food was stacked in rows on the twelve-inch-long counter between the stove and the window. I was well stocked, with two boxes of Ronzoni spaghetti, two cans of tomato sauce, a bag of Tootsie Rolls, and three potatoes that sat like a sculpture, piled one on top of two, on the windowsill. They were growing sprouts. The room filled with clouds of exhaled smoke. Coughing, Henri woke up in the mist of a Marlboro.

"Good morning," he said, turning over onto his belly, burying his head under the pillow, adding a muffled, "What time is it?"

Flatly, I told him, "It's about eight o'clock. Don't forget there's no store to open this week." I rose and poured water from the kettle into a cup, then walked over, and sat on the edge of the double bed that occupied the whole of the alcove. "Want some instant black? It's all I have." There came a quick urge to drop the scalding sludge on him, but I softened when he looked up and smiled.

He took the cup from me and nosed at it. "Smells like shit." He drank it. Sitting up higher, he asked what time I wanted to leave to see Manny for today's Shiva.

"I don't know. I guess he doesn't need us there first thing. About ten." I stood and walked back toward the snack table, pissed at him all anew for not even realizing I had not forgiven him for everything and anything he ever stood for or did or thought. He could be so simple. That observation only warmed me toward him, and my confusion was dizzying. "We have to talk, you and me. We have to talk about Jackie." I stared at Henri, expecting him to ignore my suggestion.

"Okay. So talk." He sank back into the pillows.

Surprised at his cooperation, I plunged in. "I want you to stop Jackie from seeing that devil woman. I want you to take a stand at protecting your child."

I waited, but he didn't respond. By the window, pulling my hair back into a ponytail and holding it at the nape of my neck, I said, "So talk back."

"She's not a child anymore. I can't order her around. I have no control over who she sees or what she does. Haven't you been paying attention?" He turned in the bed and stood, adjusted his shorts, and made his way the two feet to the bathroom. My lower lip was bleeding from biting it. I already felt defeated.

He finished his business and came to kiss my cheek. "You are not her mother, my Claudala. You and I may love her equally, but you hold no responsibility to rescue her from her mother, or George, or anyone else. I know you care, I know. But you have to face the possibility that we might lose her someday." He shook his head as he rubbed his chin.

"We'll try. We'll always *try*, Claud. If I could think of a different thing, or way to treat her…but I don't know what else I can do, besides lock her up!"

"She will only get *lost* if you *lose* her. You're pulling out of the game and giving in to her mother's manipulation. What kind of father are you? She may be eighteen and living on her own, if you call that living *or* on her own, but she is a child—an eleven-year-old child who is probably still having nightmares about her mother never coming home. Or worse. You know *what* worse she could be dreaming." I wanted to vomit. I gathered my breath and spoke too loudly. "And I have every right and every responsibility as a human being to rescue that person. I love her, and I will not stand by and let Monika or you—yes *you*, Henri—ignore her cries." With that, losing my breath and out of control, I ran into the bathroom to cry. Sitting on the cold tiled floor, I thought of Jackie getting sick at the Shiva. How could that girl stand to be this sick all the time? How can I allow her to be this sick all the time?

I wanted to be alone and recuperate enough to go and sit with Manny. Another one. Another puppet. Monika keeps him dancing, too. I cried out loud, "Uch!"

"Are you okay? Are you sick?" Henri ran to me.

Instinctively, I pushed him away, then grabbed his arm so he would stay with me. "Henri, please, please help me get Jackie away. Please, please," I whispered.

He lowered his chin into his chest, pouted, and spoke in the tone of a little boy. "Yes, Claudala. Yes. We'll get her away." He stood. "Let me help you up. Can you stand now?"

"Thanks. I'm okay." I heard Henri agree to help, but was not for a second fooled into thinking he was committed to the cause.

We showered, each alone, then dressed to visit Manny. I flushed with embarrassment at the thought of facing him, now that we had discussed his *entanglement*.

—✦—

"Didn't seem like I was very much loved inside the house before. Seems you have a problem with the kind of man I am. Why would you love a man you don't respect?" Henri stopped walking and looked at me.

My heart sank. I pushed my bangs out of my eyes and looked back at him and could not say I loved him. "I respect you, Henri. Let's just get to Manny. As it is, it'll be noon before we get to Brooklyn, and my mother will be having a fit." We walked to the subway station on Twenty-Third and repeated the routine we had arranged. "You take the train after the one I get on. Give me a head start to my mom's."

"I think I know the plan." He smiled and kissed my cheeks before we walked to opposite ends of the platform.

Changing trains once we got to Brooklyn, we'd have a good hour to think before we arrived at Rockaway Parkway, the end of the Canarsie Line. It was easy getting a seat at this time of the late morning, and I was able to choose the one closest to the end of the car, near the door that connected to the next car. The loud constant clang of the metal straining to stay attached, and the sparks that flew from the wheels as they turned corners kept me distracted. Between the noise and the occasional interruption of darkness as the cars temporarily lost their electrical connections, I entered a fugue that allowed me to imagine a meandering tale of horror. As an actress—an *interpreter of emotion*, as I chose to think—I could easily imagine Jackie watching Monika and Henri make love. The little girl staring in shock at the twists and turns of their bodies, the fear of God keeping her eyes open and her mouth shut, her little heart beating fiercely as she heard her father making painful groans. And her mother, caught under the body of his violent rage, pushing up and up. To escape?

The train shook and went dark, halted between stations. I evaporated into the darkness and imagined how, after Monika and Henri finished,

Jackie must have crawled back into bed, strained with her small hands to lift open the heavy window, and then bravely put her head within its metal frame, trying to close the window on herself, and banged against it as hard as she could. A baseball bat, Monika had told everyone, a halluci-nation! Now the train jerked and began to move, and I sat back watching the sparks tease the window that protected me from the burning embers.

# 5
# On Notice



At the sound of the hinged screen door, I looked up from my favorite lunch, bologna on Russian rye with mustard, to see Claudette whip into the kitchen, shiny with sweat. Hildie, aproned and neat, with yellow latex gloves, was wet up to her elbows at the sink. Fanny was out of sight in the basement doing a wash, whistling the theme song to TV's *Lassie*. I smiled for my niece. "Hi, doll. It was getting late. We were worried." I stood and gave her a welcome kiss on the cheek.

"Yeah, I figured you'd be worried. I had some stuff to do." She spoke fast, as if singing a radio jingle. "But I'm here now, ready to sit and relax." She wiped her brow with the cuff of her sweater, then removed it and hung it on a hook by the back door.

From her flushed face and damp skin, I expressed fear that she might be catching a cold and raised my hand to touch her forehead. "You okay?"

"Oh, yeah. Just fine. The train was stuffy. And then the bus. Oy. I'm good now. I'm not getting sick." She patted my hand and picked at the string around the edge of bologna that stuck out from my sandwich, sat at the table and pulled the gummy meat off the casing, "Too salty. You have any leftover tuna in the fridge?"

I watched her prance about the kitchen, pretending to be my innocent little girl. I restrained the urge to shake her and ask her for the truth. Deeply disturbed that she had been in love with Henri but more so about her secretiveness, I confronted her without premeditation. "Have you heard from Henri? I tried his apartment this morning, but there was no answer."

"Nope. Haven't heard a thing. He'll turn up," Claudette said too easily.

Is she lying? I wondered if they had just gotten out of bed, if that was why she was late; if that was why she was sweaty. My nerves were as sensitive as the insole of a baby's foot. I reacted to her response as though she had blurted a vulgarity. "Claudette, come with me into the living room, will you?" Terse, I could not pull off a poker face.

"Sure. Let me get a schemata to put on the table."

I watched her, took her plate and the dishtowel she had gotten to put under it, and carried it for her into the living room. She sat on the couch, looking so small in the empty room. No visitors had come since the night before. I sat on a chair next to her.

With the place so peaceful, I wished I had stayed here last night as they begged me to, instead of returning home to find Monika at my house. She wouldn't dare show up now and force me to break her heart right here, with the Hoffman women all around. I'd been drumming a speech in my head all morning, and was almost afraid to confront Monika alone—afraid she would fall apart when I told her. Just the thought of her appearance frightened me enough so that I turned to check the front door.

I swallowed and cleared my throat. "How have you been handling all this? Have you been sleeping and eating okay?" I watched her stuff the tuna sandwich in her mouth and realized I'd asked a stupid question.

With her mouth full, she said, "Yes, Manny," and she smiled.

"Because I want to make sure before we start talking that you feel okay, physically."

Having swallowed, she could be more eloquent. "I feel fine. Of course, I miss Nadine. Why, do I look bad or something? I have lost a few pounds, but really, I've been healthy for the most part."

"You look as beautiful as ever, sweetheart. It's just that I have some tough things to talk to you about."

Claudette looked behind her quickly and whispered, "We shouldn't talk about *her* yet."

I was surprised. I had let myself ignore her fury over Monika. "Not about her. This is about you and Henri." I heard the words escape overhead, as though coming from my army picture on the mantel.

Claudette began coughing. When she was finished, she stood up. "Let's take this to the office." Which meant she wanted to go down to the basement. After rubbing her hands clean on the dishtowel, she used it to cover the leftovers. As she looked at me following her out of the room, she fastened the top button of her blouse.

Watching her from behind, I could see her bottom had filled out like her mother's, and her shoulders were a little bony, but broad. I realized she was a woman. I'll never again be able to carry her on my back for a ride. I didn't understand why those California movie people hadn't gobbled her up with love, but I was happy for their shortsightedness. Fanny had finished with her laundry, and we went quietly downstairs. I turned on all the lights so I wouldn't see shadows of Monika, or the ghost of Nadine. We pushed past the line of wet clothes hung across the room and sat on Fanny's old bed.

Trying to measure the amount of anxiety Claudette was feeling, I scanned her face but saw more relief than anything else. The tension lines between her eyes had smoothed, and her mouth had the diminutive smile that forced a dimple in her right cheek. "You want to tell me, don't you? You want to explain about you and Henri. I can see it on your face."

She smiled fully. "I could never hide from you."

"Well, you've been hiding *something* from me. I just found this out yesterday, and from what I heard, it's been going on for some time." I assumed a fatherly pose, my eyes wide and ready to accept, my shoulders stiff enough to confront. "You were together last night. That's why I couldn't reach him. Correct?"

"Yes. It's been easier since I moved out of here." She picked at the skin on her lips briefly, then pushed her bangs from her forehead and straightened her back, and it occurred to me that she was asserting the parity of her adulthood with mine. "It started when I used to babysit for Jackie. Before I left for California. Well, years before I left for California." She fell quiet. I allowed her the time to think. "I love him. I think. And he is my cousin. It's totally embarrassing." She dramatically slumped her shoulders.

I touched her cheek. "First of all, he's your second cousin. You shouldn't feel guilty."

"I said *embarrassed.*"

"You shouldn't be embarrassed about who you love. Henri is a good man." Actually, Hildie's soap operas made more sense to me than this. Henri was not at all good enough for Claudette. He wasn't clever enough, wasn't good-looking enough, or wealthy, kind, manly, handy, or responsible enough for Claudette. Although they had not grown up together, had not even known each other as young children, it was a fact that this was her second cousin. Not being able to imagine any further, I took a full breath and went on. "I want to know if you're happy and what your plans are with him. Do you intend to marry, or go on like this, or what? You'll be thirty-one soon. You might want to think about children. Do you have plans?"

Frightened that she would say yes, yes they were going to marry, though that seemed impossible to me, I held my breath. I would not allow it. I did not believe Monika when she said Henri didn't love

Claudette. Everyone loved Claudette. There was nothing about her that wasn't loveable.

"No plans." She stood, looking down at one fingernail cleaning under another, then said, "I don't make plans. We've got other concerns, other problems. Besides, I don't even know if I ever want to get married," then said under her breath, "or have children."

"What other problems?"

"I can't say. Really, Manny, I am not at liberty to say. It doesn't have to do with being cousins or anything like that. It's more important than that."

"Claudette, if you're going to play games with me here, I really don't appreciate it. More important, less important—either tell me or don't."

Claudette shook the hair off her face, her eyes wild. "I will only reiterate that Monika is a devil and you should stop seeing her. It has nothing to do with you being with another woman while Nadine was still alive, it has only to do with the kind of monster that *other* woman is." Claudette started walking toward the staircase. "I'm going back up. This is not what we should do today. I will not continue to discuss this. I hear people. Come upstairs." She stopped and waited for my response.

I said softly, "I've decided to stop seeing her. I don't know what you mean by devil or monster, but it should no longer upset you. As of today, that relationship is over." The words jumped out of my mouth involuntarily. I pulled to loosen the knot of my tie, and inhaled my own alarm at my anger toward Monika.

"Oh? What happened, is it—? Never mind. I'm glad."

"Yeah, well." Thoughts of Monika's touch made me flinch. I felt a burning sensation on my leg and wanted to rip into my skin. Claudette let me take her arm at the elbow, "Okay? So let's go up. We'll talk about this later." I didn't know what to think. She seemed very sincere about Henri, but not entirely devoted to him. I tried to hide my disgust.

Upstairs, I found Henri in the kitchen making a sandwich. He nodded at me and blushed, sweeping his eyes away from Claudette's face. Closing the mustard jar, he asked, "Manny, Claudette, how're you doing today?"

I leaned over and whispered to him, "I know where you were last night. Cut the bullshit." Fear flew into Henri's eyes. Unsuccessful with my attempt to smile, we followed after Claudette into the living room. Some neighbors urgently paid their respects, full of sighs and head-shaking, warm hand-clasping over this terrible loss, as I tried to chat casually with them. But I couldn't stop thinking about Monika. When I told Claudette that my relationship with her was over, it was the first time that idea had seemed concrete in my mind. Now I wondered why I said it, if I meant it, and where and how I would tell her it was over. Hildie and Franny came into the room with freshly baked cookies and coffee. The women were still dressed in black, save their aprons, and the palette made me uncomfortable. They were fair-skinned and redheaded; they didn't look right in black. I wanted to tell them to go change their clothes. Nadine would absolutely hate all of this gloom.

The rich smell of cinnamon too liberally sprinkled over the cookies made me queasy. I leaned toward Claudette, sitting next to me, and said I thought I was getting a stomach flu and to keep her distance. She told me she had vomited that morning and maybe something was going around. "You vomited this morning? I thought you said your health was fine, that you felt well?" I saw both sisters comfortably seated, talking with neighbors, and knew the kitchen was clear. "Come in the kitchen with me." Lifting her by her elbow again, we went off. Hearing the words "vomit" and "morning" in the same sentence made me think: pregnant.

Henri was caught by surprise and jumped when he saw us leaving the room. He had a plate in his hand and his mouth poised to take a bite. "Should I come back with you?" he asked Claudette, looking stiff and frightened, as if she were his classmate being dragged to the principal's office.

"I don't think you have to. Does he have to, Manny?"

"Yes. As a matter of fact, it would be better for him to hear what I have to say. That way, you won't have to repeat it later when the two of you are alone."

In the privacy of the kitchen, they stood still, petrified. Henri looked at me and blushed again. "I love her. I have nothing to be ashamed of."

"Well, that answers one question. Let's sit." We took our places around the kitchen table.

At seeing Claudette stare at him, waiting for his directive, I recalled her as the seventeen-year-old so in love with the captain of the high school basketball team. She thought she would die if he went off to sports camp for the summer. "How will I survive?" she had cried. "How did you survive being away from Nadine when you went to fight?" I had laughed so hard then at her comparison. I humored her and told her I was busy doing other things.

I rolled up my shirtsleeves, neatly folding them over. "Henri, what are your plans?"

"Manny, do you think this is necessary?" Claudette interrupted. "I mean, we're hardly teenagers."

"No, no, it's all right. I would love to answer this." Henri cleared his throat. "As I have already said, I love her. I am not so sure she would marry me. I haven't even asked her yet. And there are other concerns. Issues I can't discuss." He coughed and pushed his chair farther from the table.

"Another one with issues he can't discuss." I also pushed my chair from the table and stood. "Am I missing something here? Is there a skeleton left that's still in somebody's closet?" The blood rushed to my face.

Claudette and Henri looked at each other. Claud's face clamped shut, her eyes blinked rapidly at Henri. Sending Morse code?

"What the hell is going on here? Who is this about? Monika? Is this about Monika?" I asked.

The kissing cousins sat mute.

"All right, don't tell me. I have enough on my mind." The skin on my arms began to itch, as if a hundred mosquitoes had descended for lunch. I looked only at Claudette. "You do what's right. Whatever you decide, whatever this big secret has to do with—if this problem is because you and Henri disagree on what is the right thing to do, you do what your good sense and morals tell you to do. You hear me?" No indication from either of them that pregnancy was the issue. They were too vague and relaxed. I had no clue what the two were hiding, and had to grit my teeth to stop myself from lecturing her on a matter unknown. Intuition told me to let this ride itself out. Whatever damage this relationship did was already done, and my sense was that it was nearing an end. I'd seen her in love before. This was not the lovelorn niece I knew. I bent down and leaned in close to Claudette's face. "You set a time limit here. Figure out what's going to be with you two and this *secret* by the New Year. You're not a kid anymore."

She nodded that she had heard me but without the diminutive pout of compliance I was expecting. I opened a cabinet to retrieve the hidden sticky bottle and poured a glass of schnapps. "You want?" I asked Henri.

"Sure. It's afternoon."

Henri and Claudette kept proper distance. The feeling that they were in cahoots looped around my stomach. When the hell do I get to grieve for Nadine? With my sisters constantly pampering me, rubbing me, peering at me. This Shiva is a fucking farce.

Hildie finally caught me late in the day, as I stood alone on the front porch. The sun struck her hair and brought to life the under-strands of red left tangled with the gray. She still had the sweet face of her youth: her sharp chin was tucked tight back to her throat, and her blue eyes, though small, were bright with half-moons of white around her pupils. Claudette looked like her, and she would stay this pretty as well. Hildie gave me a hug, rubbing my back before asking if anything besides Nadine was on my mind. "You looked better the day of the funeral than you do today." Her voice was direct, not patronizing.

Below the porch, the darkened corner of the garden held my attention. "What can I tell you? This isn't the way we thought it was planned, you know? We go through the horror of the war, make a good life, a good business, great family, and I end up with it all—but without her. After all her disappointment and frustration—first me going away for almost three years, the babies she lost—just so she had to suffer like this. I wish I could be with her. You know, Hildie, I wish I were dead."

She didn't pooh-pooh my words or say, "God forbid." I knew she understood the real need sometimes to be dead. "Yes, Nadine had a horrible time. But she's at rest now and someday—well, someday. I hope you find your comfort." She raised her chin, closing her eyes to the indigo sky. She was asking for something meaningful from me. Poised, she appeared intent on withstanding anything that came out of my mouth.

"What do you mean, you hope I 'find my comfort'? What does that mean?"

"Correct me if I'm wrong. And don't be mad at me if I am, because I'm only stating what I believe, not passing judgment and—"

"What!" I knew the "passing judgment" line meant she was talking about Monika, but I wanted it to come out.

She kept her poise and stayed on track. "I am not passing judgment, as I said, but I believe, from things I've been told, that you have a woman." She smacked her hands on the porch railing,—"There, I've said it. So?"—then crossed her arms in front of her stomach and turned to me.

"And I suppose you also have a *belief* as to who this woman is."

"Yes I do." She looked out over her roses. "I would have preferred someone who won't bring the pain of her past within the family, but if this is who you've chosen to bury your grief, well then," she swooshed her hand into the air, "this too shall pass."

I pulled a folded aluminum lawn chair from the corner of the porch and squawked open its rusted hinges. Hildie sat in it, and I pulled out another for myself. "Can I ask who told you?" I hoped Claudette had not betrayed me.

Hildie ran her hands along the rail of the porch, imitating smoothing linen. "Beatrice. She told me after she was with Monika. She said she had gotten into a tiff with Jacqueline about letting her into her father's apartment while he wasn't there. She ran away. Then she said she couldn't find Monika, and that she suspected she was with you, either at the hospital or somewhere. I knew you weren't at the hospital because I had just come from there. So I asked her, straight out—I asked if you and Monika were romantically involved, and she told me yes." Hildie shrugged sharply to indicate "that's it."

I mimicked her shrug. "Well, it's over with her. So in answer to your question, no, I didn't find my comfort. This too has passed." I pulled my chair closer to the railing and hung my forearms over. "You should have told me you knew. I would've liked to talk to you about it sooner."

"Why didn't you just talk? Have I ever not listened to a single thing you had to say?"

"I'm so ashamed. Nadine was suffering and I was with a beautiful woman." This was my sister, and there was only so much I could speak about. "While my wife—" winded, I exhaled a moan, then lowered my chin to my chest, crying.

Hildie reached the nape of my neck, massaged it. "I understand."

"You don't understand. Nadine *knew.* She told me she knew. And she forgave me. This feeling will never end."

"With time, and without Monika turning your head…well, you'll get on with it. I know you will."


I relived that morning, how I had left a woman lying uninvited in my bed. Scrapping the idea of going home, I instead headed toward the Belt Parkway into Manhattan. The Belt wrapped around the edge of Brooklyn along the ocean, like eyeliner defining the shape of the harbors and bays, the beaches and swamps. Once dotted with carnivals, Nadine and I would spend hot summer nights going round the Ferris wheel, eating cotton candy, and sneaking kisses behind a game of chance.

# 6

# The Break



## *Manny*

Having reached the city in record time, I parked my car on Second Avenue, a block away from Monika's apartment. I'd have time to catch my breath and think before confronting her. A jolt even to me, finding that I possessed no deep feelings for her, I shook, anticipating her shock.

Standing outside her door, surrounded by the silent, gauzy smoke of someone's unseen outdoor grill, I closed my eyes, breathing shallow breaths, and drifted into detachment. I was floating above a house. Nothing happened and nothing had to happen. I would just stand here in limbo forever. Quiet. Motionless. Floating. Then the door opened.

"Manny!" Monika threw her arms around me and kissed my cheeks, then my lips, and then pulled on my hand with both of hers, drawing me into the apartment. I offered a meek smile and walked with her to her parlor. She sat next to me on the sofa. "It's so early. I didn't even hope to hear from you until after ten o'clock." She spoke fast, her words slurred with excitement, smiling, her dimples deep in her cheeks and hair falling into her eyes.

She started to stand. "Can I prepare for you something to eat?"

I held her fingers and pulled her gently back down onto the sofa, putting my index finger over her mouth. "Monika. You don't understand why I've come. You have to calm down and listen to me." I pushed the hair from her eyes and hesitated in the glare of them, waiting for the spiked hazel to explode. "I've just come from Shiva at Hildie's. You don't walk out of her house hungry." Usually, I would have chuckled at that, but instead I sat solemnly while Monika's eyes stung my face. "Last night. I came to talk to you about last night, and about this morning." I nodded four times as if counting four second-long pauses between statements, still floating, but sensing the downdraft tugging at my feet.

"I was afraid of this. I knew you'd be angry because I slept in your bed. I knew it." She pursed her lips, and her chest began heaving.

"That's not the thing. The thing is—hell, I don't know what the thing is." I took a breath. "Yes, the thing is I'm not in love with you, Monika. I don't want to hurt you—you've tried to be there for me and for Nadine, but it's been a mistake." I folded one leg over the knee of the other as if I were settling in for a while. Monika sat again, silently, and had stopped breathing hard. I said, "Will you be all right? I mean, I don't want you to be upset. I still want to help you when I can." Though she sat perfectly still, perfectly childlike and sweet, the tears ran over her cheeks into her mouth. "Yell at me if you want to. I know you must feel used. I didn't think of it that way, I just don't feel what I should feel if this is to go on. It would be a continuation of a mistake. It can never be anything honest and wholesome."

"Honest and *wholesome*?" She barely spoke above a whisper. "What are we if not honest, and what is this *wholesome*?" She slapped the seat of the sofa, then put her finger across the bridge of her nose.

The soles of my feet started to burn. "Maybe you've been honest.

You have been honest. But wholesomeness is, I don't know, healthy. This isn't." I took her hand, holding down the pressure that rose up my legs and sat like lead in my belly. "You're beautiful and comforting. I was swept by it all. But now I feel like I've stained the memory of my marriage. Being with you now—it would be a constant reminder of how I failed my wife." My brain was splitting into fragments. "All of a sudden—I don't know where or why it happened—but when you come into my head, as you often do, the thought brings pain. It brings a heartache that's too deep for me to deal with now."

Monika started to lift herself from the sofa, wobbled, appearing weak in her legs. She sighed, sat back down, and stayed seated.

Just as she opened her mouth to speak, there was a single bang on the glass of the front door. We jumped. The sound was so powerful, it rattled a small plate that hung on the wall.

Monika peeked through the side of the curtain. "Shit. It's Jacqueline and that must be that Svengali, George." She turned to me. "Manny, please stay with me. I don't know what condition she's in, and I'm afraid of this man."

The bang had arrested my drift, and I felt even less sure footed. "Sure, sure. I'll stay. Let them in."

Monika wiped under her eyes, took a deep breath, and opened the door. "Jacqueline, what a pleasure to see you, darling." Her voice was sweet but strained, like a teenaged whore flirting with a john. She kissed her cheeks and turned to the lanky man beside her. "George, I presume?"

His straight long black hair was clean, and his eyes were bloodshot. His shirt was white and clean as well, although it had begun to get ragged around the cuffs. Jackie's hair was soft around her face, her purple shirt tucked into her dungarees. She smiled a cracked-tooth smile at George and looked to be waiting to hear him say something clever. George stood next to Jackie like a tall dark exclamation mark. His long black hair fell to his shoulders, dawdling past the upturned collar of his shirt. He turned his head as I cleared my throat; Jackie's glance followed his, and she noticed me standing there. This was our first meeting of the infamous George. If I could have been anywhere else, I would have dove through the living room window and ran for my life. The heat on my cheeks told me that the color of my face changed from guilt-ridden blush to mortified red. George played with Jackie's ear, making circles around it. Jackie took a pose, her hand on her hip, her cheeks sucked in with impatience.

"Manny? What the hell are you doing here? Aren't you still sitting Shiva or something, over at Hildie's?" Jackie tilted her head in thought and turned to look at her mother. Her eyes grew wide and her mouth gaped. "You're shittin' me. You and Manny? Holy fucking shit." Her howling laugh filled the house.

The room was an inferno. Monika jumped to put her hand on Jackie's shoulder. "It's not what you think, Jackie. Don't be ridiculous. I asked Manny to visit, give himself a break from those sisters." Monika smiled with her mouth closed.

"Manny doesn't think of them as 'those sisters.' That's what *you* think of them." Jackie looked at me with no expression on her face, but her foot was tapping. Pictures of my sisters flashed like transparent slides on the wall, and I heard them reciting kaddish, the prayer for the dead. I stood still as though buried in a vertical grave. Jackie finally blinked, "You don't lie, Manny, right? You fucking her? Because I know she'd fuck you in a minute." She tried to snap her fingers, but no clicking sound was made.

My mouth was rubber. "I'm sorry."

"Jacqueline, you're being delusional," Monika interjected.

"Oh, are you all a delusion in front of me?" Jackie asked.

"I wish *I* were a delusion," George said under his breath.

Looking at George, I said, "I think I'll go. She seems sober enough." I looked away from George and toward Jackie. "You have any problems I should know about before I leave you two here?"

"No, sir. I'm fine. Jackie just wanted to visit with her mom." I was taken aback as George answered on behalf of himself. He wasn't letting Jackie speak for herself. George just smiled and looked like the obnoxious Eddie Haskell from *Leave It to Beaver*, a polite and charming young Judas.

"Excuse us a moment, please," I said to the couple. "Monika, would you come into the kitchen?" Monika bit the inside of her cheek, and told the intruders to sit and wait.

"Is that an order?" Jackie asked. She stayed put, even as George plopped on the sofa and got comfortable, spotted Monika's cigarettes on the lamp table, and lit himself a smoke.

"Come on, Jackie," George called to her as she leered at her mother; he waved her over with the cigarette between his fingers, the smoke overwhelming the air around his face. She smiled at him and shimmied toward the cloud, falling into his lap, her face blurred with his. I used the lull to make our break from the mother-daughter-boyfriend triangle, taking Monika by the elbow and hustling her into the kitchen.

Monika leaned her back against the wall, her hands clasped and resting against her belly, and I stood next to her with my back blocking Jackie and her boyfriend's view. The hum of the fridge softened the stinging quiet. We could hear an ice cream truck ringing its bell from the street. The kitchen smelled of fish, oily and burnt. I tried not to inhale too deeply.

"I have to get out of here. I feel like my chest is going to rupture. Tell them anything, I don't care," I said.

"Even the truth? I should tell them you have been, how should I say it, *fucking* me, but now you decided you don't want me anymore? I should say that?" Her voice was rising, and I wanted to put my hand over her mouth.

It was just that kind of dismissal of all concerns—other than those having only to do with her—that irritated me the most about Monika. I spoke as softly as possible. "If that's how you see this, and I can't say exactly how else you might see it, then that's what you tell them if you want. I'll call you. Tomorrow. I'll call you tomorrow, okay?" Monika said nothing and appeared unexpectedly calm. "I need time to understand this all myself before I can explain it to you—but I don't want to leave you so distraught." She squeezed my hand, and simply nodded her head okay.

She stayed behind me as we made our way past Jackie and George on the sofa. Hesitant, looking at them, I then pointed my finger, shaking it at the two of them. "You behave yourselves. And yes, Jacqueline, that's an order." I waited a beat for George to dare give me some lip. When none came, I opened the front door, pulling it firmly shut.

The damp first night of May felt like a cool shower on sunburn. The skin on my face tingled with the light drizzle, and I felt—leaving Monika behind—I was breathing fresh air for the first time in months. I knowingly walked past my car, delaying my return home, to take full advantage of this relief.

# 7

# Thunder and Lightening

## *Monika*

Manny was gone—for now. I rejoined the two in the living room and sat on the chair facing the sofa. "So, what are you looking for? I have no money for you."

Jacqueline took a drag of her cigarette. "We need to crash here for a few nights."

"Oh, really. Well, you can't," I said, lifting my eyebrows, suggesting, "Will that be all?"

"Great! Can always count on you, *mom*. Just fucking great." Jackie stood, stamped her cigarette out on the metal base of the lamp, and pulled George up. "They're looking for him, you know." Jackie's eyes fell closed, her chin dropped, and she curled into a ball of tears. "They're looking for George, and they're gonna kill him," she bawled, and wiped under her nose with her sleeve. "Please mom, if we can't hide out here, we'll have to sleep in the subway." She dissolved to the floor, sat, and wept. George plopped down next to her and put his arms around her shoulders.

It had, in fact, been such a long time since I had seen my daughter cry this forcefully that I forgot myself, and concern for her erupted. "George, what's this about? And you better damn well give it to me straight." I wished I had the strength to kick him where it hurt. I watched him squirm. "Spit it out!"

"I sold some bad shit. Jackie's man Clifton is dead, and his friends are gonna kill me. That's it. Straight enough?" He adjusted his butt and reached into the front of his pants to reposition things.

"Clifton!?"

"My pimp!" Jackie shouted, "Remember?"

I gasped and put both hands across my chest. Before tears had time to pour over my face, I slid off the chair, kneeled, and draped myself around Jacqueline. Rocking her in my arms, her face buried in my chest, I felt the weight of a small child, and the irreparable damage of a girl on death row. George sat close by, lighting his third or fourth cigarette. I told Jacqueline to get up and sit on the sofa. I wiped the tears from her face and told her to look at me. "Jacqueline, are you listening? Because I don't have the strength to repeat myself a hundred times until you understand."

"I'm listening," George said, now sitting on the chair.

"I'm not speaking to you, am I?" I could have ripped into his smug face with my fingernails.

"I'm listening," Jackie whispered.

I held her face in my hands so she wouldn't look away. "You can stay, but George can't. I have no room for him and he'll put us in danger." Turning sharply to look George in the eyes, "You! Idiot! Look the other way." George obeyed, spinning on his skinny butt to face the blank screen of the television. Getting near enough to Jacqueline's ear to feel as much a part of her as amniotic fluid around a fetus, I whispered, "I have your fix, I got it today—not shit like he'll give you, and not enough for him." Then I shouted so he could hear clearly, "He'll have to sleep in the subway, or just leave town."

Jackie whispered in my ear, "First let me see the shit, then I'll tell him to leave. Deal?" I nodded, deal. She raised her voice, suddenly as alert as a kindergarten teacher. "George, me and my mom are going into the bedroom for a heart to heart. Wait here, I'll be right back." She walked to him in the chair and kissed him hard on the mouth. He stuck his tongue out to lick her and my stomach jumped, but I turned my head toward the window, the Mister Softy ice cream truck, and its signature song.

At the threshold of the bedroom, only a step ahead of me, Jackie stopped. What was she thinking now? The debris from Manny's visit was creeping into every pore of my body, and here was Jacqueline, my daughter, suffering. Instead of an ice cream cone with sprinkles, she wanted heroin. I grabbed her by the waist. "Come on in, will you?" Once inside, Jackie looked around my bedroom, embarrassing me as she mutely assessed my inexpensive things, making a face at my vanity table, covered with make-up and perfume. Looking disgusted, she jutted her chin toward my fake cuckoo clock with the bird that was always out of the birdhouse, ready to sing, and the pictures on the walls of children with enormous, sad brown eyes. "There's that half-finished needlepoint," Jackie pointed to a basket on the floor. "That was there last Christmas. Still unfinished, huh?" She sat on the bed, shaking her head, bouncing her foot nervously. And now she's belittling me!

Sifting through my lingerie drawer, relieved at finding what I sought, I sat on the bed next to Jacqueline. "See? What did I promise you? It's all here." I opened the cigar box on her lap. "The syringe is new, and I took these gauze pads that are already treated with alcohol on them. They're sterile." I showed her the little gray-and-blue package that held the gauze pad. I could take care of Jacqueline. At least I am efficient and professional.

"Neat," Jackie said, then unbuttoned her blouse and pulled down on her bra.

"What are you doing?" I asked. "This isn't for now. You don't need this now. Tell George to leave like you promised."

"I will, I will. Just let me have this first." She grabbed the gauze from the box, along with the used birthday candle and the metal spoon I put in the kit. "What if he doesn't leave right away? I'll have to wait. Come on, mom. *I'll let you watch.*" She said the last words singsong, teasing me with her morbid reminder—my daughter's taunting an attempt to pierce my soul with remorse.

"I don't want to watch. I'll let you do it, but I don't want to watch." I handed Jacqueline the drug and turned away to regard the needlework in a frame on the wall. "Here. Do it. Tell me when you've finished."

The bed bounced, indicating that Jacqueline was finished and was lying down, waiting for the euphoria to begin. I laid down next to her, my arm over my forehead, waiting for my baby to sit up again, knowing not to touch her now, feeling my daughter's ensuing calm spread over the bedsheet like the plume of crème over hot black coffee. Jackie did sit after a few minutes, her hands fumbling with the air in front of her, as she tried to say something that was little more than a slur.

"Go tell George to leave," I said. The room already smelled like sweat and blood. My perfume did no good covering her filth.

"Tell George to leave? Oh. Yeah." Jackie sang out, "Georgie-Porgie pumpkin pie."

I pulled on her hands and got her up. It was so easy. She was light as dust. I could have blown her into the next room. Walking with her arm in arm, Jackie strolled into the living room. "Hey George. Sorry, got none for you. Let's go."

George's face expanded in surprise to see her already stoned. "So, we can't stay?" he asked. He yawned, put his hands behind his head, and stretched his back. Then he rocked his hips, crack, crack, and looked at me.

"Stay? No man, we gotta go. Come on, Georgie." She removed her arm from me and went to take his hand. "Clifton should have come here for his shit," she giggled.

"Jacqueline!" Her skinny forearm felt like a silky ribbon in my hands.

"You are supposed to tell George to leave, and you're going to stay here with me. George, you have to leave. Now. Tell him, Jacqueline!"

"You shittin me? I'm not sending George out alone. I never said I'd stay without my man George. Let's go, George." She pushed at his back for him to move.

"But where we goin'? We can't go back downtown. They'll kill us both."

He whined like a spoiled teenaged girl, and I stretched my fingers flat against my chest, ready to rip his face off. I stepped forward and pushed at both of them. "Get out. Go ahead. Both of you go into the street where you belong."

"We're going to be killed, Mom." Then one eyebrow rose with a thought. "You think Daddy's home?" Jackie swooned a little and George grunted, straightening her up.

"Great time to get stoned. I'm gonna get fuckin' blown away and you're taking joy rides." He turned to the door. "Stay here. I'm getting out of this loony bin." He walked out, leaving the door open behind him.

Jackie looked at me and smiled with her eyes. "Bye, mom." She started out the door, but then turned to say one more thing. "This is some good shit. Thanks."

The light drizzle that fell earlier had erupted into a heavy rainfall with thunder and lightning. Wet with disappointment, the apartment smelled of damp cigarette smoke. Reaching my bedroom in complete darkness, I found the bed and crumbled into it, sobbing. My beautiful daughter, into the street, loaded up on heroin I had provided, into a situation of imminent danger. No more danger than I experienced as a girl in Paris. And she has me. I had no mother. My other baby appeared in the darkness, and I crawled under the blankets.

Manny had made it very clear he did not want me to call. Nadine was dead three days. Was that how long it had taken to come to terms with the rest of his life, to light up like a bulb and see his path? Three days! If only I hadn't gone to him last night. If only I hadn't slept in his bed or stolen his shirt or told him I loved him. Why, why had he chosen today to decide to break it off? Is the three-day wait of Jewish significance, or had his sisters or that *actress* finally gotten to him?

His T-shirt still smelled of his Old Spice. On the nights he had stayed in my bed, he'd left the cologne smell on the sheets. He'll come back. My guarantor offered its first kick in my belly, and reminded me I would not be left alone again.

Sliding deeper beneath my quilt-cover, I reached up to the night-stand and ran my hand across the pill bottles, the bobby pins, to grip the telephone receiver. Trying to get the croak out of my voice, I waited the five rings until a voice asked, "Hello?"

"Henri?"

✦

# *Henri*

"She's here. Is that why you called?" I regarded Jackie's beautiful face, minus a tooth, and George's buckteeth, and hoped dismally that this young man was who he said he was. "They rang the bell about two minutes ago." Claudette had stayed away tonight. We'd spoken little about our so-called *heart-to-heart* with Manny. The walls were still a hideous avocado, but at night I kept the lights low. But they were up high now, as I sat in the kitchen with Jackie and George and responded to Monika on the phone.

With my hand over the mouthpiece I said, "Shush," to Jackie, who was forcing herself to belch in loud, drawn-out eruptions.

"What? What is she telling you?" Monika asked.

"Uch. You don't want to know. She's stoned out of her mind." I took the phone away from my mouth again and said, "Jackie. Be quiet or else go into the other room. Let me hear what Momma wants."

"She wants to know why the fuck I'm here. Give me the damn phone." She grabbed it out of my hand, a familiar insult of disrespect she had learned from her mother. "Mom? I'm here with Daddy because you threw us out. No need to interfere. I'm good, George is good, all is well with the world." She wet her lips, burped, and smiled at George, who giggled, rolled his eyes, and shook his head, looking reluctantly amused.

"May I?" I took the phone back. "Let me hear what's happening. Hold on." The phone plunked on the table, looking at the two of them, the handpiece held by my shoulder to my ear. "So?" Maybe this is the scene of a normal adolescent crisis, telling me they were eloping or even having a baby.

"I'll tell you what's happening!" Monika was shouting into the phone. "Someone wants to *kill* them, and they're looking for a hideaway. Make her leave, Henri! I'm warning you, this is no good, Jacqueline and George there with you!" My heart jumped. I checked that the front door was locked. She waited for me to answer. "Henri, what are you doing? Say something!"

"Let me talk to them. I'll call you back." I hung up without waiting for her to say goodbye.

Jackie and George sat mute, their heads down. If they fell asleep at the table, what in the world would I do with them when they woke up? I reached into the cabinet, got three glasses, and poured them each two fingers of Schnapps. A gust of rain caught in the back alley and shook the kitchen window hard, sounding like a burglar trying his luck. Jackie twitched at the sound. "Who's that?" George shouted. He sat up straighter, probably listening for his killer breaking through the window.

Sitting still at the table with only the sound of Jackie snoring, I thought she was officially asleep now. "Help me get her into bed." I tried to imagine she'd come home drunk from the senior prom and the boyfriend and I were just a bit tickled at the task of getting this ingenue to bed. My heart crumbled under the fantasy. We lifted with our arms under her, our hands gripping each other, the drained-bottle weight of her being carried to my bed. George covered her, kissed her forehead, and stared for a minute. Her face fell back, gray and sunken. "She really was beautiful," I said to George. Tying her up and keeping her locked in this room until this tumultuous and hideous time in her life passed seemed the only sensible solution. Meanwhile, George eyeballed me up and down.

Twisting my mouth before I spoke, "So, who's trying to kill you?" Fortunately for George, I had a long-standing compassion for men who ran for their lives.

"Oh, man. It's such a fucked up story." George waved his hand to get me to move out of the room. In the kitchen, George sat back and attempted an explanation. "I gave this dude some shit, bad heroin. It killed the guy."

"Gave? Why, you had extra? Gave someone a gift, I suppose," I said mocking him.

"I sold it to him, okay? Actually, I traded it. Your daughter for it. Get the picture, daddio?"

My fist lifted, and George jolted. No match for George, I grit my teeth and rubbed my sweaty hands on my pants. "You're a piece of shit," I said, and spit in his face. "Get out of my house and leave my daughter alone. I hope someone does kill you." I held myself up on the rim of the sink.

George stood and kicked a kitchen chair at me. "You let her mother give her smack and you ridicule me?" He pulled on his tight jeans and jutted his jaw. "I'm outta here. Tell your little darlin' when she wakes up and's looking for me that I'm gone. G-o-n-e. Gone." He pushed the chair hard out of his way and bounced through the house, out the door into the blowing rain, leaving the wind trailing behind.

After the door slammed, I punched my fist into the wall. The avocado plaster splintered. Bitch Monika. If what George said is true—if she's actually given her heroin—I'll strangle her with my bare hands.

I couldn't settle enough to decide what to do first: cry over my daughter's drug addiction, or her prostitution, or leave her sleeping while I went to Monika's apartment to strangle her. Both mother and daughter, prostitutes. Maybe for Monika it had been the only way, but Jackie? I hoped Jackie had forgotten by now. I didn't fully understand why Monika did what she did or what my daughter actually remembered of her abuse.

When we first arrived in New York, I began working as a driver immediately, at least a dozen hours a day. Monika and Jacqueline would spend the days alone those first years. Macy's was a weekly ritual, but Monika had little or no money for the nice things she saw. Manny's family lived in Brooklyn, and had their work. Much as she told everyone she met—through Jacqueline's school, at the park, and in the shops—that she had moved here from Paris, they still thought of her as German. When speaking English or French, it was with a German inflection. In this mixed neighborhood of other European immigrants, Jewish and Italians mostly, she was still a daughter of the enemy. It never occurred to her when she came here that anyone would associate her with the Nazis. She made no attempt to warm up to acquaintances because she thought everyone laughed at her, at her clothes, her speech, her guilt.

It pained me so that I had not given her the life I promised. In her mind, all the world looked down on her, except Beatrice—Monika felt more a part of local society after Bea helped her get the job at the hospital. It was upsetting at first for Jacqueline, when she came home to find babysitters instead of her mother. They'd been an inseparable mother-daughter team. But my little sweet girl adjusted, it seemed. She learned to bake butter and anise cookies, to play with James's boyish toys, and time passed, lives were lived, money was earned and spent, and life occurred on schedule. And then the peace was over. Just like that.

On the edge of my bed, I listened for Jackie's breathing but heard only my own labored panting. I held my breath and heard a small whistling sound come from her nose. Before I could bend over to kiss her head, I began to choke on my own tears. She was still my darling Jacqueline, and the fear of losing her crushed me.

With my raincoat and umbrella, I walked the twenty blocks to Monika's in the storm. There was no taxi at this time of night, in this weather. While I walked, the rain pounded, setting my pace with the hard beat, energizing my temper.

The sight of her building was a surprise. Christmas lights were still blinking in a first-floor apartment, even though it was May. The main door to the building got locked after ten o'clock, so I shouted, "Let me in, witch," into Monika's intercom, raising my voice over the sound of a torrent of rain. There was loud thunder, and I was afraid lightening would follow. As a child, I had seen a girl struck with it, her stiffened little body lying in the street. This was the first time in two and a half decades I'd willingly gone out during a thunderstorm.

"Henri? Is that you?" Her voice came back high-pitched and excited.

"Open the damn door, witch, before I kick it down!" I was filled with as much fear of a lightning bolt zapping me on the front stoop as I was with anger. The morning headlines: "Man dies of lightning strike while attempting to strangle drug-dealing ex-wife." Monika whipped open the main door, wrapped tightly in a white linen robe and white fluffy slippers, like the night mistress of an all-girls' school. Once inside the vestibule, I pushed past her and shook the rain from my hair.

"You look like a drowned red Irish setter," Monika remarked. "I presume this is about Jacqueline."

"Never could fool you, Monika." My mouth opened again, but

words failed me. Now, with her face two feet away, I couldn't think of what to say next.

"Come in, then. Get dry. I'll make you tea."

"Ah, yes. Tea. That should settle everything."

Monika glared at me like a nun catching a pupil making donkey ears behind her. "If you can't be civil, Henri…"

"Go inside. I have to get back to her, and we have to talk fast." We walked into her apartment and stood in the middle of the room. I was breathless, pain digging its way in between my eyes. There were cigarette butts in ashtrays and torn pieces of facial tissue on the floor. The television showed a test pattern and hummed one note. I stomped over to shut the damn thing off.

"She came to you with George asking for asylum, no?" Monika stood, put one hand on her hip, reached behind her head to scratch under her ponytail with the other, and breathed hard.

"She's with me now, asleep. He's gone." I shook my head in short accusatory nods. "He had something to say about you." She didn't ask what he'd said; she just waited. "He said you're a sick motherfucker and you gave Jacqueline heroin. Tell me that isn't true, Monika. Tell me. Because if I find out it *is*, in fact, true, I'll…"

She sat in the rocking chair across from me, nodded right back, and looked into my eyes. "You tell me, Henri. When have you seen your daughter withdraw from that drug? Have you ever seen the shaking, the vomit, and the hysterical crying from pain? Because I have, Henri. What did you want me to do? Let her convulse in my arms? Come on now, you don't even know what you're talking about. You simply hide in that green apartment of yours, with your pretty, sweet Claudette, and leave Jacqueline to me. Really, Henri! How can *you* come here and question *me*?" Her face had turned fiery, and her jaw and the muscles in her cheeks tightened. She looked so strong.

"Did you ever think to take her to the hospital?" I threw back with fury. "Did you ever get any help, besides the shrink-heads who don't agree with your *diagnosis*?"

"Don't ask me questions before you've answered mine. You do what Manny does. Ask without answers." Her mouth quivered.

"Does Manny know about the drugs you give her?"

"Questions! Answer me first! Do you know what withdrawal is like?"

"No, Monika, I do not know what it is like. But I can tell you I would only have to see it *once*, and she'd be in the emergency room."

She mumbled, and I continued my assault. "What? Are you afraid if they take her into the hospital they might get her well, and then you'd have nothing to live for?"

My god, I thought, could this be true? "Is that it? You want to keep her sick?"

"You are the biggest fool I have ever known. Why would I want to keep her sick? She'd be a real daughter to me if she were well." Monika shook her head mournfully. "We'd talk about boys and we'd shop. We might still be married."

"Married? You think after what you've put us through that we would still be married? You're the fool, Monika. Or else you're insane." Oh my god, she's insane.

"Get out of my house. You don't deserve to speak to me. People like you exhaust me. I can see it now that I am Jacqueline's only hope!" She ran into her bedroom and slammed the door.

"Hope? *You*, someone's hope?" I went to her and opened the door, banging it against the back wall. "Where are the drugs? Give them to me, or I'll tear this place apart."

"I don't have any." She turned her face into a pillow and sobbed.

Light-headed, I was forced to sit on the bed next to her. After a few minutes of silence, Monika turned over on her back. "You should get back to her. She could wake up and run away."

I squeezed her chin hard in my hand. "Don't give her drugs, Monika.

I'm warning you. You won't have a daughter or your freedom if you give her drugs. I'll call the police and report you. I swear I will."

"You'd put a pregnant woman in jail?" She said as if proposing I'd hang a puppy by its ears.

I shut down, mind and body, collecting all of my energy to listen for the next word out of her mouth. Who was pregnant, Jacqueline? Who was she talking about? I sat dumb.

Monika scooted closer to me and held her chin high. "I'm carrying Manny's baby. The one Nadine couldn't give him. I have it in here." She rubbed her belly.

Still mute with shock, I rose slowly and stood motionless. She is pregnant and will have another child? Feeling again the pain between my eyes, the thickness of my throat pulsated as I squinted at her. "What wouldn't you do, Monika, to keep all your men? Is that it? And now you'll try to keep Manny with this child?"

"What makes you think I have to use a child to hold him to me? What has he told you? What has he said?" She sat still, her eyes red and mouth tense, as though she were awaiting some breaking official report. "Has he already announced this to the world—that he is through with *that woman*?"

She lunged at me and pounded her fists against my chest.

"Who the hell do you think you are?" I pinned her shoulders, shook her, bounced her hard off the mattress, and yelled into her face, "You won't have Manny and you won't have Jacqueline, and you won't have this child!"

"Are you crazy?" She jumped off the bed and ran into the bathroom. The door lock clicked.

I had never used the force of my body with her, and I was sorry for it even before the lock clicked. A huge wave of regret washed away the fires of hostility. After catching my breath, I went to the door. "Monika, I'm sorry." No response. "Do you hear me?"

"Those things you said." Her voice was thick from the other side of the door. It sounded like her face was wrapped in a towel.

"I know. I'm sorry I pushed you." I wobbled, retreating to perjury. "I made the decision to leave you." Backing away from the door I said, "I better go back now. She might wake up. You all right?"

"I'm fine. Go to her." She opened the bathroom door. "Never say those horrible things again to me. I know what I'm doing," she said, and grabbed a breath. "And your thinking—it adds up to a zero for what it takes to get Jacqueline out of her gutter." Seeing her without her perfect make-up—rouge sunken into her pores and dark rings under her eyes, bluish-green smudges like odd wounds across her pale lids—she looked ill. Then I realized, with nausea, that she looked pregnant.

"I'll keep her tonight, and then I'm taking her on a trip. A few days in the Catskills," deciding my intention as I uttered the words. "Manny told me to take some time away with her, and I think it's a good idea."

"She won't last until the morning. You have no idea what kind of fit she'll have."

"I'll take care of her." I felt an old yearning to take care of them both.

"She won't get through the night, I'm telling you." Monika grabbed my jacket at the sleeve. "Bring her to me. Bring her back tonight." She pulled on the fabric—one quick yank to seal her request into my bones.

"Goodnight, Monika."

Her face was streaked white by tears where her face powder had been, and she stood there before me—a sad, pregnant clown. I looked down to her belly to see if there was any visible sign. "You better get rest now," I said, wishing I could abscond with the child inside her and allow it to form somewhere else.

I walked back into the rain, without my umbrella.

# 8

# Just Another Night

_Henri_

Beatrice was standing in the open doorway to my apartment, a pink che-
nille blanket wrapped around her shoulders. The rain was dropping in
front of her face from the door overhang like strings of hippie beads, glistening from the street lamps, Beatrice staunch behind them. When I was
sure she recognized me, I ran up the stairs, the water on each step sloshing
up to the cuffs of my pants. Soaked and shivering, my curly red hair now
straight down over my eyes, I was relieved she had been standing guard.

"Come inside. Hurry. What kind of stupidity—oh, for Christ's sake,
Henri, where did you go?"

"To Monika. Never mind. Jackie. Is she all right?" I asked, already
breathless from the eight-stair run. Cigarettes.

Under the protection of the door's overhang, she told me Jacqueline
had woken after I had gone. She was thirsty and cold. She didn't remember where George was, and she thought she was at her mother's house. She
went upstairs to get Beatrice. She told Beatrice how she felt and where

she thought she was, and Beatrice took her back downstairs. "I didn't want my son James to see Jacqueline this way, both for her protection and for his," Beatrice told me. I took offense, but said nothing. The boy had been her childhood friend, but it was just as well he didn't have to look at her, and these days, I was glad when as few people as possible saw my daughter.

Beatrice pulled my arm. "Come in and get dry." She walked behind, pushing me. "And after that, she ransacked your clothes closet. Evidently, she thought she'd find some cash, which I believe she did, and she took off. No, no. She called someone first. I don't know who, but I think I know where she was headed."

"To George?" My chest tightened, and I shivered.

"I don't know, Henri. And she took the gold cigarette lighter from your bedroom."

I had brought that from Paris. It was my father's, and now she would sell it.

"That's when she made the call, from in there." Beatrice pointed to the bedroom. "I followed her in, and she told someone she'd meet them at the corner of Houston and West Broadway." Beatrice mimicked Jackie, "Houston and West Broadway, Houston and West Broadway," imitating the serious tone with which Jackie had repeated it to herself.

"Well, she couldn't have reached George by phone." I stared at the floor, as if I could scan my options. "I want to go look for her," I said. "But I don't want to call Monika to pick me up. You could drive me?"

Beatrice smiled gently and winked. "I'll take Tommy's truck. Here." She lifted keys out of her pocket and swung them in front of my face. "I'm ready. Change your clothes and we'll go."

I tried to balance on one leg while removing my pants in front of her, and she tried to find a place to avert her eyes. "How long ago did she leave?"

"An hour, at most. I'll drive fast. Just change already." She pushed me into my bedroom.

Alone in the mess of the bedroom for a few minutes, dumping my entire sock drawer to pull out two socks, I picked a shirt off the rocking chair and threw it over my head. Never even turning the lights on, I came out wearing a hooded sweatshirt that read: *You break it—we'll fix it.*

"Henri, take a rain slicker or something. You might have to chase her." She was holding two umbrellas and had tied a transparent plastic bonnet under her chin, the kind women wore when they left the beauty parlor if it rained or the wind blew. I looked at her and grimaced, still not comprehending the way American women allowed themselves to appear in public. Even during the war the women dressed better, I thought.

"What!" she shouted, "You think you look better, with those white socks sticking out the bottom of your pants?" She clucked her tongue. "Henri, let's get going. I don't know what to make of you." I shrugged. I hadn't a clue what to make of me either. We ran out the door and into the truck.

The rain had lightened to a drizzle, and Beatrice was able to drive fast down Second Avenue, her hands firmly gripping the steering wheel. I sat with my head hung into my chest, making grunting sounds that Beatrice seemed not to hear. Why did Jackie have to leave the house, her warm bed? How was I to explain this to her mother? I could hear her scolding me for my pigheadedness, for my foolish dreaming. Oh god, Monika is right about her.

By the time we got to Houston, the rain had stopped completely. "Good. We will be able to see her now," Beatrice declared, trying to sound optimistic. She made a sharp right turn and drove slowly, crawling, until a car behind her honked. It was a cop, so she picked up speed to the minimum. We rode up and down Houston four times, peering into alleys, slowing when we saw a slightly built girl or tall, lanky man we thought could be George.

"It's no use," I decided. I waved my hand in the air, coughed up cigarette phlegm, then rolled down my window and spit a wad into the gutter. "It's no use. Let's just go home and wait for her next crisis." I leaned my seat back and closed my eyes, and drifted up into the bottom of the sky, its endless pitch a weighty balm, making my skin feel slimy under my shirt. Jackie's skinny body, wet and chilled, frightened and shaking, was drawn inside my eyelids.

"Henri, I'm scared for her," Beatrice said. "What about this being in trouble with a Clifton person? She seemed to think she had to hide."

"It's for real. No delusions about some bad man coming through her window this time. Someone croaked on some shit George sold him. Uch. What did she tell you?" I opened my eyes and looked at her for the first time since Nineteenth and Second.

Beatrice turned onto Lafayette Street and parallel-parked with the calculated precision of a kid taking her road test. "Let me think exactly what she said. She said someone was going to get *whacked*. I didn't know if that was good or bad for her, and she said she would meet him or her, and that's it, really. She was mumbling a lot."

"She could be anywhere by now."

"Let's think. You want to go over to that place she's been sleeping in?" Beatrice snarled out the words, even as she nodded that she thought we should try. She made a Uturn and drove back downtown. I directed her: make a right, a left here, then told her to park. Two of the streetlamps were out, and I tensed my shoulders at a pack of dogs systematically knocking over a line of aluminum garbage pails—the clash of the metal cans like background noise from a science fiction movie. One pail, blown by the wind, rolled down the middle of the street. I opened the car door, and the dogs started to growl and bare their teeth. I got back in and locked the door.

Beatrice laughed. "You don't have to lock it. They don't know how to work the handle." She poked my shoulder. "So what now, Sherlock?"

"You got me. I'm not getting out until they're through with dinner."

"Maybe I can scare them away with the horn." She pushed on the steering wheel and honked three times. The dogs just stood there, staring at the truck, their eyes saying, *Shut up, you idiots!*

With the street so dark and the dogs so stubborn, the sidewalks—scattered with half-abandoned apartment houses—might as well have been plopped down from another dimension. "You better stop." I tapped her firing arm. "Every drug addict in creation will be out here looking to steal from us. Let's go back home."

Defeated, tired, slipping through the slicked air into exhaustion, I mumbled, "You think we should call Monika now? Maybe Jackie went back there." I really didn't believe she would have.

"*Back* there? She was there tonight?"

"Yeah. She tried Monika first, but she threw her and George out. Seems they wanted to stay a few days. Play your Bonnie and Clyde."

"I could have sworn she was high when I saw her. How'd she have time to get high running between you two? Did Monika give her—?" She stopped herself.

First I sat still, waiting for her to finish, then felt the rush of betrayal—at once a blunt and sharp ache in my lungs—and breathed in deep enough to crackle the muck in them. My voice was strong, to this day my accent still straining to sound like a New Yorker. "Did you know about this? You knew Monika supplies her with that shit?"

Beatrice turned toward me in the dim light of the streetlamp. Her voice was even and soft. "I know she did once. I thought you already knew."

"Dear god!" I shouted, grabbing at my hair and slamming my forehead into the dashboard. Demeaned by my last-to-know status, I had to acknowledge my humble rank in the hierarchy of Jackie's caretakers. "I found out tonight. From *George*." Hearing Beatrice's confession, resentment scratched up my spine. Her disloyalty drowned my resolve to search further. "I'm beat. Let's get back."

"I'm sorry I never told you about what Monika did. I was, I—"

"Beatrice, just stop. I am so angry, with you and with her, and I almost could jump out of this car—but, so help me, *I* haven't been able to condemn Monika either. So—" I patted her hand in a sign of friendship. "I'm too tired. My head aches too much to concentrate."

On the radio, we listened to a discussion on Vietnam, about Americans—kids—sacrificing their lives, and about the United States government exerting itself as the power responsible for stopping Communism anywhere in the world. "They won't send more ground troops in," I said. "Johnson would be crazy to." With my eyes closed, I sniffled, sneezed. "Nah, they won't go in."

"You know enough about war to know it's not an easy decision to make," she reached over and rubbed my shoulder.

As we passed the UN on First Avenue, dozens of national flags lay vertical, asleep with the weight of soaking rain. Beatrice told me she feared my girl was in grave danger. She felt sure Jacqueline was going to be found before the week was out, her body cold. I disagreed. I believed my daughter was a survivor like her mother. "One way or the other, Jackie will turn up and be looking for cash from Monika," I said. We decided to agree—at least to each other—that Jacqueline was with George, on the run, stoned and looking for money and refuge; she would pop up again when things cooled down. "Okay then," she told me.

"I'm going home to sleep. My daughter has returned after worse episodes than this." I scratched at my mess of hair. The shouting in my head, telling me I had absolutely no control over the women I loved, had quieted to a harsh whisper.

"Well, I don't know what could be worse than this, and I'd just as soon you didn't tell me." Coming to a stoplight, she leaned over and kissed my cheek. "This is a mistake, leaving so soon," she begged. "Let's go back downtown and search until we find her."

The simple plea was all it took to change my mind, as if I'd been waiting for her to say something. "Turn the damn truck around."

By four a.m., we were sitting on Jackie's street, the truck doors locked against all human and animal life, the sky clearing, clouds traveling markedly into the East River, leaving predawn hints of clarity behind them. The Big Dipper was still visible, and I relaxed at the sight of it; the world might be reverting to goodness again. The dogs had withdrawn from the front of Jackie's apartment building, having left only inedible remains of trash—crumpled tin foil, paper cups, newspaper. An old man in a buttoned raincoat that stretched unwillingly across his chest and torso, his hands black with life, rummaged through the remains, then kicked the garbage when he found nothing to take. I watched without comment as Beatrice reached for her husband Tommy's lunch scraps in a brown bag on the floor of the truck and lifted it to check its contents. He had not eaten his tangerine. I opened the passenger-side window about two inches and offered it to the man. He took it, nodded, and asked if he could have a dollar. She refused him, and he moved on.

We had about an hour before Beatrice would have to return the truck to Tommy for work. The street was barren. I left the car and went into the building. Stronger than any drug addict, I could fight off or argue back an attack. Fully intending to find and retrieve Jackie if she were there, I marched in. The mailbox in the front hallway had been ripped off, only four screw holes testifying that it had once been there at all. The corridor was bulbless, but light filtered in from an open apartment door at the far end of the hall. It stank of garbage and urine. Standing at the threshold of the ground floor, a memory of my hallway on Rue de Rochechouart slapped my face: *A siren had blasted and all lights had gone out. I'd been going to visit my cousin, and the hallway turned dark as my mother ran toward me from their apartment, grabbed my hand, and we squatted in a corner on the cold, tiled floor, waiting for the world to end. My father and sister were outside somewhere. The roundups were beginning.* And now here, in this hallway, I felt the darkness as it was then: unbearable.

Unable to creep any deeper into the despair, I turned to leave. Beatrice stood frozen behind me. A lamp in the window of the building directly across the street shown some light. I jumped at the sound of a cat crying. It continued, and began to sound more human: a whimper, then a sudden, forced cough. The cough seemed to release Beatrice, and she pulled me by my sleeve, back toward the open apartment. Slowly creeping toward the door, I held her arm as we stepped into the threshold and waited for someone to jump out. We took our chances and walked through.

For a second, back there in the darkness, the cough had sounded like Jackie's. But I was wrong. A breeze blew lightly through the window and wrapped a piece of waxed paper around my ankle. I bent quickly to get it off, thinking it was a rat, and saw standing beside me a four-and-a-half-foot-tall boy, about twelve years old. It was his cough we had heard.

"Are you all right?" Beatrice asked him.

The boy spit a wad of something he was chewing over his left shoulder before he spoke. "My mom told me to wait out here. She's inside doing something with some guy." He shrugged, then looked Beatrice over as if deciding whether to steal her purse. "You better get your ass outta here though. This ain't no place for you, lady."

Beatrice moved toward him and spoke loudly, wanting to show the boy she wasn't afraid. "I'm looking for Jackie Hoffman or George… something. Have you seen them?"

"Not George. Don't think he'll come around for a while. He fuckin' killed Clifton. Fuckin' shot him through the back." The boy bobbed his head and shoulders, his eyebrows rising with the sound of his voice, as though he were talking about the town hero. "George ain't comin' back here. My mom says Jackie's got some hard work to do to get her shit now."

"I thought George sold him bad heroin? Isn't that what killed him?" Beatrice whispered to me.

The boy spoke out louder. "Nope. Shot him. Police were already here and gone. Took Jak-o-leen away in the police car." He held his fingers in the shape of a gun, mimed taking a shot, fell back with the discharge, then made a wooing sound, imitating the siren.

My hand over my heart, a tear already escaping the rim of my eyelid, I asked, "They took her away? We were just here an hour ago. When did they take her?"

"What am I, a fuckin' NBC news reporter? They took her. Before you got here. But they took her from around the corner—from the alley." He pointed to the space between two other buildings. The boy held himself stout and steady, a news reporter.

Filled with my daughter's fright, as real as if I were locked in a cell right beside her, I asked again, "You know this for sure?"

"I was back there with her. Keepin' her company," he smiled and winked. Nodding his head to the left, "That your truck?"

"Truck?" Beatrice sounded confused, as though she had forgotten how we got there. "Yes, it is. You want me to take you somewhere? I can take you to a dry place." She suggested bringing him to a children's shelter, or a kindly rectory, or at the very least to the police.

His eyes narrowed as he stepped backward, "You with social service? Shit!" He ran out and down the street and was out of sight in seconds.

Beatrice and I hurried to the truck and drove home through the waking city. I could not go to the police station alone, without Monika; I didn't have the stomach for it. Having already been wrong to think Jacqueline would last the night with me, I needed Monika if I had to make a decision about our daughter. I only hoped that no one called Monika first. Since I was Jackie's legal guardian, the police usually called me. They had grabbed Jacqueline, maybe arrested her, but at least she was safe.

Now the sun was rising, cars were beginning the morning rush. We had to get home. Tommy needed the truck, and Beatrice had steps to sweep.

9

# Two and Counting

*Manny*

Rattled by Jackie and George, I had not gone home after I left Monika's apartment. I drove around for hours, from the Brooklyn Battery Tunnel onto the Belt, east past the high-rise apartments and Ferris wheel of Coney Island, underneath the elevated train tracks through Brighton Beach, then down Avenue U to Sheepshead Bay. Driving until I was almost dead asleep, I crept to my sisters' street and parked in their driveway. Without enough strength to leave the car and go inside, I slept there. Fanny saw me when she took the garbage out at seven a.m. and ran over, pounding on the car window. She told me afterward that she thought for sure I had committed suicide right there, where I would be easily discovered. Hildie had been so upset about her talk with me on the porch the day before that she had confided to Fanny what I said—that sometimes I wished I were dead. That was just as good as a suicide warning.

At nine in the morning, Hildie and Fanny entered their kitchen, dressed in varying shades of blue, chattering of Maj Jong next Wednesday night, and the monthly Ladies Auxiliary meeting at temple Sunday evening. Even amidst Shiva, their everyday gab declared that their engagement with life's rituals continued, and looking at them, I smiled. The three of us prepared brunch for visitors, including Henri and Claudette. Tomorrow, Friday, would be the end of Shiva before the Sabbath, which the women observed. Then I would have to think about returning to work, and about the rest of my life without Nadine. Right now all I had to do was whip eight eggs in a bowl without spinning it off the counter.

"Add some water to those eggs," Hildie instructed without looking, as she emptied round, flat shells of golden-fried batter from a small frying pan. Cheese blintzes were her specialty. Every half minute, batter sizzled in the hot oil and was followed by the bang of the upside-down pan hitting waxed paper on the counter, releasing the shell. Fanny would peel the dough off the paper and fill it with the pot cheese, egg, and sugar mixture, roll it up, tuck the ends, and set it down in another pan with frying butter. It was relaxing to keep track of the flour settling over the room, covering the counters, the stove, faucet, floor, and eventually, everyone's clothes. I knew they'd refuse my help to clean up during Shiva. A least they had allowed me to whip the eggs. Usually, on Fridays, they'd stand around for hours doing this, eating some as they went along, smothering the hot crepes in cold sour cream. Today we'd save them for lunch guests.

An hour passed, with only two burnt-blintz mishaps, before Henri and Claudette walked in together, later than expected. The realization that the women seemed to know about the couple was horrifying; no one asked questions about their late, simultaneous arrival. The room got duller, the patience drained from Fanny's face. Hildie was more discreet, if in fact she was feeling disapproval; Claudette was her daughter, after all.

To me, Claudette was a Dresden doll—her pastel costume striking against her china-white skin, with her light-blue cotton skirt full, ruffled at its knee-length hem, her shirt pink and crisp. The capped sleeves had a soft ruffle as well. She had learned how to iron from her mother.

Her hair was pulled back into a ponytail—a style I preferred because it exposed all of her face—and she wore looped silver earrings that lay flat against her neck. No makeup. Clean. Fresh. Beautiful. I took it all in, and for a wisp of a moment I was happy, until my eyes traveled to the man at her side. Henri was wearing a gray sweatshirt, blue dungarees, and white Converse canvas sneakers. He had not shaven. His eyes were bloodshot. I was offended for Claudette, even if she didn't object to his sloppiness, and I immediately assumed he'd been drinking.

"What the hell is wrong with you?" I asked him, then looked at Claudette and shrugged when she shook her head, "don't."

"Let's sit," Henri said. He looked serious, some grim emotion evident behind his threadbare restraint.

The women turned off the stove, wiped their hands clean of flour, and took seats at the table to hear his address. The stoic look on Claudette's face cautioned us from speaking. When the five of us had settled, expectant, Henri cleared his throat. "Well. I don't know how to begin." His face fisted itself into tears, and he put his hand over his mouth.

Claudette said, "You want me to tell them?" She took Henri's hand.

They both were so immature, my head was exploding—how they played these games with secrets and telling—but I willed myself to stay silent. I scanned my sisters' faces and guessed by their stiffness that they were waiting, as was I, to hear that she was pregnant. Within seconds, I had conjured my reaction. I'd put my niece on a farm in the mountains with food enough for nine months, a telephone, and Hildie; Henri would be sailing east on a slow boat to Siberia.

Henri coughed again and said, "I got a call early this morning from the police." He had to stop speaking while everyone gasped and asked, "Who? What?" all at once. "Jackie. It's Jackie. She was picked up last night, and they're holding her on several charges." We sat motionless. "First and most serious is, they've accused her as an accessory to murder, after the fact." More gasps.

Esophageal paralysis set in. Just the thought of Jacqueline with that degenerate George, and my mouth burst open. "Henri, why don't we—"

"Please, please, let me finish."

He looked out the window, avoiding eyes, avoiding life. "There's the drug charge, and also solicitation. They actually caught her in an alley with an underage boy."

"My god."

"Oh, my God."

"God, no."

The inside of my head felt as if it were both devoid of matter and filled with rocks. "What do we do? How do we get her out?" I never imagined—and I was a man who could imagine horrible things—that she'd be in jail, arrested with a full set of heart-sickening charges against her. I was grateful Nadine had missed this.

"They set bail at ten thousand dollars, because of the accessory charge," Claudette said. That's why she had dressed so tidily, her face so clean; she was prepared to face a court for Jacqueline, and poised to cry.

"Who was *murdered*?" Fanny and Hildie asked at once, both their voices solid. Pillars.

"George, her idiot boyfriend, shot someone. He and Jackie went to Monika and then came to me last night looking to hide. They didn't say anything about him shooting someone," Henri said. "They told me some bull about bad heroin. Anyway, that doesn't matter. What matters is she's probably guilty." His sobs escaped from his throat.

Claudette started to cry, and I went to hold her. "Shush, hon." I held her, looked at Henri, and asked, "Monika. Where is she?" The lump in my throat expanded, burrowed through my heart and settled heavily in my stomach. With compassion for Monika, I didn't know if or how to relieve her pain without the undesirable effect of again ending up in her bed. She was still not out of my mind.

Henri stamped out his half-smoked cigarette. "I haven't called

Monika yet. I wanted to, and I almost did, but, well, she's no help. That's what we have to talk about. Whether or not to get her involved now." Henri then unleashed Claudette from my grasp and held her to his chest, then kissed her head. In unison, everyone looked away. I was mortified my sisters were subjected to this display, which sickened us, and I knew if they could speak their hearts, they would attest that the intimate relationship between Claud and Henri sickened them even more. Later, I thought.

"You have to call Monika," Hildie said. "She's always been available for Jacqueline, and now, well, the girl needs her mother." Fanny nodded.

"Excuse us," I told my sisters. "Can I talk to Henri alone?" The women closed their eyes and shrugged, looking insulted, but rose and left the kitchen, single file. "Claudette, you stay," I told her.

I took out my wallet from my back pocket and shuffled some papers in its sleeves. Henri sat at the table watching, and Claudette stood behind him, rubbing the sides of his head. She made faces at me, trying to communicate something, but I couldn't read her. Finally, I found the small paper envelope I was searching for and sat down next to my cousin.

"Henri, this is the key to my safe deposit box. I have some cash in there. We'll go down right now and get it, go get Jackie out, and *then* we'll go to Monika." I nodded, trying to prompt Henri to respond enthusiastically and accept this plan.

He grabbed my fisted hand that held the key. "You're still sitting Shiva," Henri said respectfully. "You shouldn't go to the bank."

"Don't make me have to explain to you all the reasons why this Shiva is over. Just do what I say and worry about your own religious desertion."

Henri looked confused. His face turned to Claudette, his eyes asking her for the correct response. The lovers playing more eye games. What was the thing they *were not at liberty* to discuss when I talked to them about their relationship? There had been so much more between them than I realized yesterday. They had years of intimacy, years of experiences as caretakers and friends. My stomach hurt, a raw torment, both hollow and cold.

Claudette was looking to Henri now, and abandonment surrounded me. So many times, I had wished to be relieved of the burden her father left with me when he abandoned them after the war: when she was twelve and chubby, and I had to assure her constantly that she was beautiful, and later the crushes every other month, then the decision to go to California to follow her dream—which I always suspected had more to do with finding her father than finding stardom. Hildie was too old-fashioned to be her guide and advisor, and Claudette relied on me, at once as a father and as someone more of her generation. It was exhausting. I'd prayed she'd find another man to adore and depend on to replace me. Now that I wanted to pull her back into my heart, a space now doubly vacant, I felt cleaved to see myself replaced. And why, why did it have to be Henri?

We made no excuse to the sisters, just got into my car and drove to the bank. Claudette sat scrunched between us in the front seat. "Thank you for this," she said to me.

"I wish I could do more. I wish I would have stayed with Monika last night and kept Jackie home."

"You were with her last night? You said that—" Claudette started, her eyes popping.

I interrupted her. "I said that I was breaking it off and that's why I was there. Then Jackie and George came by, and I left." Stopped at a corner, I breathed deeply and looked squarely into her face.

"She still would have gotten arrested," Henri said. "They know where Monika lives—the police, I mean. They would have gone there next if they hadn't found her in the alley. I didn't realize you'd seen her last night," Henri said, polishing the chrome door handle with the cuff of his sweatshirt.

Claudette pouted and leaned her head on my shoulder. "We'll keep together the whole day?"

"Yes, of course, sweetheart," I said, patting her thigh. "A real family reunion. With Monika and Jackie as entertainment." I regretted saying that immediately. "Sorry, Henri. I don't find humor in your daughter's situation."

"I know, I know." Henri opened his window and wiped the side-view mirror with a tissue.


It was noon as we drove in silence to the police station. Carrying the bail money in an envelope in my shirt pocket, I contemplated the morning's events and what the day might bring. The tall stone arches of the Brooklyn Bridge hung like giant flying buttresses over the East River—a solid affirmation, a justification for destroying bridges in Europe, for lives expended and boys blown up in the street while playing with the war toys left in the gutter.

The station sat at the corner where the Holland Tunnel empties into Greenwich Village, surrounded now with heavy lunch-hour traffic, forcing us to circle the block and adjoining streets three times before finding a parking spot two blocks away. The city glistened in the early afternoon sun—gutters swept clean by wind and water, red geraniums bursting from window boxes, dripping with the residue of rain. Everything, from the tops of cars to the drains of sewers, shone.

Claudette and Henri walked arm in arm; I strode two steps ahead of them, hearing their footsteps but nothing else. Existing in the hole of solitary life—the never-ending, never-beginning ocean I had floated in with Nadine as she left the world—I felt a certain buoyancy. But now my feet dutifully scraped the ground, and I was dragged down and back into thoughts of how difficult this trip really was, of all the decisions that would soon have to be made. Fitfully angry with myself, I thought I would put my fist through any passing window. Imagining myself bleeding, I felt a hand on my shoulder.

"Well, let's go in," Claudette said. She hooked her arm into mine, letting Henri walk into the station ahead of us. We were sandwiched between Henri and a group of boys in handcuffs behind us, herded in from a police bus. Once inside, the cuffed group derailed to the wide, gray stairway of this ancient bank of justice, and I noted without awe the grand, high, tin-coffered ceilings, now painted over in dirty white, and below, the worn wooden railings and doors. "This is the piss pot of humanity," I whispered.

Claudette put her index finger to her sealed lips. Henri approached the main desk. He spoke softly to the desk sergeant, either out of fear or out of mere inability to speak any louder, and waited while the officer left his caged post, presumably to get Jacqueline. We waited, breathing heavier by the minute, alongside others but apart from them.

The sergeant returned alone, save for some yellow papers. He shoved them through a small metal mesh opening and started talking. "Here's her hospital transfer papers. You can sign for her belongings." He pointed to a line at the bottom of the page.

Henri stood stunned. The cop looked annoyed, dragged on his cigarette, and said, "Were you notified she'd been moved?"

"No. I haven't been…I was out. Where?" Henri was already in tears.

"Bellevue, sir." He raised his eyebrows, waiting for a response. "Your daughter had a seizure. OD'd, we suppose. She's been moved to Bellevue."

Seeing Henri disintegrate, his breath becoming labored with the sinking of his chest, the cop motioned with his hand for me to come to his aide. The man lugged himself off his swivel chair. "Wait here," he said, and disappeared again. Henri turned to me and dropped his weight onto my chest. I put my arms around him and squeezed tightly. Henri began to weep as Claudette put her arms around his waist from the back. Shielded by our two bodies, he looked like the young boy I had found in Paris.

"We'll get through this," I said.

"How could she OD while she was here?"

"Don't know. We'll get answers when we get to the hospital. Just try to hold on."

The sergeant returned with a uniformed officer. "Mr. Hoffman, this is Officer Hart," he said. "He'll meet you at Bellevue. If you want to have your daughter moved out of the prison ward to the main hospital, you'll have to post bond. Officer Hart will take care of it at the other end." Officer Hart was a young man, about twenty-two, possibly just out of the academy. He had dark hair and glaring black eyes that were checking out Claudette's figure. As for the desk sergeant, maybe it was my disorientation, but I sensed the older man was surprisingly sympathetic.

"Yes," Claudette spoke up. "We've got the bond. Let's do that, Henri." She pulled on his arm to stir him.

"I've got it here," I said, taking the envelope from my pocket. "Can we sit somewhere?" Officer Hart took us deeper into the station, deposited me at the appropriate bench to wait my turn, spoke about something to Henri, and left ahead of us for the hospital.

The traffic lights up First Avenue from Houston to Twenty-Seventh Street were timed to change at thirty miles per hour, and though I wanted to speed, I drove with the rhythm of the city. Once Bellevue's great brick mass emerged on our right, we pulled into the closest illegal parking spot we saw. Officer Hart had given Henri painstakingly exact directions to find Jacqueline, and we made our way through the labyrinth of the hospital without a detour. Henri was already familiar with the layout because of Monika's job there, and at the elevator, we all turned to each other at once and said, "Monika."

Given Claudette's fierce contempt for her and Henri's urgent need to see his daughter, in a brief, erratic conversation, they elected me to call the psychiatric floor to see if Monika was at work. I felt an urgency to get hold of her that raced up my legs as I rushed to find a pay phone. At the same time, I dreaded making the call—like an Army officer reporting a soldier missing in action. There was hope, but who knew how much. When I got within a foot of the phone booth, it occurred to me that she was probably with Jacqueline already—that someone from the emergency room would have notified her. As soon as I heard someone else answer her phone, I hung up, knowing she wasn't there.

Claudette and Henri had already ascended. Waiting again for the elevator, behind a collection of visitors—some holding boxes of candy, others holding flowers, all of them alert with anxiety. I wanted to shout at them, *That will not help! Just eat the chocolate yourselves; acknowledge that you are the ones who need the soothing gifts.* The elevator doors opened and they herded in, as if this were the last train out.

The elevator stopped on every floor, the wait infuriating as people shuffled off and on. Finally arriving on the sixth floor, I breathed deep before the doors let me out. A New York City policeman sat on a folding chair directly in front of me, a newspaper in his hand, a gun on his belt. Like Hart, he was young, but blond and blue-eyed. Separated from Henri, I had no papers, no proof of my intentions.

The policeman stood. "Sorry. No unauthorized visitors are permitted to enter the ward."

Panting as though I had walked the six flights, the heat firing up my face, I tried to swallow my fury. "Well, how can I get a message through?"

"You wait right here until someone comes along, that's how."

So this is what it comes down to: everyone who knows a drug addict is a criminal and will be treated as one. "Can I at least ask a question?"

"Ask away," the cop said, sitting back down.

"Did Officer Hart meet the Hoffmans here a few minutes ago?"

"Yes. They're back there with the girl." He looked at me now with a twisted mouth and raised eyebrows, successfully implying that he was annoyed.

"I'm a close relative, can you tell them I'm waiting?"

"I'll tell them if I see them. They might go down the back elevator, since they'll be transporting the patient, so I might not see them. I can't leave my post to deliver messages, sir. There's more than one patient up here."

"No, of course not. You said transporting. Do you know where to?" An eerie wave of hope flushed through me.

"Can't give that information. You best get going now." The cop got up and pushed the down button for the elevator.

Side by side, *buddies*, we watched the numbers light up above the elevator and bing as it rose. It seemed to stall at the third floor for a few long seconds, then climbed directly to six. Even after the *bing*, the doors stayed closed, and I jabbed three times at the button. They cracked apart, hesitated, then continued to open, exposing the broad back of a man in a suit, his arms around someone. As the door fully opened, the man turned forward, and I was stunned, hit in the chest by the boot of a ghost, to see Monika in his arms. Her pale face was blotched with mascara, her hair wet around her face, matted down on her neck. As soon as she recognized me, she cried out, *"Oh, my Jackie!"* and threw herself on me.

"It will be okay. Shush, shush. She'll be okay." I embraced her awkwardly.

Monika pulled away and sobered momentarily, with disbelief on her face. "You, you, what have they told you? Was there a mistake? Is she alive?"

"What are you talking about?" I looked at the man in the suit.

The man's eyes bulged. "I'm sorry—we've lost her."

Hit again, the boot kicked straight on, into my stomach. "Lost her? Is she *missing* or *dead*, for Christ's sake?"

"This is the deceased girl's mother," the suit said to the officer.

Monika had already sunk to the floor, weeping. The suit bent down to her. He and I each took an elbow and lifted her. The floor beneath me went soft as I held Monika's head to my chest. "Monika, Monika." We rocked back and forth.

The officer put a hand on Monika's shoulder. "Come. I'll take you to her," he said. Stunned, she pulled me to go with her. The sensation of being led away reminded me of running over a sand dune to the crashing waves on the shore, pulled by the stubborn grip of an adolescent girl. But a woman who had been given her penalty and handed her sentence was the one pulling now—pulling hard—with the grip of a woman who would have her way.

—✦—

## *Henri*

We had rushed to the hospital expecting to see my daughter convulsing or, at worst, in a coma. When we got off the elevator on the sixth floor, Officer Hart was waiting with the news we later learned he'd been notified about before we reached the hospital: Jacqueline had loaded up so fully with drugs in the alley before they found her that when she dropped a tab of LSD another prostitute slipped to her in the cell, she banged her head on the bars with such force she knocked herself unconscious, the paper tab still melting on her tongue. She was already brain dead in the emergency room. A medical team wheeled her to a room on the locked ward and tried to keep her breathing until I arrived, but they failed. By the time I met Hart on the sixth floor, she was gone.

Holding onto Claudette for balance, I stood over my daughter's bed and sensed my head bobbing, Parkinson's-like. Claudette wept first. Officer Hart put a hand to my shoulder, startling me, and I gasped, waking. I held Jackie's face, kissed her forehead, and—stunned by the cold—turned and fell into Claudette's arms.

The white sheet had been tucked in around Jacqueline's flesh-and-bone body. Her hair, trapped in a hospital cap, didn't hide the drying, baby-fine hairs around her face springing into their natural curl. If not for the crashing pain hitting the walls of my chest, I would think I had died as well.

Minutes later, Monika and Manny arrived with a man in a suit. Claudette leapt at Monika the moment she walked into the hospital room and pounded into her shoulders with her fists. "You whore," she yelled. "You murderer!"

Even as I pulled Claudette off her, I shouted at Monika, "You did this. You gave her the drugs." She pushed past me, made her way to Jackie's side, fell on her daughter's stiff body, and demanded she wake up. Then she pleaded with her to wake up.

I stared at Manny, crying through a mouthful of tears, jerking my chin toward Monika. "She said she's pregnant with your baby. Don't let her have it!"

## *Manny*

Not sure I'd heard Henri correctly, I thanked God that over her own screaming and crying, Claudette hadn't seemed to hear. Even as I stood there and watched the gurney arrive to transport Jacqueline Hoffman from the morgue for an autopsy, I was imagining putting a fresh coat of baby-blue paint on the walls of the baby's bedroom. Voices spoke over voices, and crying sounds rattled between my ears like stones of hail. Standing tall as I could between Monika and the others—guarding her against further attack—I couldn't help but look at her belly, and my heart fluttered at the sight. Detecting a new roundness, I bit down on my lower lip.

On the elevator, we stood along the entire right side of the gurney, Monika at her daughter's head, and Henri and Claudette with their hands over the part of the sheet that covered the stalks that were Jackie's legs. From above the sheet, her legs looked as though they were being held apart. Why had she been starving? I looked at Monika standing so close, touching my shoulder with her head, and thought, *My baby will not starve.*

After we let the body disappear, Claudette spat on the floor in front of Monika, visibly shivered when she looked at me holding Monika's arm, and pulled Henri away by his elbow. We walked behind them to handle the newly familial business of death.

By five o'clock that evening, I sat with Monika in her apartment, and confirmed a child had been conceived. She vacillated between everyday chatter to unrestrained tears. Although desperately confused, my mood remained outwardly even-keeled. The tales about the excitement of expectant fathers didn't seem so exaggerated anymore. Despite the fact that she was only into her third month, I was confident in her ability to carry to full term. I'd already spent a few hours with her, trying to feed and comfort her, but during times of more lucid chatter—when she seemed removed from her grief, eerily elevated—I tried to draw up a manifesto for the future. I moved a kitchen chair into the bedroom and sat next to the bed, facing her. "I plan to support you and the baby. Things will be better for you and this child. I'll be a strong father and partner for you to raise him or her. I want to make that clear."

She took my hand and held it until I gently pulled it away. "Jackie," she whispered. "I wish I'd called her that when she was here."

Beatrice was coming at six o'clock. I would have to quickly speak my mind in order to get the hell out of here by the time Beatrice arrived, aching for a place to privately express my pain and joy. Lifting soundlessly from the chair, I walked toward the window, and when Monika put her cup and spoon on the nightstand and looked up dry-eyed, I spoke from as far across the room as I was able. "I'd very much want to keep the baby with me, Monika. I want you to know that option is there for you," I couldn't look at her, "so you can recuperate properly from this horror."

After hearing this, she got out of bed and walked around the room, collecting all four framed photographs of Jackie: her first day of school, a seven-year-old Marilyn Monroe at Halloween, her junior high graduation, and a picture of Henri with her at the Bronx Zoo. She was ten. Monika sat with them, pressing them face down into her breasts. "And us?"

Surprised to hear this, I nonetheless responded readily. "No us, Monika."

She placed the frames on her pillow, reached her hand out into the room, and moved her fingers, signaling me to come hold them, but I stayed back.

"I hate what happened to Jackie," I said. Tears filled my eyes and over-flowed. "I feel guilty being this happy about our baby, but I love that this is happening." I finally walked to her. "We—we can't be together. I'm sorry." I wiped my eyes, trying not to speak further, trying to smother the crossbred selfishness and guilt propagating inside me.

Monika tilted her head and looked into my eyes, elegant, poised to accept the next dance, and placed my hand on her belly. "We need rest. Go home to your sisters, Manny."

# 10
# Babes in Arms

<u>*Monika*</u>

"Did you, in fact, give Jacqueline the dose that may have attributed to her death?" Officer Hart had asked me this before, but I'd been unable to speak at that time, feeling insane myself, practically laying over my daughter's corpse as disbelief clouded my mind. Hart stopped interrogating me, but advised me not to leave New York State. In the week that followed, and after many sessions of police questioning that left me fighting dry heaves and tears, I convinced the police I had been nowhere near Jacqueline so late into that night, that Jacqueline was certifiably schizophrenic, if they cared to check with her psychiatrists—which they did—and that my daughter often lied and fabricated, hallucinated, and became delusional, telling hideous stories about her mother. And I had an exceptionally clean history, save for the ugly divorce. Everyone who had seen me and Jackie that night swore to the fact that they saw nothing *unusual*, a term meant to stick me like the jab of a hypodermic needle, but nonetheless helped me escape the wrath of the stupid and pushy policeman. Didn't they have to look for George? "I am frustrated up to my fullness with their nonsense," I had cried to Manny. When he was questioned by the police, Henri denied that Jackie was stoned when she and George arrived at his house, and George was nowhere to be found.

Manny made every attempt to be with me for the informal interrogations and promised to stay by my side through my grief, through my pregnancy, through my life. I was happy about one thing: Henri had let Manny know—as I remained quiet behind my dignity.

Because of the damage the pathologist had inflicted on Jacqueline's beautiful body, I decided to have her cremated. Henri had no objection, saying flatly, "My parents were probably cremated in a *camp*."

I had been momentarily silenced by Henri's remark, then—contemplating my own parents' fate—I said, "God rest their souls." The Hoffman sisters spoke with gentle insistence about their family's religious laws prohibiting cremation, but Manny interceded, siding with me, reminding them I was a Christian, that the damage had already been done, and to let me do as I saw fit for my daughter. Grateful, I welcomed Manny's faithfulness.

I stood at the entrance door to the crematorium, waiting for Henri in the glaring sun, but when he finally arrived he didn't have the stomach to enter, saying only, "I think this will kill me, if I stay." So I sat alone in the heat of the mortician's small, paneled office, stuck to the leather of his guest chair, waiting for this morning to end. I wiped perspiration from my brow, tears from my cheeks, and used the wet tissue to rub ink off my thumb and index finger—ink from the pen used to sign the agreement.

A travel agent who knew me and the details of Jacqueline's death let me put a sign on the agency's bulletin board, asking anyone going to West Germany to take her ashes with them and sprinkle them somewhere beautiful when they got there—and make Jackie's dream to travel to my home country finally come true. A young couple going on their first-anniversary vacation offered to take her remains to Belgium. Close enough, I thought. Beatrice drove with me to the newly renamed John F. Kennedy International Airport, where we handed the simple brown box to the couple, who seemed unaware of anyone else in the terminal as they giggled into each other's faces. "So inappropriate," I whispered to Beatrice.

Once we interrupted them and handed over my package, all four of us cried. Watching until the plane left the ground, I stood mute at the observation window, my eyes following the stretch of black runway that led to paths farther than I could see. A hard lump filled my throat as I wondered, *Where is my little Jackie going to rest?* As the plane lifted, I crossed my heart, with the retraction of the wheels, I said a prayer, and when the plane passed through the farthest visible cloud—absorbed into the sky—Beatrice and I turned like synchronized swimmers and walked to the car.

The drive back from JFK Airport to Manhattan was perfect in its silence. Beatrice sat with her hands in her lap; not the slightest movement of her lips betrayed any prayers that I guessed she might have been reciting in her head. I could have turned downtown to bring Beatrice home with me, or uptown to deliver Beatrice to her house and thus be alone. I did miss her company. Beatrice had been infuriatingly distant and close-mouthed since Jackie's death, and I knew Beatrice had only accompanied me to the airport so she could be with Jackie this one last time. She so much as told me that.

The traffic light changed, and I had to decide which way to go. I headed downtown, and Beatrice turned her head and asked, "What are you doing?"

"I thought you'd come to my place. Have some dinner and talk." I felt myself blush, embarrassed and afraid of what Beatrice would say.

"I really can't do that, Monika. James and Tommy, you know. They expect me home."

"I don't want to go home alone. Please, Bea. We need to talk. I miss you." First whimpering and then crying in full sobs, gripping the wheel with my sweaty hands, as much for support as to steer, I said, "I've just lost my child, for God's sake."

"I'm really sorry. I can't. Let me off here and I'll grab a cab." Beatrice reached for the door handle and held her handbag tightly to her chest.

"Don't be that way. You want to go home—I'll take you." With my sleeve dabbing my eyes and then my nose, I said, "We've been friends since Jackie and I were dragged to this city. You're going to just stop talking to me without explaining for me why?"

Beatrice's voice was low and throaty. "If you want me to tell you why, I will. But I know you'll end up feeling worse, and I don't think it'll change the way I feel." She finally looked at me. "When we get to my street, we'll park. We'll talk." She turned and looked out the side window.

Double-parked in front of Beatrice's building, I shut off the engine and shifted my weight in the seat to face her. "You blame me for her death. I know that much. Everyone else does—but you, Beatrice? You, who saw how I *was* with her? What her death has done to me?"

Beatrice pressed her lips together before opening them to speak. "Listen to me carefully. This is not about how you feel; it's about how I feel about you. And I'm telling you straight when I say, I have absolutely lost all sense of you as a good person. Your motives, your tactics—you are completely centered on yourself." She was breathing hard enough that I could see her breasts rising and falling.

"Be specific when you speak such accusations. Because how I see it, I'm the person who gave up my home with my daughter, whom I now grieve for alone. I gave up living in a building with my best friend, you, to satisfy Mr. Henri's divorce demands. I work in a mental hospital and take care of patients and their families. That is how I'm, how you said, centered on myself?" I was in disbelief.

"My God, Monika. It would take all night to be specific." Beatrice let her eyes hold on mine. "Briefly? You lied to patients and doctors to get attention and favors." She paused to allow the car that was slithering by mine to stop honking. "I do talk to other people at the hospital. I know things. You gave—not the one time you told me about—but *gave and gave and gave* your daughter heroin. For God's sake, Monika! We know you gave her drugs the night she died!"

"I did what I had to do. You *never* understood!" Split open and unable to speak, I envisioned the lines on my face deepening.

Beatrice burst out, "I could sit here and argue with you until one of us is dead and it will never matter, because you are this"—she held her palm out at me—"this person that I see. And none of us can change that. Our lives. We live who we are."

I sat, forcing myself to be still. Then I pointed to the protrusion in my mid-section, tilting my head and squinting curiously. Henri surely had told Beatrice I was pregnant. He'd told everyone who hadn't been there to hear it firsthand when he blurted it out in Jackie's hospital room. Even at only twelve weeks, my pregnancy was beginning to show and wearing loose-fitting blouses was futile. I sank back cozily in my seat, then sat higher and smiled. "Yes, this." I looked down at myself. "Well, as you can see, I'm pregnant. Three months. I suppose this is selfish too. Is this selfish too, Beatrice?"

"Does Manny want this? Because if you did this to keep him, it may very well be the most selfish thing you've ever done." She put her hand on the door handle.

"Whether he wants it or not, this is a human life. I will sustain this life and protect it. *That* is who *I am*."

Beatrice gasped in amazement. "You're out of your mind. God help you and God help that baby. You are the worst mother in the world." With that, she opened the door, got out, and ran into her home.

Barely able to click on the engine, so insulted and abused, I stepped hard on the gas pedal. Crawling the twenty-odd blocks home in heavy traffic, the car heated with the stagnant city air. I was sweating and choking from thirst. The nerve. How dare she treat me with such self-righteousness? Conceited know-nothing about anything. That last awful thing she said. I parked down the street from my apartment and stomped home. My heart filled with rage—that perfect little home-nest of hers.

The apartment was stuffy, suspended in time in anticipation of my return. I moved through the still space. Opening the two back windows did very little to dissipate the dull murmurs in the air. I dug into the bottom of the hall closet and retrieved last summer's electric fan. Gulping a glass of ice water, I plugged the fan into the kitchen counter outlet in front of the window, the sun finding its way into the window and onto the blades of the fan. The steel shone with excitement as it stood ready to go, then became a transparent round frame as the blades whirred on high. And finally, the blades disappeared, the metal matter vaporized.


Feeling increasingly wronged by Beatrice, I writhed with resentment and blame. Slapping my fists into my bath water, so hard the splashing reached my face, I flung at Henri all the blame for our daughter's turn to drugs for comfort. Incapable of understanding his daughter's basic needs, he had seeded her need to prostitute herself, which caused me to have to feed Jackie drugs to ease her excruciating physical pain and mental anguish. My body grew heavy with anger, and I felt the pressure of fury weighted inside my pelvis. Fearing losing control of my bladder, I started to get out of the tub to pee. The phone rang. The jingle so startled me that my knee buckled, I lost balance, and fell on my back into the water.

While I sat stunned and breathless, my back slapped against the porcelain, my hand went to my belly to protect it, and I looked between my legs for blood. There was none. Carefully shifting my weight, I rose slowly forward and up, holding firmly onto the rim of the tub. I was intact. The phone was still ringing and I wrapped myself in a towel and caught it.

"Hello. Did you hear the phone before?" It was Manny, and I thought I detected anxiety in his voice.

"I heard. I was taking a bath and fell in the tub when I tried to get out. Praise the Lord, I seem to be fine." I pulled at the telephone cord and sat in the rocker. My rosary beads were lying on the seat cushion, and I reached under my buttocks to retrieve them.

"Are you sure? Maybe we should call the doctor."

Warmed by his concern, I kissed the rosary. "I feel okay. There's no bleeding. It was a hard fall, but I didn't have very far to go."

"I'm coming over. Just stay put."

"Okay. I won't move until you get here." Elated, I was paralyzed in my seat.

"And keep your feet up." He sounded as if he had started to run out the door already.

"Drive carefully. I love you."

He had hung up. I wasn't sure he'd heard me. Jolted by anticipation, I got up to dress in something light and roomy. He would be there for me just as he had promised. I'd have the baby and keep it in my home. He had robustly tried to convince me to let the baby live with him, which I secretly considered, even though I was unsure how that would work. Which arrangement would give me more frequent access to Manny? In all likelihood, we would share custody. He would support our child financially, through his entire life. We were not to be romantically in-volved—no more sex, no more touching, period. But I wasn't sure of his true intentions in that regard.

Before I dressed, I released the catch on the bedroom shade, letting it rise to half-exposure. Standing fully naked before the window, I exam-ined the contour of my body with my fingertips, pleased with my bur-geoning figure, my belly the even tone of palest pink, like the underbelly of a kitten. I cradled the baby in my arms, pulling it up close to my breast. Closing my eyes, I watched the infant.

—✧—

# *Manny*

I prayed and cursed and drove twenty miles an hour over the speed limit to get to Monika. The button for the doorbell was missing, and for a moment I forgot that I could knock. "Shit." Shaking my head to clear it, I then pounded too hard on the door.

"I only disobeyed you and moved in order to get up off the chair to unlock the deadbolt."

My eyes raced from her belly to her face, surveying for damage, as I spit out an uneasy "How are you?", tripping on words like I did when I tried to speak French to her and Henri in Paris. It came out, How *you are*? She walked to the rocker.

"Have a seat, Manny." Monika smiled and rocked gently.

Unnerved by the suggestion, I shook my head. "I just wanted to make sure, you know, that you were all right." I pinched my lips closed, embarrassed by my unkindness. Now we both knew, I only worried for the baby.

"The baby is fine. So. I guess you can go back to Brooklyn."

"I'll stay a few minutes if you'd like." I took a seat on the sofa. "Any dizziness or pain? You want me to get you a drink or something?" She shook her head. "Any blood?"

"Nothing. Nothing bad has happened. To either of us."

Maybe she should have some blood or urine tests. Nadine was always having urine tests. I was going to suggest it when I remembered the somber event of the day. "How was it at the airport. Everything go as planned?" I wanted to be able to tell Henri and Claudette that it went smoothly, that Jackie would be at peace by the end of the day.

"You can tell the lovebirds that she is safe with God. They need not worry about her anymore. I have seen to her final wish, and she is happy.

So then, is that it?" She cocked her head, leaned back, and kicked off her slippers.

"I suppose so." I stood, looked sheepishly into her eyes as she stared up at mine. I was stunned at the light that still shone from hers. Monika had filled her womb, eclipsing Jacqueline's death, avoiding any intervals of calm. I wanted that baby inside her. I should rip it out from within her before it grew bedeviled. "You'll let me know if you need anything."

"Anything? Like what, anything?" she said, without the least bit of levity in her tone.

"Like money, or a ride somewhere…you know what I mean." I started for the door, sorry I had come. Had she actually fallen at all? She looked fine; she looked beautiful. All at once, I was afraid of what she could do to me. "I hope Jacqueline gets to Europe safely." I wasn't sure where her mother had shipped her. I stepped closer to the door.

Monika stood and walked behind me. She cleared her throat and sighed. "I might *need* for you to keep our baby. I might give it to you."

My head spun around. She seemed perfectly calm. Not happy, or sad. Flat. "You want that?" she asked. "You want to keep our baby for yourself." She smiled, but I knew that smile had nothing to do with kindness.

I sat again, so dizzy with surprise I almost kissed her, and more frightened of her than a minute before. "Monika, please don't tease me. Are you serious? Because if you're serious, you know that this is all I want. You would be the kindest, the most wonderful…" What? Mother? She sat again in the rocker with a blank look. I had misunderstood, had imagined her offer. Was I really in the room with her at all, or was it merely my thoughts that lingered in this room and my body had never even arrived? When I asked her to repeat herself, my own voice rose from another room—no, another world.

"I don't know if I have the strength to raise the baby," she said. "No, I know I haven't the strength."

"I don't understand, Monika. Are you feeling weak? Is it that you're just not feeling well?" I held firmly onto the arm of the sofa and concentrated so very hard on listening that my head started to pound.

Monika shifted in her seat, laboring as though she were already forty pounds into pregnancy. There was the small, round ball around her waist, but the rest of her hadn't changed. Her arms and legs were still solid skin and muscle, her Bing-cherry-shaped face. "I feel *physically* strong. This is nothing so difficult to do, giving birth to our healthy baby. I just feel, after Jackie, I can't raise another. I gave her all anyone could give a child, and it was still not enough." She wiped a tear from under her eye. "I have nothing left. Nothing for this one."

Thoughts tripped over each other in my head, each wild in its eagerness to take control. She was still grieving too much to think about this baby. Her fear was temporary, based more on sadness and remorse. "You're right, Monika. After the time you had with Jackie, the love and energy you spent trying to make her well, it's natural to feel… exhausted." The adrenalin surged, and I jumped toward my dream. "I want the baby, Monika. I have nothing but love and energy to give. It would be the best thing, the most loving thing you could do, to give me and Nadine the baby."

Her eyes, pink and moist with tears, seemed to dry in an instant flash of heat. "You and *Nadine*? What are you talking about? This isn't so you can live a fantasy life." She slapped her hand against the rocker's arm and scooted toward me. "You lost her, I lost Jacqueline, and if you take this baby, it will be *only* for *you*, you understand that?" She was yelling, pointing at me, her face so close to mine I was hit with her spit.

What made me mention Nadine's name? "I didn't mean that. I didn't mean it would be *with* her. I just meant it would make her glad for me if she looked down. Just like you made Jackie happy by sending her ashes to Europe."

Monika smiled. "Yes, well, I suppose she would look down and be happy that I gave you a child." Her body fell back. "You go tell your sisters now. And tell Claudette and Henri, and the whole free world if you like." She held up one hand, spreading her fingers. "In five or so months, you will be the proud father. You will be the sole guardian."

Kissing her cheek, I smelled her skin and my legs weakened, but only for a moment. She watched me turn my head away from her, and she reached for my arm.

"I'm not going to say anything to anyone yet. But I'll hold it in my heart. This is wonderful." I scratched a fictitious itch on my face, restraining my delight—even as hers was eclipsed with contempt for the life inside her.

# 11
# More Liberations



## *Henri*

Ushered in by the aftermath of Jacqueline's death, summer brought nothing but explosions of madness. National politics battled for attention against the escalation of dissent now happening within the family. The Hoffmans were imploding with grief, disbelief, and accusation. Claudette and I walked the two miles from her apartment to the UN on First Avenue and Forty-Ninth Street, where by eight o'clock on a hot Sunday August morning a crowd of several thousand had already gathered to demonstrate against the Vietnam War.

The demonstrators were mostly young college students, protesting as President Johnson sent the first ground troops into Cambodia. But there were others like me, in their thirties—veterans of other wars, refugees, immigrants. Obscuring my view of the fisted and impassioned speakers were taller men and kids on their daddies' shoulders, playing with flowers in their fathers' hair—the lilac scent, reminiscent of the trees in the cemetery of Montmartre, like a warm memory sitting on a cold stone tomb. A wave of grief crushed around my lungs as my eyes wandered from the speakers to the strange, pale, bald men with braided ponytails protruding from the tops of their otherwise-shaved heads, wearing saffron-colored sheets for clothing. They had started appearing all through the city, handing out flyers and blessing you as you read their preachings and they sang an Indian chant—*Hare Krishna*. They looked ridiculous. Were they here to protest the war or just preaching to an already captive audience? I resented their presence, their fervor stirring up guilt about my abandonment of Judaism.

I had brought my girls to New York after the Korean War. Their Hero. I looked at Claud, knowing she was ignorant of the expectations Monika had of me when we moved here. Jacqueline would be a fine student. Monika would settle into a comfortable domestic life. I would provide. I would not have to join the French Volunteers to prove my heroism because my girls would realize I was a devoted father and fiercely ambitious husband. Now war was upon us again. Was I supposed to be making promises to Claudette? Was I supposed to forget that Jackie was ash and I had amounted to nothing but shit? Monika loved Manny, after all. Inexcusably, the grief that overwhelmed me following Jackie's death was overshadowed in the daily turmoil surrounding Monika's pregnancy.

We soon left for my place to meet Manny for lunch. Claudette had seen little of him all summer. Since the bomb of Monika's pregnancy had rumbled through the Hoffman family, Claudette's hatred for her seethed. Through June and July, I tolerated her ranting about Monika, and my free time remained available to her as she tried to avoid Manny, her anger tying us closer together. She'd begun a job as a secretary at the ABC television station, and she had no time to travel into Brooklyn to visit her mother, her aunt, or Manny. I saw Manny every day at the hardware store. Our conversations were limited to whether this clerk or that was stealing, what orders came in and went out, and who misplaced the key to the employees-only restroom. Manny always sent his love to Claudette, which I respectfully delivered, whereupon she would sulk until after dinner. She called him to wish him happy birthday but declined his invitation to join him for Carvel ice-cream cake at her mother's house. Monika would be there. They had agreed to meet today only after he'd told me that it was a matter of serious family consequence. We both knew without much soul-searching that this was going to be—directly or indirectly—about Monika, the baby, and life after the birth.

"Do you think he's going to tell us he's marrying her?" Claudette asked, as the megaphoned voices receded behind us.

"Never."

There was a powerful sense of trust between us. She counted on my truthfulness, but tearfully disagreed with my opinion. She stopped me from walking by pulling on my sleeve. "I'm giving you fair warning here. You better rely on me to get that woman out of our lives. I'll kick her the hell back to Europe if it's the last thing I ever do."

"Well *I* warn you back, Claud, don't dare use the past between Monika and Jackie. I would be disgraced in this family." I begged her, "Please. Just don't do it." She promised nothing.

We picked up bagels and lox and cream cheese. I wanted a whiskey sour with lunch, so I ran back down the street to the grocery to get orange juice. Claudette waited on the corner, watching people, her heels bouncing on the pavement. "The baby will be my cousin, Henri," she'd whined to me. "How will I be able to love it and be with it, with that she-devil as its mother?" Claudette said, torn, unabashedly, between loving and fearing the child.

I was distraught over the inevitability that I would love the child; my biggest fear, what if it were a girl who looked like Jackie? "If I have to look into the face of my daughter every time I see the baby—" Hopefully she would be redheaded, like the Hoffman side of the family. How would I allow a Jacqueline replica to live with Monika?

I whistled with my fingers in my mouth and got Claudette's attention. She walked the half block back toward me to take one of the brown bags. "Why the sad face?" I asked her when she got close up.

"Manny. I can't stop worrying about him."

"I see him every day, Claud. He's fine. Really."

"That's why I worry. He shouldn't be fine with a devil carrying his flesh and blood." She shuddered.

"Look, you're not the one to deal with her. I'm sure, as sure as I know Monika, that she's giving him a run for his dollar, but Manny is a strong man." I kissed her cheek. The feel of her skin regulated me as much as it ever had. "At least he will be a father." Smiling for her, raising my eyebrows, I revealed my truth. "But oy gevalt, it will come with such a high price."

"His money. That's another thing I worry about. She's probably got him paying for everything." She squinted.

"On that, I know you're right."

She shifted her weight to get a better grip on the grocery bag, which she held with both arms, hugging it to her chest. While she handed me the juice, milk, and fresh strawberries, she schlepped the bagels and cake and a pound of fresh coffee. We had gotten a much more elaborate meal for our lunch with Manny than we had originally planned.

From the corner of my street, we caught Manny's silhouette standing on the stoop, talking with Beatrice. Claudette knocked into me with her hip, since her hands were full, to get my attention, and whispered, "He looks wonderful, doesn't he?" Her eyes sparkled in the sunlight. She freed one hand and made an awning over her eyes.

We stopped to look at him. "You love him, Claudette," I said. "I love him."

Claudette pouted and started to cry. "Great job, Henri." She wiped her eyes on the bag.

Beatrice saw us coming and waved hello. Manny ran down the steps and grabbed the bag from Claudette, looking at her face. She offered her cheek, and he kissed her.

"Hello, Claudette." He juggled the bag into one hand. "This is heavy. Did you have far to walk?"

"No," she lied. "Are you hungry?"

"Famished." He didn't take his eyes off her.

Abandoned, I felt their connection.

"Hi, Henri." Manny grinned at me and rested his gaze back on his niece. "Let's eat."

Manny's condescension—being pushed aside as *that thing that hangs onto my Claudie*—provoked instant resentment in me. When we got to the top step, Beatrice kissed me and Claudette. "Well, the family looks well," Beatrice congratulated us. "Have a wonderful lunch." She excused herself and returned to her apartment upstairs. In the sunlight, I saw for the first time that she had lost a fair amount of weight over the summer, and I worried. She'd not been caring for the property as she always had, sweeping, hosing down. Maybe there was trouble with Tommy. I'd encountered her running late for work more than once, and had noticed a wiped smudge of mascara and tears under her eyes.

"We should support the war and the boys that are going," Manny declared. Among his vices, my cousin was a blind patriot. Rebutting anything I'd bring to his attention about the war would only result in a fiery, face-to-face standoff. Claudette and Manny set the table while I listened, as they talked casually about the weather and the war. "I'd hate to think what it's like for them, going into those jungles. Thank god at least I didn't get sent to the South Pacific after Germany. Jungles—scares me to death."

"Well, that's why we're demonstrating," Claudette chided him. "We're not against the boys. We're against war."

"That's not entirely why we're demonstrating," I added in a low tone.

"There is the question of a right and a wrong war—politically."

"Yeah. But the picture is bigger than we know." Manny said, his voice so confident, impassioned, that again I swallowed my response. I didn't want the afternoon to devolve into a political debate, especially when my views began to oppose Manny's.

When we had all started smothering our second bagels in cream cheese, I put my knife down and thought carefully before opening my mouth to speak. Should I come right out and ask Manny what the problem was—ask him why this emergency meeting had been called? Intimidated, thinking it not my place to put my cousin on the spot, I said nothing. Manny *knew* he had called this meeting; he would speak when he was ready. Yet I couldn't help feeling humbled by the affinity between my cousins. I still hoped they would someday tow me away from my childhood horrors, past the disappearance of fathers and faith, a time that remains connected somehow to my still-wishful expectancy of contentment.

Claudette lifted her shoulders and eyebrows when she blurted, "Has Henri told you we've heard from Officer Hart?"

"Who?" Manny asked.

"Not now," I said. I wanted Manny to get to his point already, but he looked at me strangely. "Officer Hart is the young cop who met us at the hospital." I looked to him for recognition, but Manny gave me a blank stare. I said softly, "When we went for Jackie."

"Oh, yeah. What about?"

Claudette said, "Seems they caught up with George. He'd gotten all the way to California. Hart said they hauled his ass back here and there'll be a trial or hearing. We might get called. Might not. Depends on the asshole's plea."

We sat chewing. I tried not to think about Jackie. "Now that we all have food in us, what d'ya say we get serious?" Both Manny and Claudette looked at me. "Well, not that that wasn't serious, you know—I mean we should talk about the thing that is concerning you, Manny."

Manny pushed his chair out from under the table and scratched under his nose. "This shouldn't be difficult. At least I hope it's not. I think it's something that will please everyone." He looked only at Claudette. She sat still, her posture perfect. He reached over and touched her hand, which lay on top of her knife. He went on, "You know, Monika is due in three months."

"How did I guess this was about her?" Claudette asked, her voice clipped and theatrical.

"Claudette," I raised my forefinger. "Fresh start." She sat back in her seat, but stuck her tongue out at me.

Manny lowered his head, then raised it sharply, most likely to get a running start. "My baby is due in three months. The situation is this. A few months ago, Monika offered to let me keep the baby. She'd literally offered to give me full guardianship." He looked at each of us.

"A few months ago?" Claud said.

"Well, I don't believe it," I continued, slapping my hand hard on the table. I assumed she'd be greedy, manipulative, give Manny an ultimatum. I was counting on Manny to hold his ground. Be a soldier.

"I waited to tell you to make sure she was serious. It seems now… well, now that the birth could happen anytime—say, if it's premature—I felt I had to tell you." He looked at his niece. "She doesn't know yet what part she will play in the baby's life."

Claudette remained unanimated, but her face was red. "Will she put it in writing?"

"Writing? Umm, I don't know," Manny said. "Maybe I should ask her." He looked uneasy about that, holding his mouth closed against a burp that sounded to me more tension than indigestion.

This was the only way to deal with Monika. I knew from experience with my own divorce battle that she could renege and cheat her way back to custody. As I declared all this, something in Manny's scared-boy face made me realize he needed more than legal suggestions from us. I stood and went to hug him. "So glad for you."

"Thanks, Henri. This is a miracle for me." He looked at Claudette. "I want you to be happy."

"Of course I'm happy about this." She too stood and hugged her uncle. "It will be wonderful." Her face seemed to force out a smile. "We'll name her Nadine, or Nathan if it's a boy."

Manny looked at me. "What about 'Jacqueline,' if it's a girl? Monika should have a say. Would you want that, Henri?"

My brain went ballistic. A fiery wall crashed before my face. "I don't want that. No, Manny," I said with a thick voice. "Let that name rest. Nadine should have had this baby. I want it to be named after her." The last thing I needed was to hear my daughter's name spoken every day. "I still can't believe…" I started to cry.

Manny put his arm around my shoulders.

We embraced for a while. "I wish she had a *grave* I could visit," I said. "I wish Monika hadn't sent her into *the air.*" To be somehow able to collect her windblown ashes and bring them home, and scatter them again like a swarm of butterflies… I turned to Claudette. "You think she ever really contacted anyone in Germany?" hopeful that she would say yes. Yes, of course she knew someone, someone who loved her.

"Yes, Henri. I'm sure she really knew people there, somehow." From the serious and solemn look on her face, I chose to believe her.

I insisted we end our visit with smiles and hugs. Manny offered to give Claudette a lift to her acting class downtown. The two of them could take this chance to reconnect, to have a normal uncle-niece interaction. The idea that Manny would keep the baby, and the wish that Monika might even live her life apart from them, was both a hopeful and an unnerving fantasy. It was unfathomable that she could be that generous, but if she reneged, did decide to keep the baby, Claudette would use any means she had to splice Monika onto the cutting room floor.

Now I had to check on Beatrice. She didn't seem the least bit anxious to visit with Manny or tell Claudette how pretty she looked in her long skirt and flowery blouse. I picked up the phone. "Beatrice, it's me. Could you come down and visit? I have things I want to talk about."

"Things? What kind of things? You know apartment matters go straight to Tommy." She sighed.

"Come on down, Bea. To be honest, I don't like how you look." I caught myself. "I didn't mean it that way. I don't like how tired you seem."

"I work hard. I'm tired."

"You've been late for work a few times, and the front steps have been covered with leaves and cigarette butts." She was silent. "Bea, I'm not complaining, I'm just worried."

"Don't worry."

"What, only you're allowed to worry about me? I can't worry for you?"

"Oh, for goodness sake. Okay, I'll be right down, Mr. Henri. But just for a few minutes." She hung up. By the time I chugged a warm whiskey sour, she was knocking at the door.

She was clean, neat, and thin. She had never been as trim as Jackie or Monika, but she had a curvy figure. Now she was skinnier than Monika had ever been. She had a plate of chocolate-chip cookies in her hand. "Here, I baked these for James's trip."

"Trip? Doesn't he start at NYU in a week or so?" A cookie from the plate went into my hand and in my mouth. "Delicious." Crumbs spilled from my lips.

"These were Jackie's favorite."

"Where did you say he's going?" She hadn't said. Beatrice's mouth changed from straight across to turned down. "What, Bea? Has something gone wrong with James?" Tears filled the whites of her eyes, spilling over in big heavy drops. I grabbed her arm. "Beatrice, what is it?"

Speechless, she tugged on my sleeve to come sit on the couch.

"My son, James—" she stopped to sniffle. "My James has joined the Navy. He's enlisted." Her head bowed, her arms fell limp at her sides. Stunned, I said, "That boy would do such a stupid thing?" A war was not a place to go voluntarily.

"He said he had to help somehow. He felt lost and useless, he said. He had a high lottery number but said he could not stand by and watch all his friends get called and not back them up. Not be there for them if he could." She nodded, as if to accept such an explanation. "He said he had to fight with them, or else he would explode inside."

Not expecting to hear anything but stupidity from a boy who had enlisted, I found this reason for going wasn't so much stupid as it was naive. "You raised a good boy." Icy, raw lament bit through my body, and I shivered in my friend's sadness.

My daughter. She had not been raised to be good. Here was James, offering his life for the absurd notion that he'd find peace by killing or being killed alongside his friends. And there was Jackie, who gave her life by shooting drugs through her veins. How many ways were there for children to destroy themselves? Startled, as I was daily by my own godlessness, I put my shaking hand on Beatrice's knee. "We'll pray."

"Yes," she said, and smiled. She pulled a rosary from her apron pocket. We got off the couch, knelt on our knees, and prayed to Jesus Christ that the war would end before James would have to go.

# 12
# Cats Out of Bags

## *Monika*

Macy's infants' department was air-conditioned, so I spent most of my summer there. Though six months into my pregnancy I was still carrying small, as I had before, the weight irritated me. At almost forty, I felt old; the swell of my breasts would be more beneficial to an ingenue looking to attract a boyfriend. My waist was nonetheless disturbingly round and my feet swollen.

At the beginning of August, traveling downtown in the heat had grown too hard. Manny paid my rent and gave me money for food and anything else I needed. Today, as most days, I needed baby clothes. It was no use searching for clothes that would enhance my own looks, so instead I would prepare to have a finely dressed child. I could not afford this one luxury with Jackie. Jackie had worn hand-me-downs from Beatrice's friends' daughters, and even from James, augmented by an occasional gift of a dress or a black, patent-leather Mary Jane from one of Manny's sisters, all of whom tried in vain to spoil the girl; she always reverted to wearing her dungarees and James's old overalls and T-shirts. She was uninterested in clothes by the time she turned thirteen—when at last Henri earned enough to buy her nice things.

The Jewish men along Houston were sure I was having a boy. Earlier in August, while shopping for baby furniture on the Lower East Side, an old Chasidic man shouted to me in the street, "It's a boy!" I believed him wholeheartedly and began to buy everything in blue. Manny had given me carte blanche, telling me to choose whatever I liked to go in the baby's room in his house. Grinning, his flushed face broadcasting such relief when I told him the old man's prediction, I felt I could have purchased a new car for the child and he'd be fine with it. That day we'd ordered the crib in pale blue wood, a changing table and dresser in pale blue wicker, and a Ferris-wheel lamp.

The baby would be born in autumn, and although I remained aware I might not be the one to dress him each morning, I wanted to be sure he would have warm things. When I looked at the zippered blanket in the store, holding it up to estimate the size of the baby, I pictured handing the wrapped infant to Manny and kissing him goodbye—the last, bittersweet scene in a movie about a war-torn city. The good-hearted streetwalker who gives her child away for a better life with the American soldier and his virgin *gal* back home. Manny would grab the child and hold it to his chest, rocking and rocking, his eyes glued to the baby's face, as I silently slipped from the picture, my slim body leaving the scene unnoticed, cold, and alone. Emerging from the image, I shuddered, and reimagined how devastating and lonely relinquishing the child would be. Blue as the baby's wardrobe, I dropped into a chair at the layette counter. In the glass showcase, a boy's silver-spoon-and-cup set—with a horse on the spoon's handle and a lasso on the cup—simply had to be mine. The sales girl wrapped it in pretty paper. "It's a gift," I told her. The purchase uplifted me.

Continuing my air-chilled spree, I bought undershirts and socks, booties, blankets, stretchies for sleep, and even a blue-and-yellow terrycloth bathrobe. It had a hood that made me laugh, a tiny prizefighter. The bags were heavy, and I had spent the five hundred dollars Manny gave me for this month's miscellaneous expenses. It was time to go home.

Going home meant being alone. Without Beatrice, I had only Manny, and he was not willing to keep me constant company. Beatrice and I hadn't spoken since the day we took Jacqueline to the airport. Neither of us had tried to contact the other. As had always been my worst fear, Henri had no use for me without his daughter. He was stubbornly holding onto the  anger of losing his child. We had spoken once during the summer, and that was in regard to police questioning upon George's arrest and imprisonment. Hildie, generous as always, had tried to be friendly, phoning me several times, but soon she told me that Manny didn't want boundaries confused. Already we were in a cold war, it seemed, with Manny maneuvering his troops as far from danger of confrontation as possible.

Since stopping work, I called a few parents of patients I had come to know, but they had lives too complicated to bear my woes. They had heard all about Jacqueline's fate, and the parents preferred not to be reminded of the trauma that might lie ahead in their own futures; their dismay was compounded by rumors of a baby conceived out of wedlock.

But today, lonelier than I had ever been, bringing home bags full of all these adorable baby things with no one to show them to, no one to share my fun, I stacked the Macy's bags on the sofa, all in a row, and decided to try to call the teenage patient, Sophia, again, to see if the girl I befriended and was so fond of was finally home from the hospital; I would see if I could catch her alone to talk.

The two kitchen chairs stood face to face, with enough distance between them for the length of my legs. Putting my feet up, catching my breath, I sat back before regaining strength to dial the phone. A sweet and childish voice answered. "Sophia?" I asked.

"Yup. Who's this?"

"It's Monika."

"Hey, hi! Wait! Mom!" she yelled, as I tried to stop her. Sophia yelled again, "It's Monika from the hospital!"

"Okay. Coming. Tell her to hold on."

"I heard," I said. "So how are you, dear, since our last talk?"

"All right, I guess. They got me on some new, anti-who-I-really-am drug, and I feel okay. Should be able to go back to school in September. Hey. How're you doin'? Why didn't you tell me? I heard you got knocked up."

I had to laugh. "Yes. It was planned. I wasn't "knocked up," as you say. I have a wonderful boyfriend, and we're very happy, thank you for asking." I giggled.

"Groovy. Here's my mom. Bye." The receiver made a swooshing sound as it transferred hands and rubbed against a body. Camille groaned as she retrieved the phone.

"Monika. How are you, dear? Oh, I'm so terribly sorry for your loss." Her voice was soft and breathy.

"I'd guessed you heard. It was gossiped all through the hospital, naturally."

"Sophia told me. She said she couldn't remember how she'd heard about it. So, what can I say? It's a tragic, horrible state of affairs, out there in the street, and this war. Our children are going crazy. An awful, crying shame."

"I don't care to talk about that, really. Thank you for your concern." Waiting to receive acknowledgement of my wishes, I said, "You know I'm having a baby." I swallowed hard, hoping this would encourage Camille to talk casually and offer friendship.

"Yes, yes. I heard that as well. Wonderful for you to have that to look forward to. Is it wonderful?"

"I can't wait." I'm a good liar.

We chatted about babies and child-rearing for a good half hour. Our exchange went so well that Camille invited me for dinner that night. As it turned out, we lived only ten streets and two avenues apart. Camille would have her husband John pick me up and take me home.

It was four in the afternoon, which meant I had an hour to bathe and dress before he'd come to get me. Excited, I cautiously stood under the shower and let the warm water travel its long and semi-circular route down my rounded body. I ran an Ivory soap bar over my arms and legs, the white foam collecting at the drain. I couldn't see my feet and laughed. Then cried.

Before getting sucked into a lasting dark mood, I stepped out of the tub, dried and powdered my body, and pulled my wet yellow curls into a bun. The baby will have my coloring, I hope, and not the red hair that ran through Manny's family in everyone except him. My new baggy underpants and white cotton bra looked rather large when I'd first bought them at three months pregnant, but as the salesgirl had predicted, they were too tight by now. I pushed the back bra hooks together with all my might. Even if I suffocate, I am never going to buy a double D cup. The bib of the maternity dress was more than adequate to cover me without an undershirt, and it was just too hot to wear another thing. The black thong sandals Jacqueline had left behind looked modern to me.

John was punctual. At five o'clock, he honked the horn and I ran out to him. He wore a white cotton long-sleeve shirt with his initials embroidered on the pocket, tucked into navy blue pants with a black belt and black shoes. I thought he looked overdressed, too warm. He drove a new white Cadillac, with red leather seats and an FM radio tuned to a classical station. I was familiar with the composer, Johann Strauss, and I pictured men marching with uniforms. An old dream threw shade across my effervescence, but I immediately blinked it away. "Do you know this piece?" I asked. John said he knew neither the artist nor the piece and drove otherwise close-mouthed. At Sixtieth and Fifth, I tried again. "This is a beautiful car, John. Is it new?"

"Just got it." He nodded.

Dumbstruck by his curtness, here I'd been prepared to tell them my whole life's story, and he was barely able to respond. I was sure he was disgusted with my condition and appearance, convinced I shouldn't bother him with any other questions or remarks. I'd have liked to ask him what kind of law he practiced, where he'd gone to school, and when he graduated. I thought of George supposedly in NYU Law School and shook my head. How long it had taken me until I doubted George? One minute was too long. Jackie, Jackie… I sighed. John turned to see if I was all right.

"If it's too warm, I can up the air," he said.

"No." Back when we spoke in the hospital, we had only talked about illness. Now I would become their friend, and they would talk to me about anything.

He parked underneath his apartment building and entered the elevator from the garage. There was a leather-upholstered seat against the elevator's back wall and a man in a uniform who tilted his hat to John and then pressed a button. There were only letters on the buttons. He pressed letter "J," which was the top and tenth button. I assumed that meant he lived on the top floor. Wrapped in the three-ply cashmere of luxury, the elevator shot upward. My stomach fell and I lost my equilibrium, swaying slightly into John. The man who had the job of pushing buttons looked amused, and then he faced front and gazed straight into the metallic, copper-colored door. His reflection revealed that his eyes were shut. I wondered if the elevator made him queasy as well.

The door opened to a vestibule lit by a delicate crystal sconce on either side of a gilded mirror, the space adorned with fresh white flowers in a vase on a small mahogany Demilune antique console. I felt as if I were back in my father's shop. Never since coming to this country had I seen such good taste.

John allowed me to walk ahead of him. Sophia opened the apartment door, a smiling sixteen-year-old in a white T-shirt, dungarees, and the same black thong sandals I wore. I could have wept, but quickly recovered when Sophia hugged me. "Not too tight," I said, faking a funny gasp.

"You look so neat! My goodness. Can I feel?" She was all over me. Camille walked out from the kitchen, talking to someone over her shoulder. Sophia whispered, "Why didn't you tell me yourself?" I shushed her with a quick kick to her foot.

"Take the roast out in ten, and then put the pie in. Thank you, Belle." Camille turned full face and embraced me. "Oh, my word. You do look pregnant." As soon as Camille let go, Sophia elbowed her way back around her mother, close again, and put her ear flat up against my belly.

"I can hear swooshing." Sophia said in a flat, serious tone.

"Sophia," Camille said, "you mustn't be so…so…*invasive.*" She pulled on her daughter's shirt to tug her back and looked at me, saying, "The medication, it makes her so *relaxed.*" She winked.

I smiled graciously. "It's fine, really. No one has even tried yet to listen to the baby." A single minute into the visit and I was already crying on their shoulders about my loneliness, and delighted by their attention.

Camille escorted me to the couch. John looked at us and disappeared into another room, urging with a tilt of his head for Sophia to leave the room as well, which she did with a skip and a whistle. The room was long and narrow, bordered by a wall of windows. The late afternoon sun filled the room with light, while the air-conditioner that poked through the wall somewhere behind the couch sang in a low electric hum. Differently shaped and upholstered chairs flanked the couch, each with a tiny table at its foot to hold a cup or ashtray. This seemed an extravagant convenience. The dining room lay at the end of the expanse, open to us, designated as a discrete room by two capital-topped columns. There were place settings and lit candles. Apparently, I was dining with a queen, a queen who would be my friend and perhaps grant pardons, a queen who would share the life of her little misguided princess, Sophia. We settled into a quiet conversation, and I filled her in on the past few months.

Within minutes, I'd related my story up to the time Nadine died. "He was distraught, of course, but so much in love with me that the pregnancy just carried him through the rough spots." I pressed my lips together to smooth my lipstick. "And then his family butted in and he was torn between us. It's because I'm not Jewish." I nodded, vehemently.

"But they accepted you when you were married to Henri, didn't they?"

"Well, Henri is not their precious Manny. And besides, Henri made his decision to be a Catholic long before he came here." I pictured him as an eleven-year-old boy following my insistence that he make the sign of the cross over his chest. "So, it's not like he married out of his faith." I blew my nose.

"I forgot that about Henri. But yes," she said and nodded several times, remembering. "It's such an unusual thing. I mean, for a man to convert for the wife. Especially a Jewish man."

"Being a Jew did him no good, or his family," I pronounced. "What would he want with them? Besides, he believes in our Lord just as strongly as we do. He's been a good Catholic." Waving my hand back and forth, I said, "This is all beside the point. And Henri's not speaking to me either." I looked up at the ceiling and shook my head again. The ceiling was painted blue. I sat speechless for a few seconds. The woman who'd been monitoring the roast, Belle, came out in a white apron and announced dinner. All smiling, we went to say grace and break bread. New friends.

Sophia had fallen asleep, John announced once we were seated, and she was not going to join us for dinner. I gleaned from his newly casual demeanor that he was relieved by her absence. Camille and I commented on the deliciousness of the meal, the oppressive heat, the war in Vietnam, and how unfortunate but necessary it seemed to be, and then she drank wine, knowing I couldn't indulge in such pleasures, while a pitcher of water sat on the table unoffered. Before Belle removed the plates, John cleared his throat to speak for the first time during our dinner. He looked at me with a calm face, his mouth relaxed and his brown eyes drooping slightly, probably from the wine. "Sophia is doing well since she left the hospital. Does she look well to you, Monika?" His tone was almost daring.

He was obviously not interested in my observation. "Yes, yes. She looks much better. You know, though, these things flare up. I'd love to spend some time talking with her. I bet she misses our talks as much as I do."

"Oh? What kind of talks? Did you discuss drugs with her?" John asked, his tone now full with insinuation.

Camille slapped her hand on the table. "John! What kind of question is that?"

"What? I can't ask what they discussed? I have no rights?" He smirked at his wife and then at me.

Stone-faced, I said, "If anyone would know their rights, certainly it would be a lawyer such as yourself." I waited a beat, tingling with insolence. "I'm sure you know about *everyone's* rights." Why was he talking about drugs? I couldn't wait any longer for any hospitality, and reached for the water pitcher myself.

Camille took a deep breath and signaled Belle to bring coffee. "We all have the same rights. Now let's talk about something else."

John's eyes flicked from his wife to me, and his storm seemed to fizzle with a deep breath, but he wasn't finished. "You'll be a single mother soon. What family have you got left in the city to help with the baby?" he asked.

"I have the father, of course. Manny Hoffman. He owns a tremendous hardware store in Brooklyn." I flattened my napkin over my belly and smiled at him. Even their blasting air-conditioner couldn't keep me from sweating.

He squinted at me as if he were a prosecutor, and I the defendant. "So, I was never sure. Are you French or German? Were you born a Catholic, or did you convert after the war?"

"I'm a Catholic *German*." Usually feeling shame making that disclosure, a sudden pinch of pride gripped my chest.

"Family in Germany?"

"John, enough!" Camille intervened. "Do you think this is appropriate now? Let Monika finish her dinner and then we'll talk, if she wants to." Her nostrils flared, revealing that she was seriously annoyed with her husband.

"It's fine, Camille," I said, in fact glad for the opportunity to speak about them. I hoped that hearing myself speak out loud might clarify the rouse masking my shameful feelings surrounding my heritage. "I don't know if I have family in Germany." An image of a dirt-and-grass playing field appeared, my cousins running in a game of tag. "I'd heard my parents had been killed during the war, after we'd been separated—because they were a mixed marriage. My father was Jewish." I looked into my lap. I had not yet been able to measure how I felt about my Jewish half, but the thought now made my heart race. "I might have aunts or uncles, maybe cousins. Certainly my father's side of the family are all dead. No one has ever come looking for me." I looked squarely at John, "I wish I knew, to be honest. I'd go back to see Germany in a heartbeat." I'd never imagined those words coming together in that way, and now they had formed and escaped my mouth. The relief was like giving birth. They all nodded.

Lubricated by the wine, John went on to speculate whether or not Manny's family would ever accept me as a Jew, since I was "sort of half-Jewish." But I was solely Catholic, as far as I was concerned, and I explained to John that for Jews, the mother was the parent who counted. My father's religion held no importance. I explained about Manny's allegiance to me and his unborn child; still, I would try to convince them that allegiance was trifling in comparison to the weight of his sisters' demands upon him, the women being the source of his unwillingness to marry me, even though he'd found love.

John made a face, "What kind of man is he?" He put his drink down. "Oh yes, a Jewish man." He laughed at his witty deduction.

The reason for his bias and hostility toward Jews was unclear. I didn't appreciate his innuendo about Manny and worked hard to make sense of his intentions. "You see," I told them, "he is the only male in the family and his sisters are all like mothers to him. His mother died when he was young, and his father just ran off." I remembered him confiding that to me when we first met in Paris, and proceeded to tell John and Camille about the initial and immediate attraction he'd had for me, when in wartime he had appeared at the door like a lost angel, pale and weary. I told them of the trust he felt in me. "But you have to understand," I insisted, my earlier fabrications drowned under the sheer rightness of these words, "in a family like his, blood relations are your first loyalty. If his sisters don't want me, well then…"

Camille pouted in sympathy. John didn't. "He took you as a blood relative when he made that child with you," John said. Then he softened as I felt myself blush, and he added, "He may surprise us all and marry you. Do the righteous thing."

My heart punched hard at his suggestion. "You really think this, maybe he will?"

John and Camille sat mute.

Self-conscious in the silence, I offered for conversation the first thing that came to mind. "How would it be for me to take Sophia to the Central Park tomorrow. Lord knows we both can use the company."

"I don't think so," John said, without taking a beat.

"Oh, you're dear. But we're keeping *very, very* close eyes on her until school starts," Camille said.

With the apple pie finished, it felt like time to go home. John leaned back in his chair and scrutinized me. "My firm is very well connected to various foreign embassies. What if I investigate a bit, see where I can dig to inquire about possible relatives back home?"

He lit a pipe, and when I inhaled the cherry smell, I felt a surge of longing for my father—the loneliness and sorrow within me so magnified that the embodiment of it was heavier than that of any baby. In a way I had never felt before, I wanted desperately to go home. Germany home.

At eight o'clock that evening, John was driving me home. In spite of the wine, the roast, and the intimate talk, John had not warmed any more to me, and I was certain it was because I had lost my figure. He'd been attracted to me at the hospital. I was sure of it. Now he was silent and had no more questions. My stomach ached from the excitement of possibly finding my family. The cousins who had been my playmates, the house with its bumpy stone-front wall and tiny, flat, green lawn, my father's pipe-scented furniture shop, with Hyman, the old upholsterer who I would watch tying springs together in worn chairs—they were shadows in my memory, gaining texture and fragrance. Maybe I had reparation for the stolen property coming and could open a business, call it Jacqueline's Antiques, and become a leader in the community. The pressure began burning beneath my ribs.

We got to my building, and John offered to wait and watch until I unlocked the door and got inside. He sat there, expecting me to open the car door and get out, but I did not reach for the handle. The burning had to be addressed. "What you said during dinner, about trying to locate my family. You'll really do that?"

"You get a list together of everything you have—names, addresses, anything that might start a lead. It shouldn't be too difficult. The Germans kept pristine records, and the records of citizens have been preserved. We'll find someone." He smiled, finally—a proud, white-toothed smile—then stepped on the emergency brake and shut off the ignition. Frightened for a moment, I sat frozen. "Monika," John began, "it would be a big, indeed welcomed, chore for me to get a hold of information on your family. That's what you want, right?"

"Yes." I swallowed and was sure he was going to ask for sex. I wouldn't have sex with him while I was still pregnant with Manny's baby. "What is it you want from me?"

"I want you to guarantee me you will stay away from my daughter." His smile turned into a malignant smirk.

My stomach kicked. "Stay away from Sophia? What do you possibly think I want with Sophia?" I thought I would vomit all over his red leather seats.

John went on, meticulously accusing me of secretly speaking with and trying to brainwash his daughter while she was on the ward. Accusing me of offering Sophia different kinds of medication, of offering her a place to stay if things were bad at home and she wanted to run away.

"What has she told you? It's all lies!" I couldn't believe Sophia had confided in him.

In a deep voice, he explained in legal and layman's terms that he would find my family, and I would not, ever again, contact his daughter. "You said you'd leave the country. Will you?"

I thought for a few minutes. How important was Sophia to me, anyway? "I'll never call her again, I swear, but I cannot promise anything about leaving the country. I have a baby to think about. The father is here." I wrapped my arms around my body and held perfectly still, to keep the baby at bay.

"You'll leave," he assured me quietly.

"I said I wouldn't promise that!"

He responded in a whisper. "You will or you'll not only have lost your family in Germany, you'll lose everything else you have here." I could see the bulge of his jaw tightening. "You purchased drugs from patients' 'friends' in the hospital. Don't try to deny it."

Opening the door, I scooted out and slammed it closed. Lowering my head into the car window, I said, "I'll start my list of relatives tonight." I wanted my family back. I wanted Manny. I wanted.

Turning down the covers of my bed, I tried to forget the nonsense of John's threats—I wasn't sure he could prove anything. I had already assembled a roster of names and addresses that was a page long. My mother had had five siblings, and each of them had children. My father's parents had lived in Berlin. I was sure they were dead. His brother was surely dead as well. I remembered every address of my aunts and uncles because they lived within walking distance of each other. I could picture the schoolbooks clutched in my and my cousins' arms across our chests as we picked each other up, one by one, for school—just thirteen the last time I walked with any of them. Three of my mother's brothers had small shops on the street level of their apartment houses. Otto was a butcher and had a meat shop, Joseph was a jeweler and watchmaker, and Frederick sold and repaired shoes. He even made me the pair I wore that last day in Germany. White leather. They were not wealthy, but they were all independent and prospered just enough. The family had been very proud, and I believed they could have kept their businesses and remained in Germany. Since they were my mother's relatives, non-Jews, their lives should have been spared.

Sleep came easily, settling so deep that I remained a prisoner of dreams that made me sweat with anguish. My last nightmare of the night was of wartime. I was young and naked and running through buildings connected by stairways. The stairs were narrow and rickety, brown in the half light, construction debris hanging and falling from them, and at every turn there was a tight opening I had to squeeze through before I could connect to the next building. I had to get to the staircase where I knew my mother waited, tied to the banister post with a cat scratching at her face. "Mama, I'm almost there!"

In the morning, the sheets were damp beneath me; I lifted my knees and the sheet lifted with me, stuck to the underside of my thigh. I peeled it away and threw the top cover to the floor. Pulse racing, my hands shook. I concentrated on my shallow breathing and waited for my heart to slow down, waited for the weight to lift from my chest.

It wasn't immediate, but it slowed, and I didn't panic—prone to having a racing heart during pregnancy, what the obstetrician called tachycardia. It was harmless, the doctor had told me, unless it persisted and worsened over a few hours. I felt better after fifteen minutes. It was the bed: The bed—broad, flat, and stately—seemingly holding the floor in place, claiming the unused empty space it occupied; its audacity reminded me of my isolation and abandonment. I would not get in it again; instead, I would sleep sitting up on the rocker in the living room, with the window shades open so I could at least see passersby and know I was not alone. But now, as Manny preferred me to do, I would call him at the store and report on my condition and make requests for assistance. That was how he put it: "Call me anytime with your requests for assistance." He sounded like an office manager or factory foreman. I was just another employee for him to oversee, until the product was delivered.

The tumult of the store rattled behind him when he picked up on the third ring. "Hello, Manny. It's me," I said, flat, tired, stung by the traffic of everyone's life. "How are you?"

"Good." He shouted at someone to keep it down. "Sorry about the noise. Tell me how you feel. Is the heat getting you nauseous?"

"I'm bearing it. I have an OB appointment today, anyway. The doctor will check everything. My tachycardia acted up this morning. So why don't I call you back after the appointment? Report for you all the vitals."

He excused himself to talk to a customer, and as I waited for him to come back, I heard a noise in my hallway and turned to see if someone had come to visit, to surprise me with company. Smiling at my imaginary relative, his blue eyes smiling back, I hoped I could find a way to accept John's offer.

When Manny returned to our call, he said he'd wait to hear from me in the afternoon. "Make sure you tell the doctor about this morning."

"Yes, of course," I assured him.

"And Monika?"

"Still here."

"I told Henri and Claudette about you letting me have custody. Full. Was that all right?"

"If I said no, it wasn't all right, it would be too late now, no?" I faked a laugh. "I bet Henri said I wouldn't be true to my word. Didn't he?"

"He's worried. But they're happy, naturally. They're happy for me."

"That's why *I'm* doing this. *For you*, Manny. I want to make you happy. And if you don't find happiness with me, then I'll give you the one thing I can to make you happy." For as long as this child lived, it would be of my blood and Manny would love the child—and so, he would also love me. The indisputable evidence of our love would lie on his heart. I smiled, happy.

His goodbye sounded uneasy. He stalled his words, "I'll pick up Chinese for dinner for us."

# 13
# That Number Three

*Manny*

For the first time in his life, Henri had an enterprising idea—the store should carry small appliances—and it actually turned out to be lucrative. We were busy all through August with sales of fans and window air-conditioners. I felt more secure that he could be left to manage things if need be, but foreboding lingered in me as heavy as ever. I had been drinking at the end of the work day, more and more, and overheard Henry fighting with Claud on the phone. I wondered what was happening in their relationship. I feared it would affect his work negatively if things between them was splintering. Busy but sullen, I spent all my free time, which amounted to three or four fifteen-minute breaks over a fourteen-hour workday, in the back storage room with a pack of cigarettes and pictures of Nadine. More lost as the baby's arrival drew closer, my heart became soft and as easily pulled apart as the white fibrous batting Fanny had bought to stuff the dolls she was making for the baby. What was I going to do with this infant?

Afraid I would need to love the mother to love the baby, I tried intently to find something in Monika to love—something besides her beauty—but she could do nothing right for me. Her sweetness seemed saccharine, her humor sarcastic, she walked too slow and ate too fast. She spent money in waves of excess, and she never said a genuinely kind word. Though I believed in my heart this couldn't be true, for no one did everything wrong, my disdain—revulsion at the way she misused her child, home, even her beauty—left me feeling detached. The disconnection pervaded my general mood so that just trying to love her separated me from all things I once had known were real: family, work, love.

In September, I spent more time in the dark and smoked upwards of two packs a day. I tried to visit Monika once or twice a week, to retain some semblance of friendship. She was finally large enough to tease open the seams of her early maternity clothes, and could do little more than waddle around her apartment and fix herself simple meals of pan-seared fish and cooled potato salad. Inexplicably, she insisted on sleeping on her rocking chair. I'd also bought her a rose-and-petal needlepoint footrest with a matching pillow and comforter. When I found it while passing an antique store, I was overwhelmed with the delicate details that Nadine would have loved.

During the third stage of her pregnancy, Monika developed a habit of calling me in the middle of the night. I was usually awake, either lighting a cigarette or squashing one out. One late-September night, a thunderstorm threatened and the two of us, separate in our own lives, watched in our dark rooms as the lightning stung the blackness. Monika called me during the initial onslaught of thunder—she only wanted to hear a voice, she said. On the phone with her, I counted the time between the flash and the boom, hoping that the angry sound would jolt the ground, cause me to lose grip and fall away from the sadness, or at the very least stir me to move from one rumination to another.

The rain finally fell, and the sky quilted. I wanted to get off the phone. "It's over now, Mon. There's no more thunder to scare you. You'll be able to sleep now, okay?" I finally yawned.

"Thank you. I'll try. Manny?"

"Yeah."

"You'll be a wonderful father." She hung up.

Waiting for her labor, I took the second week of November off from work and moved into Monika's apartment. I slept on her bed; she dozed in the rocker. The first three days were busy for me as I watched her pass through her day, her naps and discomfort filling her life like a full-time job. We talked in sparse exchanges. I shopped for food and cleaned the house, prepared light meals, and watched TV. During a typical quiet supper at five twenty-eight on November ninth, the clock on the wall stopped, the TV went off, and every light in the apartment blinked out. Turning on a faint transistor radio that Jackie had left behind, her fingerprints still smeared on the metal casing, I heard that the entire eastern seaboard from New York City to Canada had gone dark. Searching in disbelief for a light from another building, she waddled to the front window. "It's all black!" she yelled. There was a power failure, a blackout, the likes of which no one had ever experienced.

Monika was hysterical with fear—she would go into labor and be unable to get to the hospital, or would somehow get to the hospital and they wouldn't be able to help her in the dark, she'd get lost in a stairwell, or at worst, she would give birth on the dark street in the dead and dirty city she hated, and she and the baby would die. I remained calm for her sake, but I shared a dose of her fears. Forcing her to lie down on the bed, I put pillows under her feet to keep them from swelling. I lay with her for the next twelve hours, talking constantly, maintaining a monologue about everything from my first trumpet lesson at ten years old to the first night I blew taps for the army base. While I talked I felt her belly, feeling for contractions, kicks. The baby was wild with activity that night and every movement sent me soaring into anticipation. Monika groaned because the baby's foot or a hand felt stuck in her ribs, or she sensed pressure in her bladder and had to get up and down ten times to urinate. Every hour, I asked if she felt any pains, but she didn't, and by three in the morning it was clear her delivery would not come before the light of dawn.

Monika fell into a deep, snoring sleep, and I went in and out of a shallow rest until the sun lifted into the room from the uncovered window. When I opened my eyes, I found myself as far as possible at the opposite edge of the bed. Even in sleep, I had avoided her.

I rested, watching her, beholding the fullness of her body, the way her chest rose and fell with her labored breathing, how her belly stayed firmly put, hunkered down with the weight of water and flesh. Hildie and Fanny were there in my head and kept repeating, "As long as it's healthy, it doesn't matter if it's a girl or a boy." But I wanted a boy, and my wanting worried me. I didn't want to look into the face of my daughter and see Monika.

We still hadn't worked out all the details of custody. I hoped Monika would grow weary of being around the baby once I showed no interest in her. Just about every day at the hardware store, Henri warned me about the lengths she'd go to, to keep me in her life. He reminded me that she had supplied Jackie with drugs, just to keep their *family problem* alive between them. And through her sheer power of conceit, she manipulated fate and tried to mold a life new for us.

The lights went back on. The elevators ran. Traffic lights, washing machines, refrigerators—everything we had taken for granted, that had been pulled from our easy lives so suddenly, were all back at work. People were buying food to freeze. The city was alive with pre-Christmas madness. Each of the last three days, I left her to make an early morning check on the store, before hurrying back to the city by nine o'clock. On the third day, I found Monika had awakened with the kind of pain she knew meant only one thing.

She was sitting in tears, rocking and sobbing, when I walked in at one minute after nine. In the three hours I'd been gone, she went from her first labor pain to breaking her water. She sat in her wet pants, afraid to move until I came back. Jacqueline had been delivered after only three hours of labor, so she told me she was sure that if she stood, the baby would just fall out and be strangled by the umbilical cord.

The ambulance arrived within minutes, and we were off to New York Hospital. Holding my hand during the ride, Monika cried out, "Marry me, Manny. Please don't take this baby and leave me." She screamed from a contraction, and the attending medic helped her lift her legs as he spread them apart to check her progress. Even so, as I sat at her side, I was reeling from her pleas. Seeing what the medic had just inspected, I did wish she weren't suffering like this. The medic ordered the driver to move faster.

"She's got a few minutes, but I'd really like to see the entrance door to that emergency room." The medic, who was a man in his twenties, told us he was doing his internship rotation in emergency medicine and this was his first ride.

"Oh, that's great," I said. "Move this piece of tin!"

Finally there, Monika was wheeled into the emergency room. The attending doctor called out orders and pushed her gurney into a cubicle. "You the husband?" he asked me.

"I'm the father." The doctor looked at his clipboard and raised his eyebrows. "I know." I said, "We have the same name. It's a long story."

The doctor shrugged, then smiled to himself and mumbled, "As long as you're not her brother." He didn't look at me again until I finished reading the form. "You can watch this if you want, but it's gonna be quick and bloody." The doctor spoke while he gloved his hands and tied a mask around his face. I declined and backed out, finding a corner in the hallway to shiver in.

She screamed and stopped, screamed and stopped, then nothing, then a man and woman's voice urging, "push, push," then a cat cry, then applause. A nurse peeked out from behind the curtain and found my eyes. She mouthed, "It's a girl."

I walked tentatively toward the cubicle, then stopped and listened to the sounds coming from the other side. There were nurses laughing and cooing, and I heard Monika say, "Can you call in my husband, please?" I was embarrassed for her, because I'd already told the doctor we weren't married. I shook out the knots in my mind and pulled the curtain aside.

The baby was wrapped in a white blanket meant for an adult that spilled off the table onto the floor. Our daughter lay on Monika's bare chest and looked at peace. I loved this baby so much so fast that I feared if I disturbed her angelic pose and kissed her, I would take her into my arms and never let her go. "She's so beautiful," I said to everyone. Just to Monika, I said, "Thank you, thank you." I bent down to kiss her cheek, leaning over the white bunting on her chest.

"Hold her," Monika said to me. "She's your daughter."

I looked at the nurse, then at the doctor, who was busy writing in a chart. The doctor must have felt my stare, because he turned, smiled, and said, "You can pick her up. Wash your hands and get a gown." He nodded to a nurse to help me, adding, "Just watch her head." He resumed his paperwork. The nurse motioned to me to come to the other side of the table, where she tied on my gown as I washed my hands.

Never taking my eyes off my daughter as I walked around Monika's feet, I stopped in front of her, reached down, put my hand under the baby's head, and slowly lifted her to my face. Her cheek was flush to mine. With the first touch of her softness, the first sense of her smell, I melted into the deep way I remembered feeling after having survived a battle, enveloped in relief, and excruciating fear. "I love you," I told the baby.

She whimpered and yawned. When I saw the inside of her mouth—the smooth pink cavern that would take in her nourishment, help her to breathe, speak, laugh, and cry—I tasted her warm, delicious breath and began crying.

"Oh, now look and see what you've done to poppa," the nurse cooed at the baby as she took her from my arms. "We're gonna get your mom up to her room and put you to sleep in the nursery," she said to the baby. She laid her on a flat table and rewrapped her in a smaller blanket. I watched dumbly and in awe as she diapered her, tucking the end of the wrap tightly into itself and leaving the baby looking a bit squashed. She put her into a bassinet and began to wheel her away from us. Blowing my nose, I didn't hear what the nurse asked.

"I'm sorry, what did you want?"

"I was just wondering if you have a name yet. We could put it on the pink tag if you already picked one out."

I looked at Monika. We had not decided this. She shrugged, and I answered, "I don't think just yet."

"That's okay. You got two weeks for that one. Let's go, little Miss Hoffman."

The baby was gone. Monika was able to reach far enough to take my hand. I squeezed hers, and moved closer to the table. "How're you feeling? It sounded pretty rough from the other side." I cupped the top of her head over her cap.

"It was worth it. She's a beauty." She kissed my hand and put it to her cheek.

"Monika." I didn't know what I was going to say, but I was panicky and wanted to run away from her, run up to the nursery and steal the baby, move to Alaska, and hide her in an igloo. "We'll talk later, later when you're in your room. I told them I'd pay for a private room, okay?"

"You're not going to, are you?" she asked, dropping her eyes and grimacing in some sort of pain.

"If you mean marry you—no, Monika. But we can talk when you're not so uncomfortable."

Monika spoke softly, her voice raspy from screaming, and she gazed into the green room. "If you're not going to marry me, and if you still—I pray—want to take her, then give her any name you'd like. Name her Nadine. I don't care." Tears rolled down her cheeks, but she made no crying sounds.

Speaking slowly and gently, I responded with the steadiness I thought a father should. "You're weak and not thinking straight. I don't want you to make rash decisions that you'll regret."

She turned her face toward me, but didn't smile. "Okay, Manny. Be the gentlemen you were brought up to be. But I won't change my mind. I'm not a good mother. I give birth to beautiful babies, but they never live when I keep them."

Jolted and saddened by such an exaggeration, I pulled my head back. "Monika, you're not being fair. I'm sure there are a hundred reasons for what happened to Jacqueline." I pulled the blanket to her neck and tucked it in. Two male transporters came in to move Monika to her room. I said goodbye, telling her I'd be back in the afternoon to see her and the baby.

Departing, she moved her index finger, calling me to come close. I thought she was going to say again that she loved me, and I didn't want to hear it, but lowered my ear to hear her whisper, "You don't know everything about me. There was another child."

# 14

# Nadine

*Manny*

I parked my car in the emergency zone in front of New York Hospital and hurried in the main entrance, loaded down with a new pink bunting, booties, and a knitted sweater and bonnet that Hildie made in the last four days. I would make a trip to Macy's sometime during the week to trade in all of Monika's blue merchandise for the same in pink.

Four days after my daughter's birth, I was still trying to decide if Monika had been delirious or deceitful after she'd given birth, talking about another child. Henri would have known, would have said something. She'd not brought it up again; I buried it along with all the other miserable things I'd heard connected to her during the war.

Netted glass obscured the clarity as I peered at mother and child in the nursery. Monika was dressed in a loose white sweater and blue hospital pants. Her hair had been swept up in back and tied with ribbon, and her face was awash with her natural pinkness. Little Nadine was wrapped in a blanket printed with cows jumping over the moon. Her mother held a bottle in her mouth and rocked her. I didn't want to disturb this. Not just this particular mother-and-child moment, but also the future I'd be taking from them, the shopping trips and parties, the dancing school, and the sharing of clothes. The baby's name rang in my head like an unexpected guest at the door, and I gritted my teeth and bowed in remembrance of my wife. I also mourned Jackie. As I watched them now, the innocent infant in the cradle of her mysterious mother's arms, I grew taut with resolve to raise Nadine and stung with urgency to protect her from Monika and the kind of life she could inflict on her.

I tapped on the nursery's glass window. Monika looked up; her lips moved, calling a nurse to take the baby. The nurse took Nadine and set her in the curve of her arms just as Monika had. She rocked the same, held the bottle the same, and the baby looked just as peaceful. Witnessing that, I felt more certain I could rear his child without Monika.

We walked back to the room together, where I spread the pink loot on the bed for Monika's approval.

"Oh, this is all very sweet." She lifted the sweater Hildie had knitted and touched it to her face. "Yes, this is soft enough."

"So, they're all at my house expecting us," I said, putting my hand on her shoulder. "I want you to stay with me, a few days, until you're up and running at your usual *full* speed." I offered a wide smile, hoping her flat affect would fade into liveliness before we got home.

The scene of their welcome played in my mind all the way home from the hospital—Hildie and Fanny standing in a row like a royal receiving line, spiffy in their finest clothes, their skin beaming from anticipation as much as from over-scrubbing—joyously, cautiously awaiting the arrival of the next princess of Brooklyn. Monika sat next to me in the car, staring out the front windshield. Hearing my tiny creature of a daughter making sucking sounds in the car-bed behind me, her glow permeating my skin, my joy was dimmed only by the dull and distant mood of her mother. When Monika, Nadine, and I parked in the driveway, we waved to my sisters, who were sitting by the front window watching for us. If they were dogs, their tails would have been wagging.

Sure enough, the receiving line was at the door. Fanny the first one, holding her hands out as though preparing to catch a large ball. She smiled a broad, dimpled smile, shining with the sweetness I always treasured in her. She was only four years older than I was, and at forty-seven, she looked ten years younger. She had had an easy life, living with her sister, sharing Claudette, but I read the pining in her eyes as her niece grew away from her into adulthood. Though being single never appeared to interfere with her happiness, Fanny had been more afflicted by her childlessness than even Nadine had, so I relished seeing her radiance today. The baby, Monika, and I stood on the porch, the winter sun scolding our backs, as the welcoming committee clambered from just inside the door. Henri and Claudette stood off to the side, but in full view.

"Come back and see the room!" Hildie said, clapping and then waving her hand, ostensibly scooping the three of us up to come in.

I kissed Fanny's cheek, then Hildie's. "Fanny, you will be the first one to smother this baby, but just let me and Monika be the ones to walk her in." Monika had Nadine in her arms and handed her to me. "Are you sure?" I asked her.

"Yes. This is your house. You be the one to cross her over the threshold."

"Oh, for goodness sake," Fanny said. "She's not his *bride*." And with that, Monika's face froze in a dead gaze, and I flashed an annoyed look at Fanny.

"I didn't think. Forgive me," Fanny said, her face suddenly pouty.

I looked beyond my sisters to see Henri shaking his head, making a sour face as he raised his eyebrows. "Henri assembled the *blue* crib," Hildie yelped from behind Fanny.

"It was non-returnable," Henri said apologetically. "But I also hung an animal mobile from the ceiling over it."

We made our way into the house—our auburn-haired baby girl looking hauntingly like Jacqueline. Claudette spoke to me as we walked through to the living room. "I made the crib up in sheets and bumpers with matching yellow- and pink-colored balloons and kites." And rushed to add, "My mom shampooed the carpet."

Relief lifted through me when I surveyed their faces.

Quickly after giving Fanny first dibs on undressing Nadine, Hildie grabbed the bonnet and sweater she had knit and carefully folded it for storage. "We'll save this for her own child. This will be her coming-home sweater."

"Oy gevalt, she has the baby having babies already," Claudette rolled her eyes at me and shook her head, smiling. I could not discern whether Claudette was actually finding it bearable to be in my house with my baby and the *she-devil*, or if she was pretending for my sake and would ultimately explode the way she had in the basement that day during Shiva.

The women passed the baby until all had smooched her cheeks and studied her face. Fanny melted into tears when Nadine instinctively turned toward her breast, opening her mouth, searching. Hildie took the baby then, promising to feed her pot roast and carrots in about a year. I watched from the couch as Hildie handed Nadine to her daughter. "My turn?" Claudette asked, as she put her hands to her cheeks in a performance of surprise.

Take the baby, Claudette, I thought, afraid she would actually have the gall to decline. Finally her hands reached out to Hildie, whereupon she gently placed Nadine in Claudette's arms. Yes, that's it. As if magnetically pulled, Claudette's face lowered to Nadine's, and then she put her lips on the baby's forehead, holding them there long enough to take her temperature.

Claudette brought the baby back to me and mouthed, "I love her."

Monika had retreated to my bedroom, while Henri and I went into the kitchen to sample the pot roast. "So, what do you think?" I asked Henri.

"I think you're going to have more help than you want. But I'm curious—why are you letting Monika stay here? Your sisters, you know, they don't really want her here." Henri dipped a chunk of challah bread into the pot and soaked up some gravy, stuffing it whole into his mouth.

"She can't be alone yet. She's still in some pain, you know. I don't want her to be alone right away." I followed Henri's lead and dipped some bread. "Claudette will come around."

"She'll come around about the baby, but if Monika tries to stay? I don't know. Just make sure Monika knows she's leaving, or you could have her here for a very long time." Henri cast his eyes downward, and even as he spoke, his mouth remained in a frown. He was obviously hurting, and I was torn. Along with all the pleasure, it seemed the birth had caused so many people pain. I wrung my hands, but the action did nothing to alleviate my frustration. I walked out of the kitchen, back to the baby and the women.

When night fell, after my sisters, Henri, and Claudette left, Monika and I sat at the kitchen table, sipping coffee and dunking Hildie's cinnamon cookies. It was uncomfortable having her at the table. She looked beautiful. When she spoke, she spoke quietly. My hand shook as I lowered my cup back into the saucer. The coffee spilled. I cursed.

"That's okay," Monika said, and wiped the table with her napkin. "I think it went well today, no?"

"Yup, it went really smooth."

"So why are you so shaky? Someone say or do something to upset you?"

"Nothing in particular." We sat in silence briefly, and I reflected on the family's reaction to having Monika in this house. "You know, this whole scene is pretty unreal. Sitting here with you, the quiet, our baby sleeping in a bedroom a few feet away." I looked at her, shaking my head, thinking how different everything was from just a year ago. "It is a bit unbelievable."

Monika lowered her gaze and rubbed her cheek on the back of my shoulder. When I didn't move to touch her, she lifted her head and cleared her throat. "I'm not a fool. I know what I said to you the day Nadine was born, about another child. Why haven't you asked me about it? You're afraid?"

"I didn't think it was true, I thought you were dazed, that's all."

"Well, ask me." She waited, staring at me.

"Okay, tell me what you meant." Braced, uncomfortable, I stood and took her hand, gently pulling her. "Come. Let's go sit on the couch."

Slouching with my feet up on my wife's needlepoint hassock, I was poised to endure a horror story as Monika ushered me into her past. She took my hand again, and I allowed it to stay in my palm. She felt cold, and I was starting to feel sick to my stomach.

"In my first months in Paris," she began, with a hard sigh. She then reminded me that she had just barely turned fourteen when she'd started having sex with Germans in exchange for food. I knew this, of course—she told me the first night we'd met. But throughout the years we lived in New York, neither she nor Henri had ever so much as intimated anything about that fact. Watching this movie reel develop in front of me as she described the situation in detail, I felt myself sliding closer and closer to her. At fourteen, she knew close to nothing about birth control, and the men probably didn't think she'd survive long enough to worry about her conceiving—if they thought about it at all. But she conceived quickly, giving birth in 1941. A baker/midwife had been feeding and giving her shelter for months and delivered the baby the last week of October in her backroom. She allowed Monika and the baby to sleep there for another week after the birth, but then the elderly husband—having just returned from some resistance effort—threw Monika and the baby out.

"Oh, it was such a scene," she told me, and I watched her eyes float away from my face. "The wife was screaming at him to have mercy, and he screamed back, 'prostitute's blood in the bread is not good for business!' He kept yelling, 'Send her back to Germany! She's a collaborator, and we'll be killed because of her!'" Monika had to leave.

She nursed the baby girl the first month, but soon her breasts grew dry because she had so little to eat, and she had to start prostituting again. She'd gotten by this far by begging, but the streets were getting cold, it was the end of November, and she didn't want the baby outside.

At some point during her story, I tightened my grip around her hand. With no resistance, sympathy had quickly grown, and I found myself praying for her. "Did the baby have a name?" I asked.

"Ursula, my mother's name. It was the only one I could think of. But it turned out that every time I said it to her, I started to cry." She went on, trance-like, the way a conductor would, reciting directions to a well-traveled destination. She had left the baby asleep in a blanket on the floor of a dirt storage barn she'd found to stay in. It had no heat, of course, not even a pail with sticks to burn. She'd covered the windows with stray newspapers, which kept the wind from blowing in. She lined the dirt floor with paper as well, but it was barely warmer inside than out. She had a wool coat, which she grabbed from the first train station stop after her mother abandoned her, when a woman left it behind as she ran from the train, screaming after someone. Monika laid that coat on top of the newspaper, under the baby, nestling Ursula's head within the plush lamb's-wool collar, tying the sleeves around her to keep her covered in case she moved too much. She thought it was the best thing to do. "I was only fifteen at the time," she reminded me, her voice even-toned, her words factual.

"It was the right thing to do," I said quietly. *Where is this baby? What is she telling me?* More nausea.

"Yes," she continued. "I was gone for three hours. I'd made enough money to buy some milk and cheese. I'd been lucky, you see, to find a truckload of Nazi troops in front of the old theatre." She raised her eyebrows, remembering. "I knew I could ration myself and make it last a week." When she'd gotten back to the barn, she found the baby still asleep on the floor. It was dusk. Intending to lie down next to Ursula—to get inside the coat with the baby, where together they'd be warmer—she looked down in the dark room to unknot the sleeves. As she got closer, her eyes adjusting to the minimal light, she saw that the baby had turned her face into the lamb's-wool collar. When she touched her daughter, her cheeks were cold. "She must have twisted in her sleep, or cried out for milk, or just moved inside her dream, and got caught," she said, still flat, removed, reciting an ordinary recollection. "I wrapped her in the coat and buried her in the floor."

I immediately hugged Monika, but I needed something to stabilize me. All through the story, I had been picturing little Nadine's face, the pale and delicate skin of any baby Monika would conceive. Then a heated panic flashed through me. "I'll be right back," I told her, and in one movement, lifted off the couch and marched urgently to the nursery.

Nadine was on her stomach, her cheek flush against the mattress, her lips pursed in a sucking gesture, her hand, tiny and chubby, near her mouth. Soon enough, she would find her thumb. Claudette sucked her thumb until she was ten years old. I put my index finger to Nadine's cheek to feel her warmth, test if she was too hot. I pulled her light blanket down from around her shoulders to her waist, then bent closer to feel her breathe, turning her instinctively onto her back.

"She's still asleep," I told Monika, finding her back in the kitchen. I motioned with one arm outstretched and one hand waving her to come close. She moved only when I pulled her toward me to kiss her cheek. "It was one of the tragedies of the war, Monika. So many babies died." I held her for a quiet moment. "Does Henri know this?" I asked earnestly.

"Only you know now. I was afraid to tell anyone then. I didn't under-stand that at the time no one would have cared, that everyone expected prostitutes' babies to die. I thought I'd killed her. I thought I'd be arrested for murder. I was still only a girl." She stared straight away, showing no emotion, save for her exorbitant emptiness. Numbed, I could only think of all the world's dangers awaiting my child.

Nadine woke twice in the night to be fed. I rose to the sound of her cries and went to her room to sit with Monika as she fed her her bottle. When I woke again at seven in the morning, I was astounded that the baby had slept through the night, since two a.m. Monika and Nadine were sitting at the kitchen table, Monika sucking on a Charms lollipop and the baby on a bottle.

Nadine's first week followed the same schedule of sleeping and eating, visitors and quiet. Hildie and Fanny were rotating around their work schedules to get a rhythm for their new lives as aunty-mommies, and the baby was easily accepting bottles and attention from all of them. Claudette had not been back this week to see Nadine, but she called each morning, lunch break, and at night, both to check in and ask if Monika was still there. Oddly, Henri had come home from work one night to visit and stayed through dinner until we put the baby to sleep for the night. He and Monika cooed over the little girl in the blue crib, talking about the facial similarities to Jacqueline, and Henri hugged Monika, very hard.

After a week of this, it became time for me to return to work, and time for Monika to go back to her own home. Our days together here in my house had brought me more sympathy toward her, and her history, but still I could not absolve her for her part in the destruction of Jackie, the malicious and self-serving actions she took, exploiting her power over Jackie's addiction. There was no way to summon or invent any rea-son in the world for Monika to have supplied Jackie with heroin.

On the morning of the eighth day, as I diapered Nadine on her blue wicker changing table, between powdering her bottom and slipping on her pajamas, I told Monika it was time for her to return home. She stiffened and her breathing thinned. I put Nadine in her crib and reached around Monika's shoulder to grip her. "You're always welcome to visit. I want you to know that."

"I know. But it may be a while before I come to see her. I have things I have to straighten out in my life. I have to find a job, maybe move to a different place. In that place," she whispered, "I fear the visits from my own mind coming to haunt me." She began to cry.

Monika lifted a cotton diaper to her eyes and dried them. "I'm so afraid, Manny, so afraid that I've made another mistake. Right now, I want so much to be here with you and Nadine."

She stopped to exhale an extended, "Oooh. I can't bear your rejection of me. It will come to me wanting to run away, with her, or not. I don't want to hurt anyone anymore." She blew her nose into the diaper.

"Of course you don't." Anticipating this conversation, I knew she'd give it one more try before she officially left our daughter with me. Still, I had not composed a prepared response. I acted as though I knew she'd never take Nadine away. "You'll come and go at will, Monika. Some nights, maybe you'll watch her overnight. We'll see each other all the time." I lowered my head to see her eyes and have her look at me. "And in time, you'll see, we'll become friends. We'll have a lifetime of friendship."

We packed the few items she had me bring over for her—a few shirts, pajamas, underwear. Hildie had brought Monika's car to the house the day before so she would be able to drive herself home. She waited for the baby's eleven o'clock morning feeding, then she and I, my heart pounding, walked to her car. An early morning blast of snow had painted her yellow Pontiac white. I squinted at the car, the radiant noon sun shimmering on the snow. The white heat surrounded me, hugged me, and I was fully warmed. Nadie.

# 15
# Plan B

*Monika*

My landlord knew I'd be gone for a few weeks and had not kept the heat on for my return. The apartment was freezing. I sat in the rocker, coat on, not moving even to rock. I sat frozen until my episiotomy became uncomfortable and I had to stand. Walking around the small space, taking stock of my meager possessions, I listed disposable things in my head: tattered towels, wash-worn dishes, Jacqueline's clothes. I then called the landlord. When he answered, I said, "It's Monika Hoffman. Put on the damn heat."

On the kitchen counter was a note from Manny, propped against a grocery bag. It read, "Monika, I tried to think of some of the food you'll need right away. Hildie and Fanny came by and dropped them off. There should be bread, milk, and eggs in the fridge and some cheese and produce. Make sure you eat and keep your strength. Manny." I folded the note into fourths and put it in the drawer with cooking utensils, the drawer I would go to every day. Staples. The kettle still had water in it from the morning I gave birth. I turned on the gas beneath it and waited for it to boil.

I stood at the counter with my cup of tea, dipping a spoon into the honey jar and letting the excess drip back in. I took a sip of tea and put the wet, hot, sticky goop in my mouth. After four or five spoonsful, a shot of anxiety stuck in my throat, the problem being who to call first, Beatrice or John.

"Beatrice? It's me, Monika." I expected a chill in her voice, but when she spoke, it was warm.

"Hi, Monika. Where are you?" Beatrice coughed. "Congratulations. Manny called me. Did you know?"

"Well no, he didn't say he spoke to you. I would have loved to see you. Did you know I've been at Manny's house?"

"Yes. Henri told me everything." Beatrice waited. Her voice remained warm, but I sensed by the coughs and the pauses that she was holding something back. "I'm sorry for not coming or calling. At our last meeting, I was too abrupt with you. I'm sorry. I was just so upset, you know?"

"I know." My throat tightened. Why was Beatrice coming back this easily after being so angry about Jackie and the baby?

She asked me to hold on while she got a drink. I took a few deep breaths until I heard Beatrice's faucet stop running. She cleared her throat and spoke up cheerfully. "Are you still at Manny's? If you'd want me to, I'd love to come and see Nadine." She sounded breathless.

I snickered. "So, Henri didn't tell you everything after all. I'm home. Why don't you come over and we'll talk about it? Are you free today?" Please Lord, let her be free today.

"Oh, Monika. My James is being sent for training in New London, Connecticut." She sighed and let out a whimper. "He's joined the Navy and he's leaving tomorrow and we'll be together for the last time tonight. I can't…"

My eyes opened wide. "Beatrice, I had no idea. Not one person said anything to me. I'm sorry. Is he okay?" James, a sailor?

"This is what he wanted. It's in God's hands now." She blew her nose.

My upper body caved inward as I closed my eyes, clamped my jaw, and thought about the killing I had seen on television. "Will he go to Vietnam?"

"I just keep praying."

"Praise the Lord. Keep him safe." I crossed my chest, picturing Beatrice doing the same.

Then Beatrice spoke again. "Tomorrow would be perfect though."

We agreed on that, and as soon as we hung up, I sat on the couch and dialed John. Unfortunately, he was not the one to answer. Camille burst out, racing her words, my voice the starter pistol. "You will not believe what's been happening, all day yesterday and this morning. Monika!" Camille exclaimed. "We have found your cousins. Oh, I've forgotten the city. They're in Germany. But there are lots of them, and John said he will be in touch with them within the week."

I became dizzy. "My parents? Has he found out about my parents?" Hyperventilating and faint, knowing he had threatened me in exchange for this favor, I gripped my knees. I had not called Sophia again, but could I follow through and leave the country…and Manny?

"Monika dear, there's been no word of your parents. Not one way or the other. I'm sorry. But you know this investigation has not been going on that long. What, a few months? And possibly—well, very likely—your cousins will know something of their fate." We were quiet for a few seconds, and I heard the ping-ping drip of the kitchen faucet. "Monika? What about the baby? How is she? I saw that woman Beatrice when I took Sophia to the hospital for her therapy appointment, and she told me it's a girl. How wonderful for you. Sophia told Beatrice she would love to babysit. Oh, her name?"

"Nadine, after Manny's deceased wife."

"I see. Well, very nice. Very Respectful."

Uch. I stood and circled the coffee table several times, dragging the phone wire, wrapping it around my hand, pulling it until I felt the pressure against my bones. I didn't know if John would be enraged if I so much as discussed Sophia with Camille. Breathing hard, I said, "Yes, she's a beautiful baby. She's with Manny. I don't want to discuss this right now, I'm so tired, but she's with him for now." I begged silently, *Don't ask about his intentions.*

"I see. Well, for the best, sweetheart. All is for the best. And with this news, perhaps you could take a trip to Germany and see your cousins?" Camille gasped at the wonder of that suggestion.

I sighed. "That would be a dream, to find them and be with them. But I can't afford a trip like that." Yes, I would plead to John that the cost was prohibitive. What could he say to that?

"A 'giving-birth' gift! It will be our giving-birth gift to you! A recuperative trip to your homeland. John's idea, actually—after all you did for our daughter in the hospital. Please say yes."

My God. Who would have thought John would be so cunning to make such an offer? "Let's see if John can get in touch with them first." I bit off the tapered nail-tip from my pinky, the polish long gone.

"He will. And when he does, we will put you on a plane, and in seven hours you'll be home again. Oh, I'm so excited." She must have been holding the phone with her shoulder because I heard her clapping.

After the assault John made on my character and good-hearted efforts to help Sophia, I deserved every last penny it would cost them to give me this gift. But could I really go? Could he arrange to keep me out for good? Have me exiled? What else will his investigators dig up? I envisioned myself getting onto the plane. It would be my first flight, but I could hear the engines and feel the plane lift, see the tarmac below—I could feel my body in the air, as if I'd been thrown from a roof. "And what comes next?" I asked, forcing myself to swallow.

"I'm not sure. I think now that they've confirmed the names and whereabouts, they'll try to get current addresses and phone numbers. That can't be very hard to do."

"Camille, you and John—I don't know how to thank you."

"You deserve this. You poor dear, all the heartache you've endured."

"Yes. From the beginning of time." I laughed a little. "I wonder, even if you found my parents, if I really could make that trip—go back to Germany and leave everything else behind." I would dish up this last tease to see how much Camille knew, and how resolute John was about sending me away.

"I hope you find them. I'll pray for you, and for your baby, that she will come to know her grandparents and you will all be together again. Take her from Manny and raise her to be the good Christian she was born to be." She cleared her throat. "She should be what you are. They have no right to take her. I've discussed this with John. He absolutely agrees. They have no legal rights."

"This would be my decision. Everything has been my decision. Please don't go any deeper into this with John." Camille was being so presumptuous, so annoying—insinuating that she and John shared my disapproval of Nadine being raised Jewish. What did she know about how much it meant that Manny was grateful to me, grateful that I stayed long enough in this forsaken country to fulfill him with my warm and generous accommodation? What did she know about what it meant to give Manny the choice to raise our daughter as a Jew? My back went rigid. I wanted to shock Camille, cut into the bigotry I had found so offensive, and told her sweetly, "Funny, my father was a Jew, Jackie's father too, and now little Nadine's. Life is funny." I wanted to shout, *ha-ha-ha*, and hoped that idiot Camille was bright enough to feel contrition.

Camille seemed convinced Nadine would have a cleaner, more cultured life if she grew up in Europe, the kind of opinion uttered by a New Yorker who had only seen Europe through the gauze of lavish vacations and expensive Parisian holidays. I knew where Nadine would have a better life. But would her life be even better, wherever she lived, if raised by this mother? By the time our conversation ended, I was furious enough to defy John and wanted to call Manny and beg him unceasingly until he agreed to let me live with them.

But I didn't.

By nightfall, the apartment had warmed. I was nagged by the thought the place looked different, until finally I realized Hildie must have straightened up when she brought the groceries. There was not a speck of dust. All my clothes had been hung, and the perfume bottles on my dresser were lined up in a perfect, horizontal row. Some new fashion magazines were spread out at the foot of the bed, where the blanket was tucked into the mattress.

I changed into a fresh nightgown, one that was silky and wasn't big enough to house a milk cow—even though I feared I might soil the gown because my nipples still leaked—then slipped under the cold sheets and thumbed through the magazines. Dozing within minutes, I slept like death through the night.

The seven o'clock light woke me. I leaned forward in bed, trying to remember where I was, understanding soon enough that I was alone and without a family. My breasts were still full of milk and ached when I sat up, reminding me physically, before it had come to mind, that my baby had been given away and the man I'd loved almost all my life has taken his gift and thrown me out.

I lay motionless in bed, thinking of Cologne, though knowing I confused the smaller streets with Paris. There were wind gusts in my head. My mother's face was lost within one of those autumn storms. Did I resemble my mother or my father? No memories of the finer details remained: if they were small or tall or fair or dark, hairy, smooth, big-assed, small-boned, straight, crooked, good souls or bad. I tried to envision myself standing next to them in front of our house and to remember where I measured against them in height. It was a rush that day. Even so, how could I forget the waning sight of my mother's eyes as the train pulled away? *How?*

But I had.

Thinking about leaving home with them—when I thought we were all leaving Germany together—I hadn't packed any pictures to take on the journey. A book, and a comb, I even remembered my collection of rhinestone bracelets. Now I tried to retrieve any glimpse, a fragment: my mother's shade of lipstick, the shape of her blue eyes, the perfumed smell of her hand as she kissed me goodnight. I was left with only my own face to remind me of my ancestors. The palm of my hand found my forehead, and I pounded it. And while I chewed on my nails, it seemed criminal that I should go on without knowing more, that they should go on not knowing where I have gone, what I have done. That I was even alive. And I wanted to show them my family.

The shaft of light coming through my door was blindingly bright across the lower portion of the room. Rising and stretching, holding my breasts to keep them from pulling as I lifted off the bed, I shuffled barefoot into the shower. The heaviness that had pressed like an andiron on my chest for the past months lifted; the burn in my stomach had soothed. Right there and then, I decided I'd be out of this apartment by the new year.

Beatrice called to say she'd be there by noon. I hard-boiled the eggs the women had brought and made egg salad for lunch. Still stored in the basement were the suitcases I had taken when Henri told me to leave almost seven years ago. As soon as I heard from Beatrice, I felt easy about leaving the apartment. I had to get the landlord to unlock that creepy space. Bringing the cases into the bedroom, unzipping them to air out, I put sachets in them and began to pile my clothes on the bed. No time like the present. Even if the clothes had to sit piled in the suitcase for a month, I would be packed and ready when the time came. I closed the bedroom door to hide my plans from visitors.

At precisely twelve o'clock, the doorbell rang. A light snow was falling, and the morning sun had disappeared behind the noontime winter sky. I opened the door to find my only friend in a red winter coat, the shoulders covered with a fine mist. The flakes on her black velvet kerchief melted like sugar. I kept my grin broad and proud, but I was nervous and small in her presence. We stood looking at each other, a weary smile on Beatrice's face. "What? Am I gonna have to catch pneumonia for you to let me in?" Beatrice shuddered at a blast of wind, and with a nice laugh, pushed me aside and barged into the apartment.

I relaxed some, giggled, hugged her, then squeezed her tight, and held on until she cried out. With an umbrella still in one hand and a package with pink bows in the other, Beatrice stood still as a scarecrow until I let go. She then walked around the apartment, looking as though she were officiating a ceremonial recapture of the capital.

"Come into the kitchen. I don't have such a gourmet lunch, but it doesn't look to me you've eaten a bite since summer. You're so svelte," I said, leading her to the table.

"Since this whole to-do with James leaving, my appetite is not what it used to be. But this looks nice." She poked a fork into the egg salad.

It took several minutes of chewing and drinking before I harvested enough nerve to speak. "You think you'll go to see Nadine? Manny would love the visit."

"Of course. I have a gift for her. I brought it with me. After lunch, I'll show you."

"Great. But *you'll* bring it to her. I don't know when I'll get over there." I stared at Beatrice, realizing this was the opening I'd been waiting for. I tried to stay calm and focused, preparing for ridicule and disapproval, as I had gotten with everything surrounding Jackie. Beatrice was completely misinformed, almost ignorant, when it came to raising a child with problems. Look what she had done with James. He must have been so unhappy, he joined the Navy just to get away from her.

Beatrice wiggled in her chair a bit, seeking the right spot for the bones in her behind. When she settled and sat tight, she looked back at me. Her lips parted, at the ready.

"You might as well begin, " I said. "Whatever you have to say—let me hear you out." I put my hands flat on the table.

"You're expecting me to argue with you about the baby, about her living with Manny. I don't want to argue, Monika. I think it's an opportunity, really, to give you time to understand yourself."

"I don't understand *you,* Beatrice. Understand what about myself?"

"Your *life.* When I thought about all the ways you were, possibly, not a fit mother for Jackie, I was so angry with you. I thought about all the attention it brought you. You know how you told me how happy you were to have Henri all those times?" Her hand was poised in the air, ready to elaborate, when I interrupted.

"What are you saying?" I stood, my face hot.

Beatrice waited calmly for me to retake my seat. "Okay, okay." She got quiet and rested her chin on her clasped hands. "What I *really* wanted to talk about is that I've had time to think, to think about what would lead a person like you to make such poor judgments."

"Poor judgments in your opinion."

"Well, that is the opinion I'm referring to." She rubbed under her nose. "I know you lost so much—" Beatrice's voice was full of sincere empathy, and I was listening carefully. "You might have grown up more deprived, you know, and felt more insecure, because you'd been through so many atrocities—that's all."

Silence. My heart was full of relief, not knowing what I was most grateful for. Had Beatrice just offered me kindness? "Thank you, Beatrice. Thank you for taking the time to think about me. You've given me…" All at once, sand clogged my head from ear to ear. This time, Beatrice came to hug me.

"You spend time away from Nadine if you have to. She'll be in very safe hands."

"All I want from my own life is to be sure Manny knows I have given him the purest part of me. The joy."

"Monika." She took my hands. "You keep the lines open. The baby needs to know her mother loves her. Don't punish her with your absence." Beatrice rolled her shoulders back. "If you leave her to be raised by Manny, make sure she knows where you are and that she can have access to you."

"Yes, my goodness, of course she'll *know* me," I told Beatrice. "Manny has insisted, beyond insisted—he's made me promise to think about living with them."

Beatrice cocked her head. "Are you serious? Henri never mentioned anything about that."

"Things change constantly," I said.

Once Beatrice left me alone, the emptiness of a Europe I had fled with Henri filled the apartment. A continent I would return to without him. So much of our misfortune was not his fault. He was not a weak man. He was an ignorant man, a stunted man. I kept him a child, and now, when I leave him here, I would leave him with my pain, without knowing my demon.

"Henri?" The hand that held the phone shook. "Please come over. I couldn't leave without talking to you."

"Leave? Where are you going?" He waited for an answer but got none. "Monika, I am not helping you with any devious plans you have. My allegiance is to Manny and, though it does upset me somehow, you are on your own now."

"Just come, Hen. I'm leaving America. I promise."

It was midnight before Henri walked through my front door. I remained in my rocker, trying to stay calm, until he finally sat and faced me. I stoically relayed my story about Ursula, without shedding a tear.

Henri was crying. "When exactly? Why didn't I know? Why are you telling me now?" He covered his eyes.

"Jacqueline. I couldn't leave until you understood. All that searching for her disease was really trying to protect her. All those drugs I gave her. I couldn't bear to see her shiver. The war, my parents, the Nazis, they did not destroy my soul. I am stronger than anything the world outside can do to me. Ursula. That's what broke me. I could not speak of it until now. All the lives I've destroyed trying to understand, fix it, and forget it. Always I was wrong. But you tried. And I will always love you, Henri. You were my child too. You must be a man in my absence. I want you to be the good, great man you were meant to be."

# 16
# Mommas

## *Claudette*

Insulated feet sweated inside my snow-covered boots as I climbed the stairs to my apartment, my hair damp under the argyle scarf wrapping my face and head. As the December holidays approached, my job at the television station was becoming depressing. I'd had enough of my mother's "Good things come to those who wait." Had enough of life moving forward without friends, marriage, and babies. Babies and babies for everyone, including the most horrific person I had ever laid eyes on having her baby like some sordid magic trick. Monika's existence, her shadow in this city, was driving me so crazy my heart thumped every time I saw a blond woman with an infant in her arms.

It was eight o'clock on a Friday night. Working overtime to earn extra cash had turned me into a TV dinner fiend. Fried chicken with whipped potatoes; I was consuming packages of frozen salt. I'd kill for fresh scrambled eggs right now, but who had time to buy eggs? As I stomped my boots on the door mat, Henri opened my door, and I startled. He stood smiling, wearing his coat and hat.

"'Bout time. I was just going to leave." He kissed my cheek.

The apartment was dark, save for the light that shone through the frosted window, lending glitter to the long tail of the snowy scarf I pulled from my neck. I slid passed Henri without a word, dropped my coat to the floor, and headed straight for bed. Crashing down onto it, I looked up at Henri, and it occurred to me—with a potent trepidation I had felt for years—that he was my cousin. Abrupt terror was so strong that a stranger might as well have been standing there threatening to rape me. At first only a tear escaped, but soon I was sobbing. Covering my face with my hands, I bent into my knees and wept a minute or so until I could breathe long enough to sniffle it back and raise my head.

Henri knelt at the side of the bed. "What, Claudie? What are you crying about?" He scooted onto the bed and pulled my hands into his.

His breath of tobacco and spearmint filled the air between our faces, his narrow nose pointing at me like a scolding finger. I was saddened more by the wintry trap that his touch snapped around my heart. I wanted to release myself, but didn't resist this temporary grip he had on me. I clamped his hand in mine, as much for strength as to secure his attention, and said softly, "Henri, why are you here? I'm tired, and you should ask before you enter my home."

"Sorry. I am slow to learn your new rules," he said and stood. "It's just that I overheard Manny on the phone at work. I guess talking to one of the sisters."

"And and and?" I shook my hands at him.

"And, Manny might have taken our advice and tried to get Monika to sign some custody thing. I heard him say on the phone that she still hasn't returned the *documentation*. And also, that *her lawyer* is impossible to get hold of." He huffed and began to unbutton his coat. "So, that is why

I ran to you and entered your apartment unannounced. I believed this is something you'd want to know about."

"That dirty bitch," I said. "Monika has got to let go of Manny. We can threaten to tell him about what she did to Jackie." I held Henri's gaze and waited.

Henri smiled sympathetically. "He already knows about the drugs. It seems he doesn't give a shit."

"Not the drugs, you fool. About the sex! About her torturing Jackie!" I ripped open my top shirt button. "She has a choice, Henri. That fucker will either get the hell away from him, just leave the country and never come back, or I can tell him about her." I pointed my finger at Henri. "Let me see him not give a *shit* about that!" I raised my hand and snapped my fingers. "He'd kick her right overboard!"

"Claudie, by you telling him these half-truths—"

"Half-truths? Are you out of your mind!" I pulled at my hair, making a show of my frustration.

"We don't know what happened, damn it! My child is dead! She's dead! Do you have to keep her pain alive through to the next generation? She has suffered. She's lost more than you know."

"You, you..." I couldn't bring myself to call him a fool again. "It's retribution. Jackie deserves to get back at Monika."

"She's dead." After wiping his nose with a hankie, he stood more erect and cleared his throat gently. "*You* want retribution, Claud. You want to punish Monika for having Manny."

"Because—because she doesn't deserve him! He's blinded by that baby, and someone has to look out for him. He'll lose everything if she doesn't get out of his life." I was furious. "I need some quiet now. Why don't you just leave?"

"Yes, yes, of course. But if you indict Monika, you also indict me."

"Oh, Henri. Go, go now. I'll keep away from Monika until I talk to you tomorrow. Promise." As Henri left, I stared at the room window, covered with condensation from my anger.

At nine o'clock the next morning, I met my mother and aunt in Brooklyn to observe the Sabbath/Chanukah service at temple. Following, we all had great fun watching the children get bags of gold-covered chocolate money. We walked together in locked arms through the cold streets, gossiping about this lady and that, and laughing. It was a blessing to get to Hildie's house and find the cinnamon cookies already on the table. In no time, Fanny had made potato pancakes with apple sauce. "If the Rabbi stops by, don't let him in the kitchen," Hildie warned me, as though I had been gone so long I'd forgotten that they couldn't let him see them turning on the gas on Shabbos.

The heat in this house was always set too high, and the warmth, along with my suppressed stress over the night before, made me jumpy and ready to peel away my clothes.

"Go put on a housedress of mine if you're too warm," my mother told me. "I'm not lowering the heat."

I did just that, and when I came back to the table, I felt unencumbered enough to incite a family conference. The same word that had been a virus in my thoughts last night resurfaced. "Monika." I blurted out, without realizing I was thinking aloud. "What do you think? I can't stand it anymore."

Fanny was quick to speak. "Did you see her legs when she was in her bathrobe? The woman doesn't shave."

"You never noticed before?" I was smug.

"She is from another world."

We drank ginger ale in unison with sly looks and shrugs that said, what else would you expect?

"She is not like us. We have to make allowances. But she will never fit in smoothly with us." Fanny confirmed.

I knew all they didn't need to say—she was a German. She had odd ways. Growing up, I often heard them murmur in Yiddish about Monika's relationship with Henri and how bizarre it had always been—marrying him when he was a child, after she had cared for him as a mother—but they spoke little of this in front of me since I started up with him myself. I would have to keep his name out of this conversation. Nonetheless, I would do whatever it took to assure they were willing to send Monika into exile. How could I possibly speak about Monika's disgraceful deeds to these gentle women? Still, they had to see that she was trouble beyond her grooming issues. Keeping her harshest offense from the two of them, I would not betray Henri's confidence. I would start with the matter of generalized promiscuity. "You know, she's been with lots of men. I mean, I suspect that after she and Henri split, she ran around." I bit the inside of my cheek. "Not exactly a good example to set for a daughter."

"You *suspect* she ran around? Look, Claudette," Hildie said, "She gave us Nadine. Let's not dream up a scandal around her." My mother offered her reproachful tone, which had more to do with Henri and I being *one* scandalous love affair too many for this family. I wished I could talk to her about her confused feelings about Henri. Not here. Not now. No… not ever.

"Right, right. But you know," I eased into my sing-song voice, "if she wants to make trouble for Manny, she could pull that baby from under his pink, his pink, oh, *everything,* faster than he can finish saying, 'I won't marry you.'"

"She wouldn't." Fanny tried to assure us.

I laughed sarcastically at her naïveté. "Oh, but she would, Fanny. She most definitely would."

Explaining to Henri that I had to help my mother and aunt straighten out their end-of-year accounts for taxes and such, I avoided him by staying with them Saturday night. The next morning, I dressed to leave the house and make my way up to Forty-Ninth Street. The subway was empty on a Sunday morning, and the quiet let me think about what on earth I would say, and how to begin. As the train thudded, the words would not come. I remembered Henri accused me of seeking retribution for myself. For what? For her screwing my uncle and giving him a dream come true? For staying here and making my life miserable? What do I want from her, really?

Was the issue between me and Monika, or Monika and Henri, or Monika and Manny—or was it just Monika? As the subway car clanged along, my back hit the hard seat, and I relied on that movement to keep me alert, sharp. Monika—I began to rehearse in my head—*You are a beautiful woman. You should ask for more out of life.* No, no, no. I started again. *Monika, Manny is a good man and deserves better than you.* Uch. And again. *Monika, are you willing to leave Manny and Nadine and start over somewhere else?* That's it. I'll give her the choice—first—to explore her options. That way, I'll be able to judge just how permanently she's hunkered down—if she has any intention of relinquishing custody *soon*—before I give her an ultimatum.

From the street, I saw the former Mrs. Henri Hoffman looking out her living room window. Monika noticed me. She leaned closer to the glass, so I smiled, waving to her—her new friend.

Monika opened the door just as I was about to knock.

"Hi, Monika. Busy?" I kept smiling, and waited, bouncing on my heels a little and clapping my mittened hands in front of her nose in a show of frozen discomfort.

Monika had to look up to meet my eyes. After a moment, she seemed to decide to be cordial. She waved me in. "Did you come to this block to see me, or you simply enjoy to do *streetwalking* in the cold?" Monika took a seat on the sofa and held out her hand, offering me the same.

I sat, ignored her come-on, and refused to let the debate battling it out in my head disrupt the purpose of this mission. Drawing a breath, I counted to ten. Just looking at Monika reminded me of Jackie and was enough to rile the devil in me. I inhaled deeply, and proceeded to orate my monologue. "I came just to see you, about Nadine. She's six weeks, Monika. I was wondering what your plans were. When you plan to move away." That came out wrong. It sounded threatening.

Monika looked at me and smirked. "What in heaven are you talking about, *Claudie*? Who told you I'm *going* anywhere?"

"You did. You said, you told Manny and he told me, you had to look for a new place. Bad memories. I just thought it would be out of the city. Maybe you'd go to, I don't know, Florida."

"Florida?" Monika laughed. I knew she was mocking me. I'm an actress, for God's sake.

"Yeah well, maybe you are too young for that. But lots of people do get tired of this weather and move south." I wished Monika would go south of hell. "I know you haven't gone back to work yet. What about plans for that? And those papers? What about your impossible-to-reach lawyer and those papers?" But what papers had Manny been talking about? As long as Monika thought I knew, I had a chance.

Monika stood, straightened and cinched her belt, which by now could show off her narrowed waist. "What in hell are you doing here? Did Manny send you?"

I could see tears forming. Good, she's weakening. "Are you afraid he did? Are you unsure of his motives; unsure of his *word*?" I figured he had probably made some ridiculous promise to Monika. Needles poked one at a time into my temples, and I imagined the floor buckling below Monika. I sat deeper into my seat. And I watched now, as Monika lost balance and sat again.

"Why are you here?" Monika asked again.

"I think you need your life back. I think—" I could not think.

"What! You think I'm beneath him. You think you and Henri and your little house games you played with Jackie can be equal to what I went through with her! You think you have a right to ask me to leave

Manny, who I love more than life, and leave our beautiful child! I won't!" She threw her shoulders out and her head up.

"You will!" I kept breathing until my respiration evened out. I then casually sauntered off the cliff. "You will, or I'll tell Manny about you and your daughter. How you had her watch you with Henri." Having already lost my senses, I spit at her.

Monika reached for her cheek, where the attack had stuck. She slapped me across the face. The sting was no less brutal than the story Henri had told me months ago. As I felt the pain travelling from my cheek to my eyes, I started to cry.

"Claudette, oh Lord, I'm sorry." She went to touch my arm. "But you *spit* on me!"

"You didn't have to hit me, for God's sake." I caught my breath and walked to the kitchen sink. Monika retrieved a dishtowel, ran it under cold water, and applied it to my cheek.

"Jeez, this stings."

"I've been spit at before. It is intolerable for me. You should have instead hit me. I would have been less offended."

Under other circumstances, with other people, I would have started to laugh at the stupidity of all this, but it was Monika, and that hadn't changed. "This makes no difference in how I feel. You can't stay and raise that child with Manny. I want you to leave him alone, and I want to hear you say that you understand."

"And what makes you think Manny doesn't know already these cockeyed stories my daughter made up? She was insane. He knows that."

"Don't start that shit with me, Monika. I helped raise that girl. She wasn't insane. I know my uncle never would have tolerated you if he knew. I'll tell him. I swear I'll tell him."

Monika's mouth fell into a frown as her skin turned sallow and her shoulders drooped. "I don't believe you. And I don't care." Monika said doggedly.

Her body was trembling, betraying her words so definitively that I realized Monika would collapse if she thought Manny lost all respect for her. And I knew how Monika worked, knew how good she was at getting people to think they needed her. Monika's gift to Manny came with the expectation that it made him think kindly of her—that thoughts of her kindness and generosity would bring him warmth on lonely nights, and that one of those nights he will turn to the empty side of his bed and yearn to hold her. Now her collapsed body begged me to keep that sentiment alive. She sat across from me at the kitchen table, her entire face quivering. A pang of pity. I didn't know if I could threaten Monika again, not today, but I had to go one step further. More softly, I asked, "Do you at least have an explanation why you did that to Jackie? For the life of me, I can't imagine—"

"I would have to explain a hallucination."

"You're lying, Monika. You might as well give it a rest." I looked deeply into her face, searching for a fissure in her tenacity.

Monika's face settled into a yellow, round, emotionless mask, her features drawn as if they were finger-painted on a ceramic dish. When she finally spoke, her voice was as flat as her face. "The girl was out of control. I'd seen her with James, the boy upstairs. He was trying to feel her tiny breasts." Monika's eyes clicked closed. "She would be a woman soon, and she had no idea what that would mean. I wanted to show her how little sex meant. How ordinary a thing it would be for her. How easily she could do it without noticing."

I whispered, "But you were her mother."

Monika woke. She raised her voice. "That's right, Clau*dette. I* am her mother. I had the right to do as I thought best."

It was Monika who had been insane all this time. "You look beat, Monika. Let's call an end to this meeting." I threw the towel in the sink. "You'll think about what I've asked. You'll think about what's really best for that innocent child." Monika's eyes welled, and I felt my own welling up too. "I'm not going to say anything to him yet. I'm not telling you to leave town *tomorrow*. Just give some thought to where you should go. Next week is Christmas. New Year's would be a good time to start a new life for yourself." I walked to the front door, taking in the small rooms, the places where Jackie might have spent time, where she had slept and watched TV, dizzy from the sweet, God-awful French perfume Monika loved.

# *Manny*

It was December twenty-sixth, Nadine and I were on our way to have lunch at my sisters' house. We did this every Sunday, but today we were having extra company. Besides Claudette and Henri, Monika was joining us. She told me during the week that she had to see the family, together if possible, to discuss something that had come up. Something important that would change everything. I tried to get her to tell me over the phone, but she wouldn't. "And don't think I'm trying to be coy and tease you into coming here, because I'm not," she'd told me when I got angry at her evasiveness. She insisted they all gather so she wouldn't have to explain herself more than once. The family had all confessed their morbid expectations. Henri thought she was taking Nadine back. Fanny said she would ask for more money and a bigger apartment. Hildie thought she merely wanted more time with the family, as a whole. Claudette had remained mysteriously quiet.

Hildie's house smelled sweet and sour, which meant stuffed cabbage, a favorite of mine. She would have spent the night before tearing the large leaves from a cabbage and folding them around a mixture of chopped beef, and boiled them in her brown-sugared tomato gravy and sour salt for hours. She would only have to heat the meal for an hour before serving. This was her menu for meals she didn't want to fuss with once company arrived.

By one o'clock, the appointed time, all the Hoffmans were seated at the dining room table, all except Monika. Henri and I shared white wine while we eavesdropped on Claudette and the other women, who sat huddled at the far end of the table, concocting stories about what Monika was coming to tell us. "I know she wants Nadine back," Henri said to me. Henri's shoulders were slumped, and he didn't look like he was ready for battle.

"You sound like Claudie," Fanny said. "She's not taking that child. She probably just wants to *share* a little more, maybe start visiting on a regular basis. She's seen Nadine exactly one time since she's gone back home. She doesn't want her full time." A sharp stab of hope cut into my chest. She continued, "Who knows what kind of mothers German women are? Maybe they give their children away easier than we do." She shrugged.

"German mothers are the same as any mothers," Hildie said. "Don't talk foolishness like that. It makes me sick. It's not her *nationality* that you should be worrying about. It's her. She is a different sort. Different." She swirled her finger next to her temple.

Fanny whispered into my ear, "She married Henri when he was a child. She needs to have men around her. She's the sort that needs to be fed that nonsense. Get that kind of attention. Very European. Like the Italians." I looked at my sister in disbelief, my upbringing being the only thing preventing me from telling her to shut up.

"Should have your lawyer here," Claudette finally said.

"You honestly think I should have my law involved today?" Then I turned to Henri. "You think this is gonna get that messy?" I asked him, with a flash of fear, looking for an answer from someone I ordinarily wouldn't rely on to choose my socks.

Alas, Henri just shrugged and said, "I told you that from the start. Monika's not a person to do business on the honor system. She's determined when it concerns her own wants." Henri had already started eating the half-grapefruit first course.

"I'm with you," I said, forcing a smile, throwing my arms up. "I'll throw myself bodily against the door." We all laughed nervously. I looked out the window to see her coming up the walk. "Attention, all ye. Madam cometh," I announced, as my stomach rolled over.

As I got the door, the women scampered to change their seats at the table. Nobody wanted to be the one to sit next to her. Having departed the dining room to give her pot one more stir and check on the sleeping baby, Hildie lost her spot next to Claud. The exhibition of their apprehension temporarily pinned my feet to the floor.

The door opened to a calm and lovely Monika. Unsure of how to greet her, I saw her face lean toward me and felt compelled to kiss her cheeks. Her perfume ravished my nostrils. I had to swallow hard to collect my voice. "Come on in, Monika." The cold air washed our faces. Taking her coat from her shoulders as soon as she entered, I walked into the dining room behind her, waving my left hand above the back of her head, with my right index finger vertically stuck to my lips for the family to stay quiet.

"Manny, get Monika a warm cup of tea," Hildie said, her voice furiously pleasant.

"Just what I want. Thank you, Hildie. You know me so well." Monika blushed, her face and body suspiciously deprived of pomp or arrogance.

Struck by the incongruence of her shyness, her beauty also moved me. She had never looked this whole and healthy. She was more rounded than before her pregnancy; I guessed that was natural, and it was becoming. Soft red plums had sprung on the tops of her cheekbones, and her hazel eyes had streaks of green, but more salient, the color of a fresh blade of grass.

"Can I go in and peek at Nadie?" Monika asked me.

"Go, of course. I tried to keep her up, but she fell asleep in the car. We've been out."

"Oh. How nice for her." She lowered her head slightly, and we withdrew into the nursery.

The mother of my baby stood next to the crib, her hands on the side rail, completely immobile except for the subtle swell of her shoulders as she breathed. After a few seconds, while I hoped she would at least touch the sleeping baby's sleeve, all she did was inhale deeply before turning to me. "She's perfect," Monika whispered.

When we all sat and dug into the half-grapefruit sections, Monika coughed to get our attention. "We don't have to go through the whole meal all tensed up and worried about me. I can talk and eat. I'm more talented than you think." Thus, she extorted a small laugh from us. Monika smiled. "Now, this is going to come as a surprise to you all. I haven't mentioned this to many people, and since no one here has asked me about it, I assume you haven't heard."

"Please, Monika. You're making us even more nervous. Spit it out," Henri muttered.

Monika's face went petulant as a kindergartner's. "Okay, okay. You don't have to yell at me."

"Henri, let her speak at her own speed," I commanded.

Monika's eyes swept us. When she was satisfied, she continued. "Well, as Manny might remember, I had some friends whose daughter was a patient at the hospital. Their first names are Camille and John. He's a lawyer."

"Oh, God," Claudette groaned. I felt the buzz of electricity travel between Claudette and Monika and held my breath.

Monika looked at Claudette and smirked. "I only tell you what he does so you can follow this. I don't want to expose their last names, for their privacy as much as for my own." She again addressed the whole table. "Anyway, I knew them from the hospital, and we got to talking—actually, we dined together." She put her hand on her chest. "They hold me very close in their hearts and treat me like family." She sighed as though fulfilled. I already doubted her truthfulness. She continued as though we were waiting to hear about her day at the zoo. "One thing led to other things, and he offered to look for my family in Germany." All eyes focused on Monika. "Yes, well, you see…he has found some of them."

"Your parents?" I asked, amazed.

Monika looked at just me. "Some cousins, an aunt, and," she took a deep breath, "he has found my mother, but she's very ill."

Hildie was closest and grabbed her hand.

"And what does this all mean? Why are we all here?" Hildie said, erect and stoic as always, but I saw tears forming, "Are you taking Nadine to her? Are you taking her away to Germany?"

"Because you can't do that!" Claudette interrupted. "I'm giving you fair warning!"

I stood. "Would everyone shut up?" I turned to Monika and saw by her tensed mouth that I had to think fast. "This is good news for you. God knows you've ached—not knowing, but—" I closed my eyes against the dizziness—"what kind of news is this for us? *Are* you thinking of taking Nadine?"

Claudette stood up.

Silenced by all the attacks, I watched Monika swallow repeatedly to get her voice back. "I'm—I'm not taking her. I would never take her from you all." She glanced at Claudette. Then Monika continued, "Please. All I want to tell you is that I'm leaving for Germany this week, December twenty-ninth, and I'm going to stay there. I came to say goodbye."

Monika held tight onto small details and revealed only the big picture. The family was scattered in different German cities, her mother in a hospital in Cologne. She would visit her mother first.

I pictured her going to a bombed-out church. This was not anything remotely related to what I had hoped for Monika. When I asked what she would do after she visited and reconnected, Monika said she had no idea. Eager to have Monika map out her life, I was left as lost as she was. Everyone started to fidget with their napkins, looking at each other, trying to stay calm.

When Nadine starting crying, waking from her nap for lunch, I asked everyone to finish their meal and settle in the parlor. "I'd like for me and Monika to tend to the baby." My ambivalence about my daughter's relationship with her mother was giving me cramps. She and I prepared the bottle in the kitchen silently. I tested the temperature of the formula on Monika's arm, satisfied that her "good" was good enough.

Smiling meekly as she wiped her arm with a tissue, she told me what I had been too polite to ask in front of the others. "My lawyer, John. He's got the signed papers for you. He'll mail them once I've left," she said, looking at me squarely. "He said that's the way it should be." A grin erupted, and so I leaned over to obscure my excitement by pressing my lips to her forehead.

Thinking, *stay calm*, I put my arm around her shoulder. We walked into Fanny's bedroom where Nadine lay in a bassinette. "Pick her up," I told Monika.

She did, lightly touching her lips to the baby's cheek. Monika fed her on the bed, watching her daughter gulping, and listening to her hum.

"You think I'm not human, how I can leave her," Monika said.

"It doesn't make me think you're not human. I don't know what to think of your plan." I ran my hand through my hair. A fragment of respect for Monika and responsibility for our child tripped over one another in my mind. "I never meant to take Nadine away from you totally. I only wanted to be the one to raise her." Monika's eyes swept my face, not able to land. "I want her to know her mother. But I also want you to go see *your* mother, especially now that she's ill."

Switching Nadine to her other arm, Monika stretched out her neck in a circular motion. She cleared her throat and I expected an outburst, but she spoke softly. "She's been *ill all* these years." Her tears fell on Nadine's scalp. "She's been institutionalized." Beads of perspiration formed along her upper lip, and her shoulders fell with heat, as if still carrying the baby inside her. "After the war, when she could be reunited with her brothers, after my father was killed, she lost her mind. This is how they tell it."

"They who?" My brows pinched and hurt. She had just pronounced her father was definitely dead, and to hear her speak, soft, flat, she sounded as though she made these announcements every day.

"I spoke with my mother's brother, Otto. He was the one she lived with until he couldn't handle her anymore." Monika's voice fell even flatter—the same tone when she told me about Ursula. "Otto said she cried and cried for me, and still thinks to ask now if he's heard any news of me." Monika popped the baby's suction from the nipple and handed her to me. She began shaking with tears. "I love you and I want you to be happy with Nadine." She cast her eyes on the baby as if she were a chore too dirty for her to tackle. "Tell the baby your wife Nadine was the mother and died in childbirth. Don't ever tell her what a monster her mother really was." Now her cries were coming in heaves.

I needed both hands for Monika, so I put the baby in the bassinette, wishing she would drift into a deep sleep and not hear any of this. "I will not do any such thing. You're not a monster, and your daughter will know that. You'll see us all again, Monika. Planes go both ways over the Atlantic." I held her and she shook her head.

"Shah. Yes, you will see her again. Shah." She had called herself a monster; my niece called her a devil. My body flushed with an eerie suspicion that she had committed some deed more heinous than giving her teenage daughter heroin or allowing her baby daughter to smother during wartime. If that were true, I hoped I never found out. We rocked back and forth as my gaze fell from the top of Monika's head to the face of Nadine, as she slipped into the doldrums of infant slumber.

In the three days before Monika's departure, I caught myself calling her several times a day, urging her to buy a roundtrip ticket. As much as I wanted Nadine to be reared by me and my sisters, I didn't want her to grow up without knowing that her mother loved her, which I was convinced she did. Solemnly, I prayed that Monika be drenched with love by the family she would reunite with, drowning her years of grief with her own mother's relief.

By Wednesday afternoon, I felt desperate and drove to the city, stopping first by Claudette, to leave Nadine for her to tend. Claudette answered her door inside the dimly lit corridor, with a smile for the baby that zipped itself into a look of frustrated resignation for me. She lifted Nadine from my arms, kissing her hard on the cheek, then pursed her lips and squinted her eyes, saying, "I won't ever say terrible things—outright terrible things—about Monika in front of Nadine, but you know what she's capable of. Why are you trying to keep her here? Let her go."

I kept a poker face while Claudette baited me, nodding as if in agreement; I let her finish before shaking my head. "How many parentless family members do we have to have before we realize it's a dreadful way to live? I want Nadine to have her mother here. And as soon as she knows enough, she'll want her mother here too, in school, for concerts and dance recitals. I could have invited every last woman in the family to attend your graduations and performances, but I know you were looking for only one man, and that one wasn't there. I *want* her to be there."

Claudette burrowed her chin into Nadine's bunting and closed her eyes. The faint glistening of tears appeared on her lashes. "My father," she whispered.

With Nadine squeezed between us, I hugged her and said, "I don't want to miss her before she goes to the airport. I'll be back by dinner time."

"Go." She pushed me with her free hand.

I kissed Nadine's head and left.

—◇—

# *Claudette*

Separation from Henri started when Monika left for Germany; that day, I watched Nadine for Manny and came to understand why he had to try to stop her. Kneading the lump of doubt that had been rising inside me, I resolved that I could never marry Henri and have children with him. The thought of intimacy with Henri became intolerable. My infatuation, if that is what it was, was over. Too much mess, too many doubts about his loyalties and devotion.

Later that afternoon, after Manny returned for Nadine, I called Henri, and then my mother, announcing my official breakup. When I learned Henri was going back to France as well, I was too easily pleased. His American *stint*, as he referred to it, was over. He said that without me, facing Manny with Monika's child would be unbearable. He would search for his true identity. It was my mother's suspicion that he was going to search for Monika. What else did he have in Europe? What else did he have anywhere?

Reviving myself with coffee and cookies in the kitchen, I vividly remembered another kitchen, my childhood kitchen, and the day Manny left for the army, could still feel the ice-cold skin of his hand, the rough green blanket he had draped around him. I could see myself dancing for him to make him smile, then being scolded for it and sent to my room by Fanny. I felt embarrassed by the memory of that girl with a lampshade on her head in a hot kitchen in Brooklyn.

I was only a few years older than Nadine when my life turned upside down, and inside out. Crumbled. I thought about being a little girl, and about Nadine living with so many surrogate mothers. Of course, I had no father. Nadine, sweetheart, you have a father.

"If I knew where he was, I could send him a card," I told no one, straightening my posture. I reached into my pants pocket for a Tootsie Roll, unwrapped it, and shoved it in my mouth. And now Nadine without her mother. And it's a lifetime after the war, but still, the baby with no mother. I actually had some feeling for Monika that wasn't purely ugly. My voice low but clear, I said to no one, "I think, Nadine, you should know your mother."

# 17
# ETD



*Manny*

The traffic was light midday, and I breezed up to Forty-Ninth Street. I parked and walked north, wind blowing hard against my body, plowing forward, my shoulders tensed, as if I were a football player going in for a tackle. After buzzing Monika's apartment, I felt physically relieved, could sense my pulse slow down as soon as I heard her voice.

Monika came to the door dressed in a smart, pale-blue pants suit and a turtleneck sweater, wearing matching pumps, a silky yellow-and-blue scarf thrown across her shoulders. "Come in, Manny. Come in from the cold." She kissed my cheek.

"How long before you have to catch your plane?"

"I have a few hours. Sit. We'll talk again." She walked closely, clutching my arm at the elbow with both hands, holding me against her side, leading me to the sofa. I recalled how she sat with me on the sofa the night of Nadine's Shiva. The venom that memory had once produced was gone.

With hands folded in our laps, we sat and talked about what she had packed to take with her and how Beatrice had agreed to dispose of her other things. Monika had reserved a small wooden cigar box. "Maybe Nadine will like these one day." She handed the box to me and tried to smile.

"Can I open it?" I asked. She reached over my arms and opened it for me. I found three carefully folded squares of tissue paper.

"Open them," Monika told me. "Open that one first." She pointed to a square.

I made sure I was gentle, so as not to rip anything. With the first sight of the aged white cotton cloth, frayed around the edges, I broke into tears. "This is the cotton you used on my head that first night in Paris when I found you and got so sick," I said.

"Nadine will love to hear the story." She took it from my hand and wrapped it up. Also in the box was what I surmised were the few pieces of jewelry she owned, a small emerald ring I knew Henri had given her one Christmas, and a pearl hatpin.

"Monika. This trip, this escape, is all so drastic. Say that you will at least *think* about when you will be coming back."

She sat motionless for a full minute. When she did move, she leaned her head to me. "It never *occurred* to me that she could actually die. I never *thought* she would end up so broken." She lowered her head, remaining still.

"You mean Jackie?"

She nodded.

"That's exactly why I want you to come back. Don't you see? Just look at the facts here." I put up one finger to start to count them, to explain how she'd have another chance, with me doing the everyday work while she could just enjoy Nadine. She grabbed my finger and took my hand to her face.

"You look at these facts, Manny. I've lost two children. I don't know how to love them. Manny, I am not a fit mother." She patted my hand, which lay numb in my lap, and looked at me, making sure I'd heard.

It had been only two days since Monika left, having signed her lawyer's release of custody papers the day before. I itched with self-doubt. I should have married Monika. That absolutely would have kept her in New York. Yet I agreed she was unfit to be a mother—as she herself had groped to articulate—unless she miraculously changed to her core. I scratched feverishly at the side of my face. Monika had not called when she got to Germany, but before she left, she gave an address and phone number for John and Camille. They had, as instructed, called me to confirm the information was available in case of an emergency, and John would be the one to determine whether it was an emergency. John did say she was well and was visiting her mother.

On New Year's Eve, I stayed home alone with Nadine and somber-ly waited for the ball at Times Square to drop hazily on the television screen. I thought I should see the new year dawn. Then I went to sleep. It was a Friday night, and I'd promised my sisters I'd start lighting Shabbat candles for Nadine. I hadn't. She wouldn't have known, and I really didn't care—sure the women would teach Nadine well about the discipline of our religion in due time.

Nadine had been sleeping through the night—a solid seven hours— and I'd put her down after her last feeding at eight. This gave me plenty of time to ruminate and prepare for whatever the new year would bring. I had made some plans. Expand the business, buy another store closer to home, carry a full line of appliances, and take more days off to be with Nadine. Hildie spoke with her managers at the department store where she worked and got on alternating schedules in order to split the days with Fanny taking care of Nadine. Fanny worked in a bank, so she was always around after three p.m. in case of an emergency. Since coming home from Europe, I fantasized and dreamed about joining a local combo. Finding an ad from a musician at the local grocery store, I called the guy and joined an ensemble. I took Mondays off and Claudette babysat two nights a week, when I went out to jam with my little group. No matter what, the management of Nadine's life took precedence.

# 18

# Balance


## *Manny*

During the distraction of the family's restructuring, Fanny started dating the bank's accountant, Mr. Siboni, a mature, widowed Moroccan Jew. Having retired at sixty-two, he at last found it proper to date a *former* co-worker. They had flirted with each other for years. He saved his money, and now he and Fanny decided to marry and travel through the British Isles for their honeymoon.

On the first Monday in May, I was off from work and home with Nadine, as was our routine. I was up half the night, on the phone with Fanny, trying to warm the cold feet she'd developed, her wedding less than one week away. I sat on my bedroom floor with only the streetlight filtering through the window for illumination. "What if he isn't clean?" she dared me when I said how wonderful it would be to live with a man like Mr. Siboni. "How do you know? You never *slept* with him."

I laughed at that, but in general, I had lost patience and wanted to hang up on her. Nadine must have felt the tension in the house, because she refused to sleep for more than thirty minutes at a time all through the night. This morning, she sat strapped in her seat on the floor of the living room while I lay on the couch, my hand waving bunnies and rattles, making funny faces, and trying to keep her from crying long enough that I might be able to entertain her with my eyes closed.

When she started screaming at a pitch I had never heard come from a human being before, my heart clubbed inside of me, and I jumped off the floor to unstrap her and hold her tight. As I lifted her, she looked into my eyes and pouted; her lower lip quivered, and she whimpered. I touched my lips to her forehead. No fever. I did as Hildie suggested and rubbed whiskey on her gums. When I removed my finger from her mouth, she quieted for a brief moment, puckered her mouth, and wailed out a cry for all of Kings Highway to hear. I held her up above my head, and her pout turned into a giggle, her outstretched arms trying to fly. I started to swirl with her and dance while I sang off-key, a tune from *Porgy and Bess*: "Oh, I got plenty o' nuttin', And nuttin's plenty for me." Held snuggly against my chest, Nadine lowered her head, and when I crooked my neck to see her face, she was sucking her thumb, wide-eyed and alert, and I felt her tapping feet against my stomach, bouncing in perfect rhythm to Gershwin's tune.

I danced her into her room, and sat her against a pile of blankets in the corner of her crib. "Don't cry," I held one finger up, as if she understood that that meant, *one minute,* and ran out of the room. I returned to her in seconds, my leather trumpet case in tow. Placing it on my lap as I sat in the old rocking chair Monika had left behind for Nadine, I carefully removed the shiny brass horn, inserted the mouthpiece, shook it to clear the valves of spit, and blew one long and even note to warm my lips. Nadine was rocking on her clumsily pinned diaper and smiling around her thumb. Moving a little closer to her, I fit my lips to the mouthpiece. "Gershwin," I told her. She released her thumb from her mouth, gaped at the sight of me and my horn and waited, her little chest rising and falling. With the trumpet held to my mouth for a few seconds, gazing at my baby, my heart turned to clouds of lightness at her willingness to turn off her cacophony of distress and fall into the world of melody I would make for her. I proceeded to play "Summertime," against the warm, slow afternoon.

# Epilogue

## *Nadine*

In June 1995, fifty years after the end of the war, the remaining members of the Hoffman family, in New York and abroad, arranged to meet at the upstate home of my adored cousin, Claudette, and her husband Barry. Claudette had married the divorced father of a toddler son, at her *advanced* age of thirty-nine. More than a cousin, she'd been a surrogate mother to me, and Manhattan without her was not the same. I missed her doting, but we stayed close after I grew out of childhood.

My father sat on a wicker chaise that jutted into the middle of his niece's small cottage living room—the best position to watch the arriving guests. Both of us still unmarried, I was very close to my dad. I sat crossed-legged on the floor in front of him, watching the front door.

The French and German entourage were expected to arrive in a van from the city. The group consisted of: Henri, an aunt he found from his mother's side who had survived the camps, her husband, their two daughters, and a distant cousin of Henri's father. Henri and my mother hadn't remarried, but they'd shared a home once he found her in West Germany over twenty-five years ago. The intimate details of their relationship were unknown to me; the mere cohabitation made me uneasy. I had invited my mother by letter, but our relationship was less than constant. We exchanged birthday cards every year, and I visited her twice in Germany as a teenager. Henri was an odd sort, always around with not much to say, and my discomfort, more than anything else, kept me away. My dad kept in touch with them, but never mentioned the arrangement.

As the unfamiliar faces slid past, I looked over their shoulders, searching behind them. Henri at last walked in, alone, a man in his sixties with all his hair, bright blue eyes, and rugged jeans held snug against his thin stature. There was no one behind him. Henri ran directly to my dad. Their hug was tight, seeming to engulf each other's bodies. When they let go, they joined hands. Turning toward my ear, my dad whispered to me, "I hope you're not too disappointed that Monika didn't come." In truth, I was not. When I see her again, it will be just the two of us. I was actually relieved.

I resembled my mother, but no longer my half-sister, Jaqueline. No resemblance in temperament or coloring, from what little bits the family shared about her life before I came and she departed. I did sometimes imagine life as if we had been real sisters, friends; if my love for her would have made a difference in her future. Petite, blond hair, large hazel eyes—there was no mistaking that I was Monika's daughter. I also wondered if my father secretly wished I looked like his wife. I have her name, and his memories.

Henri kissed both our cheeks. "Ma belle jeune fille." Still the Frenchman. Then he turned to my dad. He clutched the crook of his elbow, took my hand, and led us to the backyard. Positioned in a quiet circle of three, Henri reached under his collar, slipped his fingers through a chain, and brought a gold mezuzah over his head. "You gave this to me fifty years ago to keep me safe. It is time I return it to you. It has done its job."

I stood in awe as my dad took the piece in his hand and felt around the rough edges, the open back, ran his hand around the chain. "I can't believe you kept this all these years." He began to cry. "Our survivor."

"You are the survivor, my dearest cousin."

# Author's Note

My father served overseas during World War II. He was a soldier in the US Army, private first class, trained in demolition engineering. He blew things up. But before he was drafted, my father was a musician, playing the trumpet with some of the jazz heroes of his time, and a self-taught artist. And when I came along, he was a doting father who tried to teach me about music, art, and philosophy. He was a high school dropout who read more than anyone I knew. When I began to write, at age seven, it was a story about him teaching me how to sew a doll's dress.

This book is a tribute to the man he was during the war, having left behind the love of his life, my mother. Unlike Nadine, my mother—who was loving, compassionate, and strong—remained married to my father from 1945 to 2011, the time of his death. The Hoffman family events in the book are fictional.

The story in this novel that refers to his time stationed in Bath, England, awaiting the attack on Normandy Beach, is true. Since he played the trumpet, and the professional musician who came to entertain the troops had the flu, the powers that be kept him back a few days to play with the USO. He crossed on D-Day, plus six.

I now own the trumpet he pulled from a wreckage in Bonn, Germany, where he did witness the boy being blown up in the street, shortly after the death of President Roosevelt. Any war-related story in the book was as he described it to me.

Upon Paris's liberation, my father went there to find his parents' sisters and brothers who had not immigrated to the United States before the war. He found one young boy. His name was not Henri, but he was living, hiding in plain view, with a Christian woman. He was a teen. This cousin married a German woman many years after the war and converted to Christianity.

The entirety of the stories in New York is fiction, though some personalities were based on my Brooklyn family. I have a beautiful cousin who tried to become a movie star, wonderful aunts who were unique in their quirkiness, and I knew well a woman who procured heroin for her very sick and addicted daughter, as Monika did for hers. The rest is my imagination, based on historical events, and the culture I witnessed in the 1960s.

I was present on that June day in 1995, up in the country (anything out of Brooklyn we called "the country"), when I met the person whom my father discovered in 1945. I learned during the car ride home from the reunion that [Henri] did indeed return the mezuzah he had received as protection. Among all the treasures of the horrible war, I am the keeper of that mezuzah, and the trumpet, and the memories.

# Acknowlededements

My work is a tribute to my belief that life is strange, all people are flawed, and the unthinkable actually happens. If it weren't for all the amazing, unique, and loving people I've met and known, I doubt I would have the courage to write about such haunted characters.

I have to thank the internet for supplying me with every minuscule historical factoid in order to tell about these time periods authentically. Paris in the 1940s and New York in the 1960s were historically significant for their specifically horrible events. Though I was alive in the 60s, living in New York City, there are details I could never have been personally privy to. Weather, store names and products, cross-streets, etc., are all recorded as vital information, and can be discovered and verified on the internet.

Vast appreciation to all my literature professors who mentored and inspired me at Brooklyn College, especially Susan Fromberg Schaeffer, and the psychology professors during my post-graduate studies at Kean University—helping to fulfill my unquenchable database on theories of personality disorders, PTSD, and the psychological effects of abuse.

My father's war stories were the basis of finer details on the battles of World War II, and I thank the journalists and eyewitnesses who lived through it for their personal observations. *The Paris I Love* (Tudor Publishing, 1963) provided rare photographs and cultural content, as did old family photographs.

When it came time to publish (ten years after starting the manuscript), my team of editorial professionals were critical and immensely patient. First, I have to thank editor and esteemed poet, David Groff (*Clay*, Trio House Press, 2013) for continuing to be there as a sounding board and for his astute advice on the direction my work should take in its early drafts. His introduction to editor and author Alice Peck (*Around the World in 80 Spiritual Places*, CICO Books, 2022) proved to be my lifeboat, steering me and introducing me to the rest of my team. She and her recommendations for copyeditors and designers guided me through the long and difficult path of publishing under my own name. My graphic designer, Duane Stapp, not only produced a beautiful cover, accepting my desire to use one of my father's paintings as a backdrop, but typeset and designed the interior of the book. The computer is not my friend, so he also took over in times of my uploading hysteria. Copyeditor extraordinaire, Crystal Sershen, meticulously read and cleaned my manuscript, asked many questions, understood my voice, and was a wonderful source of confidence and enthusiasm for my work.

I thank my local library in Morristown, New Jersey, for its reference room and solitude.

Of course, I robustly thank my two sons, Rosh and Steven, for their computer savvy and endless technical rescues, at all times of day or night. For their encouragement and patience, my early readers and trusted confidants, in order of time known: Henriette Tadman, Myra Weinberg, Mari Jaffe, Shari Korenstein, Valerie Sterlacci, Roger B. Granet, M.D., and Sande Boritz Berger (*The Sweetness*, She Writes Press, 2014). I hold them tight as my friends and allies, always.

Most of all, I thank my father, Julius (Jussie/Yussle) Schorr. Although this novel is a fictional portrayal, he inspired the writing and telling of this story. He not only served in World War II and the many conflicts mentioned in *The Hoffman Affairs*, he was also able to remember and relay his experiences to me, in fine detail, though the memories caused him great despair. His death has left a hole in the universe. My hope is to honor the survivors, both civilian and military, and the victims, both during and after the wars.

And my ever-tolerant, often-neglected husband, Len, who not only loved and encouraged me but made it financially possible to have the time and place to write. I am forever grateful for the opportunities that comfort and security afforded me. I could not have written without that freedom. I will always love and appreciate you.

www.ingramcontent.com/pod-product-compliance
Lightning Source LLC
Chambersburg PA
CBHW031140160726
47991CB00004B/1494